Dear Jane

Dear Jane

Erin Sullenberger

Copyright © 2021 by Erin L. Sullenberger

To request permission, contact the publisher at erinsullenberger5@gmail.com.

ISBN 978-1-7369280-0-4

Library of Congress Control Number: 2021906700

First paperback edition April 2021

Erin Sullenberger
Philadelphia, PA

erinsullenberger.wordpress.com

This book is dedicated to Jane Austen.

Additional thanks to the following:

My English teachers, particularly Ms. Patterson, who taught me British Literature, and Mr. Brady, who taught me so much beyond the curriculum in addition to the vocabulary word around which my first finished novel was based.

Mr. Threston, who taught me about a subject I love—the material of which is included in this text. Mrs. Larkin, who taught me life lessons I will never forget, and Mrs. Berthin, who dedicated so much time to teaching me calculus, and for whom I will forever be grateful.

My teammates and coaches at SJEB Rush, who continue to challenge me in the first of my two passions: football.

Ms. Negri, who encouraged my love of writing, and Mrs. Lehr, who encouraged my love of learning.

All my friends and family, who support me in all aspects of my life—particularly my parents, Uncle Leon, Avery, and Kai.

Chelsea Football Club, which has never failed to bring me happiness, which has been the foundation for my "endless, romantic dreams," and which has allowed me to connect with people across the world, some of whom I now consider wonderful friends.

Author's Note

Writing a novel has been my dream since I was five years old. I always intended to publish one of my many books before I graduated high school, so when the opportunity to publish *Dear Jane* arose, I took it. I began to write this book on the afternoon that I returned home from watching Greta Gerwig's adaptation of *Little Women.* I had never read the book, but I fell in love with Saoirse Ronan's portrayal of Jo March. On the ride home from the theater, I was filled with excitement, and when I finally reached my house, I ran to my bedroom and sketched a tentative outline for this novel. And by the end of my first draft, I had created a Jane Austen-inspired story that starred three protagonists whom I believe represent myself. Additionally, I think this novel unveils the idealistic and almost romantic sides of me. I did my best to create a 19th-century society in which it is a woman's responsibility to marry. I did my best to exaggerate and romanticize the details of the Phillips sisters' lives, but I hope that my underlying message became clear. My hope is that people realize they can be anyone that want to be. I hope that women, for example, realize it is beyond okay to attend a ball by themselves. It is an amazing feat to dance your heart out before a crowd of ladies and gentlemen, such as Bess did alongside Miss Henwood. I'll save my other messages for my readers' interpretations, but I hope that my main point is clear. Lastly, (minor spoiler alert!) I'd be lying if I conceded that my ending to *Dear Jane* was how I envisioned it to be. Perhaps I'll publish another version in which the finale is less satisfying to my readers, but I hope it brings everyone peace of mind, despite how difficult it was for me to type that final period.

This book is my biggest dream and my biggest fear. I love it, and I hate it, but I put too many hours into it not to publish it.

Dear Jane

Part I

Chapter 1

The inhabitants of Kent knew that the eldest daughter of the Phillips family and the only son of the Cawdor family were destined to marry. Each mother had spent their young adult lives alongside one another; therefore, when their children were born in the same week, they officially declared the resolution: Mr. Alexander Cawdor and Miss Jane Phillips must wed.

As time passed and the two children grew into adults, their expectations of marriage drew nearer. Eventually, a ceremonial clink of glasses announced their engagement, and Mr. Alexander Cawdor clasped his fiancée's hand and promised that his affection would never wane. Both partners met their parents' gazes, and with a mutual understanding, they nodded and initiated the first dance of the evening.

As she gazed onward at her sister's happiness, Miss Elizabeth Phillips, or Bess, considered the circumstances surrounding the engagement. Of course, Jane and Alex were perfect for each other. Not only was it their familial duty to wed, but there was no better conclusion to adolescence than marrying a childhood friend. While admiring her sister and future brother, Bess felt a perplexing idea come upon her. *How interesting it is that my dear Jane and Alex resemble one another—yet again, a sign that they were meant to be together.* After all, Jane was a gorgeous brunette with glimmering blue eyes—a breathtaking anomaly in their brown-haired-brown-eyed society. As irony would have it, Alex, too, possessed these attractive features, but Bess couldn't help but pause and chuckle. *Although Jane and Alex could be mistaken for siblings, the manner they tend to themselves substantially differs.* Jane always wore her hair up in a tight fixture that made her look intimidating, but contrasting her uptight appearance was Alex with his ruffled hairstyle—an oddly perfect indication of his disorderly personality. *How intriguing a marriage they shall have, for one is so organized and the other not so much.* And although Bess wanted to make light of the evening, she could not help but imagine how she might look dancing alongside her friend. Whereas Jane was almost twenty years of age, Bess was eighteen, and if Alex had been born a year later—oh, but she couldn't continue. The thought of marriage—the idea of conforming to anyone's expectations—was enough to make her turn away.

Bess shifted her gaze to her younger sister, Abigail, who was only fifteen—approaching sixteen—years old. She was seated at the edge of the ballroom floor, eyes glued to the figures of her eldest sister and Alex. She wore a yellow gown of Jane's, and although a stranger might mistake Abigail for a younger, less mature version of her eldest sister, it wasn't hard to tell the two apart. Abigail was very handsome, but she was young, bright-faced, and flighty. It was widely acknowledged that no one could match Jane's beauty and poise, but Abigail trotted about their home, Laurel Manor, imitating her sister in whatever manner she could. She painted, sang, and dressed up, but when it came down to it, she hadn't a talent or niche for herself.

Once, Abigail painted a portrait of Jane and Alex's future children to garner praise from her role model. However, when Bess laid her eyes upon this artwork, her face puffed up, and her eyes gleamed as she tried to hold back laughter. She opened her mouth to inquire where the heads of these blotchy, indistinct "children" were, but Jane's condemnation quieted her. Following her reproach, Jane remarked that the children looked more like awkwardly shaped trees than actual people, but because she said it in such a tender, light-hearted way, she made her sister laugh, not turn upset.

Nevertheless, this engagement was brilliantly timed, for just five weeks prior, Mrs. Emily Phillips, the mother of the Phillips sisters, had passed away from scarlet fever. The moods of Phillipses had thus shifted from catastrophic to cheerful, and Jane's mournful countenance had uplifted to one of happiness. Finally, her future of settling down and marrying—a typical, conventional wish for ladies in England—was in sight. And hopefully, she would become a mother—the pinnacle of her endless, romantic dreams. Not only was the official engagement lovely for Jane, but the other Phillipses were delighted. Alex had served as a brother for the younger Phillips sisters and a son for Mr. Phillips, so he was practically family already!

Two weeks after the engagement ball, Jane announced that her wedding was to occur in three months. Naturally, both Bess and Abigail were beyond intrigued about the event, and that night, while preparing to attend a local dance, they desired to satisfy their curiosities.

"Where do you suppose it shall take place?" Bess remarked, rummaging through a chest to find a suitable gown to wear. Giving up, she hopped onto Jane's bed and received a cringe from Jane, who did not want her perfectly set sheets to wrinkle. Yet, Jane ignored her untidy sister, for she was too excited to see Alex to reprimand Bess. She sighed, turned back to her closet, and removed a blue gown, which she passed to Abigail, who was also present.

"Oh, well," Jane started, turning back to Bess while managing to conceal a smile. "Alex said that he wouldn't mind having it here at Laurel Manor. I wasn't certain about having it at home because of the trouble in preparing it, but that might be all right." Jane turned to Abigail again, pointing to a pretty but outdated dress. With hesitation, for she hadn't formed an opinion on this style, she asked, "Do you think Alex will like this, Abbie?"

Abigail, who was hoping to dress like her sister, replied that this gown would not do, for there existed no other dress of a similar color in Laurel Manor.

Bess turned to examine Jane's dress and replied in such awe that both Jane and Abigail started. "Oh, no, Abbie—that dress is gorgeous, Jane! If I had one of any resemblance, I would never hesitate to wear it. Besides, as I hope you've learned by now, Alex loves dark-colored attire, *and* dark blue complements your eyes—or does it?" She paused. "You see, I can never remember colors that go well together. You mustn't listen to my awful fashion commentary, but I assure you that my advice *is* valid!" Bess returned to her pile of dresses and finished her statement with a smirk. "Try it on then, and you'll see I'm right." Jane shrugged, reluctantly dressing herself. After all, if Bess (whose fashion sense wasn't ideal) had suggested it, she could *never* fancy wearing it.

"Bessie," Abigail began, hoping to match Bess if she couldn't match Jane. "Can you please wear pink? I have one that is—"

"Oh, for Heaven's sake!" Bess interrupted, and Abigail stopped. "None of these dresses suits me!" Bess threw the dress she had taken off onto a pile on the floor.

"Oh, Bessie," Jane sighed, noticing Bess' messy pile of dresses scattered across her bedroom.

"I cannot wear one of yours, Jane," Bess started.

"But yours are so—"

"Unconventional? You've told me," Bess remarked, trudging toward the bedroom door. She touched her hand on the doorknob before turning around and remarking, "Jane, you ought to wear that dress. And Abbie, wear the blue one I just tried on."

Once Jane and Abigail exchanged a glance to acknowledge Bess' rude character, the door slammed shut.

"She's nervous, I believe," whispered Jane to her youngest sister. "I asked Mr. Augustus Ashford to accompany her to the ball this evening, and if she chooses to wear one of her embarrassing gowns and act so out-of-place as she normally does, I fear she'll lose his attention. A certain Miss Barlette will be there this evening, and I heard that she's been smitten with him for much longer than poor Bessie has."

"Oh, but Bessie doesn't like—"

"We mustn't surmise whom we think Bessie likes and doesn't like because that strategy would get us nowhere," began Jane, hanging a dress in her closet. "I know she's stubborn and practically hopeless in the romantic world. So, to increase her chances of finding someone, I've decided that she must fancy everyone we meet. Eventually, I may be right."

Abigail shrugged, choosing not to disagree with her eldest sister. She then picked up the blue gown Bess recommended and eyed it with distaste.

Chapter 2

Bess trudged through the hallway to avoid listening to her sisters' shallow fashion talk, and as she descended the staircase leading to the entrance hall, she justified a proper reason for abandoning them. *The Westfield Ball isn't for another few hours. I suppose I'll change my dress later—there's no need to be ridiculous and waste time doing that now.* Once she reached the ground floor, she glanced up from her concentrated state and immediately drew back. In front of her stood Mr. Phillips *and* four unexpected guests.

Bess' gaze first landed upon Alex, who wore a tailcoat with his usual ruffled hair. She froze, exchanged a warm smile with him, and then turned to her other visitors. With a curtsey, Bess introduced herself, but it did not take long until she noticed how awkward her companions stood. Confidently standing in the center of the hall was a large man, showcasing a great, boastful grin. He had jet black hair that was turning grey at the edges of his scalp, an oddly small mouse-like nose, and a rugged smile that made him look like a charlatan. Beside this man stood two petite girls. The older of the two must have been in her early twenties, for her bright, golden hair and icy blue eyes radiated youth. The younger of the two sisters, who was cowering a few yards away from her friends, stood next to Mr. Phillips. Like her sister, she had the same attractive features of golden hair and blue eyes.

Mr. Phillips shuffled his feet, cleared his throat, and stammered, "Bessie, uh—this is Alex's friend Mr. Charles Henwood, his fiancée, Miss Emma—uh," he said as if he had forgotten Miss Emma's surname. "And well, this is her sister—uh—oh yes—Miss Rachel," Mr. Phillips reported.

Once he finished speaking, he returned his hands to his sides and peered down to the floor.

Neither sister mentioned their last name, so to break the awkwardness, Bess exchanged a faint smile with her guests before Mr. Phillips, fumbling with his words, insisted that everyone take a seat. As he led the way to the drawing-room, Mr. Henwood gloated about something that Bess ignored before sitting himself between the two sisters on the most ornate sofa in the room. Bess sat across from them on a small loveseat, and Alex and Mr. Phillips shared a smaller sofa situated between the two.

After asking a servant to prepare a pot of tea, Mr. Phillips wondered when the wedding between Mr. Henwood and his fiancée would occur.

"Oh, we plan for it to be very soon," began Mr. Henwood with an icy smile that caused Bess to raise an eyebrow, "for dear Emma's mother can hardly wait for her daughter to become one of the famous Henwood brides." He clasped his meaty hands together before coughing to clear his throat. Bess opened her mouth to reply, but for fear of being interrupted, she refrained from speaking. When it became clear that Mr. Henwood had finished his reply, she devised a proper response.

Leaning on her seat's edge, Bess asked with a hint of sarcasm, "What makes them famous?" However, Mr. Henwood did not seem to pick up on her tone.

"Well," he began after a long, enthusiastic breath in which he unclasped his hands and pounded them down on the upper thigh of Miss Emma, who winced. The servant returned with tea, and Mr. Henwood grabbed a cup and dumped the contents down his throat. With tea still puddling in his mouth, he asked Mr. Phillips, "Do you have something to drink, my good gentleman?" Mr. Phillips hesitated before nodding to his servant, who went back to the kitchen to fetch their guest his requested beverage.

"The famous brides, sir," Bess interrupted, raising an eyebrow.

"Oh, yes," Mr. Henwood continued hurriedly. "My family is very wealthy, my dear, *very, very* wealthy indeed. That's all there is to it." He cleared his throat again and shifted his weight toward Miss Rachel, who reacted with a half-smile.

"I see," said Bess, frowning. "But if I may ask, upon what grounds do you consider yourself to be wealthy? By money or by good circumstance? Because I am a firm believer that money alone does not deem one wealthy."

"Then that is the point at which we part," Mr. Henwood chuckled, and his round belly shook. "Because one cannot be wealthy without having a good sum of money. Why, my money, I'd say, is my best feature!" he beamed. His grin looked like a child's, but Bess couldn't help but scowl. She turned to Miss Emma and Miss Rachel for any sign of humiliation at their near relative's ignorant remark, but they sat expressionless.

"But how can you say that, Mr. Henwood?" Bess continued. "Although my family *does* possess a large sum of money, as you should know, I do not consider myself wealthy simply because of the number of pounds I possess. Rather, I have a beautiful family to consider my source of wealth." Bess exchanged a smile with Alex before concluding, "And as my family continues to expand, my definition shall only grow stronger."

"Oh, such a childish remark!" exclaimed Mr. Henwood. He pressed his large hands onto Miss Emma's shoulder and stumbled to his feet. "So naïve, so disappointing, my dear."

"Please do not call me *my dear* again," Bess shot back, taking a deep breath to keep her wry remarks from sounding argumentative. Yet, Mr. Henwood stared down at her with such disdain that she stood to match his stature. Although she was clearly a half a dozen inches shorter than he, they no longer stood on uneven footing. Bess placed her hands on her hips, and from the corner of her eye, she saw her father's face crinkle with fear.

A squeal emerged from Mr. Henwood's mouth, and suddenly, Mr. Phillips exclaimed, "Oh, Bess doesn't mean you any harm, Charles! We quarrel like this every day during breakfast!"

"No, we don't," Bess mumbled, but the only person who heard her comment was Alex, sitting an arm's length away. He chuckled.

With a fading grin, Bess caught a glimpse of Mr. Henwood's waning red face. He took a menacing step in her direction, expecting her to recede, but she stood firmly. "Listen, *my dear*," began Mr. Henwood, and Bess frowned again. "A person is not wealthy until they can reach into their pockets and pull out handfuls of gold coins. Your definition is nonsensical, and I wish not to be plagued with the ugly idea that you are calling me poor."

"I never said that," Bess calmly interrupted.

"Of course, you did!" cried Mr. Henwood, shaking his fists.

"She didn't, Charles," Miss Emma mumbled while reaching outward to rub her fiancé's large arm.

Mr. Henwood took a deep breath. For a moment, he appeared to have collected his emotions, and Miss Emma sighed with relief. Mr. Phillips comfortably sat back in his chair before realizing that he had done so too soon. Mr. Henwood clenched his fists together and exclaimed, "Perhaps you are all deaf then!" He pushed Miss Emma's hand away, causing her to recoil in either distaste or fear—Bess could not decide.

"I wouldn't say that you *are* wealthy, however," Bess muttered. Again, only Alex heard this comment, and this time, he burst with laughter.

"What did she say?" demanded Mr. Henwood, pounding his fists on his thighs.

"I didn't say a word," Bess said, raising her eyebrows.

"That's a lie!" cried Mr. Henwood.

"No, it isn't."

"Don't quarrel with me, young lady!"

"I never intended to quarrel, Mr. Henwood. Rather, I thought we were simply *arguing* using proper logic," Bess chuckled, and she found it difficult to conceal a slight smile.

Mr. Phillips muttered his daughter's name under his breath while Mr. Henwood tensed. Hardly able to contain his laughter any longer, Alex pinched himself and asked if he could escort Bess upstairs to fetch the remaining two sisters. Bess felt a pang of disappointment come over her, for a part of her did not want her fun to end, but she knew that she would only make her father more uncomfortable.

"*Please* do," Mr. Phillips said with a blush.

Alex jumped up from his seat, and Bess led him away from the drawing-room. A second after they had left, Mr. Henwood screamed some loud, obscure complaint, and Alex burst into laughter. Bess admired him with a smile.

"What's so funny, Alex?" she teased.

Alex couldn't respond, for he was unable to articulate any words. He managed to walk upstairs without a problem, but once he reached the top of the staircase, he doubled over howling. Bess smirked at his high-pitched cackles. He cried, "Bessie, I *love* you! You're hilarious!" Bess blushed.

Hearing Alex's voice, Jane left her bedroom to greet her fiancé and sister. When she noticed how hard Alex was laughing, she exchanged a suspicious grin with Abigail, who had just arrived in the hallway. Abigail shrugged, and Jane chuckled, "What's wrong with you, Alex?"

"Your," Alex laughed, "sister," he continued, "is unbelievable," he concluded during an exhale.

"Who? Bessie?" Abigail asked, and Alex nodded. "Why? What did she do?"

Jane kissed Alex on the cheek and said, "Doing Bessie things, of course."

Bess, who would have usually taken offense to this remark but was too happy to argue, rolled her eyes. She took a step toward Jane to explain but was beaten to the task.

"She made a fool out of Mr. Henwood," Alex continued.

"Mr. Charles Henwood? Your friend?" Jane asked as she began to play with Alex's hair. "Alex, you *must* do something with this crazy hair. You look ridiculous—"

"I wouldn't say *friend*," Alex replied, ignoring Jane's comment on his appearance. "He's that distant cousin who offered me the small sum of money to perform that favor."

"Alex, that's awfully vague, and you know it. What favor?" asked Bess, and she crossed her arms.

Jane proudly piped up, "He cannot say. He said that information is between me and—"

Bess rolled her eyes. "It ought not be a *secret*. You're not Mrs. Alexander Cawdor yet, Jane."

Having taken offense to this attack, Jane whimpered, but Alex, who was still vulnerable to Bess' humor, laughed again.

"Alex!" Jane exclaimed, turning red. "That isn't funny!"

"Yes, it kind of is," he laughed, causing Abigail to chuckle as well. Then he turned to Bess, whose eyes were still glazed over with annoyance. "He asked me to introduce a friend of mine to his sister this evening. That's all, Bessie."

Frowning, Jane resolved, "Let's carry on. We should greet our guest."

"*Guests*," Bess corrected. "His fiancée Miss Emma and her sister are also here."

"Lovely," Jane replied, starting forward. "Will they be accompanying us this evening?"

Bess nodded. "But don't expect to get much more than a word from them. They're like dogs—they'll do whatever Mr. Henwood, their owner, wants. I'd be much happier staying up here, but of course, Father would not appreciate that clear sign of disrespect."

Abigail glared, Alex chuckled, and Jane, doing her best to appear professional, faked a smile, and led the party down the hallway.

"Jane, you can't ignore me," Bess called.

"Bessie, please be quiet. They'll be able to hear you soon."

Bess rolled her eyes. Alex laughed.

Chapter 3

Approaching the top of the staircase, Bess could still hear Mr. Henwood's loud criticisms about her behavior, but as she descended the steps, his voice quieted. *How pointless that he wastes his time and energy talking behind my back when I was only teasing him.* Bess shrugged and chuckled, for Mr. Henwood's ridiculousness was humorous.

Bess' thoughts ceased when she entered the drawing-room and seated herself on a wooden chair beside her father. She peered toward her sisters and watched them stand in the doorway with bright smiles plastered across their faces. She groaned, unable to believe that after all she had just articulated, they and their servile heads had no ears to listen.

"These are my other—uh—two daughters," stammered Mr. Phillips.

Mr. Henwood sighed, "I hope they have pleasanter attitudes than their sister."

"Whatever she said, sir," began Jane, and Bess took a deep breath, "was probably meant to be harmless. Please do not take her comments personally. I've learned not to," she chuckled, and Bess slumped back in her chair and rolled her eyes. Jane curtseyed, which signaled to Abigail that she ought to curtsey as well. Jane tucked a lock of her smooth brown hair behind her ear, and Abigail peered over and mirrored her sister's actions. If it was possible for Bess to slump farther down in her seat without appearing completely impolite, she did so.

"And your name, my dear?" asked Mr. Henwood. The outer edges of his lips curved up into a disgusting smile, and Bess muttered a swear word under her breath. Not even Alex seemed to have heard (or have taken amusement in) her annoyance.

"Miss Jane Phillips." She paused. "This is my sister, Miss Abigail Phillips," she replied before squeezing between her fiancé and father. Abigail, though, perched on the edge of Bess' seat. Bess shifted her position, and Abigail attempted to crawl beside her sister, but she nearly fell off the chair while doing so. Abigail gasped, and her face turned a bright red, but nobody seemed to notice other than Bess.

"Pretty names for pretty girls," Mr. Henwood praised with his obnoxious smile.

Bess completely forgot her younger sister's humiliation and turned to Miss Emma, hoping that she would convey *some* expression from listening to her fiancé talk about *other* beautiful women. But Miss Emma remained emotionless, and Bess sat back in astonishment.

Upon receiving no response, Mr. Henwood took a deep breath before adding, "With whom will you be attending the ball?"

Jane placed her hand on Alex's knee and replied in perhaps the most light-hearted manner, "My fiancé Alexander."

"I'm going with a gentleman named Gus," interrupted Bess, who could no longer tolerate the sweet-tempered tone of this shell of a conversation.

"Mr. *Augustus* Ashford," Jane muttered, correcting her sister's informality.

But it was too late. Mr. Henwood's eyes narrowed, and he spat back, "I asked your sister, *not* you and your uncontrollable mouth!" he barked, and the angrier he grew, the more his plump facial features shook. Bess smirked, and from the corner of her eye, she noticed a change in Alex's

30

countenance. His silent laughter was more fuel for her amusement, and she crossed her arms with a smile.

After watching Mr. Henwood's red face slowly fade away, Bess enunciated the words: "I beg your pardon. However, the question was rather ambiguous."

Comprehending Bess' thoughts, Jane frowned. She sat upright in her seat, took a deep breath, and whispered, "Bessie, please."

"Please *what*, Jane?" Bess snapped for the first time that afternoon. She whipped her head toward her elder sister and grimaced upon seeing Jane's furrowed brow.

"*Please* go on, Miss Jane," grunted Mr. Henwood as he folded his arms across his chest.

Catching Bess' scowl, Jane hesitated to reply. She took a deep breath and said, "It's nothing, Mr. Henwood."

Silence circulated throughout the room. Mr. Henwood opened his mouth to reply to Jane's disappointing remark, but something within him must have refrained him from doing so, for he remained quiet. Mr. Phillips twitched with anticipation, but after realizing that nothing would be said, he suggested that his daughters return upstairs to finish preparing for the ball. Bess was the first to jump to her feet and lead her sisters, trailed by Alex, out of the drawing-room. Mr. Phillips looked longingly after his daughters' male companion, for he did not want to be left alone again with Mr. Henwood and the speechless girls.

Bess mounted the staircase with great swiftness, for she did not want to have any more verbal encounters with Jane before the dance. From ahead, she listened to Abigail whimper, "Jane, my dress is in your bedroom. Can I prepare with you? I'd also like to wear that lip-coloring item you were mentioning."

31

"Of course, Abbie," Jane replied. She paused before projecting her voice to reach Bess' level. "Bessie, *please* wear one of my gowns. I've heard that a certain Miss Barlette fancies Mr. Augustus Ashford, too, and I do not want him—"

"Jane," Bess sighed. She reached the top floor and turned to speak down at her sisters and Alex. "First, will you *stop* acting like Mother? *Do not* reprimand me in front of others, and *do not* command me to go against my wishes!" She took a deep breath but continued with increasing volume. "And second, I hardly know who Gus is! I shall wear what I like, and if he is not fond of it, then I do not care!" Bess turned away and stomped down the hallway to her bedroom.

Jane covered her face in her hands. She shook her head and sighed, "Please, Alex." Alex glanced toward his fiancée, and Jane tucked a strand of hair behind her ear. "I loathe to ask this of you because Bessie is acting like such a nuisance, but can you go and calm her down? Sometimes I fear that you're the only person to whom she'll listen."

"Of course, Jane," Alex said without a second thought. Jane bit her lip and turned away.

Once he reached Bess' bedroom, Alex tapped on the door. A moment of hesitation elapsed before the hardened expression of Bess emerged and accused Jane of *making* Alex visit her. There was nothing more Alex could say but confirm her suspicions, yet Bess allowed him to enter anyway.

As he crossed the threshold, Alex teased, "Mr. Augustus Ashford, hmm?"

"*Please* do not remind me." Bess frowned as she began rummaging through her wardrobe to find something suitable to wear. Bess' bedroom was small. A bed, decorated with white pillows and blankets, sat in the furthermost corner surrounded by a bright red rug. To the right of the bed stood a large wardrobe carved from a light-colored wood. There was not much detail engraved on to the exterior of the wardrobe, and there were not many other pieces of furniture in the room. However, scattered books and clothes lying in every cranny made the room look full and homey.

Alex stepped over a pile of Dickens books sitting in the center of the room as he replied, "Yesterday, Jane told me you were practically in love with him."

"Me? Did she?" Bess turned around immediately. She looked neither embarrassed nor upset; on the contrary, the frown planted on her face conveyed a look of utter annoyance. "*She* was the one who fancied him when we were younger. She made me agree to go with him tonight because *she* said that it would be 'good for me' to have someone with whom to go." Bess removed a crumbled dress from her closet and threw it onto her bed.

After a pause, Alex said, "Perhaps it would be."

"Alex," Bess turned to face her friend and sighed, "I've met about two proper gentlemen in my entire life. Of those two, I would consider spending time with one of them." Bess rolled her eyes and continued, "*Besides,* I don't think that balls are authentic representations of cordiality. I think they're used to hide the hosts' secret motives, and overall, create a group of people who *think* that they are friends. *Going with* people to balls only extends the false friendships the entire idea of a ball represents. Therefore, I hate the idea of participating in this messed-up societal trickery!"

Alex took a step back and whispered, "May I comment?"

"Of course," Bess smiled and returned to her wardrobe.

"Although your perception *may* prove true, I believe you're overcomplicating the matter. View this evening as an opportunity to acquaint with others."

"But I don't know Gus, and I'd rather not associate with him!" complained Bess, throwing a wrinkled brown dress on the floor. She looked up, pondering, "Well, I saw him once, but I don't *know* him. After all, he's just a part of this *societal ball scheme*."

"Why do you call him *Gus,* not Mr. Ashford?"

Bess smiled. "In short, I learned of him as Gus, but your honest answer is… to bother Jane, of course."

Alex nodded but did not reply. Bess pursed her lips—there was certainly another reason for her informality, but Alex would not press her further. He sighed and cast his eyes to the floor, "Well, regardless, perhaps you'll meet someone else."

Bess shrugged before announcing that she found "the most perfect" dress to wear. With a large smile, she turned to face Alex, who, upon seeing what Bess had found, drew back. Between Bess' hands was a light brown dress that looked fashioned out of old curtains. Alex frowned, replying that no gentleman could like that gown. Bess was about to respond with a rude comment, but she refrained.

"Then what shall I wear?" she asked, turning away from Alex's penetrating gaze.

Bess stepped aside so Alex could explore her wardrobe. When he saw how untidy her closet was, he drew back. Hangers were stacked on the floor in countless piles, dresses were torn and tossed everywhere, and there was not a matching shoe in sight. With humiliation coursing through her body, Bess collected a couple of misplaced tops, but it wasn't long before Alex addressed her.

"You're really messy, aren't you?" Alex laughed, but Bess didn't smile at her friend's bluntness disguised as humor. Alex shrugged, adding, "Let me borrow one from Jane." Without replying, Bess watched her friend depart from her bedroom quietly. Once he shut the door, she hurriedly sorted through some of her dresses, and when she heard him re-enter, she hasted upwards and whipped around. Held between his hands was the same blue dress that she had tried on earlier.

"I thought Abbie was going to wear that," she feebly remarked.

"She's wearing something pink, and so is Jane."

Bess wrung her hands together and looked up at the ceiling. She composed herself and frowned. "They haven't any good taste, and besides, I don't like this dress on me." She paused. "Somehow, my sisters think that I'm not fashionable, but in truth, *they* are just too conventional. (Of course, I admit that I don't know basic ideas, such as what colors go well together and which do not.) They wear what society *expects* them to like to wear and—"

"I think that this would make you look lovely," Alex interrupted, and Bess closed her mouth and nodded.

A smile flickered across her face. "Well, get out of here, so I can try this on again," she beamed, and Alex stepped out of the room.

Once Alex had left, Bess threw on her dress, tied a few laces, and managed to completely dress herself in under a minute: a massive feat for women of her era. She did not mind that she tore a string in the process; she was simply excited to see Alex's reaction to her appearance. So, she tossed open her bedroom door, allowing her friend to re-enter. She twirled around, watching the ends of her dress created a wide circle. When she settled, Bess noticed Alex's charming smile, and she agreed to wear this dress.

"Do you plan on wearing your hair up?" asked Alex.

Bess shook her head and turned away. She said, "But Abbie will play with it while we're sitting in the carriage."

Alex laughed, "Abbie is so much like Jane."

And as if the thought had been perched on the edge of her mind for a while now, she sputtered, "Do you like her, too, then?" When she heard her remark, Bess covered her mouth and added, "I apologize. I didn't mean—well, you don't *have* to answer."

"Do I like Abbie?" he repeated, neglecting her distress. "Of course, I do. She'll be my sister soon!"

"Not like that." Bess hesitated, turning to face her mirror to mend her broken string.

"No, not like that. Jane is prettier," Alex remarked, watching his friend carefully tie the two ends of her string together.

"Do you only like Jane because she is pretty?" Bess murmured, quitting her unsuccessful task of fixing her dress. She turned to her friend and fully expected to face criticism for her bluntness. Yet, she was surprised when Alex ran his hand through his hair and shrugged.

"She's attractive, but she's also a great person—"

"Who deliberately embarrasses me," Bess added.

Alex shook his head and chuckled, "Besides, we're the same age, and our parents have set us up since we were children," he said, ignoring Bess' sigh. "Do *you* like Jane?"

"Do *I* like Jane?" Bess mocked, but upon noticing Alex's face turn red, she lowered her temper. "How could I not like Jane? She's my sister." She took a deep breath and walked to her bed. She picked up a dress lying on top of her sheets and as if it had been rehearsed, she added, "But she and Abbie are a different breed than I am. Sometimes

36

Jane acts too orderly, and I'm sure you can easily comprehend my emotions regarding that matter, but—"

Alex interrupted, "I hope you know she loves you and Abbie more than she loves anyone else, including herself."

Bess raised an eyebrow. "What makes you say that?"

"She told me," Alex answered as he ran his hand through his hair and looked away. "She's jealous of your individuality, Bess, and she's jealous of Abbie's youth."

"Ha—I am flattered—truly." Bess smiled in disbelief. She turned to her mirror, brushing her hair with her fingers. "But from a secondary source—from someone who admired my individuality already—" Alex's face brightened, and Bess laughed. "Alex, it's a tease! Yet, my *individuality* and Abbie's *youth*—of all things—which will soon fade, are nothing to commend. Beauty, well, *that* is certainly applaudable in this society. Jane is superior in *that* aspect; and besides, I dare say she possesses another trait that is better than mine and Abbie's: responsibility." Bess paused. "Why would she say what you claim she did, Alex?"

Alex shrugged. "I don't know."

Bess turned around with a smile and replied that she was ready. She and Alex left her bedroom and reconvened with Jane and Abigail, who stood at the edge of the staircase. As always, Janes was the picture of beauty; she wore a light pink gown and colorful cosmetics that highlighted her natural charm. Bess glanced sideways at Alex, who was admiring Jane and frowned. Then she turned to Abigail, who wore the same color as Jane, but her dress was much longer. She had identical make-up to Jane, but because she was only fifteen, Bess thought the cosmetics made her look a bit too old. Already, she was ruining the trait Jane praised in her: youth.

When the four of them were ready, they returned downstairs, where two carriages awaited their arrival. In the first coach sat Mr. Henwood, Miss Emma, Miss Rachel, and Mr. Henwood's sister, who had recently arrived. Mr. Phillips prepared to ride by horse (for there was too much inconvenience in requesting a third coach) while Alex helped Jane and Abigail into the second coach. When it was Bess' turn to enter, she took Alex's hand, smiled, and hopped inside. However, the size of Abigail's dress took up two full seats, leaving no room for Alex, and he was forced to ride on horseback with his future father-in-law.

Alex and Mr. Phillips prepared their horses as the carriages started toward Westfield Manor. Bess peered out the window to watch them mount their horses, and when Jane noticed her looking, she accused, "Bessie, I *do* hope that you are not admiring Alex."

"Oh," Bess answered, "I'm not. I'm watching out for Father's safety. His elderly figure should not be put upon that animal. I should have opted to travel on horseback instead."

"But your dress—"

"My dress would then better represent my temperament to *Mr. Augustus Ashford.*"

But before Jane had the opportunity to reply, Abigail said, "Oh, I hope they'll be all right. It would be all my fault if one of them got hurt!"

Jane glared at Bess then turned to Abigail, reassuring, "Do not fret. It's my dress, Abbie; therefore, any fault would be mine alone." She perked up, "Besides, it looks splendid on you!"

Abigail smiled, and Bess closed the curtains on the carriage window before shutting her eyes, listening to her sisters discuss the eligible bachelors attending the ball.

Chapter 4

The rocky road leading to Westfield Manor awoke Bess from her nap. She rubbed her eyes, opened the curtains, and admired the grand scenery. Unlike any other dwelling Bess had seen, Westfield Manor possessed massive marble pillars at its entrance. An ornate fountain sprang water into a pool that ran across the property. Bess shifted her position to catch a glimpse of the manor's interior, and when her eyes set upon a large crystal chandelier, she gasped.

Jane recognized her younger sister's awe and replied, "It *is* lovely, isn't it?"

But it didn't take long before Bess snapped out of her wonderment. Mr. Ashford would be arriving shortly, so it was her absolute duty to avoid him. Neglecting all gestures of propriety, Bess slipped out of the carriage and sprinted up the manor steps, nearly tripping over her dress while doing so. After making her way behind one of the giant pillars, Bess peered back and noticed her sisters eagerly greeting their hosts. *Oh, I suppose I ought to have said hello.* She paused. *But Gus could be nearby, and I cannot let him see me.* She turned back to the manor and headed inside.

Once she took a step into the entrance hall, Bess stopped, gasping in awe. The crystal chandelier she had seen was a trifle in comparison to the rest of the interior. Chinoiserie paper lined the walls, proving an excellent backdrop to the hundreds of guests. Ladies lathered in gowns with sloping shoulders and bell-shaped skirts pranced beside their male counterparts dressed in waistcoats. Pearl tiles decorated the floors, providing a lovely complement to the ladies' lavish attire. And to complete the image, a gentleman in a top hat played a grand piano forte.

Bess took a step toward the instrument, ready to examine its design, when she heard a nasal voice echoing behind her.

"Miss Jane Phillips," the voice called. Bess turned and found Mr. Ashford approaching her elder sister. She took a step back, preparing to hide, but she paused upon hearing her suitor again. "Congratulations on your recent engagement. For the past week, it has been the talk of Kent—I'm not sure if you were aware. I'm not certain you've lately ventured outside of Laurel Manor; and quite honestly, I hardly see a problem in *that*. That abode is absolutely—"

Jane laughed, "Thank you, Mr. Ashford. I'm flattered by your commentary."

Mr. Ashford managed a small grin. "As of late, I have been searching for a beautiful lady to marry. If only you were not engaged," he said sweetly, and Jane laughed once more. "I'm sure you understand then why I am eager to spend this evening with your sister. Society has been pressing me to wed soon, and—"

But Bess hardly cared to listen to Mr. Ashford's conclusion, so she continued walking. Soon, she encountered a large woman with a tall, flowered hat sitting on a bench beside the piano forte. The woman dangled a glass of champagne between her thumb and forefinger and laughed to herself. Bess kneeled behind this intoxicated guest.

From her view, Bess watched as Mr. Ashford pushed past the guests, asking if they had seen a "beautiful lady in blue." Bess was caught between humiliation and disgust, and she ducked farther down in her hiding spot. When Mr. Ashford came close enough for Bess to examine his features, she recoiled with further distaste. His face possessed no symmetry—it was entirely crooked, and she determined that he had a duck-like nose, for it stuck too far forward. Bess scrutinized the remainder of his countenance, and she concluded in a whisper that he was "perhaps the ugliest man I've ever encountered—aside from Mr. Henwood, of course." *How could Jane ever have fancied Gus?*

Amid her thoughts, Bess forgot about avoiding Mr. Ashford, and a moment later, she was greeted with a familiar nasal tone. Bess blushed and slowly stood to face her suitor whose bright smile diminished upon seeing her up close. He tilted his head sideways, comparing Jane's beauty to her's.

"I dropped," she stammered, neglecting Mr. Ashford's strange demeanor, "my—uh—hat," she panicked, "and I cannot seem to find it. But no worries. It was hardly worth the amount it cost. I could easily do without it. In fact," she continued, forcing a laugh, "it was rather ugly. I'm quite glad it disappeared."

"Miss Elizabeth Phillips," Mr. Ashford started, clearing his throat.

Bess exchanged an apologetic look with him before casting her eyes aside and mumbling, "Oh, good evening, Gus."

Mr. Ashford pulled his shoulders forward and continued, "I would appreciate being called *Augustus* or *Mr. Ashford*—or, preferably, *Mr. Augustus Ashford*—in case anyone overhears us."

Bess clenched her jaw, no longer feeling apologetic. She brought her lips upward, forming a fake smile, before replying, "Of course. And oh, I absolutely *adore* all alcohol. *Mr. Augustus Ashford*, could you please get me a glass of something—anything?" Bess managed to whimper, and Mr. Ashford frowned. Bess had vowed never to drink, but she would say *anything* to make him leave.

"Later, Miss Phillips," he replied, reaching for Bess' hand. "I have been awaiting this day all week! I am so pleased that Miss Jane set us up."

Bess exhaled and yanked her hand away. Without a change in expression, she stated, "You may simply call her Jane."

"But it is *so* informal, my love," Mr. Ashford replied with a sheepish look.

"We aren't acquainted enough to refer to each other as *loves*," Bess snapped before turning around to search for an escape.

Mr. Ashford's face turned a brighter shade of red. He cleared his throat, rubbed his palms together, and said, "Oh, Eliza, I didn't mean to offend you."

"Did you know that I am called Bess?" she retorted with a small laugh, starting to find Mr. Ashford's humiliation entertaining.

"Yes, of course," Mr. Ashford continued, collecting himself. He mumbled, "I thought Eliza would sound nicer and *a bit* more feminine."

"I like my name the way it is—thank you." Bess frowned, growing more serious.

"Oh yes—of course, Bess," he remarked, and a period of silence ensued. Mr. Ashford displayed a false smile, doing his best to appear civil while Bess anxiously glanced around, looking for an escape. Mr. Ashford cleared his throat, and afraid he would say something intimate, Bess asked about a gold bracelet he wore around his wrist. Mr. Ashford glanced down, eyes enlarging as he admired this piece of jewelry. "Ah, yes," he started. "My bracelet." Bess shifted her body weight from one foot to the other, crossed her arms, and reluctantly listened to her suitor. "I am an apprentice of Mr. Westfield, this evening's host," he continued with a broad smile (*Oh, how ugly he looks*), "and he rewarded me with this for my hard work. It's costly and thus delicate, but I like to wear it."

"Why do you work with Mr. Westfield?" Bess asked, only half-interested in his response.

"I'm interested in his trade," he answered.

With genuine curiosity, Bess inquired, "May I inquire what his trade is?"

"Yes." Mr. Ashford smiled. "Although I'm not entirely certain, I know it is related to money."

Bess glanced away and smirked, "Of course it does." But Mr. Ashford ignored her comment, either due to miscomprehension or annoyance—Bess could not tell. He opened his mouth to change the subject, but Bess exhaled and interjected, "When did you begin having others call you Augustus instead of Gus? I've always known of you as Gus, and I like the latter much better. If you listened to what I said before, my name is Bess, not Elizabeth, and certainly *not* Eliza. Shortened names are personal and easier to pronounce," she continued, despite Mr. Ashford's confused stares. "For instance, my younger sister's name is Abigail, but I see no reason to call her that unless I become mad at her. Instead, I call her Abbie."

Having tolerated enough of Bess' rambling, Mr. Ashford groaned, "But it's *so* informal. At least Eliza sounds like it *could* be a full name." Bess opened her mouth to argue, but Mr. Ashford didn't allow her the time. "Besides, I was told that I do not look like a Gus."

"By whom?" sighed Bess, stepping away from her suitor.

"Miss Barlette."

"Ah," Bess said with a smile. "I heard from Jane that she's quite smitten with you, and Jane certainly knows her gossip."

Mr. Ashford's face lit up. "Are you certain?"

"Well," Bess started, "as I said, Jane is usually accurate when it comes to rumors and gossip. I wouldn't put *this* piece of news past being true." Mr. Ashford cast his eyes to the floor, realizing that he was with

Bess, not Miss Barlette. "What is her first name?" Bess continued. "Have you seen her yet this evening? Is she pretty? I wonder if I know who she is."

"Rachel," Mr. Ashford answered hurriedly. He scratched his head and added, "I believe she has a sister named Emma."

"Oh, I *have* met Miss Rachel Barlette," Bess thought aloud. "Although I've never heard her speak. I'm not certain when you arrived this evening, but she came from Laurel Manor with my family and me. Indeed, she's a beautiful girl, and I'm sure—*most* sure—that she *must* fancy you." Bess exhaled. "You may be able to find her with her sister and Mr. Henwood. I do not believe she intended on meeting anyone this evening."

Mr. Ashford's face lit up, and he exclaimed, "Yes, Mr. Henwood! Such a delightful gentleman!"

"Oh," Bess groaned. "What makes you say that?"

Mr. Ashford's grin doubled in size, and his eyes scrunched as he explained, "He's always cordial, and he bought me a gold watch when I was *his* apprentice."

Bess shook her head and sighed, "Well, Miss Rachel Barlette is here if you would like to greet her. In the meantime, I plan to find my sisters and ask them how their evenings have fared thus far. Perhaps I'll see you later tonight, *Mr. Augustus Ashford*." Bess curtseyed and began to prance away, but Mr. Ashford reached out and caught her arm.

Blushing, he interjected, "Miss Phillips—oh, Miss *Bess* Phillips—I didn't mean to offend you when we were talking of Miss Rachel Barlette! I was simply curious. How could a young gentleman not wonder when a beautiful lady is rumored to like him?"

"Please," Bess laughed. "I was *not* offended."

She turned away to look for her family when, suddenly, she noticed Mr. Ashford leaning toward her with his lips puckered. Once her reflexes allowed, Bess knocked her suitor in the side of the head and cried, "Haven't you any manners?"

Mr. Ashford nursed his new mark while attempting to apologize, explaining that he had "misread" Bess' intentions.

Bess stomped away, and from the corner of her eye, she caught Alex's tall figure and ruffled hair. She pushed through the crowd of dancers to meet him with raging thoughts racing through her mind. *How discourteous that young man is! All he cared for was being an apprentice to enrich his status!*

Jane was the first to notice Bess, and with concern, she inquired, "Where is Mr. Ashford? He was looking for you a few minutes ago."

"I met him," Bess huffed, "and he tried to kiss me right away. I escaped because it was very impolite, and you *must* agree, Jane." Bess concluded her story with a great exhale, which caused Alex, who was eavesdropping, to chuckle.

Jane bit her lip and asked her fiancé to fetch the family some champagne. Once Alex had gone, she returned to Bess with a sympathetic look. She extended her arms and embraced her sister, adding, "Oh, I apologize, Bessie. I did not mean for you to have an unfortunate evening. I was just trying to help, and although I know you detest courtship and anything related, I figured you might like Mr. Ashford. Normally, I think he's well-mannered." Bess frowned. "Nevertheless, I am to blame for your regrettable evening, and I am truly sorry."

"Thank you, Jane," sighed Bess. "Of course, I know your good intentions." She squeezed her sister harder, and for a moment, the two sisters stood arm in arm until Alex arrived with a tray holding filled champagne glasses.

"Champagne, Jane? Bess?" he asked, hurriedly passing around the glasses so they would not spill.

From a few yards away, Abigail perked, "I'll have some!"

Jane took a glass and laughed, "You're too young, Abbie."

"Bess?" Alex asked again.

"Oh, no. I do not drink," Bess answered. Alex shrugged, and Bess watched Jane take a sip from her glass. She licked her lips before setting her drink down on a ledge sitting against a large ocular window. Bess approached the window and glanced into the dark sky. She admired the beauty of the stars, and something deep inside of her yearned to meet a nice gentleman this evening. Snapping out of her dreams, Bess turned around to face her sisters and Alex, who had already finished his first glass of champagne and had proceeded to Bess'.

Jane raised her eyebrows. "It's strong, Alex. I couldn't take more than a sip or two of mine."

Alex chuckled and suddenly announced, "Bess, I want to dance with you first."

Jane gasped, looking anxiously to her sister who, moments before, she had caressed with unparalleled love and sympathy. To her relief, Bess, who was hardly paying attention, replied, "You're with Jane, Alex." She paused. "Where did Father go? I'd like to sit in the carriage if I cannot go home."

"He's with Mr. Henwood," Jane said with a sigh. "In any case, I advise you not to go over there. Try to enjoy yourself, Bessie. Perhaps someone will introduce you to a gentleman of interest."

With a shrug, Bess returned to the window to stare at the night sky. She listened to Jane eagerly accept Alex's offer to dance. Turning around, Bess watched Abigail follow Alex and Jane to the other dancers. She watched Alex's ruffled hair disappear among the crowd, and she returned to the window with a sigh. *Oh, what am I doing here? I suppose that having a male companion would be nice. I'd be much less bored, but then I'd be conforming to society's expectations for me—for women.* She paused. *I cannot do it—I cannot be a trifling pawn in this naïve society.* She frowned. *Yet, how lovely it would be to have someone like Alex with whom to spend time. Unfortunately, everyone else is dull, bothersome, small-minded, or some combination of all three, and I would never be able to associate with them. They wouldn't understand me.* She shook her head and returned her gaze to the dancers. *Oh, but Alex is my friend, so I cannot think of him romantically. Besides, he's taken, and not only for this evening but for eternity!*

"Miss Elizabeth Phillips," a male voice called. Bess shifted her head to where the voice had originated and found an old gentleman approaching. He wore a tailcoat, a top hat, and a few gold bracelets that were so small that they did not come across as gaudy. Bess smiled before noticing a younger gentleman trailing behind her addressor. "I would like to introduce you to my nephew, Mr. Jackson Elmsworth," said the man. After a moment of hesitation, Bess recognized this man to be Mr. Westfield. She opened her mouth to reply but the gentleman added, "I don't believe I had the opportunity to welcome you this evening, my dear. I apologize. I must place the fault on my aging mind."

"Oh!" Bess nervously laughed. "No, the apologies are all mine. But truly, you must believe that I had a probable cause for doing so—for so *rudely* finding my way past you."

48

"There's no reason to worry, my dear," laughed Mr. Westfield. "I saw that you were spending the evening alone, and I thought to introduce you to Jackson." He nodded to Mr. Elmsworth. "And," he continued with sparkling eyes, "I've heard plenty of admirable stories about your good character, so I can trust that whatever motive it was that kept you away from introducing yourself earlier was for good reason." Mr. Westfield concluded his monologue with a bow, and he moved aside to showcase his nephew. Bess started to apologize again, but Mr. Westfield added, "I hope you have a wonderful evening." He tipped his hat, and before Bess was able to thank him, he left.

"Oh," Bess sighed, turning to her newest acquaintance. But when her eyes landed on Mr. Elmsworth, she froze with enchantment and giggled. Before she heard him say his first word, Bess had devised that Mr. Elmsworth was most certainly a few years her senior. He appeared mature, but this supposition made no difference in her judgment of him. Mr. Elmsworth was perhaps the most attractive person Bess had ever laid her eyes upon. He had dark hair, hazel eyes, freckles dotting his cheeks, and a warm smile. For the first time in forever, she had the sudden urge to reach out and kiss him—only the thought of Alex restrained her.

And amid her stares, Mr. Elmsworth knelt to kiss her on the hand, and upon his rising, he whispered, "May we continue our introductions outside?"

Bess smiled, and Mr. Elmsworth led her to the corridors outside of the ballroom. She glanced around and frowned at the dozen guests who were wandering around. Mr. Elmsworth must have sensed Bess' frustration, for he took hold of her hand (causing her heart to skip a beat) and guided her to the front porch, where nobody stood.

49

"Why did you lead me here?" asked Bess, trying to conceal a giggle. She covered her mouth with her hands and chastised herself for acting foolish.

"There's fresh air outside," answered Mr. Elmsworth with a grin. Bess hardly heard his response, for she was lost in thought. *Oh, what a smooth, masculine voice. And he's awfully handsome.* She gazed toward the night sky and thanked the stars (despite how cliché it was) for granting her wish. But Mr. Elmsworth interrupted her fawning. "Also, I saw you sitting in the corner, and I thought to ask you to dance. However, I observed you seemed uninterested in dancing, so I figured I ought to talk with you instead."

"What made you believe I was uninterested?" Bess asked, unknowingly twirling a lock of her hair around her finger.

"You hadn't a partner, and a lady as captivating as you would *never* be alone unless by choice."

"Then this is where your judgment falls," she perked. She let out a laugh and fancied herself almost *in love*, for nobody had ever complimented her beauty before. She straightened her posture and added, "I am a lover of dances, especially of the traditional art; however, the reason for why I have fallen short of engaging a partner is because I have none. I arrived here with my father, my two sisters, and my sister's fiancé."

Mr. Elmsworth's eyes brightened. "What a pleasant surprise, for that is exactly the response I wished to hear! However, I *did* notice you were speaking to a certain Mr. Ashford—"

"Oh," Bess started, "in that case, there are two points upon which I must reply. To begin, for you to have seen that, you must have scouted me out from the ball's beginning. And at that thought, I wonder if you were simply smitten with me or if you know me from some prior engagement," Bess said, finding it hard to contain a chuckle—*how intelligent I sound!* "If the instance was the former, then I cannot lie, but I feel a sense of defensiveness coming upon me. On the contrary, I apologize if the answer is the latter, for I do not remember seeing you before. And I believe I would remember a face (*as handsome*) as yours."

Mr. Elmsworth exchanged a smile with Bess before assuring, "It was the former, but do not fret. This evening, I have seen your elegance and have simply wanted to engage you before Mr. Ashford returned."

At the thought of Mr. Ashford, Bess laughed. She caught a glimpse of Mr. Elmsworth's sparkling eyes and replied, "I appreciate your remarks, Mr. Elmsworth, since nobody else has ever spoken of me in such high regard."

"You must call me Jack!" Mr. Elmsworth laughed. "Mr. Elmsworth is a name reserved for those who do not know me well, and I have a feeling that we will soon be remarkably acquainted." His fascinating eyes flashed across Bess' countenance again, and Bess turned red with embarrassment.

"And I am Bess," she giggled, "not Miss Phillips, as Mr. Westfield had courteously introduced me."

"Well, would you care to dance with me, Bess?" began Jack, who no longer exhibited a confident stature but rather a timid one. This sudden change in behavior perplexed Bess, but she ignored its connotation and answered with such excitement that it caused Jack to start forward.

"Absolutely!" She blushed again at her sudden and unconcealed emotion, but Jack did not seem to notice. Bess took a deep breath and followed her newest acquaintance back to the ballroom, which she discovered was booming with music from the piano forte and noise from cheering and clapping. Bess hardly had time to process the scene before Jack took her hand and pulled her into his arms. Her heart (if it was possible to do so for the dozenth time) skipped a beat, and she jumped closer to her partner, finding her rhythm for the current dance.

Swinging around, Bess admired Jack's deliberate and graceful steps. She watched his strong, broad shoulders loosen and stiffen at different intervals, and during her admiration, she hardly noticed when she stepped on his foot. Jack quietly squealed, and Bess' eyes widened with a rushing sense of fear. She sincerely apologized for her errors, but Jack's laughter relieved her of her guilt. With a giggle, she complimented his amazing dancing abilities.

"I've always been athletic—at least my mother says so," he replied coyly. Bess opened her mouth to tease him, but the next dance, which was of French origin, began, and she completely forgot about her plan.

Lost in thought, Bess missed the first few steps of the dance, causing Jack to inquire, "Do you know how—?"

"Ha—yes. I'm not as awful as you might think." She smiled. "If I hadn't a sister who was remarkably well-raised in the art of dancing and courtesy, then my nature would certainly never have learned it. But for your luck, my sister Jane taught it to me about a hundred times when I was a child, so it is ingrained into my memory. Now, I quite enjoy it," she finished with a smirk, and to prove her dominance in this French dance, she focused on perfecting her remaining moves.

Jack laughed, "Thank God for Jane then."

With a chuckle, Bess couldn't help but roll into a whirl of daydreaming. *Oh, how lovely Jack is! He is the only stranger I've ever met who referred to Jane simply by her name rather than Miss Phillips. What a pleasant idiosyncrasy, and it had nothing to do with my prodding! How delighted I am to have met such a handsome, proper, and, most importantly, genuine gentleman.* Suddenly, Bess' thoughts ceased, for a new song began to ring about the hall. Soon, she was engaged in a line of hopping, clapping, and continuous spinning. By the end of the dance, and thus, after Bess' heaven-like gaiety, she felt so dizzy that she nearly fell into Jack, who gladly offered to sit down and continue conversing.

After sitting down by the ocular window where they had met, Jack took a deep breath. He took hold of Bess' hand and said, "You have a sister named Jane."

"Yes," exhaled Bess, breathing heavily to catch her breath. She watched Jack take a deep breath, and she giggled. *Oh, quit it, Bess. You're acting ridiculous.* Bess slowly slipped her hand out from under Jack's, and she continued, "And Abbie, but she is so young, and all she does is mimic Jane, so I do not think there is much I can say about her. And what about your family?"

"I have an elder brother and a younger sister, who is ill. I anticipate leaving early tonight, so I can attend to her needs," Jack replied. "And in case I forget to mention: my home is Elmsworth Manor, which isn't far from here. Please visit, and any of us Elmsworths will be happy to welcome you inside." He paused. "Perhaps I could take you to town on my horse whose name I shall reveal to you later."

Bess smiled, for she understood how Jack was trying to gauge her interest and bring her into his home. To confirm her suspicions, Bess continued, "Are there any women of whom I must be aware? Any marriage proposals or the like?"

Jack answered, "My brother Curtis is married to a certain Mrs. Lydia Baldare, but that is all."

With excitement running through her, Bess could only manage a nod. She felt weak with giddiness, so she did not realize that Jack had led her to the ballroom floor until she was halfway through a waltz. She was consumed with utter bliss, so she laid her head on Jack's chest. His height was impressive, and Bess felt comfortable near him. Never did the thought of being seen with a *gentleman* by her sisters cross her mind. She simply enjoyed her dance for the next half an hour before Jack requested to take a break. When she reached the ocular window, Bess sat down and watched the other dancers. She spotted Jack gazing at her from the corner of her eye, and she blushed. She tested to see how long he could stare at her without becoming bored and after feeling a slight sense of insecurity, she turned to face him, remarking, "Your brother Curtis," she began. "Tell me about him and your sister."

"Well," Jack sighed. "As I mentioned, Curtis is married to Mrs. Lydia Baldare—"

"Oh!" perked Bess. "I hadn't realized, but I know that name from somewhere."

"She's the daughter of one of the wealthiest men in southern England," he remarked with an eye roll so fast that it was almost nonexistent. "He doesn't love her," he bluntly concluded. "We're wealthy, but not *that* wealthy, and Curtis thinks he'll inherit the Baldare fortune after Lydia's parents pass away." He lowered and shook his head. "I believe the money will go to their only son Isaac." He paused to rub his eyes. "Lydia has perfect table manners, but she possesses a repulsive character. I cannot stand holding a conversation with her, for all we seem to talk about is the latest fashions. She refused to take our surname upon her marriage to Curtis—and that fact alone should detail her character." He sighed, "I try to ignore both her and Curtis as best I can," he continued. "I am much closer with my sister Liza."

"Her name is Elizabeth, too?" asked Bess.

"No." Jack shook his head. "Her full name is Adeliza Lucille Elmsworth."

Bess nodded. "How pretty—"

"She has a precious heart, but she has always been a child of sickness. There has never been a moment within the past few years where she has not been plagued with some sort of disorder, illness, or symptom. She has a contagious fever right now," he added, "but I've had it before when I was an infant, and the doctors believe I can care for her without becoming ill, unlike the rest of my family."

"Oh," Bess began, recognizing this illness. "Not long ago, my mother passed away from scarlet fever. Because I caught it as an infant as well, I was able to hold her hand when she died. My sisters were out of town because my mother did not wish to pass it to them. My father, who also had it before, was with us, too." Bess paused. She stared into the crowd of dancers, and for a split second, her ignorant bliss faded as the recollection of her mother returned. "Oh, how Jane and Abbie were devastated after Father had me write and ask them to come home."

"Indeed—scarlet fever! But how unfortunate," remarked Jack.

"Yes, but we have great news that can distract us from this sad occasion. My elder sister Jane is engaged to our friend Alex. Their wedding is upcoming, and I know that nobody will be able to think about Mother with all the preparations and festivities."

"Well," said Jack as his eyes drifted off into the crowd of dancers, "if I can be of any service, please do not hesitate to ask."

"I will not," Bess replied, exchanging a warm smile with her new friend.

After a period of silence, Jack said that he had to depart, for Miss Elmsworth was undoubtedly in need of his care. He made Bess promise to keep in touch, and Bess reluctantly wished him a farewell. As soon as his handsome figure escaped Bess' view, she rotated and started making her way toward the ocular window.

"Bess!" a voice remarked, and Bess turned her head, hoping to see Jack. Instead, she found Alex stumbling toward her. Her heart dropped, and she looked around and noticed that Jane was not beside him.

"Alex," she started, "where is Jane?"

"Who was that?" he answered, ignoring her previous question.

"Are you drunk?" exclaimed Bess. Alex did not reply, and she shook her head. Quietly, she added, "Mr. Jackson Elmsworth. And where is Jane?"

"She's finished dancing. She's not the liveliest person, so I asked her if I could ask you to dance." He paused. "And no, I'm not drunk *at all*."

Bess smiled, ignoring Alex's intoxication, and she replied to the affirmative.

Soon, Bess and Alex engaged in a fast-paced dance throughout which Alex stumbled over his feet. When the song ended, both friends were so out of breath that Bess nearly collapsed with fatigue. Alex laughed, which caused Bess to laugh as well, and he took this light-hearted opportunity to lead her into the corridor. Bess grabbed hold of Alex's arm and pulled him toward the front porch. Alex tripped over the threshold, but Bess caught him and guided him to a seated position on the floor. She stood above her friend and shook her head.

"Well," Bess started after a moment of silence ensued, "are you excited for your wedding?" The moonlight briefly flashed over Alex's ruffled hair, and Bess blushed.

The shadow cast across her face prevented Alex from seeing her embarrassment, but he nevertheless added, "Of course I am. Why do you ask? Are *you* excited?"

"Ha—it's great timing." Bess smiled, and she turned away to gaze at the stars, which had already blessed her that evening with the introduction of Jack. She closed her eyes and prayed that neither she nor Alex would say anything crass. She sighed, "But I do not want Jane to marry. She is too young, and I don't want to lose a sister. But if you say that you are excited, then I shall uphold a sense of pretense to satisfy you and everybody else."

"I don't want you to behave unnaturally," Alex slurred, and Bess couldn't help but smile at how ridiculous he sounded.

"Oh, Alex, you know that wish cannot be granted."

The two of them shared a long pause before Alex took a deep breath. He stroked his hair and asked, "Did I startle you this evening when I came upon you? I didn't mean to cause you harm—"

"Oh, please, no harm was caused. I am having an exciting evening and—"

"Bess?"

Bess looked up but did not respond. For the first time in the past few minutes, she noticed the stars reflecting in Alex's sparkling eyes. She caught a glimpse of his striking grin, and she turned away.

"I *really* care about you, Bess," continued Alex in his drunken voice. "If Jane did not exist, then there would be no other person with whom I would rather spend my time than you. Throughout my life, I've considered you as my best friend, next to Jane, of course, and I want you to know how I feel." He paused. "After I am married, I feel that my words will not be mine but bound to God's words and His laws. I will not be able to tell you that I love you, Bess. I love you—I suppose—like a brother loves a sister; therefore, I am glad that we will soon be brothers and sisters, but I—I cannot—"

"Thank you, Alex, but you should not continue," Bess interrupted.

"I need you to know it, Bess," insisted Alex, "because I don't know who Mr. Jackson Elmsworth is, but I must admit that I do not want you to fall for him."

Bess' face turned a darker shade of red, and she frowned. "Well, I may do as I choose. You chose Jane, and if I choose Jack, it should not matter."

"I know it shouldn't," said Alex. He opened his mouth, but no words emerged.

For another moment, Bess refused to reply. She took a deep breath, calculating the most appropriate response that would upset neither Alex nor her family. She prepared to walk away, but something inside of her sputtered, "Alex, I like you, too.'" She faltered. "I apologize, Alex. I didn't mean…," she stammered, regretting this sentence immediately. She had never voiced her true feelings about *anyone* before, nevertheless *Alex*. Emotions rose within her again, and she exclaimed, "But you chose Jane, and you cannot continue to hinder my relationships, Alex! You just cannot!"

Then Alex kissed her. He pressed his lips onto hers, and all that Bess could taste was champagne and his stale breath. For a moment, their teeth clicked, and Bess pulled away in disbelief. She stepped away from Alex, whose eyes looked lopsided. A thought flickered over her—*if only*

I could reach out and kiss him again—and she caressed the top of his head.

"Alex," Bess murmured as a tear rolled down her cheek. "You can't," she insisted. "You can't do this to yourself, you can't do this to Jane, and you can't do this to *me*." Bess stared at Alex's glimmering eyes and sighed, "You won't remember this tomorrow morning. You should know you'll have an awful headache, Alex."

Bess started to walk away, but Alex took hold of her arm and whispered, "Don't marry him, Bessie."

Bess' recoiled at the smell of his breath., and with growing anger boiling within her, she cried, "Alex, you're acting ridiculous! Now, let me go." She tugged her arm away from Alex's grasp and marched back into the ballroom. To her delight, she did not encounter him for the rest of the evening.

Chapter 5

The next morning, a ray of sunshine beamed through Bess' window and awoke her. She pulled her blankets over her head, hoping to return to sleep, but her efforts were to no avail. She sat up and groaned, for she had been awake all night thinking about the Westfield ball. *Had Alex meant what he said, or was he too intoxicated to think properly? Did he even remember what he had revealed?* She tucked a lock of her hair behind her ear and forced herself to stand up. She wandered over to her wardrobe, selected something casual to wear, and headed downstairs for breakfast.

When she arrived in the dining hall, Bess found her sisters munching on toast and relating gossip from last evening's ball. Most of the conversation was led by Abigail, who hardly took a breath during her loud, chirping monologue of the "the handsome young gentleman" she had encountered. Bess shook her head and slumped down beside her talkative younger sister. She started to spread marmalade over a piece of toast when Abigail's sudden increase in volume startled her.

"Oh, and Jane—Bessie—there was a certain Lieutenant Chapman who fancied me—I'm sure of it! He danced *twice* with me and only *once* with Miss Mathilde Frocker!" she exclaimed, sitting on her seat's edge.

"I believe I met him," Jane remarked, handing Bess another slice of toast. "Is his first name James?"

Abigail shook her head and grinned, "No, I believe it's Theodore." She paused. "Jane, did you happen to see Mr. Melvin Godfrey? He was perhaps ten times *more* handsome than Lieutenant Chapman. He brought a date—Miss Charlotte something—but he *still* managed to dance with me!"

Jane smiled and replied, "How lovely."

Bess, who had rushed to finish her breakfast, abruptly remarked, "Where is Father?"

"Oh, Bessie's bored," laughed Abigail, who nearly fell off her seat's edge.

"In his study, I believe," Jane said.

Bess started to rise from the table, but Abigail exclaimed, "Oh, Bessie! Sit back down!"

"Fine," Bess murmured. She rolled her eyes and sat down. She glanced over to her sister, and suddenly, her face turned red. She watched her sister's eyes glisten and feared that she would mention Alex's kiss. Bess bit her lip and held her breath.

"With whom were you dancing last night?" Abigail asked, raising an eyebrow.

"Oh!" Jane's face lit up, for this was a topic in which she was truly fascinated.

Bess exhaled with relief, and a smile grew across her face. She stood up, planning to find somewhere else to go. "Who do you mean?" she teased.

"Bessie, don't be silly!" Jane laughed. She placed her hand on Bess' side to keep her from departing. "What's his name? Even *I* think he's handsome."

Bess rolled her eyes, but she couldn't manage to conceal a smile at the memory of her newest acquaintance. Her heart began to race as she said his name, "Jack."

"Jack who?" Abigail demanded.

Bess stepped back to examine her sisters' eager countenances. Both sat on their heels, leaning toward her. They giggled and grinned, for they had never seen their sister show outward affection for *anyone*, nevertheless a gentleman from a ball!

To further bother them, Bess teased, "I won't say."

"Oh," whined Jane, "but he was beautiful! Won't you tell me?"

"And me, too!" cried Abigail. "I would have danced with him had he asked!"

"Do you know where he lives? I would love to greet him!" Jane exclaimed.

"Oh!" Abigail squealed. "*Can* we meet him?"

Bess smiled and shook her head. She collected her sisters' dishes and said, "No. You two are acting ridiculous."

Abigail's smile disappeared, and she retorted, "We'll be on our best behavior! We promise, Bessie."

"Yes, and I can bake Mother's cake as a gift for him!" added Jane.

"It can read: *To Jack, My Mysterious Romantic, Love Bess*," teased Abigail.

Bess set the dishes back on the table and laughed. "This is why I don't talk to you about my love life!" But upon speaking these words, she gasped and covered her mouth, realizing that the term *love life* was sure to send her sisters on a long investigation into her past "romances."

"There *have* been others?" Jane asked.

"Who? You ought to tell us, Bessie!" Abigail exclaimed and fell off her chair, causing her sisters to burst into laughter. Abigail clumsily regained her footing and chuckled.

"I can't tell you," said Bess seriously, thinking only of Alex. She collected the dirty dishes and carried them to the kitchen before returning to her pink-faced sisters, who were talking about something else.

"Well, *obviously* because I liked him, I think he's handsome," Abigail mentioned, but Bess had missed an integral part of this conversation.

"Who are you talking about?" she asked.

"Alex," Abigail said, and Bess' heart skipped a beat. "I used to like him before he engaged Jane."

"He's hard not to like," Jane added with a complacent smile.

"Don't tell me *you* didn't like him, too, Bessie," Abigail said, eyes widening.

"No," Bess quickly answered. "I didn't."

"That's a lie!" insisted Abigail. "And now you're making me sound silly."

"I promise," Bess softly replied.

"Well, I don't believe it," Abigail remarked. She stuck her nose in the air and smirked. Bess shook her head and left the room without hearing her sisters call her back. But it was not long until Abigail found Bess, sitting in the garden reading a book her father had recommended. Bess turned her gaze toward her approaching sister, for her book was not interesting. "What are you doing?" Abigail asked with squinted eyes, for she was trying to read the front cover. She took a step closer to her sister and sat down.

"Reading," Bess answered as she shut her book. "Why are *you* here, Abbie?"

"I'm bored," Abigail sighed dramatically. "Sometimes Jane can be too bland for me."

"I thought you liked Jane more than you like me," Bess said bluntly. "She's better at fashion and the stuff you care about."

"Oh!" exclaimed Abigail. "*Please* don't say that I'm like Jane."

"But you imitate her," Bess interrupted, and her eyes narrowed.

"I imitate her *style*, but I do not wish to *be* her. I pray I'm not *that* boring," Abigail said, concluding with a dramatic eye roll.

"Now, you're acting crass." Bess shook her head and returned to her book.

"*Don't* start acting like Jane!"

"And what if Jane is nearby to hear you?" exclaimed Bess, who was bothered by Abigail's seeming insult, for she slammed her book on the bench beside her.

"She's with Alex," Abigail muttered, and she turned her gaze half-heartedly toward the garden.

"You talk to Jane," began Bess, "with such interest in the most shallow, romantic topics of which I can think. *Alex* is the only person to whom I can truly talk without getting into—oh, I shouldn't go into that, for you couldn't comprehend." Bess took a deep breath. "You say, Abbie, that you are unlike Jane, but you are, rather, her shadow—that's all. I'm sure you'll grow out of it when you're older, but you're only fifteen—oh, please don't whimper," Bess said when she noticed Abigail pouting. "See, Abbie? This is what I mean! You want to be independent, but you cannot have a mature conversation without whimpering when your elder sister reveals such obvious truths to you!"

"Bess!"

"If a gentleman of good fortune and good appearance met you last night and proposed, perhaps, a bond of marriage, I do not doubt you would have innocently accepted. And oh, how utterly foolish that would be—and you'd cry the next day, for you'd realize it was a mistake—I know it."

"No, I wouldn't!" defied Abigail.

"Oh, but you would!" said Bess, standing up. "And *don't* insult our sister, Abbie. We're all different." She paused. "Besides, *you* haven't even developed your personality yet!"

"Me?" exclaimed Abigail, standing up to match Bess' stature. "*I* haven't developed my personality yet?" she blushed. "Says the befuddled eighteen-year-old who cannot seem to keep her eyes off her *darling* sister's fiancé! At least *I* can articulate my true feelings as a mature woman should—*I* don't have to rely on such obvious lies because I cannot *comprehend* what I'm feeling."

"Alex?" Bess blushed, hurriedly picking up her book and preparing to march away.

"You kissed him last night, Bess. I saw, and I'd thank God if I were you that I was the only one who did."

For a moment, silence filled the garden. Bess nearly threw her book on the ground as her mind boiled with anger. Her heart pounded blood into every inch of her body. She stepped closer to her younger sister and murmured, "It was not me who initiated it. I told him to stop."

"Is that so?" Abigail crossed her arms. "It seemed to go on for thirty seconds!"

"It did *not*." Bess' nostrils flared.

"I counted it." Abigail stepped onto the bench where she and Bess were previously sitting to obtain a sense of physical dominance.

"I don't like him like that, Abbie." Bess turned away from her sister's penetrating glares. She took a deep breath, trying to contain her frustration.

"Then whom do you like, Bessie? Jack?"

"Abbie, there you go again!" Bess whipped back around to face her sister. "Your life is fraught with romantics and gossip when it should be

65

consumed with books and studies. You believe you're much older than you are, and you shouldn't meddle with business that you cannot comprehend!"

"I comprehend perfectly, Bess!" exclaimed Abigail, jumping off the bench and tearing Bess' book from her arms. "Besides, books are for those who have nothing else to do." She stared down at the dull cover of *Othello*. "Why do you think Father always reads? *You* read to hide away your true emotions about everything!"

"*Everything*?" Bess seethed.

"Everything!" declared Abigail. "Alex! Mother!"

"What does Mother have to do with this?" cried Bess, grabbing back her book.

"I haven't seen you shed a tear since!" Abigail fumed.

"One doesn't need," murmured Bess, fighting back tears, "to be so clear about his or her feelings when they ought to be assumed."

"You have a *right*," whispered Abigail, starting to calm down, "to like Alex. To like anyone, in fact—I don't care—just be honest and respectful about it."

After a moment of silence, Bess snapped, "I didn't kiss him. He was drunk." She looked away and rubbed a tear from her cheek.

"But you have feelings for him," Abigail said. Bess did not respond. "It's plain as day, Bess."

"I value him as a friend—more than anyone else." She shook her head and wiped her eyes. "Regardless, I alluded to the fact that I took a fancy to Jack, so that should be enough to satisfy your need for drama. That's more than you've gotten out of me before!"

Abigail looked to the ground and clenched her teeth. She muttered something about Bess *just not getting it* before starting to walk away.

"Abbie!" cried Bess, and Abigail turned around. Bess ran to her sister and noticed that she had been crying. She lowered her voice and said, "Please do not assume that everyone fits into one mold. Jack is the first person I've ever liked, and perhaps he's the last I ever will. You shouldn't concern yourself with my business any longer. I shall visit Jack, but neither you nor Jane may come along. And concerning books... do your work your teacher Miss Camelot assigns. We're blessed as a wealthy family with wealthy connections, but that doesn't mean we are to act spoiled and take everything for granted. Suppose our house catches fire, and we lose almost everything dear to us. At least Father and I could read our way into learning a trade, and Jane could paint to earn herself a living—"

"Bess," Abigail intervened, "do you mean to say that I lack talent?"

"If one doesn't have an innate talent like Jane does, then we all must commit to our societal responsibilities of being educated in both social conventions and independent studies, such as literature and arithmetic. In any case," she continued, despite hearing Abigail's whine, "if neither of us marries well (and I define *well* as us being happy), then we must occupy ourselves with something stimulating of the mind. We cannot spend the rest of our lives gossiping at evening balls and not leaving our marks on the world."

Abigail let out a cry and began to march away, "Bess, you preach so much of happiness but neglect that what brings *you* happiness may not bring it to the rest of us!" She aggressively turned back to her sister and declared, "I would be perfectly glad if I could just have a husband! I don't need to rely on my father and sisters. You are so *against* love and healthy gossip that I fear you'll drive yourself from happiness! If all you think you need is your family and books, then I'm afraid that you'll be in for a harsh wake-up call someday, Bessie." She paused and lowered her voice. "If you opt to stay home forever, it won't be long until you're the only one left." Abigail took a deep breath. She opened her mouth to speak, but no words emerged. Finally, she choked, "Not all of us want to change the world, Bessie. Perhaps I should remain with Jane. Despite how boring she can be, at least she understands the simple concept of *respect*."

Without allowing her sister time to reply, Abigail turned around and ran back to the house. Bess exhaled as she watched her sister go. When Abigail was no longer in sight, Bess returned to the garden and collapsed beside a wall of roses. A pang of regret shot into her chest, and she let her face fall into her hands, doing her best to hold back the waterfall of tears streaming from her eyes.

Chapter 6

Breakfast the next morning was rather dull, for, when she arrived in the dining hall, Bess found herself alone. She prepared herself a bread roll, and just before she was about to sit down, Jane strolled into the room, examining an article in the local paper. Jane looked up, exchanged a brief smile with her younger sister, and sat down at the table. She flipped through the leaves of her newspaper until landing on the final page.

"Upon my word," she murmured, and Bess glanced toward her.

"What is it?" Bess asked as she took a seat across from her sister.

"Oh," Jane started, looking up, "Mr. Matson—the young gentleman who helped with Mother's funeral—well, according to the news, he married Miss Delilah Ramapo. Have you heard—?" Jane skimmed a passage before returning to her sister. Upon noticing Bess' oblivious expression, she continued. "Well, she has *no* inheritance, so *no* money, and she has hardly a family to call her own. They're an intriguing match, for I didn't even know that they knew one another."

Unsure of how to respond, Bess looked down to her breakfast. Jane frowned and returned to reading her paper. Bess opened her mouth to remark that a financial situation should not be the sole cause of marriage (as evidenced by Jane marrying Alex, whose family owned not a fifth of the Phillips family's fortune), but she looked up and examined her sister's concentration instead. *Does she know about my disagreement with Abbie?* Bess paused and bit her lip. *Besides, where is Abbie?* She returned to fumbling with her bread roll until, as if on cue, a knock sounded on the front door. From upstairs, Abigail called, "I'll get it!"

Bess heard footsteps march into the dining hall, and her younger sister appeared. She tossed a letter addressed to Bess on the table, and before Bess could thank her, she walked away.

"Perhaps you should talk to her," Jane commented without looking up from her reading. "Abbie and I spoke yesterday—"

Bess exhaled and rubbed her eyes. She clenched her teeth to withhold her emotions, but eventually she spat, "To hell if you did." In one swift motion, Bess reached across the table and snatched the letter.

"Bess!" Jane cried, looking up from her paper with eyes the size of golf balls.

Bess tore open her envelope and stomped out of the dining hall. Jane glanced up and shook her head before returning to her paper. Ascending the staircase to her bedroom, Bess read—

Dear Bess,

Please forgive me for writing so soon, but I could not bear the thought of being without you for so long. I miss you, Bess, so it would be my greatest honor to invite you and your family to dinner this evening. Invite your sisters, father, and eldest sister's fiancé. My parents intend on inviting other guests, and they'd like to dedicate this dinner as a "feast to new acquaintances." Perhaps I may have the pleasure of introducing you and your sister to my horse. I'm certain that Abigail would enjoy meeting her. In any case, I'm sending a servant to deliver this letter, so that you will receive this note shortly. Please return a reply if you can come as quickly as possible.

Until tonight,

Yours,

Mr. Jackson Elmsworth

Bess returned the letter to its envelope and crossed the hallway to her bedroom. *I suppose I shall go, but I won't invite my family.* She paused. *I'll say that they're unwell. Yes—I'll say we spent the day in town, and they each grew too weary to join me. There should be no further questioning thereafter. I will only have to ask the Elmsworths to pardon them.* Bess smiled. When she arrived at her bedroom, she stepped across her threshold and tossed the letter onto her bed. She found a pen and paper in her desk drawer and crafted her reply to Jack. She scribbled her neatly manufactured reply before returning downstairs and handing her note to a servant to deliver to Elmsworth Manor. After a moment of consideration, Bess turned around and resolved to spend the remainder of the morning and afternoon with her father—someone who couldn't possibly upset her.

With excitement brimming inside of her, Bess knocked on the door to her father's study. Upon hearing a quiet, sleepy welcome, she pushed open the door and found her father sitting dreary-eyed behind a Shakespearean work. Bess, smiling at the idea that her father was sleeping at an hour so late as ten o'clock in the morning, sat down in a chair next to him.

"Bess, my dear!" Mr. Phillips half-consciously blurted. He started forward and said, "How are you?"

"I am doing well, Father," Bess replied as she reached out to touch the cover of his book.

"It's *The Tragedy of Julius Caesar*," he said, placing it down on his desk. "I must admit that it is certainly *not* one of my favorites, but I appreciate all of his works nonetheless."

"Nor was it mine," Bess replied, happy to have a normal conversation with a member of her family again. "And *Othello*, which you recommended, was not much better. In fact," she said with increasing volume, "I drew many parallels between the two." She paused. "Yet, I still believe I liked the former better. I enjoyed Mark Antony's character (mainly his intelligence and rhetoric), but not one character of *Othello* was particularly striking. I found the characters unrealistically blind to Iago's schemes."

Bess looked up from the cover of the book and watched her father's eyes glaze over in recollection. She raised an eyebrow, and Mr. Phillips said, "Your mother said the same thing."

Bess smiled. "About Iago or—?"

Mr. Phillips placed his spectacles on the bridge of his nose. His face consisted of bone and skin alone, so it did not take long for them to slip off into his lap. Bess chuckled as her father picked them up and set them on his head. "About both stories," he answered. "Your mother turned me into an avid reader, Bess. Before I met her, I never took a particular liking to the activity, but when she taught you and your sisters how to read, listen, and imagine, I found enjoyment in it as well." He sighed and touched the cover of his book. "To Emily, reading was an art. She was beyond pleased that you learned to appreciate it as much as she did."

Bess could not help but to reveal a wide grin. "I told Abbie to finish reading her book for school, but I hardly believe she will. Not only does she loathe reading, but *Jane Eyre* is quite boring—one of my least favorites, in fact."

Mr. Phillips' smile broke into a chuckle as he said, "She's on a break now. Let her enjoy her rest, and trust that she will finish her work in time."

Bess frowned but neglected her father's defense of her younger sister. Instead, she selected another book sitting on her father's desk titled *A Tale of Two Cities.* Flipping through the leaves of the novel, she read, "Dickens."

"Your mother's favorite," Mr. Phillips recollected, and when Bess glanced up, she noticed that he had shed a tear. "Go on and read it."

Bess pursed her lips and reached out to collect her mother's favorite piece.

After a few hours of reading, Bess returned to her bedroom and found her envelope just as she had left it. She tossed it on top of her clothing chest and began to prepare for the evening. Upon every other occasion, Bess felt indifferent toward her fashion selection, for she never had anyone in mind to impress. The only person whom she ever felt that she had to please was Alex, and Bess always thought he liked her the way she was. She could wear anything, and he'd be satisfied. *It was very peculiar, though, how he didn't seem to like my brown dress from the other evening. I've always been under the impression that he didn't mind anything I wore.* Nervously, she sorted through her options but found herself at a loss. She owned nothing suitable to wear. *If only Jane could lend me a dress, but oh, she doesn't know about the dinner!* Bess paused and bit her lip. *Perhaps I could take one anyway.* But she shook her head. *However, Jack cannot see me in one of my own gowns. He'd think they're hideous, and he'd never invite me to Elmsworth Manor again!* She sagged her shoulders and quietly snuck into Jane's bedroom. She tiptoed across the floorboards and found a nice yellow gown, tried it on, and decided that it would do. When she returned to her bedroom, Bess attempted to emulate Abigail's braided hairstyle, but her efforts failed, and she left her hair down.

When she had finished preparing her appearance, Bess stood at the edge of her threshold. She poked her head out of the door and listened for anyone who might see her in Jane's dress. After a minute of complete silence, she shouted, "Father, I'm going to visit a friend!"

She dashed down the staircase, nearly tripping during the process, and fell over in shock when she saw her family and Alex dressed in their neatest attire by the front door.

"Where are you going?" Bess stammered as her eyes grew twice their size. Her heart thumped, and she turned to Abigail with flared nostrils.

"To Mr. Elmsworth's," replied Jane, and Bess blushed.

From the corner of her eye, Bess watched Alex grin, and she did her best to avoid glancing his way. Instead, she tugged onto the ends of her hair and glared at Abigail.

"I may have read your letter," Abigail said with a coy smile, "and I thought it impolite for you not to extend the invitation, so *I* did."

Bess opened her mouth to protest, but the thought of Alex watching flickered across her mind, and she remained silent. And then, recalling the kiss, she tensed and turned away.

Jane twirled a strand of her hair around the tip of her finger and added, "I know you didn't want us to come, Bessie, but I love evening dinners, so I couldn't refuse Abbie!"

Bess lowered her head and shrugged. She ignored her family's presence and walked out of the house, heading toward the farther of the two carriages.

"And Bessie," Abbie's voice called from behind, "had it not been for me, you would have ruined your dress walking there. I know you wouldn't trouble the coachman for a one-person ride, but now, there are two coaches for the five of us!"

"It's actually my dress," Jane murmured. Bess' face flushed, yet she dared not respond.

"Elmsworth Manor, I gather?" inquired Mr. Phillips as he entered the larger of the two carriages. Abigail followed him, so Bess entered the other. After a moment of hesitation, Alex followed her inside and nestled himself between the far wall and a large, ornate pillow.

"Alex, there's room in this one," Jane said, popping her head inside the carriage in which Alex and Bess were sitting and pointing toward where her father and Abigail were.

"I don't think Bess wants to sit alone," Alex answered, avoiding eye contact with both sisters.

"Oh," Jane murmured. "Of course." She hesitated before leaving.

Once the horses started to pull away from Laurel Manor, Bess' heart pumped. She wanted to talk to her best friend, but she remained silent. Her mouth could not form the words she wished to communicate, but she yearned for something to be said. *Does he remember when he kissed me, or was he too intoxicated to remember even that we danced?*

"A few minutes' ride, eh?" Alex suddenly said to break the quietness.

"I think so," she replied, refusing to make eye contact.

Yet her curtness failed to silence Alex, for he continued. "Isn't it strange that now I get to meet Mr. Jackson Elmsworth?" When Alex realized that Bess wouldn't respond, he continued, "You know, when Jane stopped by my house to invite me to this dinner, I wanted to say no." He hesitated before whispering, "I remember Saturday night, Bess—fully. How could I forget it? I know I was drunk, but I had enough sense to control, to an extent, what I did!" He paused to take a deep breath. "I apologize if I caught you off guard—I won't mention it to you ever again—I'll forget about it the best I can."

"That would be best," sniffled Bess. She felt her body sink as she replied, "Alex, you can't do that to Jane."

"I know," he sighed. He ran his hand through his hair and asked, "Did Jane say that's her dress?" Bess rolled her eyes, for Alex did not understand the depth of his mistake.

"Yes." She eventually nodded. "She didn't have to make it so obvious."

"Well," Alex said. "Why did you wear it?"

"Jack wouldn't like my dresses," she answered. "Besides, Alex, you recommended Jane's blue dress for Saturday because you *know* my dresses are—"

"Bess," he interrupted and extended his arm to touch hers. Bess pulled her arm away. Alex took a deep breath and returned his hand to his side. "I figured the blue dress would better fit Mr. Ashford's liking." He paused. "But I like your dresses more, Bess. They're unique." He shrugged and looked toward the window.

Bess blushed. "If only Jane thought the same way."

Alex did not reply, and Bess sighed. She hated herself in this moment for falling into peer pressure, which she had always tried to avoid. *Alex had made it clear that I should have remained my own person—I should have worn my own dress, and I should not have acted differently to impress someone else. Perhaps Abbie* was *right—but oh, I could never admit this!* She wrung her hands and folded her arms across her chest. *Perhaps* I *am the one who truly needs to develop my personality.*

Silence encompassed the remainder of the ride. When they reached their destination, Alex pushed open the door and said, "Go on."

Bess shook her head. "I don't need to go first, Alex." She took a deep breath. "I cannot go ahead any longer. It isn't right," she said in a muffled voice. *I can no longer bear the thought of Alex being a gentleman. I must reject all his forms of gentleman-like etiquette, such as the cliché* ladies first *and anything else to that degree.* Alex hesitated to exit the carriage, but when he finally did, he held the door open for his friend. "I've got the door," Bess said, and Alex let it swing shut.

When Bess emerged from the carriage, she saw her family greeting the Elmsworths by the entrance to the property. She watched the figures of who must have been Jack's parents, brother (*Miss Elmsworth must be too ill to present herself),* and his brother's wife introduce themselves. She searched for Jack but could not find him. Suddenly, she heard a voice exclaim, "Bess! I am delighted that you made it here safely!" Bess turned around and found Jack approaching her from the road. Without being able to contain it, she felt a massive smile spread across her lips. She laughed as Jack approached, and when he was within a yard of her, he leaned forward and wrapped his arms around her shoulders. Bess remained still, for she was not used to new acquaintances greeting one another with such casualness. *However, I* am *pleased that Jack is rejecting typical societal rules to convey his own feelings and beliefs. It's rather admirable.* She returned the gesture.

Bess finally pulled away and tucked a strand of hair behind her ears. She smiled and pointed to the road, which was opposite to where the remainder of Jack's family stood. "Where were you?"

"Purchasing medicine for Liza," Jack answered. And before Bess had the opportunity to introduce Alex, Jack turned to him and said, "And you must be Jane's fiancé?"

Alex nodded. "Yes. Mr. Alexander Cawdor."

"Pleasure," Jack remarked before turning back to Bess. "Oh, Bess, I must show you around! Since you've had scarlet fever before, you can safely meet Liza!"

Alex raised an eyebrow before heading toward the other Phillipses and Elmsworths.

"Is that your brother Mr. Curtis Elmsworth?" asked Bess, pointing to an unfamiliar gentleman standing by her family.

"Yes, but please, he deserves no other introduction than *Curtis*!" Jack started. "I apologize. I almost forgot to introduce you to everyone."

Jack grasped onto Bess' hand and led her to his family. Interrupting his father, who was speaking of a renowned Italian winery, Jack excitedly announced the arrival of Bess, who blushed and introduced herself. Mr. Elmsworth frowned at his son's lack of manners but welcomed Bess with a smile and shake of the hand. After Bess had greeted everyone, she stood back and admired the Elmsworths. Mr. Elmsworth was a man whose white mustache, beard, and balding head revealed his older age. His wife had hair that was whitening at the edges, and she wore bright diamond earrings and gold jewelry that made Bess raise an eyebrow. When she turned to Curtis and his wife, Bess took a step back. The former possessed jet-black hair and a handsome face, but a furrowed brow indicated that he was a serious, uptight gentleman. The latter was stone-faced, plain, and not very pretty, and her excessive amount of jewelry did not improve her appearance in the slightest.

Growing bored at the chatter, Curtis and his wife headed inside. Bess and Jack followed.

Elmsworth Manor was much more gorgeous than Laurel Manor. When she entered, Bess thought she was in a castle. Marble floors and lavish, red carpets decorated every corner of the house, and portraits of the family heritage added to its beautiful decor. As Bess gazed around the manor, Jack, who did not notice her awe, remarked, "And my cousins, the Wheatleys, should be arriving shortly, but they won't be troublesome. I don't mind the children, Juliette and Leonarda, at least. Juliette is seventeen, and Leonarda is thirteen, but they're both very agreeable." He paused. "We have other guests coming as well (I believe I wrote this to you), but we don't need to spend much time with them."

"Fantastic," murmured Bess as she admired a portrait of a man who closely resembled Mr. Elmsworth.

Jack glanced toward her and noticed that she was talking about a portrait, not the guests. He tapped the artwork and chuckled, "That's my father."

"Your house is fantastic," she repeated, for she was too distracted to think of a word other than *fantastic.*

"I'm glad you like it," Jack laughed.

As she walked upstairs to Miss Elmsworth's bedroom, Bess admired more portraits hanging along the way. *They all have such precise details.* She sighed. *But upon my word, Jane is a painter! And to think that she wastes her time on such a trivial... oh, will her life be wasted away just to leave its legacy on a window-sized picture on some rich man's wall?* Bess took a deep breath and shook her head.

The room in which Miss Elmsworth sat was perhaps grander and more elegant than the entrance hall. Velvet curtains draped the windows, a refined carpet laid across the floor, intricately carved wooden furniture decorated the room, and the girl on top of the bed matched everything perfectly. Miss Elmsworth's hair was neatly tied back into a large white bow, and she wore a long blue dress that neatly fell off either side of her bed. The dress was embellished with countless ruffles and sparkles, and Bess' first thought was that it was rather hideous (even though it probably cost a fortune). Aside from what she wore, Miss Elmsworth possessed an ashen complexion, blonde hair, and light blue eyes. Her facial features closely resembled Jack's, and she appeared to be around Abigail's age.

When Bess and Jack entered the room, Miss Elmsworth did not stir. Jack cleared his throat, which caused her to glance up, but she refused to say a word. Jack shrugged, and Bess watched the exchange with amusement from the doorway.

"Liza, I have someone I'd like you to meet," he said, approaching her. He outstretched his arms and caressed her long blonde hair with the back of his knuckles. Miss Elmsworth decidedly raised her head in Bess' direction.

"Her?" she snapped in an airy tone.

Bess raised her eyebrows. She clenched her teeth, trying to hold back an outburst. In any other situation, she would have voiced her frustration, but she remained quiet. *If I lash out, I'll upset Jack and elevate Miss Elmsworth's physical distress.*

After a moment of silence, Jack helped his sister stand up. He murmured that her health was improving, and Bess responded that she was happy to hear him say so. Then Jack seated his sister at a table near the doorway and found a chair for himself. Bess glanced around before finding an old wooden chair in the far corner. She dragged it to the table.

Perhaps he's just nervous that I'm here. He was polite at the ball. I suppose this uncharacteristic behavior in not finding me a seat is due to his nerves.

When Miss Elmsworth settled, she tilted her head to the side to examine Bess' appearance. Blushing, Bess mustered an awkward smile and looked kindly in return. She wanted to condemn Miss Elmsworth's rudeness, but she did not wish to ruin her chances with Jack by speaking out of line.

"When I was younger," Miss Elmsworth started after taking a deep breath, "I enjoyed attending balls. I loved to dance, and because my father said I was *too* young to bring a partner, I would dance with him, Jack, or Curtis. I remember the first ball I attended with Curtis' wife Lydia. It was a lovely day, and Lydia and I got along well. She was not the prettiest spectacle, but she seemed sweet-tempered and well-mannered, so I was able to tolerate *her* presence." She pursed her lips and glared at Bess before continuing. "However, there was one girl with whom I urged Curtis to dance. She was the most captivating human being I have ever laid eyes upon." She took a deep breath. "When I heard our guests arrive, Jack, I peered out of my window." She pointed to a large, circular window above her bed and said, "I saw that girl again. I suppose she's one of the Phillips sisters."

"*My* sister?" Bess started.

"Perhaps you're speaking of Bess?" suggested Jack with sparkling eyes.

Miss Elmsworth ignored Jack's compliment and continued, "I still remember her name. *Everyone* at the ball knew it then—and for the next month, in fact. She was the most elegant person in the room—Miss Jane Phillips." Bess clenched her teeth and nodded, boiling with envy. *Of course, out of everyone, Jane would be regarded as the most beautiful creature at a ball! I should have expected nothing different.* Miss Elmsworth added, "I watched her dance all evening, and I can say with full confidence that *to this day*, I have never seen anyone more charming than she is." She pursed her lips and refused to continue, ensuring to give a particular glare in Bess' direction.

Jack turned to his sister and said, "I think that Bess is the best dancer I've seen since *you* were last dancing!" Bess' eyes widened, and she laughed to herself, for there was certainly *no* way Jack had a truly positive evaluation of her dancing skills.

"Oh, Jack," Miss Elmsworth sighed. "I never danced as often as I would have liked. I was always plagued with some illness." *Perhaps Miss Elmsworth's apparent ignorance of me isn't due to her character.* Bess tilted her head. *She's likely too ill to act with proper courtesy.* "But Miss Jane—*Jane*! She is the most beautiful creature that I have ever seen. And your other sister," she said, giving a condescending glance toward Bess, "is also pretty. However, I do not know her name, so perhaps you can later enlighten me. Nevertheless, I *must* say that I thought her dress was too large." *It's strange how hypocritical Miss Elmsworth can be, for her dress is just as large, if not larger than anything Abbie wears!* "And I suppose that Lydia is pretty," she sighed. "The other ladies soon to arrive—the Miss Barlettes; Miss Catherine Henwood, the sister of the elegant Mr. Henwood; and our cousins Juliette and Leonarda are adequately beautiful as well."

Bess nodded, trying to agree with the odd logic of Miss Elmsworth. *I have now resolved that her rambling is entirely caused by her illness.* Bess frowned. *Yet, her peculiar recollection of Jane is somewhat unsettling. I could never remember such a thing*! Bess turned to Jack, who wasn't fazed, and shrugged. "You said that Mr. Henwood is elegant," said Bess, who was unable to hold her tongue much longer.

"Yes, he's certainly well-mannered," she answered. "He possesses lots of money, and oftentimes, manners come paired with money."

These strange opinions must be the illness, not this young girl, speaking. No sensible person could genuinely think of Mr. Henwood in any high regard. Bess frowned. *I shall therefore excuse Miss Elmsworth. And if Jack ever mentions anything positive about Mr. Henwood, then I shall have to forgive him as well. He would probably just be delusional after spending so much time with his sick sister.*

"That's certainly what I thought!" boasted a loud voice that reverberated through the upstairs floorboards.

"That's Mr. Henwood," Bess muttered.

"Then you must go and greet him. It's only polite," Miss Elmsworth concluded before rising.

While Jack assisted his sister, Bess returned the old wooden chair to its proper location. When she turned around to leave, Bess noticed that Miss Elmsworth waved both her and Jack goodbye, not neglecting to add a carefree "Oh, I'm sorry, dear. What's your name again?" Bess closed her eyes, repeating that this behavior was *just the sickness.*

Yet, her emotions got the better of her, and she smirked, "It's Bess, and it was very nice to meet you, Elizabeth." Bess smiled to herself and escaped before she could hear Miss Elmsworth's wrath. Jack opened his mouth to correct his friend, but Bess interrupted. "Jack, if your sister has scarlet fever, then why is everyone else in the same house as she is? Has your entire family had scarlet fever? Have all the guests? Are they immune? I know that Jane and Abbie are not," she said with concern.

"Oh." Jack frowned. "Liza—not *Elizabeth*, by the way—won't give it to anyone. Besides, she didn't want to be sent away."

"But if I carry it to someone who hasn't had it like Jane or Abbie—"

"You won't," Jack said. Bess raised an eyebrow but ignored her friend's naïvety. Although Bess was naturally skeptical, she nevertheless attributed Jack's ignorance to his being so often with the sick Miss Elmsworth.

Chapter 7

When Mr. Henwood laid his eyes on Bess' figure descending the staircase, he sighed and turned away. Bess frowned, but she ignored this behavior and greeted everyone else. Alex widened his eyes to capture Bess' attention, and he silently laughed at Mr. Henwood's immaturity. Bess turned to her friend and smiled, but when Mr. Henwood caught this exchange, he delivered Alex a reproachful look. Mr. Elmsworth then invited everyone to the dinner table, and as the party headed to the dining hall, Alex stayed behind to walk with Jack and Bess.

"Mr. Henwood doesn't like me either," Alex murmured to Bess with a cheeky grin. Bess wanted to remain angry at Alex because of what had passed between them at the Westfield ball, but she shrugged, opting to treat him kindly for a generous moment. The time spent with Miss Elmsworth had made her act so unlike herself—so passive and uncharacteristically agreeable—that Bess just wanted to act naturally again. *Just this once I will be friendly with Alex. For the remainder of the night, I'll be deservedly coarse.*

"That's because you keep laughing at him," replied Bess matter-of-factly. Alex opened his mouth to reply to Bess' seeming indifference toward their conversation, but Bess light-heartedly added, "But I'm pleased that I'm not the only one he dislikes."

Relieved that Bess sounded playful, Alex sighed, and upon receiving a call from Jane to stand near her, he wished Bess a good evening before catching up with his fiancée.

After a moment of silence, Jack turned to Bess and inquired, "You don't like Mr. Charles Henwood?" And Bess, who had forgotten that

Jack had been present during her brief conversation with Alex, blushed. But Jack, noticing Bess' red face, calmed her nerves by adding, "He's not the most impressive. It's his whole family, I think. His sister Catherine is only slightly tolerable, too."

Bess exhaled, and her tenseness vanished as she entered the dining hall and took a seat to Jack's right. Once she settled, she placed her napkin on her lap, but she was not long seated before a confident female voice captivated her interest.

"Good afternoon," greeted the voice, and Bess, curious to see beside whom she was sitting, glanced over and noticed one of two unfamiliar-looking girls. After a moment of deduction, Bess resolved that the sister who addressed her was Miss Juliette Wheatley, Jack's eldest cousin.

Lost in thought, Bess forgot to reply, and instead, she turned away to examine the other guests. Across from her sat Alex with Jane and Abigail to his left. Upon seeing Bess turn toward him, Alex waved, but Bess, remembering her decision to avoid him, looked away. Soon, her eyes landed upon Mr. Henwood, who was commanding the head of the table. It was evident that he had impolitely stolen Mrs. Elmsworth's hostess privilege by sitting there, so Bess shook her head. Rolling her eyes, Bess turned to Jack, but she was caught off guard when Miss Wheatley tapped her on the shoulder. Bess pursed her lips, for she had forgotten to return Miss Wheatley's greeting, and she opened her mouth to apologize, but no words emerged. Miss Wheatley's curly golden-red hair, gleaming blue eyes, and pearly white smile distracted Bess. *She's certainly not as beautiful as Jane is, but she had such beautiful features. She must be livid that I ignored her!*

"Hi," started Miss Wheatley with a bright smile. "I know that upon most occasions, it isn't proper to outright introduce oneself, *but*

86

considering that this is a family environment, I figured I'd take the liberty to do so anyway." She extended her hand, indicating that she wanted to shake Bess' and added, "My name is Miss Juliette Wheatley. And please, I already *feel* so well-acquainted with you—call me Juliette! What's your name?"

"Oh," Bess chuckled. "Bess Phillips, but a simple *Bess* will suffice."

Immediately, Juliette continued, "I'm *so* glad there's another person with whom I may speak this evening." Bess sighed, for she realized this conversation would not be short-lived. "My younger sister Leonarda follows me around everywhere (she's even sitting beside me right now), and I can never talk with anyone else. I hope I am not bothering you, really, but unless I talk with you during these dull moments of intermittent silence, Leonarda will bother me. *So* then," she exhaled, "where do you live, Bess?"

Reluctantly, Bess exchanged a warm smile with Juliette, and acting on her best behavior, she replied, "Laurel Manor. It's not far from here."

"We're neighbors of the Elmsworths," added Juliette despite noticing Bess sigh. "They're our cousins, you know. Mr. Elmsworth is my mother's brother. This is the house where she grew up, but right now, we live at Churlington House. It's smaller, but my mother didn't inherit much money when our grandfather passed away."

"I'm sure it's still lovely," intervened Bess, turning away.

"Oh yes—it has a beautiful garden with a nice pathway through the woods. You ought to come over to visit!"

"Perhaps," Bess whispered before being interrupted by Mr. Henwood, who told the server to make him steak, which was not on the menu.

After a moment of hesitation, Mr. Elmsworth stood up and thanked his guests for coming. Mr. Henwood inquired about the evening's plans to which Mr. Elmsworth responded that there would be a three-course meal with the main dish being some sort of meat and vegetables. Bess sighed, for she figured that Juliette would talk throughout the entire evening, but to her luck, Mr. Henwood started a table-conversation.

"Will there be dancing after this?" he asked. "Emma and I are soon to be married, and we must practice our waltz!"

There was an almost unanimous agreement to this suggestion, and Mr. Henwood laughed. His round belly shook, and Bess glanced toward Alex to see if he, too, was amused, but her observations ceased when Jack leaned over and whispered, "You didn't realize there would be so much excitement this evening, did you?"

Bess caught a glimpse of Alex's occasional gazes toward her, but she exchanged a smile with Jack instead, replying that she did not. *What an exciting evening it is! If my family hadn't come, I would have felt lonely among this large crowd, but I can never admit this to Abbie. She would never let me forget that she was right!*

"And what a grand party we have!" announced Mr. Henwood, disrupting Bess' thoughts. "Thank you, Mr. Elmsworth, for hosting us! Look here—we can pair up the dancing partners right now!" Mr. Henwood analyzed the guests and added, "Emma, Miss Juliette Wheatley, and Miss Jane Phillips—help me! I assume you are all well-versed in proper matchmaking!" Nobody immediately responded to his idea, but Mr. Henwood carried on nonetheless. "Emma and I shall take the first dance since we are soon to be married! Of course, Mr. and Mrs. Elmsworth shall join us because they are the hosts. Mr. and Mrs. Wheatley will dance in the second, and—"

"I shall dance with Alex," Jane said and turned her warm gaze toward her fiancé. Bess flickered her eyes across Alex's countenance, which was pointed with longing in her direction.

"Yes, Miss Phillips—yes! Carry on, my dear. Who else?" exclaimed Mr. Henwood, whose increasing volume caught Bess off-guard.

"Leonarda can play the piano forte. She is excellent, and anyway, she's not old enough for a proper partner," remarked Juliette.

"Oh, of course—Miss Leonarda Wheatley on the piano forte! I had almost forgotten about the music. Thank you, Miss Juliette!" he cried. "See? I pick the best matchmakers!"

"My sister Rachel and Mr. Ashford," Bess heard Miss Emma Barlette murmur. Bess turned and caught a glimpse of Mr. Ashford, whom she had not previously noticed. She frowned and turned away.

"Yes, oh, yes! My future sister-in-law with Mr. Ashford! What a perfect match, my dear!" Consequently, Bess glanced toward Mr. Ashford to see his reaction. His disproportionate face turned sideways to form what appeared to be a smile, and Bess still couldn't fathom *how* Jane had once found him attractive!

"Curtis and his wife, of course!" exclaimed Juliette. Bess looked over to Juliette and frowned. *Even* she *seems to follow the treacherous lead of the ugly Mr. Henwood. Is there anyone else besides Alex and me who do not?*

"And Mr. Jackson Elmsworth with my dear sister Catherine," Mr. Henwood remarked, glaring directly at Bess. Bess returned the dirty glance, and Mr. Henwood cried out, "What hideous manners, Bess!"

"Oh!" startled Mr. Phillips from the other end of the table. "Bess must not have meant any harm, Mr. Henwood. Please forgive her!"

Mr. Henwood glared at Mr. Phillips, ignoring his apologetic words, and said, "*You*, Mr. Phillips, haven't a partner yet, have you?" Mr. Phillips shook his head. "And you cannot possibly dance with the only two left—Bess and Miss Abigail Phillips—since they are your daughters. Is there anyone else in this house?" Mr. Henwood asked the Elmsworths.

Anger flooded through Bess, for if Mr. Henwood addressed *her* improperly one more time…

"I haven't a partner," Juliette remarked. "But I needn't one. I don't care much for formal dances," she added, and Mr. Henwood asked if anyone else would be *willing* to dance.

"Liza is upstairs," Curtis mentioned after a moment of hesitation.

"Mr. Henwood," began Bess, for she was startled that Curtis even *considered* inviting a sick person. "Miss Elmsworth is ill—she cannot!"

"Liza is a perfect solution! Invite her for dinner, Mr. Elmsworth. We must not exclude her!"

"She will get someone else sick!" exclaimed Bess, rising in her seat.

"Please, Bessie," Jane cooed, which only further irritated her. "Do not yell."

"I won't have anyone getting sick!" Bess announced, sitting back down in her chair. "Not if it can be prevented."

"Bess, I assure you that it will be fine," Jack replied, placing his hand on hers. His sparkling eyes' caught Bess', and she calmed down but not without wondering if Alex had noticed their moment of intimacy.

"I won't have my father dance with her," Bess whispered.

"She's getting better, Bess," he replied. "Your father will remain well, and Liza will keep him good company."

Over the next few minutes, Bess sat in silence, wishing that somebody—*anybody*—would agree with her and prohibit Miss Elmsworth from mingling among them. When Miss Elmsworth finally arrived, a servant collected another chair from the kitchen and placed it beside Abigail. Refusing to greet anyone, Miss Elmsworth took her seat. Bess opened her mouth to suggest Miss Elmsworth's sitting elsewhere, but she felt Jack's arm brush against her side, and she startled, momentarily forgetting her distress. Once she sat down, Miss Elmsworth neglected to say a word, and Mr. Henwood continued to speak of his dance and matchmaking.

"And you mean to say, Mr. Henwood," intervened Bess with frustration, "that Abbie and I are to be alone?"

"You said it yourself," he smirked, "the *richest*, by your definition—that wealth is equivalent to a person's character—may deservedly have partners. Otherwise, the *poorest*, again by your definition, will sit alone. And Miss Abigail," he turned, addressing the youngest Phillips sister, "I am excluding you from this remark. You are rich in character, but there aren't enough gentlemen. Perhaps you can dance when one of the ladies retires."

Bess glared at both Abigail and Mr. Henwood, but before she could reply, she was interrupted by a team of servants, presenting the first course. For a moment, she forgot about the disagreement, instead choosing to indulge in her meal, but once she heard Mr. Henwood's voice reemerge among the guests, Bess dropped her fork and frowned. Comprehending Bess' irritation, every guest (including Jack and Juliette) avoided speaking with her. Bess hardly noticed this blatant disregard, for she was focused on Abigail and Miss Elmsworth, who were quietly chatting across the table. She was pleased to see that the two were entertaining themselves with badinage, but she could not help but worry about Abigail's possible contraction of scarlet fever.

When the second course arrived, Bess had still not spoken a word to anybody. Jack, who was yearning to hold a conversation, turned to Mr. Henwood and Miss Emma Barlette, who sat on the other side of him. Bess refused to listen, so she eavesdropped on Alex and Jane instead.

"*One* dance, Jane. That's all I ask. She can't be alone all night," Alex insisted.

Of course, they're talking about me! Bess sighed. *But they shouldn't; naturally, I'd love to dance with someone but not Alex—not now, at least. And upon any other occasion, I'd gladly take the opportunity to dance with Abbie as a demonstration that ladies do not have to dance with* just *gentleman, but of course, Abbie, I'm sure, is in no mood to dance with me today—not after our quarrel!* Bess took a breath. *Perhaps I'll enjoy a waltz with Jack after he dances with Miss Henwood.*

"She deserves it, Alex," Jane retorted, interrupting Bess' thoughts. "She can't control her temper."

"Jane, that doesn't matter to me—please," Alex pleaded, and Bess tensed.

Jane hesitated. "So long as you dance with Abbie, too, not *just* Bess."

Alex agreed, "I was just about to ask about Abbie anyway."

Soon, the subject of their discussion altered to the lighting and other details regarding one of Jane's paintings. Bess shifted her focus to Juliette and Leonarda, who seemed to be holding a pleasant conversation. Juliette laughed, which caused everyone to startle, and Mrs. Wheatley angrily tried to quiet her daughters. Juliette ignored her mother, opting to whisper another provoking thought to Leonarda, who exploded into giggling. *It seems she gets along well enough with her sister, despite what she says.* With a sigh, for she did not hear Juliette's joke, Bess turned to Jack, who was still in conversation with Mr. Henwood and Miss Emma Barlette. They seemed to be discussing the upcoming wedding, but to Bess' surprise, Jack seemed to be an active participant in this conversation.

"Of course, *you're* invited," Mr. Henwood told Jack. "Everyone here is invited, but I do not wish to invite your friend," he added, nodding to Bess. Jack rotated to see if Bess had heard, and although she wanted to make a sharp reply, Bess remained silent.

"Yes, but if *you* don't invite her, *I* will," Miss Emma Barlette insisted "It's only right."

"As a sensible man, I *know* that, Emma," said Mr. Henwood with a scowl, "but she'll ruin the whole day—I'm certain of it. What if," he began after a momentary pause, "we just don't invite the Phillipses?"

"And invite your friend Mr. Cawdor without his fiancée?" inquired Miss Emma Barlette.

"We aren't friends. Just mutual businessmen," Mr. Henwood corrected. "I offered him some money to introduce his friend to Catherine on Saturday."

"Who was his friend?" Jack asked.

"I don't know his name." Mr. Henwood shrugged. "She didn't care for him. And yes, Emma," he said, turning back to his fiancée. "I don't want to slight the Phillips family, especially Jonathan—he's sure to give me an expensive wedding gift—but Bess! How will I handle her?"

Bess, having heard all of this, clenched her jaw to avoid lashing out.

"Miss Phillips will be a lovely guest," Jack whispered. "I'll make sure of it."

"Thank you, Mr. Elmsworth," Mr. Henwood said.

"You must keep your voice down, Charles," Miss Emma Barlette murmured, glancing toward Bess, who was not fazed by this commentary. Of everything that filled her mind, Bess couldn't fathom *how* Jack could cope with Mr. Henwood's inconsiderate character. *Again, I suppose Jack's awful acceptance of this horrid man must have something to do with the effect of Miss Elmsworth's illness upon him.*

"You know," Mr. Henwood continued, "Catherine came from Derbyshire to see you, Mr. Elmsworth."

Bess' ears perked up as she heard Jack reply, "Really? Not to meet Mr. Cawdor's friend?"

"No," added Mr. Henwood. "Not from my comprehension."

Miss Emma Barlette, who acted as the voice for Bess' confusion, intervened. "What's your relationship to Miss Henwood, Mr. Elmsworth?"

Jack sighed, leaning back in his chair. "Years ago, we befriended one another in school. I'd rather not delve too deeply into what passed between us and what made us part our separate ways, but essentially, I met Charles through his sister," he concluded.

"And it's such a shame," added Mr. Henwood, "that you exchanged your friendship with my sister for that with Bess—"

"Shush!" exclaimed Miss Emma Barlette, nodding to Bess, who pretended not to notice.

"—for I wanted you to marry Catherine, but if you continue on with Bess, I may have to find another gentleman for my darling sister."

Bess rolled her eyes and decided to ignore Mr. Henwood, for nothing good could derive from eavesdropping on his conversation. Instead, she turned her attention to her future meal, wondering how delicious it ought to be. More pressing issues eventually replaced this thought, for she could not help but ponder on the idea of Miss Henwood and Jack's secret relationship. And of course, the thought of Alex was inextricably tied to the thought of Jack—such a complicated situation!

Mr. Henwood made it sound like Jack is preparing to offer himself to me. If this is the case, I would not know how to respond! Marriage is something that everybody expects of me—something that is expectant of all ladies in society, and I could not possibly conform to society's desires. Of course, I like Jack, but to what extent? Would I be willing to give up my independence to be with him? A life away from my sisters and Father seems unimaginable. But perhaps Abigail was right—if I remain home for so long, then eventually I may be the only one left. She paused. *And naturally, I could never settle with that! Or perhaps, if that ever occurred, I could occupy myself by reading Mother's books. I suppose I'd be happy enough.*

Still, it's becoming increasingly pertinent that I comprehend my feelings. I suppose the reason I've denied fancying anyone until now is because liking gentlemen has always been expected of me—oh, but yes, I'm a nonconformist—and indeed, I have *fancied people before, but I could never admit that.* She took a deep breath. *I gather that Jack came in at the perfect time—just when I needed someone to distract me from Jane and Alex—no, not Alex, I do not like Alex.* She hesitated. *But do I truly like Jack, or is it just the idea of him that entertains me? Until I know, I suppose it'd be best to continue spending time with him. Even if I don't end up loving him, perhaps having a really good friend wouldn't be* that *horrible.*

Oh, but Alex—Alex! He's soon to marry Jane, but he's the only person I suppose I've ever liked—well, perhaps not "liked," only admired—but loved? Certainly not. Well, I'm not sure. Don't I love him like a brother? Besides, it's right for Alex to marry Jane, for she yearns for a family! I haven't a clue what my future holds for me, and I'm sure Alex wants a family. Bess shrugged. *I just want to spend time with my sisters, friends, and father. But when Jane and Alex marry, they shall move to Alex's home—away from Laurel Manor, and essentially, I shall lose half of my sisters! Wouldn't it be best for me to decide now that I'm fine with Jane leaving—that I, too, want a family so that I won't be the only person remaining at home?* She hesitated. *But no—who could I see myself marrying? And I couldn't fall into society's traps. It's something I've always been against.*

The third-course meal arrived and disrupted Bess' thoughts. After taking a bite, she agreed with everybody else that it was delicious. She complimented Mr. Elmsworth on the selection and told Jack that she enjoyed it.

Soon, everybody moved into the drawing-room to dance. Once the guests helped move aside the furniture, Leonarda sat by the piano forte and began practicing chords. When the room was prepared, Mr. Henwood took his fiancée's hand and commanded that Leonarda play an opening song. Mr. and Mrs. Elmsworth joined Mr. Henwood and Miss Emma Barlette, so Leonarda began to play an elegant waltz. Over the course of the song, Bess glared at Mr. Henwood, who occasionally snickered. When the first dance finished, Jack remarked, "Bess, I am going to dance with Miss Henwood now."

"Well, I suppose you must." Bess scowled, recalling Mr. Henwood's comment about Jack and his sister's former friendship.

Jack sighed, recognizing her disappointment. "I shall dance with you later—I promise," he said. "She came from Derbyshire to reacquaint herself with me. We used to be good friends but nothing more. As I said before, she's *just* tolerable."

Bess nodded, turning away to fixate her gaze on the dancers. Her eyes landed upon her father, who was laughing beside Miss Elmsworth. Mr. Ashford danced with the younger Miss Barlette, whispering about what must have been his apprenticeships. Curtis and his wife moved stiffly in the corner. And Jack and his partner rocked side to side in deep conversation. Bess looked over to Leonarda, who was playing beautiful music, and she noticed that Juliette was sitting beside her. For a moment, Bess could not remember Juliette's partner before recalling that Juliette said she did not like formal dances. *Perhaps she's a bit unconventional, too.* Bess smiled with approval. Then she redirected her gaze toward Abigail, who was sitting alone in the far corner. She was frowning, obviously unhappy about not being asked to dance. And although Bess was angry, she reluctantly approached her, so both of them would not be incredibly bored.

When Bess was within an arm's length away, Abigail lifted her eyes and muttered, "You've finally come."

"Yes," Bess answered and sat beside her sister.

"Alex wanted to dance with me, but I said no," Abigail said.

"Why's that?"

"I'm *not* like Jane," she replied, "and now you see that." Bess shook her head but refused to respond. "You should not react so aggressively toward Mr. Henwood. Everyone knows he's a bit absurd, but your pointing it out makes you seem quick-tempered." Bess stared ahead and felt a fire boiling within her. *How can I* not *respond to Mr. Henwood? His remarks are so obviously wrong and ill-informed?* "And," Abigail faltered. She bit her lip and changed the topic of conversation. "Well, what do you think of all the guests?"

Bess looked around to ensure nobody was eavesdropping. She whispered, "You know what I think of Mr. Henwood. Other than him, Miss Emma Barlette is well-mannered; however, I cannot fathom why she's marrying Mr. Henwood. I believe she deserves much better."

"Father said Mr. Henwood is providing money to the Barlette family for Miss Emma Barlette's hand in marriage," Abigail interrupted. "Mrs. Barlette is sick, so they need assistance. I already asked," she concluded, and the two sisters exchanged a smile.

"Yes, I have no doubt he thinks Miss Emma Barlette is a suitable bride—she's beautiful. Another jewel to add to his collection." Abigail smirked but did not reply. "Anyway," she continued, "Miss Rachel Barlette hasn't said a word all evening, so I haven't any clue what she's like. Gus is obsequious, and I cannot believe Jane once liked him!"

"I think," Abigail hesitated before saying, "she told you that so you wouldn't judge him so harshly."

Bess smirked and said, "Jane knows me too well." Abigail laughed, and once she quieted, Bess continued. "I don't know the older Wheatleys well, but Juliette is rather interesting. She complains about Leonarda, but they seem to get along well. Leonarda is a terrific musician." Abigail nodded in agreement. "Curtis and his wife are very reserved, but I sense that they think they're better than everyone else. Miss Elmsworth is sweet, but I don't agree much with her opinions." She paused in thought. "And I don't know much about the other Elmsworths."

"And Jack?" Abigail asked.

"I like him, of course," Bess replied. "But I'm unsure to what extent." Abigail crossed her legs, wondering if she should put forth the prospect of Bess' marrying Jack. But she remained silent, for Bess had experienced enough emotions for the day. Instead, she inquired about Miss Henwood, the only person about whom Bess had neglected to remark. "Miss Catherine Henwood," Bess started, considering Jack's previous remark about her only being *tolerable*. "Well, I can't say *too* much, but I don't like her."

"I find her quite agreeable," Abigail remarked, turning her gaze to the subject of their conversation, who was prancing alongside Jack. "She sat next to me at dinner before Miss Elmsworth sat between us." Abigail hastily added, "And I feel fine, Bess. Anyway, Miss Henwood was very courteous. We spoke of Derbyshire. She came all this way—"

"For Jack, I know," Bess intervened.

Abigail exchanged an irritated look with her sister before continuing. "Yes. They used to be good friends—nothing more. And Bessie," she added, "you don't know if you like Jack, so you shouldn't be jealous of Miss Henwood. She's a lovely—"

But Abigail couldn't finish, for a red-faced Bess seethed, "You shouldn't scold me, Abbie, especially after what you did to me tonight."

"What *I* did to *you* tonight?" exclaimed Abigail, standing up. "Bess, I just—"

"I didn't want you to come!" cried Bess, rising to match Abigail's height. "Abbie, not inviting you should have relayed the message that— oh well," she faltered. "You did it as vengeance for what I said yesterday!"

"Perhaps," Abigail began, lowering her voice, "but it was wrong for you to—"

"I don't care what's right and wrong, but I care to be respected!" Bess exclaimed, and when the Wheatleys turned their way, she led Abigail outside.

Time passed as Bess gazed at the evening sky. She felt Abigail to her left, but she had no desire to argue. She shook her head and looked down. She opened her mouth to ease the emotions, but Abigail started. "You know, with the mindset you just demonstrated, you'll get everyone who loves or likes you to hate you."

"You hate me then," stated Bess, whose heart resumed racing.

"No," Abigail insisted. "We're sisters."

"Well, it certainly seems like you hate me!"

"I am *only* bothered by you right now because you're so *insulting*!"

"I'm just defending against being *insulted*!" Bess shot back.

"Nobody," Abigail began, "is trying to insult you."

Abigail sighed while Bess stepped away. The latter took a long, dramatic breath, and as Abigail opened her mouth to respond, Bess exclaimed, "But even your last comment is an insult! You're assuming that I get insulted too easily, and that's a negative trait, Abbie! You must think before you make such outward accusations! Besides, you have *no* right to give me such advice because you're the younger sister!"

"So, Jane can talk to you, but I cannot?" Abigail interrupted. "Because you wouldn't listen to her either."

"That's just it, Abbie! *Insult* after *insult* and no apology! You're so immature—*so* immature! And then you try to ruin my prospects by seeking unwarranted vengeance on me!" Abigail's lips quivered, and she lost her breath. She threw her arms to her side and started to march away. "And not even an apology!" Bess declared.

"I'm sorry then!" Abigail cried, continuing to stomp into Elmsworth Manor. Bess didn't wait for her sister to escape the premise; she collapsed onto the steps beneath her as soon as her legs gave way. *I can't return inside now. Nobody can see me like this! Even the thought of dancing, a generally exciting activity, vexes me. If Jack were to ask me to dance, and I agreed, I'd utterly miserable! Oh, how distressed Abbie can make me!* Bess turned back to the darkness in contemplation. *It's still a few hours away from midnight, and I will have to go inside eventually. I should ask Father if I can wait in the carriage. If I was forced to stay, I'd suffer and make those around me dreadful.* She returned inside but what she saw took her breath away. Whispering into her father's ear was the infamous Miss Catherine Henwood! Bess' jaw dropped, and she took a step back, yearning to run back outside before anyone noticed her arrival.

"Bess," Jack's voice called. Bess' eyes widened, and she whipped around and caught a glimpse of her friend's characteristically charming grin. It was clear that he was about to ask her to dance, but before he was able to make another remark, Bess interrupted him.

"I sincerely apologize, Jack. I would love to dance, and I would love to see your horse, but I'm not feeling well. I'm going to sit in our carriage until everybody is ready to leave. I don't want anyone to have to leave early because of me," she decided, not wanting to interact with anyone who could further upset her.

Jack froze and cocked his head to the side. At the Westfield ball, she could have danced with him *all night*, but tonight, she didn't want to dance at all. He frowned and asked if she wished for company. Bess shook her head, and with hesitation, Jack kissed the back of her hand and escorted her to the carriage. Bess watched him walk away before closing her eyes as anger, disappointment, and confusion flooded her mind at once.

Chapter 8

Bess stirred a pinch of sugar into her bowl of porridge while staring at Jane, who sat a few feet in front of her. She watched her sister read a thin red book and chuckle every now and then. Throughout Bess' entire time in the kitchen, Jane had refused to acknowledge her younger sister's presence, so Bess took a seat at the opposite end of the table and cleared her throat.

"How are you feeling?" Jane asked. She set her book aside and smiled. Bess frowned at Jane's unusual friendliness before taking a spoonful of her breakfast.

"I'm fine," she answered. But it wasn't long until Jane prodded Bess further, so Bess resignedly remarked, "Abbie got me into an awful mood last night, so I couldn't deal with dancing or Mr. Henwood or anything else." Bess turned to Jane, who, lost for words, pursed her lips and returned to her book. "How was the rest of the party?" Bess asked, trying to gauge her sister's attention.

"Oh," Jane stammered, "it was all right." She smiled again, but Bess didn't buy her delayed answer. Jane lowered her book and concluded, "It was decent. Once you went to the carriage, most people sat down to talk, for they were tired of dancing. Father danced with Miss Henwood, but that was all. They seemed to be the only two unaffected by exhaustion." She sighed in recollection. "Alex wanted to check on you, but I said he shouldn't because you weren't feeling well."

Bess' face lit up, but Jane didn't notice, for she had returned to reading. As she prepared another bowl of porridge, Bess murmured, "Is Abbie asleep?"

Jane shook her head and said, "If you must know, she's reading for Miss Camelot's class. This morning, I heard her wake up much earlier than usual, and after inquiring further, I learned that she's trying to get ahead. She returns to school next week, you know."

"Mhm," Bess replied, figuring that Abigail's reading was due to their disagreement.

"Bessie," Jane added, setting her book aside. "I don't wish to upset you, but you ought to apologize to Abbie. She's not the same after last night. I've never seen her be so uninterested in dancing, especially with a good friend like Alex." Bess opened her mouth to respond, but Jane continued, "I don't know what happened. I asked Abbie, but she didn't say a word. However, I know the two of you well enough to gather my judgments."

Bess tensed. She narrowed her eyes and bolted upright. *How could Jane take Abbie's side on this argument, especially without knowing the situation!* Bess opened her mouth to defend herself, but her exhaustion from the previous night overcame her, and she sat back down. *I suppose I do feel bad about hurting Abbie. But if I am to apologize, then Abbie will most certainly return to her usual, annoying self. She would be so irresponsible—never getting her work finished—and incredibly bothersome. She'd act silly, and she would become engaged before I could comprehend the passage of time. Perhaps I shouldn't apologize then... for the good of everyone.*

After having disappointed both of her sisters, Bess spent her day walking about the garden while intermittently reading *A Tale of Two Cities.* Frequently, her boredom overcame her, so she often took breaks to pass by the drawing-room where Jane was painting. During her second venture through Laurel Manor, Bess noticed that Abigail, too, was occupied in the drawing-room. Interestingly, she wasn't painting like Jane; she was *still* reading.

It was not long until Abigail returned to school. Laurel Manor hardly seemed emptier, for, over the past week, Abigail had been so quiet that she seemed nonexistent. And Jane's newfound disappointment in Bess led the two eldest sisters to rarely converse. Bess, for she was quite social, often tried to chat with Jane, but Jane was never willing to convey more than a phrase or sigh. Even when Alex visited, Bess could never exchange more than a smile with him, for Jane would pull him away, determined to occupy him in some trivial matter.

As a result of Jane and Abigail's absences, Bess had resolved to improve her relationship with her father, who, lately, had seemed unusually happy. He had not mentioned Bess' mother in a few weeks, which contrasted his usual behavior, which consisted of quietly sitting in his study while reading and mourning. He had gone outside more so than ever, indulging in walks about the garden or even outside Laurel Manor property. Since Abigail had returned to school, Bess and her father had enjoyed countless strolls where they spoke of books and politics, which mostly centered around the American Civil War.

When she was not with her father, Bess made frequent visits to Elmsworth Manor, where Jack and his parents were often more than eager to welcome her inside. On her first visit since the dinner gathering, Bess made sure to apologize for her "curt actions last Saturday evening." Jack was quick to accept her apology, and once this awkward exchange was complete, the two friends felt comfortable with each other once again. As promised, Jack introduced Bess to his horse Monte. After a bit of discussion, Bess discovered that this horse only met Jack's "closest friends." Naturally, Bess' curiosity led her to inquire who else had met

Monte, and with a little sigh, Jack recited a list of people, including Mr. Henwood and Miss Henwood. Bess' heart sank when she heard the latter's name included, but Jack was quick to remark that he *had* to show the Henwood family because of an order his father made.

During her visits to Elmsworth Manor, Bess found herself routinely playing card games with Jack and his sister, who said she felt well. Bess was surprised that Miss Elmsworth deigned to associate with her, but she didn't think much of it. And because three-person card games tend to become dull, Jack eventually suggested inviting friends to compete in a tournament. Bess, who was yearning to socialize with a new set of people, agreed, and after Miss Elmsworth spent a moment in hesitation, Jack made plans to compete the following day.

"We shall make the gathering small," remarked Jack. "I'll have my parents come, and Bess," he said, turning to his friend, "you ought to invite your eldest sister and her fiancé."

On the day of the card tournament, Bess was surprised to discover that Miss Henwood would be joining the party! With curiosity, Bess inquired who had invited her, and Jack, startled by her outward interrogation, replied that he was unsure. *I suppose he could be lying—his relationship with Miss Henwood is still unclear; therefore, he cannot be fully trusted.* Bess shook her head. *Oh, but Jack could never lie. He's too good of a person!*

Once all nine guests arrived, they seated themselves in the dining hall. Mr. Elmsworth offered tea and appetizers, but after the introductory remarks, the first card game began. By the end of the tournament, Miss Elmsworth earned the most victories, crowning her the afternoon's champion. And since everyone was still in high spirits by the end of the hour, Mr. Elmsworth invited his guests to stay and drink more tea.

"I shall return to my bedroom, Father," Miss Elmsworth said, standing up. "I don't feel especially well."

Mr. Elmsworth excused his daughter, and despite Bess feeling anxious about everyone's safety, she made no comments. Unfazed by Miss Elmsworth's behavior, the guests retired to the drawing-room, where they could chat on warm, comfortable furniture. A brief period of silence followed Miss Elmsworth's exit, but Jane, who possessed an animated grin, broke the pause. She hopped up from her chair and announced, "I wish to share some exciting news." Anticipation spread through the room, and everyone turned their attention to Jane, who added, "I've heard that Mr. Augustus Ashford and Miss Rachel Barlette will get married! I am exceedingly happy for the two of them, but I do not know the date upon which they plan to wed. It will most definitely be *after* Mr. Charles Henwood's marriage to Miss Emma Barlette. I'm sure that the eldest Miss Barlette couldn't bear it the other way, for *no* elder sister could stand having her younger sister married first!"

Bess, who had no previous knowledge of this news, sat with skepticism. *If this rumor is true, then I cannot imagine it is good news. Gus would only marry Miss Rachel Barlette because of her association with the wealthy Henwood family.* Bess sighed, sitting back in her chair before forming another consideration. *Perhaps—oh, but this would be silly—Gus is just marrying her as revenge against me. Anyway, I had blatantly rejected him at Westfield Manor, and perhaps he wants to prove to me that women* do *like him (and his obsequiousness).* Bess chuckled to herself. *Besides, he seems immature enough for this supposition to be somewhat reasonable.*

Although Bess' reaction to this news was cynical, everyone else laughed and agreed that they would make a good couple. Naturally, Jane carried on surmising the details of their wedding, which eventually led to the discussion of her upcoming marriage. "It will be in a few months, and do not fret," she replied to Miss Henwood, who had inquired what day their wedding was to occur. "All of you shall be invited."

After listening to Jane talk of the wedding for weeks, Bess now found the topic dull. She turned to Alex, whose hand was settled on Jane's leg, to decipher his reaction. He exhibited a wide grin, but anyone who knew him well enough could quickly figure that this outward delight wasn't authentic. Alex looked up, caught Bess' eye, and turned away.

It was not long until the gentlemen of the party separated into the kitchen to find something to drink, leaving Jane, Bess, Mrs. Elmsworth, and Miss Henwood in the drawing-room. This combination of guests was a bit strange at first, for Mrs. Elmsworth and Miss Henwood were not extensive talkers, and Jane, who often initiated conversations, had run out of gossip to report.

To break the silence, Miss Henwood smiled and remarked how wonderful a hostess Mrs. Elmsworth had been. This compliment was warmly received, but Bess, always skeptical, immediately determined that Miss Henwood was simply acting servile. *The core of this compliment must derive from her unknown history with Jack. Despite what Jack says, if they were once romantically involved, I can only suppose that Miss Henwood is trying to overcome some old disagreement relating to their separation or (and I sincerely hope not) impress her future mother-in-law.*

After thanking Miss Henwood for the compliment, Mrs. Elmsworth replied, "The three of you are welcome to visit any time. Curtis is never around, but Jack and Liza are always home."

"Jack doesn't busy himself with an occupation?" asked Miss Henwood, sitting up.

Mrs. Elmsworth shook her head and answered, "We've encouraged him, but he enjoys looking after Liza, for she is often unwell."

"Ah," replied Miss Henwood, nodding. "But does he have any interests? Law like his father? Business like my brother?"

"Our father," Jane intervened, "used to work in law, but now he manages a business. He's often able to work from home, so perhaps Jack could pursue an occupation like that—one where he can work *and* provide for Miss Elmsworth."

Mrs. Elmsworth accepted Jane's suggestion with enthusiasm before adding, "But I wish he would settle down and marry. At his age, all gentleman and ladies must—"

Bess, who was only half-heartedly paying attention, heard the word "marry," thought of Miss Henwood's former relationship with Jack, and interrupted her hostess, asking, "Are you engaged, Miss Henwood? Have you ever been? Are you planning to be? A lady as elegant and well-mannered as you shouldn't be single for long, I imagine."

Jane blushed, for Bess' discourtesy often embarrassed her. Miss Henwood hesitated but soon replied, "No, Miss Phillips. I am not. However," she continued with a reddening face, "there is a certain man whom I foresee proposing soon."

"Oh!" exclaimed Jane, glad that her sister's rude interjection led to some intriguing gossip. "*Do* tell us!"

Miss Henwood smiled and glanced at the ceiling. She readjusted her seated position and remarked, "Oh, Miss Phillips, I couldn't ruin this gentleman's right of privacy, especially considering that he may *not* propose."

109

"I understand," said Jane, leaning forward. "I apologize for my prodding, but my natural fascination with news has gotten the better of me," she continued with her usual amount of zeal. "Could you at least tell us if we are acquainted with this gentleman?"

Miss Henwood smiled again before replying, "I shall answer this question only because I am very hopeful that I will soon be married to him." She paused, watching Jane lean farther forward in anticipation. "Yes," she added, "*quite* acquainted."

Jane squealed, "Oh, I cannot wait! And I hope for the best, Miss Henwood. I just wonder who this lucky gentleman may be!"

Mrs. Elmsworth and Bess agreed with this remark, but the latter couldn't help but grow more anxious. *As of this morning, Jack and Gus were the only two eligible bachelors. But since Gus is rumored to be engaged, Jack must be Miss Henwood's future husband! And oh*—Bess exhaled, turning in her seat—*how crass I must have appeared... fancying Jack while he had already made up his mind to marry another woman.* Bess shook her head in frustration.

Amid Bess' thoughts, the gentlemen returned to the drawing-room, each holding a glass or two of wine. The glasses were passed around, and Bess, buried in thought, startled when Jack tapped her on the shoulder and said, "I would have returned with a glass for you, Bess, but Alex said you would never accept alcohol."

Bess replied with a half-hearted smile.

Over the next few hours, the gathering engaged in a plethora of pleasant conversations while indulging in a bit too much wine. Bess, who was the only person not drinking, became bored and eventually recommended that she and her family return home, for Abigail would soon be back from school.

Jane agreed, adding, "She mustn't be alone for so long. And she would hate to hear that we had a party without her!"

When the Phillipses and Alex returned to Laurel Manor, they noticed that Abigail was not home. Wearing a worried countenance, for Abigail was never late, Mr. Phillips sat down and trembled. To keep him company while he waited, Bess, Jane, and Alex joined him. An hour later, Abigail opened the door, announcing her entrance. Her face was bright with energy, and she was breathing heavily. She had wind in her hair, and the attire she wore was torn and dirty.

"Abbie, where have you been?" Jane exclaimed. "We have been so worried!"

Abigail opened her mouth, but upon seeing Bess, she refused to say a word. Mr. Phillips was the first to speak, surmising that she had stayed late to do additional schoolwork.

"Exactly," Abigail agreed. "Sometimes Miss Camelot offers after-school lessons. I think I'm going to take advantage of them more often. They're good for me."

Upon seeing that Abigail was all right, Bess headed to the garden to read, Mr. Phillips returned to his study, and Jane and Alex, both intrigued about these lessons, followed Abigail to her bedroom to further question her.

Chapter 9

Constant card playing soon turned dull, so Bess, Jack, and oftentimes Miss Elmsworth (when she felt well) chose to visit the local village. Bess enjoyed walking through the village streets because the shops nestled between beautiful trees and neatly groomed gardens were lovely spectacles. She liked to imagine that she lived among the busy, bustling, and entertaining environment. She would love to awaken every morning to the sounds of children scurrying to school or gentleman and ladies heading to work. It was a life she never had yet desperately wished to experience, for there was an element of excitement in the idea that her current situation lacked.

"What a lovely day," Bess remarked as she and Jack crossed over the creek that signified their entrance to the village. Jack heartily agreed, adding how the birds chirping was a surefire sign the weather would bode well for the remainder of the week.

The first shop Bess and Jack routinely entered was called Miss Penelope's Antiques. Jack crossed over the threshold but froze upon entering. Standing in the corner of the shop was Jack's brother and sister-in-law. He gasped, and Bess inquired over her friend's animation.

Jack stuck his finger out and whispered, "Curtis tries to avoid us as best as he can. He's concerned that our family's appearance will ruin his new reputation of being a part of the Baldare family." He paused. "I haven't seen him since the dinner gathering." Jack's nostrils flared. He straightened his shoulders, marched to the corner of the shop, and announced, "Curtis! What a surprise it is to see *you* here!"

Upon being addressed, Curtis froze before turning his neck to exchange a grin with his brother. His wife was shuffling through what appeared to be a stack of cards, and she didn't seem to notice or care to greet Jack. Curtis widened his eyes as if to communicate that Jack ought to leave before his wife overhear them.

But Jack was having none of his brother's nonsense, for he exclaimed, "Good afternoon, Lydia! It's been weeks since I've last seen you, despite my father's inviting you to dinner two evenings ago."

With a scowl plastered across her face, Mrs. Baldare turned. She sighed, "Jackson, for your information, I'm not available for every one of your father's beckoning calls. Sometimes I enjoy leisure aside from my familial burdens." Bess raised an eyebrow. "And," she continued, glaring at Bess, "I gather that you're Elizabeth? A Phillips, is it?"

With a nod so that she appeared cordial, Bess replied, "Just Bess. But yes—my father is Mr. Jonathan Phillips."

"Lydia," Jack intervened, "you danced in the same room as Mr. Phillips two fortnights ago! Don't you recall, or are you too—?"

Mrs. Baldare scoffed, "As if I can recall every detail of your little family's life."

Jack, who was taken aback by this insult, turned away. He took a deep breath, and once the color in his face dissolved, he added, "I didn't realize the two of you came downtown. Bess and I visit a few times a week."

"Oh, we normally don't," Curtis said before his wife had the opportunity to make another disparaging remark. "Lydia's mother asked us to pick up a gift for the wedding."

Voicing Bess' confusion, Jack inquired, "Whose wedding? Mr. Ashford and Miss Rachel Barlette's?"

Mrs. Baldare's eyes shot upward, and without her usual disdain, she said, "They're getting married? Now, *that's* news I haven't yet heard."

113

Jack shrugged, remarking that this was *only* a rumor, and Mrs. Baldare rolled her eyes. She stood up straighter and readjusted her frame. With a deep-set frown, Jack folded his arms across his chest and inquired what her air of disapproval denoted.

Mrs. Baldare shifted her body to examine herself in the shop's mirror. She folded a lock of her hair behind her ear, touched her lip, and sighed, "I always thought that Rachel girl could do better."

The words *that Rachel girl* played over in Bess' head. She could not believe that Mrs. Baldare had the arrogance to refer to someone in this manner. It was so uncalled for, but interestingly, nobody mentioned it. Considering that Jack had already seen her act out and would not be surprised, Bess curtly replied, "She's probably twenty-some years old or some age to that effect; therefore, I believe the term *lady* would be most suitable." Bess paused, never having addressed Curtis' wife before, and added, "Mrs. Elmsworth."

And once Bess uttered this final phrase, Mrs. Baldare's eyes widened. She took a menacing step toward Bess, who noticed that both Jack and his brother seemed to shrink back into the antique shop. Bess turned to Jack for support, but his anxious expression indicated that Bess had crossed a line too far.

"Mrs. *Elmsworth*?" Mrs. Baldare huffed. "Mrs. Elmsworth is Curtis and Jack's old mother residing at Elmsworth Manor!"

Bess blushed. *Am I wrong in that Mr. Elmsworth and Mrs. Baldare are married? No, they most certainly ought to be. Jack said—*

"I," continued Mrs. Baldare, interrupting Bess' thoughts, "am Mrs. *Baldare*. Hasn't Jackson told you, or haven't you the proprietary to ask, why I didn't take Curtis' surname?"

Bess shook her head slightly, fearing to make any provoking movement. She started, "I didn't—"

"Because that family—Curtis and Jackson's family—is practically filth," she retorted. Bess glanced over to the Elmsworth brothers and noticed that their faces were bright red. Jack seemed to be on the verge of retaliating, but his mouth was glued shut. "Curtis possesses refined tastes and a handsome facade, which initially attracted me. At the time, I was caught off guard by his external appearance that I neglected all other necessities. With a clear-minded conscience, such as I have now, I would never have fallen for him as I did then, but I suppose he's lucky. I'm not so horrid as to divorce him after what he and his family unveiled to me regarding material possessions." A smile flickered across Mrs. Baldare's face, but a trace of penitence for her insolent remarks was undetectable. "I thought I made my opinions clear when I opted to reside in *my* mansion instead of his. I suppose, Elizabeth, your ignorant mind has blinded you from the obvious facts of my marriage. And if you dare to invent an argument reliant upon my spending time at Elmsworth Manor, I have a solution for that defense as well. Familial duties must be completed; otherwise, my noble acquaintances would wonder what sort of lady I am!" She chuckled to herself. "Do not consider for half a second that I *enjoy* stepping across the Elmsworth Manor threshold! I cringe at the prospect, but it is a necessity to uphold my good standing in Kent's aristocracy. I cannot afford to taint my reputation again—not after my lowly marriage." Bess watched Curtis and Jack's faces grow pale. She opened her mouth to protest, but Mrs. Baldare did not take a breath. "Now, let us consider their cousins, the Wheatleys. I assure you that *none* of my acquaintances are cognizant of my partial relationship to them. My, they live at Churlington House, for God's sake! When I was

115

informed that they would be present at the dinner two fortnights ago—you say, Jackson—I nearly fainted at the prospect of it! Curtis fell to his hands and knees with entreaties, but my excellent role as a wife led me to put his anxieties to rest, and I reluctantly agreed to come. However, I later told him that he should be glad the Phillipses were not aforementioned, or I certainly would not have come. I'm disappointed in you, Jackson," she said, turning toward Bess' ill-looking friend. "You've befriended a *Phillips* girl. Nevermind their greater wealth, they're even worse off than the Wheatleys in my opinion—their ancestors didn't even establish Laurel Manor. Mr. Jonathan Phillips II bought it off Sir Anderson Laurel XI over a century ago." She then paused, rotating to face her entire audience. "I have nothing more to say aside from the fact that you should be proud to know me!" she scoffed. "I imagine I am the wealthiest and therefore best person with whom you somewhat regularly associate." She turned back to face the mirror and smiled at the reflection of herself. She caught Bess' glare from the silvery image and added, "If you must know, the gift for which Curtis and I are searching is for Mr. Charles Henwood and Miss Emma Barlette's wedding. And I hope," she snapped, "that I *don't* see you there, Elizabeth." Before Bess had the time to reply, Mrs. Baldare grabbed hold of her husband's arm and dragged him out of the antique shop, saying, "Let's carry on, Curtis. I want to purchase one of Ms. Primstone's jewels for the wedding before they're sold out."

Bess followed Curtis and Mrs. Baldare with her gaze, and once they were out of sight, she turned to Jack and blushed. She opened her mouth to eject a most degrading exclamation regarding Mrs. Baldare, but Jack silenced her, saying, "You mustn't say anything here. I comprehend perfectly—Lydia is always like that. I apologize for not warning you."

Before he finished, Bess cried, "*How* did Curtis ever marry her?"

Jack sighed, placing his hand on his forehead. "As I believe I once mentioned, he's perhaps the most obsequious person I've ever met. Many people would pay millions to *see* Baldare Mansion nevertheless *live* there."

Bess shook her head, not fully listening to what Jack had said, "I never want to see her again. I absolutely *cannot* go to that wedding. I might explode if I see both Mr. Henwood and Mrs. Baldare in the same room again."

"Well," Jack began, "we cannot ignore our obligations. I'm sure you noticed that I turned impulsive when I saw Curtis. Unfortunately, we have to bear with these troubles."

Bess nodded, and not in the mood to peruse the remainder of the village, she and Jack returned to Elmsworth Manor. Once they arrived, rain started pouring from the sky, causing Bess to insist she return home before a storm appeared. Jack ordered a servant to prepare a carriage, but Bess offered to walk like she usually did. She didn't want to inconvenience the servants and the coachman, but Jack would hear none of her argument. It was too dark and damp for her to walk—it was too dangerous. Once the coach arrived, Bess thanked her friend for the effort, and then she bid him farewell and rode home.

When she arrived at Laurel Manor, Bess thanked the coachman for his time and headed inside. Once she shut the door behind her, Bess was pounced on by Jane, who was shouting something at Abigail.

"Jane, what?" Bess asked, trying to step aside from her elder sister, who was trying to hide something.

"Oh, it's hideous!" she exclaimed, lunging toward Bess again. "You don't want to see it, Bessie."

Nevertheless, Bess pushed her sister aside, and upon first noticing Alex, she joked, "*Alex* is hideous? Now, I know he can be obtuse sometimes, but—"

Alex laughed, leaning forward and pushing Bess into Jane, who hit her on the side of the head, exclaiming, "No!"

Jane then thrust her younger sister toward Abigail, who was standing a short distance to the right of Alex. Everything about her appeared normal, except her hair, which hardly passed her ears!

"Oh my God," Bess murmured, trying to contain her laughter. Abigail had a look of absolute annoyance planted on her face, especially as their father examined her new style, commenting on how unevenly it was cut and how it would just *have* to grow out before the upcoming weddings. "What happened?" Bess asked, unable to hide a smile.

Abigail opened her mouth to respond, but Jane retorted, "*She* did it by herself!"

"What?" Bess responded, looking over to Alex, who nodded. "Why?"

"I wanted to," Abigail said, pushing her father aside. After examining her sister for a moment, Bess tensed. *Of course, the real reason for Abigail's doing this is because she wants to look different than Jane. She's taking my advice to be different literally, making this all my fault. Now, every time I look at her, I'll feel penitent, having forced her to look like this.* Bess huffed. *Like inviting everyone to the Elmsworth dinner party, she's doing this as revenge against me!*

After making this resolution, Bess gave Abigail a dirty look before running upstairs to her bedroom. Jane called after her sister but to no avail.

Bess envisioned Jane placing her hands on her hips as she sighed, "Whatever you two said to each other must have been horrid." Abigail must have simply shaken her head, for Bess could not hear her. Only Jane's following remark was audible: "Well, I cannot conceive a plausible plan with regard to the weddings. Wigs are out of the question; they'd make you look old and too formal." She paused. "Oh, and what about school? You can't possibly let Miss Camelot see you like this! What will she think of us—your family? That we're animals, I presume!"

"I don't care what Miss Camelot thinks about my hair!" Abigail seethed. "And nor should you—you've never met her, for God's sake, Jane! You and Bess had the governess before she passed away; you've never even stepped foot into my school!" Then Bess heard some rough movement and a bang before Abigail dashed upstairs to her bedroom. She then slammed the door, and although Bess was down the hall, she could still hear Abigail's soft whimpers through the walls.

"Am I the only sensible sister in this family?" Bess heard Jane ask once Abigail had left.

In a softer voice, Alex responded, "Actually, I like it."

"That's because you're a *boy*!" Jane cried.

Alex added, "Jane, what does it even matter? It's not *your* hair!"

"But she's *my* sister, and I'm supposed to look after her."

Alex raised his voice and retorted, "Look after her *how*?"

Bess could almost see Jane blush when she responded, "I have to make sure she's safe. She must also be well-regarded. She must eventually find a husband, and by the look of her right now, I cannot imagine that *any* gentleman would *ever* want to marry her!"

At this comment, Bess heard Abigail's cries heighten for a half a second before they quieted down again.

"Some good-humored and well-mannered gentleman would most certainly find her attractive, Jane," Alex responded. "And you also ought to be proud of her. She's starting to develop her personality. She's no longer following your lead on everything."

"But she'll start acting like Bessie," Jane moaned, and Bess frowned.

"And that's a bad thing?" Alex asked.

A sudden silence filled Laurel Manor. Bess heard footsteps approach the doorway, and eventually, she heard the latch unlock and the door swing open. Then Jane sniffled, "Alex, please go home. I'm going to finish my paintings." Bess listened to Alex slowly leave Laurel Manor after neglecting to wish his fiancée farewell. Moments later, the front door shut, and Jane passed the drawing-room where her paintings resided, and sprinted upstairs. Bess heard muffled cries dash past her doorway, and she listened with intensity for more as she found comfort on her bed.

Chapter 10

Silence was never so loud as it was then. Bess' heart pounded with anticipation as she heard her father sift through the house. He ascended the staircase and entered Jane's then Abigail's bedroom. Soon, Bess heard a soft knock on her door, and quietly, she permitted her father to enter. With a great degree of gentleness, he walked over the threshold and gave her a tired smile.

"Bessie," he sighed as he made his way to her bed. "Shall I inquire what the matter is or would it be of no use? I've uncovered pieces from Jane and Abigail, but this whole affair seems quite obscure and frankly *silly*."

Bess took a deep breath, not wanting to discuss her disagreement with Abigail. Instead, she spoke of the bitterness she faced today. "Father," she answered as she pointed to a corner of her bed, where he could sit, "quite honestly, it *is* silly. But Jane and Abbie aside, my frustration today largely had to do with Mrs. Lydia Baldare, whom Jack and I saw in the village. She was so insulting and well, *you* know I cannot easily forgive people who act ill-mannered."

"But how does this relate to Abigail's situation?"

"Oh," Bess murmured, "it doesn't; however, these other issues have been plaguing me and...," she tried to continue her train of thought but caught a glimpse of her father's furrowed brow and narrowed eyes that indicated a loss of concentration. "Well, we had a disagreement," Bess conceded, "but I'd rather not go too deeply into it."

He nodded, shook off his confusion, and said, "Can you do something for me, Bess?"

Bess nodded in return. "Of course, Father. However, I don't believe that—"

"You should make amends, or at least, check in with Abigail," Mr. Phillips interrupted. "I'm unsure what all of these fervent emotions signify, but the most appropriate resolution would be to discuss whatever your matter is. After speaking with Abigail, I felt as if she was more frustrated with Jane than with you, so you would be the perfect candidate to initiate reconciliation of some kind."

Bess nodded again and rose from her seat to mark the conclusion of their conversion. "Fine. I cannot promise anything; however—"

But Mr. Phillips had already left the room. With a disappointed sigh, Bess followed her father into the hallway, making a right to Abigail's bedroom. When she approached her younger sister's door, she knocked twice, and after a moment of hesitation, the door swung wide open. Bess took a step over the threshold and met the back of Abigail's head.

"Father told you to talk to me, didn't he?" Abigail asked, avoiding eye contact with Bess as she returned to her bed. Bess hadn't the time to respond before Abigail added, "It *is* hideous, isn't it?"

Bess turned to examine her sister's new style, and after concluding that it fit her rather nicely, she replied, "No, not really."

"I just *had* to do it, though," Abigail continued as if she hadn't heard her sister's remark. "I can't tell you why, but I *had* to."

"Well," Bess smirked, "*that's* helpful."

"And Bess, I know you think I did this because of you, but I didn't," she said with hardly a breath between each of her thoughts. "I did it for a reason entirely separate from the issue of our last few conversations. So please don't think any of this is your fault."

Upon any other occasion, Bess would have taken Abigail's answer as confirmation that this *was* her fault. Yet, the sincerity and authenticity in every word she spoke conveyed her genuine honesty, and with a sigh of relief, she replied, "I appreciate your remark, but how come you can't tell me why you cut your hair?" She paused and raised an eyebrow. "Has this anything to do with Miss Camelot's extra lessons?"

Abigail blushed but refused to say another word on that matter. Instead, she started, "Jane keeps telling me—"

But Bess, moving to sit beside her sister, interrupted, "Abbie, don't mind, Jane. I'm sure she's got a lot on her mind right now with her upcoming wedding. I heard what she said to Alex about you and—"

"No, it's not that. Just listen," intervened Abigail, shifting in her seated position. "I've meant to tell you this, but I was afraid you'd be too upset to speak with me and—"

"What is it, Abbie?" Bess interrupted.

Abigail took a deep breath and continued, "Jane keeps telling me she's frustrated with Alex. They keep setting wedding dates, but Alex keeps pushing them back farther," she sighed. "Also, she believes he's in love with you, which, obviously he is; however, I don't think she knows that for certain." Bess was silent. "I don't know what's going to happen with them, but I thought I'd fill you in. Anyway, Mr. Henwood and Miss Emma Barlette are getting married in a week—"

"In a *week*?" exclaimed Bess, who couldn't help but smile, for her focus was mainly on the confirmation that Alex was *in love* with her.

"Yes," Abigail chuckled. "Jane says she thinks Miss Emma Barlette just wants to get married before her sister, but I'm unconvinced. The early date must have been Mr. Henwood's doing... for whatever strange reason he may have devised."

Bess and Abigail shared a laugh, rekindling their friendship. But soon, Bess' voice died down, and she remarked, "I cannot go."

"Oh, sure you can," Abigail resolved, leaning toward her elder sister. "So long as you refrain from making any provoking remarks." Bess sighed, knowing that Abigail's advice was valid no matter how much she wished to protest. "I suppose you could spend the afternoon with Jack," continued Abigail. "You keep each other company fairly often, so why not think of the wedding as *just* another normal day?"

"If I spend a presumably important day as if it's typical, then I shall just be reliving my monotonous lifestyle. The least I could do would be to spend time with the other guests, and perhaps," she added with a smile, "quarrel with one or two."

"Bess!" exclaimed Abigail, full of laughter.

But upon noticing that her sister's happiness lasted no longer than a moment, Abigail quieted, and Bess took a deep breath, adding, "Well, in all seriousness, my concern is true." Abigail's bright expression suddenly dulled as a look of worry cast over her sister. Bess tucked a strand of her hair behind her ear and exhaled. "Sometimes I imagine myself ten years from now, living the way I currently do, and I shudder. Abbie, I'm unsure what I ought to do with my life, and if my existence is simply meant to play cards and ride a horse with a neighborhood friend, then, well, I'm afraid. I don't know what to do, Abbie. I exercise my intelligence by arguing, but that just gets me into trouble and—"

"You could become a schoolteacher," Abigail suggested, reaching her hands out to wrap her arms around her sister. "Miss Camelot always complains about how they need more." She said this final remark with a hint of humor, but Bess' sudden despondent attitude caused her to not comprehend—or care to comprehend. Abigail slowly let her arms drop to her side.

Bess shook her head, crossed her arms, and looked away. "It seems that, these days, a schoolteacher is virtually ineffective—in comparison to the *whole* world, one schoolteacher makes no difference. Children will listen to her for the assigned period of time, but then after that, they'll entirely forget about her." She took a long breath and bit her lip. A half a minute must have passed before she continued. "I want to do something that will have a lasting impact in this world, but I just don't know what it should be. I want to do something that nobody expects me to do. I want to become somebody whom nobody expects me to become."

Abigail sat, thinking for a moment before saying, "I know you do, Bess, but I don't know what occupation fits those requirements."

"Jane will be a famous painter—"

"No," Abigail interrupted. "You give her too much credit. She's good but not *that* good."

"She'll be a great mother someday, and with Alex as her husband, they will have a sweet, lovely family," Bess sighed, and a tear ran down her cheek. Abigail's eyes widened, for this tear was confirmation of the gravity of Bess' present emotions. "*You* are going to marry someone with as many spirits as you have, and you'll both live such exciting lives," she continued with a shaky voice. "*I,* though, refuse to marry anyone, and I'm wasting my time with Jack because I'm sure he thinks otherwise. He will probably propose sometime in the next year or so. The logical part of me will dearly wish to accept, for he's very handsome as you know (and he's a good person, of course), but the Bess part of me will inevitably decline his proposal, and all of my days spent with him will be for naught. I'm wasting every day of my life, Abbie, and I don't know what to do! You're right," she admitted, "I *can't* read my way through life. I just wish that we could all be children again. I wish that Mother were here to tell me what to do."

The room filled with stillness that lasted for a long time. Neither sister had outwardly mentioned their mother's name since her death, and it was difficult to talk about her again. Bess closed her eyes, and another tear ran down her cheek. Abigail looked up, for she had hardly ever seen Bess cry before. She took Bess, who was visibly shaking, in her arms and held her through the remainder of the evening.

Chapter 11

As the Henwood wedding drew near, Bess learned that the groom had invited almost everybody in the entire town and surrounding area. This prospect seemed unfathomable, for how could Mr. Henwood possibly know this massive number of people? Certainly, Miss Emma Barlette could not be the cause of this invitation expansion—she hardly talked, so there was no way she could have *so* many acquaintances. Therefore, upon next meeting Mr. Henwood, Bess, with a subtle tone of mockery, asked if he knew each guest. With his chubby chin pointed in the air, Mr. Henwood scoffed that he was *not* well acquainted with everyone. Bess opened her mouth to reply, but Mr. Henwood had already changed the subject.

From the remainder of his jabber, Bess gathered that Mr. Henwood had plenty of money to spare on a large wedding. It was the appearance of a great number of guests that pleased him. With an ear half-listening to the groom's monologue, Bess discovered that although Miss Emma Barlette preferred a small, close-knit wedding, her mother and fiancé would not concede to the idea. Bess rolled her eyes as she listened to Mr. Henwood's chat about how his sister had coordinated the bridesmaids and groomsmen, for he had neither the time nor desire to do it himself. Well, he *did* suggest (to Miss Emma Barlette's passionate but failed refusal): "So long as Bess isn't involved in the ceremony."

With this stipulation, Miss Henwood named herself, Mrs. Baldare, Miss Rachel Barlette, Miss Elmsworth (who was miraculously feeling better again, although she had been *too ill* to see Bess yesterday), the Wheatley sisters, and the Phillips sisters (except Bess) as bridesmaids. Had this wedding belonged to anyone other than Mr. Henwood, Bess would have been outraged at her exclusion. But now, she was rather pleased to remain in the audience with Alex, who was also not included in the ritual. For the first time in the last fortnight, she could spend time with her friend without Jane's influence. Alex, too, didn't mind being excluded, for he would rather associate with Bess than the groomsmen: the Elmsworth brothers, Mr. Ashford, and Mr. Henwood's younger half-brother, a certain Mr. Benjamin Roberts.

On the eve's eve of the wedding, Miss Henwood arranged a trip to select bridesmaid dresses. Each bridesmaid, including Bess, for she had nothing else better to do, walked to Lady Madeleine's, a dress shop downtown. Mrs. Baldare and Jane, who were not too pleased about having to walk on dirt roads from Elmsworth Manor, their meeting place, to Lady Madeleine's, groaned but begrudgingly consented, wishing not to upset the bride.

"Miss Emma Barlette," Jane called, approaching the bride with her typical, cordial smile. "Although Miss Henwood made the arrangements, I wanted to let you know that I am honored to be your bridesmaid. I look forward to celebrating with you on your special day and eventually becoming closer friends."

After a pause, Miss Emma Barlette turned to Jane and replied, "I'm glad you're awaiting this day with pleasure, Jane, and yes, Miss Henwood chose a lovely group of bridesmaids."

Glad to be on a first-name basis with the bride, Jane giggled. "And how is your mother, Emma? I understand this wedding was planned in exchange for the medicine to treat her illness."

"She feels a little better," Miss Emma Barlette replied. "The medications Charles was able to afford slightly improved her health."

Jane commented that she was pleased to hear that Mrs. Barlette was doing well, but just before Bess caught Miss Emma Barlette's response, she heard a voice behind her.

"Bess, are you even *in* the wedding?" A little chorus of snickers echoed behind her, and as she turned around, Bess noticed Mrs. Baldare and Miss Elmsworth laughing.

"No," Bess began, "but I'm invited, and I don't find anything humorous in my not being a part of the ceremony."

Mrs. Baldare's eyes narrowed, for she had not anticipated receiving a direct remark, and Miss Elmsworth blushed. *At least I quieted them, but what an interesting reaction from Miss Elmsworth! Mrs. Baldare's rudeness is justified, for she has an awful character, but I never really supposed that Miss Elmsworth did, too. This rare discourtesy* must *be an effect of her ongoing illness. I shall allow her behavior to pass today, for Jack's sake, but if—*

"The decision was against my wishes, Mrs. Baldare. If it were my choice, I'd have Bess second to Rachel," Miss Emma Barlette intervened, startling Bess and the others.

Mrs. Baldare's face turned a dark shade of red while Miss Elmsworth grew pale. Jane pouted, feeling affronted at not being mentioned as "second to Rachel" even though *she* was the only person making an effort to please the bride.

Bess turned to thank Miss Emma Barlette but found that she was again engaged in a conversation with Jane. *How intriguing! That may have been the first time Miss Emma Barlette ever spoke to, or of, me. I wonder what the motive for her sudden change in behavior was, for I never took her as someone who would speak out against anyone. Well—* Bess paused—*perhaps this had* always *been her real character, but I*

129

had never noticed because of her quiet nature. If not that, then I suppose she could have values that align with mine, and perhaps she just never had the opportunity to express herself. If neither of these suppositions is correct, Miss Emma Barlette must be fond of me, and therefore, would want to stand up for me. It's not difficult to dislike Mr. Henwood, and perhaps she enjoys my rude, but frankly funny, comments. Whatever the reason was for Miss Emma Barlette's change in behavior, Bess was pleased.

"I heard that Charles' half-brother Mr. Benjamin Roberts is coming," Jane said. "What is he like?"

"Oh," Miss Emma Barlette began, turning to her younger sister, who was standing a short distance from Abigail. "Rachel and I have very different opinions about his character. Mine is based on observation, but she has her reasoning." After a moment of hesitation, in which Jane inquired further, Miss Emma Barlette said, "I believe he's much more handsome than Charles. Well, to be precise, he's much more attractive regarding facial appearance, but he's still not really *in shape*."

At this remark of Mr. Henwood's appearance, Bess could not keep from laughing. Miss Emma Barlette noticed this reaction and returned a chuckle, and at this minor conveyance of similar opinion, Bess grinned.

"Well, what does Rachel think?" asked Jane, attempting to rekindle Miss Emma Barlette's attention.

"You ought to ask her yourself," Miss Emma Barlette replied before calling over her sister, who had been daydreaming. Then she prompted her sister to put forth her opinion of Mr. Henwood's half-brother.

"Not so handsome—high-pitched voice—nasally—reeks of a horrid odor—and attempted to seduce me once" were all the vague and laconic descriptions that Miss Rachel Barlette provided.

The final two points were enough to make Abigail, who had been silent thus far, cringe and cry out, "Body odor! Seduce you!"

"Yes," Miss Emma Barlette continued. "According to Rachel's account, I gather that he's rather immature, but I have had no personal problems with him, and I haven't come close enough to smell his odor to judge."

This discussion soon died down, and Bess, who was bored walking by herself, turned to engage the only bridesmaid not involved in a conversation: Miss Henwood. Bess sighed, for she was rather indifferent toward Miss Henwood but determined that her company would be better than none. At any rate, Bess could further inquire about her potential fiancé.

Once her step aligned with Miss Henwood's, Bess began, "You are good friends with Jack?"

Miss Henwood, startled at being directly addressed, turned away from the meadow she had been admiring and replied, "Yes. We spent a lot of our youth together."

Bess awaited another remark from her companion but found that there was nothing else to be heard. Being quite displeased with Miss Henwood's lack of explanation, Bess prodded, "Jack told me that. Are the two of you close?"

"To a degree," she answered, and Bess, who thought that she had finished speaking again, frowned. However, Miss Henwood continued. "Bess, I know where your head is. Yes, I danced with Jack, but I am in love with somebody else."

And at Miss Henwood's outright assurance of her indifference toward Jack, Bess sighed with relief; yet she could not help but blush. *I must have seemed so crass to believe something untrue!* But her happiness in Jack's integrity overshadowed her humiliation, so it was not long until she inquired further.

"Can you provide any more hints as to whom he may be?"

Miss Henwood shook her head and replied, "I cannot, but I *can* assure you that the proposal shall take place rather soon."

Bess returned Miss Henwood's smile before replaying the available bachelors through her mind once more. But after running through the names thrice, she was at a loss. Unless someone had recently concealed a divorce, then there was *no one* whom Miss Henwood could marry within their social circle.

And how ironic it was, that at that moment, Abigail came running to Bess, exclaiming, "Oh, Bessie—what fascinating news I have gathered!" This excitement was enough to turn Jane around, and Abigail cried out, "Miss Rachel Barlette is *not* engaged to Mr. Ashford! It was a false claim!"

As soon as Abigail uttered these words, Miss Emma Barlette's reaction was clear. "To Mr. Ashford? Whoever supposed this?" She turned to her sister, who shrugged. Bess glanced toward Jane, who had suggested this rumor, and noticed that she was red with embarrassment. *Is it possible that Jane fabricated the entire engagement? If not her, then who?*

Bess was indeed shocked! She concluded that Mr. Ashford *must* be Miss Henwood's lover, but she found herself at a loss upon further supposition. She had never seen Miss Henwood and Mr. Ashford dance, or even speak, to one another! With a look of bewilderment plastered across her face, Bess glanced over to collect any hints from Miss Henwood's expression but saw only a trace of laughter fading from her lips.

Full of excitement, Abigail recollected how she discovered this piece of news, "First, Miss Rachel Barlette and I were discussing the wedding, and out of sheer curiosity, I inquired about her engagement. There was hardly a moment of hesitation before she vehemently denied the rumor, saying she *did* once admire Mr. Ashford, but that was all. She said he's, to quote, a *commendable gentleman*," but then Abigail stopped. It was almost as if her mouth had glued shut. Her eyes cast downward, but Jane could not help but prod, asking why she had ceased to detail the story. "No matter," Abigail mumbled while flickering her eyes in Bess' direction. "I'd rather not go on."

Bess watched as the enthusiasm faded from her sister's cheeks. Quietly, Abigail returned to her place alongside Miss Rachel Barlette, and Bess halted, for she suddenly understood that Abigail's change in behavior was on account of their ongoing quarrel. With a sigh, Bess watched her sister initiate another discussion with her companion, and after concluding that she would be all right, Bess returned to Miss Henwood.

"How long have you and Mr. Ashford known each other?" she asked.

But to Bess' embarrassment, Miss Henwood only laughed. Without providing an adequate response, she mentioned that she would like to speak to Miss Emma Barlette, for she had something important to report. Bess shrugged and decided to join the laughing Wheatley sisters at the rear of the party. Besides, they had recently passed the creek, so Bess knew that they had almost arrived at the shop, and thus, Juliette couldn't talk *so* much in such a short period.

"Oh, Bess!" exclaimed Juliette, lighting up as she watched her friend approach. She widened her eyes, glancing sideways at her sister, which was supposed to reference her previous remark about Leonarda being bothersome. But Bess, not wishing to involve herself in Juliette's silly situation, shrugged. "Have you ever been to this shop before?" Juliette continued. "I have never been a bridesmaid, and I haven't even ever been to a wedding!" But Juliette hardly gave Bess a second to respond, for she added, "Leonarda, though, has played the piano forte at one, maybe two, weddings. She said this dress shop is nice."

"Yes. It's nice," Leonarda quietly repeated.

And just as Bess raised her head to reply, the sight of Lady Madeleine's stood before her. The exterior resembled a stone cottage, for it was small and surrounded by beds of flowers. Vines clung to the facade amid each stone, and the roof was covered in long grass that blew with the wind. The steps leading up to the doorway were crooked, and upon seeing the appearance of the shop, Mrs. Baldare drew back, but Bess didn't mind. It was beautiful.

"Oh, it's a delightful shop!" announced Juliette, who ran to the front door with her sister trailing behind her.

Juliette and Leonarda were the first two to enter Lady Madeleine's, but shortly thereafter, everyone else except Bess and Abigail followed. Ascending the steps, Bess continued to admire how beautiful the exterior was, when, suddenly, a voice exclaimed, "Abbie!"

Turning as if it were her name called, Bess found a handsome boy approaching her sister. She stood back, watching as Abigail whispered that he ought to go away. The boy refused, shaking his dirty blonde head of hair. And before Abigail could tell him to leave again, the boy glanced toward Bess and asked, "Abbie, is this your sister?" Without receiving an answer, the boy climbed the steps to stand a yard away from Bess, who blushed, for he was quite handsome. He possessed deep-set brown eyes and a crooked countenance, which gave him a unique and attractive look. Despite dirt smudges spotting his face, he gave off a charming aura, and when he extended his arm to shake Bess' hand, Bess did so immediately, not wishing to disappoint this good-looking friend of Abigail's.

With a bright smile, the boy introduced himself as Callum Lewis, the son of the owner of a local pub. Everything he said was spoken with such confidence as if she already knew who he was, so Bess turned to Abigail, who ascended the staircase, and tilted her head sideways. Comprehending her puzzled countenance, Callum looked at Abigail, who shook her head to convey some discreet message. "You haven't told her?" he asked.

And before Abigail had time to open her mouth, Bess replied, "Haven't told me *what*?"

Both Bess and Callum turned to Abigail, whose face turned red. She cleared her throat and with her eyes cast to the floor, she said, "My after-school lessons are with the boys. They learn more, and I'm advanced. Callum and I are good friends from class."

Bess glanced sideways at Callum, who nodded, but still skeptical, she crossed her arms. With a sigh, she replied, "Very well." She wished Callum farewell and then turned to enter the shop.

Over the past couple of minutes, Bess had forgotten about how excited she was to see the interior of Lady Madeleine's, but when she opened the front door, she stood back in awe. In addition to there being stone walls decorated with vines and a large assortment of flowers, a lavish, purple carpet ran through the center of the shop. Dresses of all shapes and sizes were artfully arranged about the room, and an aroma of lavender wafted through the air, creating a home-like feeling.

Bess hadn't much time to continue examining the shop before a red-faced Abigail entered. With a sigh, she took one look at the shop before turning away.

"Is something the matter?" whispered Bess. "I don't have to tell Jane anything—"

"He didn't like my hair," Abigail snapped. "That's all."

Bess sighed, comprehending that Abigail would refuse to reveal anything more. And even if Bess hadn't decided to ignore her sister's apparent secrecy, Juliette arrived to call Abigail away anyway, for Miss Emma Barlette had chosen a dress she liked.

As the bridesmaids tried on their dresses, Bess stood by the entrance of the shop. Jane exited the dressing room first, remarking in the politest way imaginable that she was "not in favor of this selection." She thought that a bride would need bridesmaids with just a "bit more fashion." Miss Emma Barlette shrugged, and Jane, seeing this as permission to find a different dress, began to peruse Lady Madeleine's, looking for something that *she* deemed more suitable.

After a few minutes had elapsed, Bess observed that the only person who seemed indifferent toward the selection was Miss Henwood, who was sitting on a red sofa and thinking about what must have been Mr. Ashford and their future marriage. Bess thought of pressing the issue of marriage forward again, for she was bored, but then Juliette spoke.

"It is unfortunate," her younger companion began, "that Mr. Henwood would not allow you to be in the wedding. His hatred toward you is so unjust. *You* always seem to be the sensical one. I must say, Bess, that I admire you."

This compliment forced Bess to smile, for she was flattered that Juliette thought so highly of her. In return, Bess praised Juliette's good manners before explaining why she was rather glad to be excluded from the wedding preparations. Juliette nodded along to Bess' remarks, but when she caught a hesitation in Bess' speech, she abruptly changed the subject of the conversation.

"Are you planning on having a wedding any time soon? I was thinking, and I hope my bridesmaid days will not be over after this," she said, exhibiting a most satisfying smile that made Bess ache. *These days, people hardly ever compliment without expecting something in return, and Juliette's behavior is living proof of this supposition!*

Despite feeling disheartened, Bess shook her head and replied, "No, I haven't one in mind." After a pause, she added, "Are you asking because you want me to inquire about *your* future plans? Or, shall I say, are you anticipating—?"

But Juliette interrupted, "What about Jack? Did he propose yet?"

"Jack!" exclaimed Bess. "I had not even heard that our engagement was possible! Did he say something otherwise?" she replied in one breath. And as she listened intently, her face turned red, for she hoped she hadn't provided a false impression of her marital intentions to Juliette.

However, Juliette shook her head, explaining, "Yesterday, Father, Mother, Leonarda, and I dined at Elmsworth Manor. The evening was rather uneventful except for one topic of conversation in which Mrs. Baldare brought up how ill-mannered you seemed to be. Naturally, for I am your friend, I exclaimed that you were *not* as ill-mannered as she may suppose, and Jack passionately agreed with my remark." She stopped to take a deep breath. "When Mrs. Baldare asked him what he found so appealing in your character, he explained that he liked your individuality and vivacity. Afterward, I asked him if he fancied you or anyone else, and he answered that there *was* someone he liked. Of course, that *someone* must be you!"

Bess' heart fluttered, but she shook her head, not wishing to get caught up in the idea of marriage. Instead of basking in this supposition, she vehemently denied any suspicion of an engagement again. After Juliette admitted that she was in disbelief, Miss Emma Barlette called her away to try on a new gown.

Everyone, including Jane, resolved this dress was suitable. The dresses were purchased and ordered to be sent to Henwood Mansion the next day. As Miss Emma Barlette prepared to leave Lady Madeleine's, Mrs. Baldare moaned that her feet hurt and that she would need a carriage to escort her back. After quarreling, a decision was made for Miss Emma Barlette, Miss Henwood, Abigail, and Bess to walk back and have a coach sent for the others.

Abigail stared at her feet during the entire walk, hardly saying more than a word when addressed. On the other hand, the conversations between Miss Emma Barlette, Miss Henwood, and Bess were intermittent. But after a prolonged period of silence, Miss Emma Barlette cleared her throat and said, "Catherine, forgive me for this upcoming remark, as it is a slight against your brother, but—"

Miss Henwood interrupted, "There's no need to apologize, Emma. We all have our foibles, and my brother just happens to have a lot of them."

With a chuckle, Miss Emma Barlette paused before asking, "Would it be okay if I said no at the altar? My mother is getting better, the money has already been spent," she continued, eyes brightening, "*or* if I run away, then it will save me the outward humiliation!" When she had concluded her outburst, Miss Emma Barlette exhaled a sigh, but none of her companions said a word. After another moment of hesitation, she frowned. "Oh, but how crass that would be! I couldn't blacken my good name, and besides, I can try to like him. I *do* try to like him."

Miss Emma Barlette sighed again but continued to complain about her fiancé's character. The remainder of the walk was fraught with these complaints, but when she entered Elmsworth Manor, she quieted and sent for a coachman. After apologizing to a servant for the inconvenience of his traveling to Lady Madeleine's, Miss Emma Barlette bade her guests farewell, explaining that she ought to return home and rest (her sister had other wedding-related obligations, so she wouldn't leave until much later anyway). A quarter of an hour passed before the others returned, and once she spotted her sisters, Jane asked if they could return to Laurel Manor, for she was tired. Abigail and Bess, who had nothing to keep them at Elmsworth Manor, agreed, and after warm goodbyes, the Phillips sisters left.

Chapter 12

On the day of the wedding, Jane and Abigail planned to leave an hour earlier than Mr. Phillips, Bess, and Alex since they were involved in the ceremony. The girls spent their morning running around Laurel Manor, fetching clothing and accessories, and causing a disturbance to their father, who was concerned that they would be late. While she was reading in the drawing-room, Bess caught a glimpse of Jane, who, despite having slightly disheveled hair, looked exceedingly gorgeous. She found Abigail and whispered that Jane would look prettier than the bride, and for it was likely to be accurate, Abigail agreed.

After watching her sisters depart from the manor, Bess returned to her bedroom to find something suitable to wear. While picking through her curtain-like gowns, she resolved to wear something that would neither stand out nor offend Mr. Henwood. Eventually, she selected a plain blue gown that Alex quickly approved.

"I see you've taken my advice to wear your style," he remarked while examining her dressed figure in the mirror.

Bess sighed, "Well, I suppose so." Then she smiled and added, "But if Jane says it looks hideous—perhaps like curtains—you ought to defend me. My rhetoric is no match for her fashion rages." Alex exhaled with a laugh but did not respond, and Bess frowned.

A quarter of an hour passed before Bess, Alex, and Mr. Phillips found themselves pressed together in a carriage heading to Henwood Mansion. So long as her father was present, Bess did not feel comfortable enough to address Alex with her usual playfulness. She opened her mouth to initiate a different type of discussion, but Mr. Phillips first spoke.

"The Americans ought to be tearing themselves apart now," he began, referring to the American Civil War. "I've heard in the newspapers and by word of mouth that the Confederates have the upper hand, but who can truly know what side is ahead when our post is slow to inform us?"

Alex replied with a shy smile and the shaky response: "I still hold the belief that the Americans should never have left our country."

"Yes, and many do," Mr. Phillips agreed. "Perhaps if the Americans destroy themselves, we can reinstate what we once had."

"Yes, yes," Alex answered as he turned to the window.

Bess cleared her throat. "I hardly believe that the so-called American spirit would shatter due to one war. They might separate into two nations, but neither would ever let us Englishmen take them over again. I'm certain of it."

"Oh, my dear," Mr. Phillips continued, "I *do* believe you—yes—but a handful think otherwise. No amount of reading and learning about the war could properly give anyone a realistic prediction for the future— don't you think so, Alex?"

"Oh, yes," Alex started. "Entirely."

Bess smirked at Alex's naïvety and replied for him. "Father, Alex isn't well-versed in politics. Can we change the subject? Besides, I don't care to think about the war. It hurts me to think of something so gruesome."

Alex muttered an appreciative remark to Bess before Mr. Phillips apologized. "Oh, I didn't mean to start a conversation where you had not much knowledge, my boy! I thought it was practically a universal topic—perhaps not."

Alex blushed. "My apologies, Mr. Phillips. I *should* know more." And after a moment of hesitation, he suggested, "Why don't we talk of this wedding instead?"

"An excellent substitute, Alex, an excellent one, indeed," Mr. Phillips applauded, and Bess could not help but chuckle. Her father was always remarkably cordial, yet he lived to please others. He didn't know about anything he didn't read, and as the talk of the wedding had been mostly confined to ladies' gossip, Mr. Phillips didn't know how to begin this upcoming conversation. Bess saved her father from humiliation by starting for him.

"Although you know, Alex, that I don't like to gossip, I cannot help but reflect upon the guests today," she began, hardly knowing how else to start. If she and Alex were alone, their talking would be much livelier, but instead, they had to conceal their real judgements in front of Mr. Phillips. And as Bess and Alex both shared a clever nature, they opted to voice their opinions in disguise. "Mr. Henwood's *large* wedding will be most suitable for such a lovely bride," Bess said, trying to hold back her laughter. Alex immediately picked up on her pattern of using keywords to convey different meanings, and it was hard for him to avoid laughing as well. Luckily, Mr. Phillips did not notice.

"Mr. Curtis Elmsworth and Mrs. Lydia Baldare should be *awfully* proper wedding participants, I may also add," Alex said with a grin, and Bess nearly squealed.

She managed to reply, "Yes, they ought to be. Oh, but Gus will be *terribly* good, too!"

Alex's reaction was the same as Bess', and he added, "And as will Miss Elmsworth!"

Then Bess paused, forgetting all their humor and neglecting her father's presence. With hesitation, she questioned, "Miss Elmsworth? Why did you mention her?"

"Have you not observed her character, Bess?" Alex blushed. "Or have I misinterpreted it?"

Bess did not know how to reply. She had always agreed with Alex's judgments, but now, she had no idea to what he was referring. *Yes, Miss Elmsworth seems a bit too partial toward Mr. Henwood, and she can act a little selfish and materialistic, but her flaws have never been so significant as to be categorized among the likes of Mr. Henwood, Mrs. Baldare, Curtis, and Gus.*

"What would make you say such a thing?" Bess genuinely wondered. Mr. Phillips looked up and noticed his daughter's minor distress and hesitation. But soon, the horses halted. A coachman swung open the door, and the occupants stepped outside the carriage. Mr. Phillips mindlessly walked ahead, noticing Miss Rachel Barlette and Miss Henwood talking among one another. Bess turned to Alex and said, "I do not mean to say that your assessments are incorrect. I just mean to ask why you think so."

Alex seemed relieved at her confirmation of his sanity and began to relate a few incidents that had led him to make his remark. First, when she became acquainted with him, Miss Elmsworth seemed only to care about speaking to Jane, who was standing beside him. She hardly ever showed any interest in Alex or his well-being, but Alex concluded that she must just be a feminist. Bess questioned this conclusion but let him continue without intervention. Second, Alex remarked that she always seemed to put others' health at risk, considering that she, who has or had—no one knew for sure anymore—scarlet fever, often spent time

143

with those who weren't immune. Perhaps, he thought, she was just misguided while growing up and didn't know any better than to think of *only* herself, which, of course, wasn't her fault *at all.* Third, he mentioned a brief conversation where she was the only one who ever spoke, and of course, the subject was on comparing Jane's beauty with the other Phillips sisters'.

"I've observed that she's rather vain," Alex concluded. "And her brothers seem very flawed as well."

This final remark angered Bess, but she could not help but agree (to a slight extent) with her friend's words. Yet, she frowned and retorted, "*Very* is a convincing word, Alex. Without it, your judgment would have been fine."

Alex blushed, but before he could reply, he was saved by Mr. Phillips, who called his daughter and future son-in-law over to accompany him to the garden. Miss Rachel Barlette and Miss Henwood had been sent away on bridesmaid duties, and he needed someone to guide him to the ceremony.

When the garden of Henwood Mansion was within her view, Bess gasped. Primroses, irises, and other colorful flowers decorated the landscape. Neatly trimmed bushes with red berries lined the perimeter, a stone walkway formed the path to the altar, and not even a blade of grass existed that was not groomed to perfection. Within the designated area sat hundreds of marble benches, which already hosted approximately three-quarters of the garden's capacity. Upon closer inspection, Bess nor her two companions could recognize a single face, but they ventured onward and seated themselves between the Wheatleys and the Elmsworths.

"Why aren't Miss Phillips and Mr. Cawdor in the ceremony?" Bess overheard Mrs. Wheatley whisper to her husband, who, in turn, shrugged.

"I don't think they enjoy social events," Mr. Wheatley replied, and not wishing to hear the Wheatley's poorly concealed remarks, Bess turned to Alex.

Without knowing how else to start a conversation, she asked, "Did you notice how beautiful Jane looked this morning?" Alex sighed and cast his eyes downward, but Bess continued, "Abbie looked rather plain, yet I thought her dress matched her hairstyle rather—"

"Abbie looked beautiful, too," Alex interrupted. "I find it's hard to compare the two of them—they're both gorgeous."

Bess held her breath and hoped that Alex would compliment her beauty, but he did not. She sighed and hastily remarked, "Abbie has grown a lot lately."

"Yes, and I'm happy for her," Alex said, lowering his voice as the priest strode down the aisle. Bess closed her mouth and remained silent.

Throughout the ceremony, Alex stared absent-mindedly forward, almost forgetting to clap when Mr. Henwood concluded the wedding by kissing his new wife. Bess watched as the latter escaped from this gesture as soon as possible, and she desired to mention her amusement to Alex, but he remained motionless, hardly registering the gravity of Miss Emma Barlette's, now Mrs. Henwood's, actions. As the bridesmaids returned down the aisle, Bess sighed and admired how beautiful they each were.

The clock struck to indicate that an hour had passed since she first arrived, and Bess swam through the endless crowd of guests to reach the newly wedded couple. She extended her hand to congratulate the groom, and Mr. Henwood thanked her for attending. Bess shrugged at his decision *not* to insult her and started to turn away, but the new Mrs. Henwood tapped her on the shoulder to request a private conversation.

Once she had isolated Bess, Mrs. Henwood's smile transformed into a frown of apprehension, and she started, "Bess—"

"Are you not feeling well, Mrs. Henwood?"

Mrs. Henwood nodded, and for the first time that afternoon, Bess noticed how pale the bride was. With a scratchy voice, she added, "I cannot tell if I am sick of my husband and this wedding, which is highly possible considering my complete reluctance toward the entire marriage, or if I am truly coming down with some illness. Can I entrust you with the responsibility of covering for me if I must leave sometime this evening? I do not think I can remain highly sociable all night."

Bess remained speechless but nodded and escorted the bride back to her husband. She received Mrs. Henwood's gratitude with pleasure and turned to find Alex. Wearing a look of concern for her acquaintance, Bess pushed through the crowd and came upon her elder sister and her fiancé. She frowned and started to search for Abigail but heard a familiar voice remark, "What a pleasant wedding, and the post-celebration should be equally as delightful."

Recognizing Jack's voice, Bess smiled. She turned and felt relieved to have a friend with whom to spend time. She said, "Yes, I hope so."

"The bride looked amazing," Jack continued, "and I am honored to have been selected as a groomsman. I only regret, Bess, that you were not part of the ceremony."

Bess grinned and shook her head. "If I had been, I would have been too exhausted to celebrate afterward. And I presume that the seated view was better than the standing one, so I am not unsatisfied."

Jack exchanged a charming smile with his friend before suggesting to walk around the garden. Bess agreed, for she had nothing else to do, so they started their stroll during which they commented upon the natural beauty of the scenery. Jack admitted that he was unsure how Mr. Henwood could have managed such a picturesque landscape.

"Well," Bess began, "I suppose he'd settle for nothing less than the most famous gardener in the world." Jack laughed but could not devise a suitable reply, so he remained silent. And as a painful period ensued where neither friend talked Bess turned her attention to a small pond where, to her utter astoundment, she found her father seated beside Miss Henwood! She tapped Jack on the shoulder and relayed her observation. Jack's eyes shot toward the duck pond, and he drew back upon seeing this spectacle. Bess frowned and said, "Shouldn't they acquaint themselves with someone their own age?"

Jack shrugged. "I saw them dancing during the dinner party. I think they're both lonely creatures, so they're naturally drawn to one another."

"Or perhaps she was a friend of my mother," Bess resolved. "They must be discussing her recent passing."

After a sigh, Bess checked to ensure that Mrs. Henwood appeared healthy. Upon seeing that she was enjoying a lively conversation with Juliette (although no discussion with Juliette could *not* be lively), she calmed down. But before she had time to think, Bess' eyes landed on Alex and her sisters, who were skipping rocks by another pond. She took a deep breath and returned to Jack, beginning a conversation regarding books. Jack had read and enjoyed *Othello*. Bess laughed and said that Shakespeare, since it was wrapped up in ploys of murder and sabotage, ought to be a "gentleman's liking." Jack chuckled and conceded that she *might* be right. The two of them enjoyed a few more minutes of discussion before circling back to the altar where most of the guests had gathered.

Not caring to involve herself in other social obligations, Bess recommended that she and Jack take another walk around the garden. Jack agreed, but as they began another lap, a large man emerged from the gathering of people and called out Bess' name. At first, Bess deemed this man mistaken, but he continued to call after her, persistent in attaining her attention.

As Bess took a step toward this gentleman, she recognized him as Mr. Benjamin Roberts, Mr. Henwood's half-brother. During the ceremony, she had noticed him but hadn't intended to introduce herself, for Miss Rachel Barlette's account of his character was not appealing. In any case, Mr. Roberts' figure was large like his brother's, but fortunately, he possessed a much more handsome countenance. Upon further inspection, however, Bess decided that she could not call him *handsome*, considering that, due to his plumpness, all of his facial features were blown up to an uncanny size.

"Miss Bess Phillips!" he exclaimed, approaching her with a wide smile. "How happy I am to make your acquaintance! I have heard much about you!" But Bess was hesitant to respond. Any description of her that Mr. Roberts could have received from his brother was most definitely *not* positive.

Bess finally replied, "And I have heard about you as well. Mrs. Henwood and Miss Rachel Barlette were most happy to report upon your character."

Mr. Roberts' face lit up as he replied, "I hope they spoke highly of me!" Bess opened her mouth to respond, but Mr. Roberts pulled her aside. In a much quieter voice, he said, "I apologize for that obnoxious introduction." Bess raised an eyebrow, but Mr. Roberts added, "I am the reserved brother, but I figured today I ought to act as a more outgoing version of Charles to distract the guests from his obvious flaws. And from what Charles said about your behavior toward him, I figured you'd be a wonderful confidante for my secret." Bess exhaled and brightly smiled. If not for his size, Mr. Roberts was *almost* charming. "And anyone sensical (like myself) would entirely agree with your perception." Again, Bess opened her mouth to respond, but Mr. Roberts hurriedly added, "This evening, I'd like you to accompany me in the first dance."

"Oh!" Bess laughed, and neglecting to remember Miss Rachel Barlette's assertion of Mr. Roberts' attempting to seduce her, she accepted his invitation. Then Mr. Roberts pulled away and loudly remarked how happy he was for his brother. With a wink, he left Bess to introduce himself to the Wheatleys.

Later that evening, after every guest had settled inside the ballroom, Bess apologized to Jack for having to first dance with Mr. Roberts. Jack forgave her, so Bess reconnected with her newest friend, who invited her to join his brother and Mrs. Henwood in their second waltz.

During the dance, Mr. Roberts hardly spoke to his partner, choosing to gaze behind her instead. He briefly mentioned having met Jane and Abigail, but when the waltz ended, they parted, having other obligations in mind. Bess watched Mr. Roberts escape her grasp, and she thought: *Miss Rachel Barlette must have been mistaken. Although he is an intriguing man—first charming and then ignoring me—I cannot see how he could be a seducer. And he certainly doesn't reek a horrid odor!*

Not minding Mr. Roberts' blatant disregard toward her, for she never *really* felt attached, Bess wandered around in search of Jack. After passing by crowds of dancers, she found him drinking champagne alongside Miss Henwood! *She always seems to be in peculiar locations.* Bess blushed. *But what could she be doing? She promised that Jack was not her future fiancé.*

Upon seeing Bess approach, Jack startled and nearly choked on his champagne. He stood and exclaimed, "Oh! Catherine, I promised Bess the second dance. I will speak to you on this subject matter later!"

Bess glanced toward Miss Henwood before hurrying away. She raised an eyebrow and asked, "On what subject were you and her speaking?"

Jack hesitated before saying, "As of now, it is of no concern to you. It was on her potential fiancé."

"And it's not you?" Bess asked, hardly being able to contain her curiosity and temper.

Jack shook his head. "You will discover who it is in due time. She simply wanted some advice, so we talked during the first waltz. How was Mr. Roberts?"

As they reached the crowd of dancers, Bess replied, "Surprisingly agreeable for having the same parent as—" but her response was cut short once the music began.

After taking a moment to catch her breath, Bess finished her statement, and Jack nodded. He appeared, however, to be looking over her shoulder. When the song's natural movements shifted the two of them around, Bess looked behind him and noticed her father and Abigail speaking together. She looked for any sign of Miss Henwood but could find none. Bess sighed and gazed around the room before catching a glimpse of Jane and Alex, who were dancing together. They laughed and spun, and Bess could not help but feel as if she was missing out on the fun. Turning the other way, she ignored her elder sister and fiancé, and instead, she found Abigail, who was sitting alone. Bess wanted to stay beside Jack and try to emulate Alex and Jane's good time, but she could not help but pity her younger sister. Against all her natural desires, she said to Jack, "After this song, I'd like to chat with Abbie. If time permits, I shall dance with you later, Jack, but until then, out of sheer intrigue, may I ask with whom you will dance?"

Jack recognized Bess' reluctance to leave him but interpreted her generosity as admirable. He smiled and decided to return her kindness. "Well," he began, "since you entreat me to find another partner—you wouldn't mind if I asked Abigail to dance before you sit with her, would you? She looks awfully in need of a friend who isn't her sister."

Bess smiled, admired Jack's manners, and consented to his request.

After she finished dancing, Bess led Jack to Abigail, who was quietly playing with a torn piece of her gown. *She looks just like I did at Westfield Manor…all alone until Jack came along. And how ironic it is that he, yet again, has come to the rescue!* Interrupting her thoughts, Jack asked Abigail to dance, but to Bess' surprise, her sister declined the request, remarking that she was busy observing the other dancers. In response, Jack bade Bess farewell and promised to dance with her later.

Half a second after Bess sat down, Abigail asserted, "You want to dance with Alex." The idea of quarreling never entered Bess' mind, and she admired Alex and Jane's dancing figures. Every step taken and every movement made was in perfect alignment. "I know the feeling," she murmured, and after a moment of confusion, Bess asked *how* Abigail knew this feeling. Abigail looked up, denying having said anything at all, and although Bess questioned her sister, the interrogation was to no avail. Again, Bess' eyes fell on Jane and Alex. Now, they had ceased to dance and seemed to be arguing. Abigail sighed and muttered, "Alex wants to ask you to dance, but Jane won't allow it. I've seen them quarrel over you before. Don't be too surprised," she replied upon seeing Bess fake astonishment. "Also, you've taken another strange interest in Jack. You seemed pleased with him at Westfield Manor, but then, for a while, I thought you were indifferent toward him. Now, you seem fascinated with him once again, and I cannot begin to comprehend why." With a sly smile, she added, "Unless your observations of Alex's apparent affections toward Jane have—"

Bess blushed, but not wishing to cause a big scene, she replied in an irritated tone, "I thought I made my situation with Alex very clear to you."

"I'm a lot cleverer than you suppose me to be, Bess," Abigail said matter-of-factly. "I don't want to quarrel," she added. "I just wish to relay my observations."

Bess clenched her jaw and said, "I've never seen you *not* take an interest in the private affairs of guests at dances before."

Abigail hesitated before saying, "A while ago, I would have voiced these judgments for everyone to hear, but now, you're the only person to whom I've confided." Bess shifted her position before glancing up and noticing Jack dancing alongside Miss Henwood. "Yes," Abigail perceived, "I'm unsure of what Jack's business is with Miss Henwood, but to satisfy your concerns, I don't believe he is her future fiancé. If you must know—we think he's attached to *you*."

"With me!" exclaimed Bess. "Who—?"

"While you were dancing with Mr. Roberts, I was speaking with Jane, Alex, Mr. Ashford, the Wheatleys, and the Elmsworths, excluding Jack, and our discussion revolved around the prospect of his marrying you. His parents remarked that he seems livelier than he has been for years, making them believe he's in love."

"Uh," started Bess with widened eyes.

"However, Miss Elmsworth doesn't think he'll propose—not until he's older."

"So, the possibility of his proposing *did* come up?"

"For a moment. But—don't fret—everyone thinks you're indifferent and would decline." Abigail sighed, turning toward Jane and Alex, who were dancing again. "I'm sorry, Bessie, but Alex is going to be with Jane. Say nothing about your opinion on that matter—I know it all, but I think the best thing you can do is move on."

Suddenly, Jack returned and asked for Bess' hand in another dance. She accepted, so they returned to the ballroom floor across from Jane and Alex to perform a dance of Italian origin. Throughout the remainder of the evening, Bess made herself have a brilliant time with her partner. She mirrored Jane and Alex's seemingly happy movements, and she made herself laugh even during moments that humor did not appear appropriate. And by the end of the evening, Bess fancied herself completely in love with Jack. *If he asks me to marry him, I would be most happy to say yes. Nevermind my former opinions on marriage; if Jane and Alex are to marry, then, I suppose, Jack is the only tolerable gentleman left. Yes, I'd be conforming to what society wants of me, but that doesn't matter anymore. If Alex is to marry Jane, then I, too, can marry someone who isn't my first choice.*

Chapter 13

Bess could not take her newly-developed love of Jack out of her mind until the arrival of an unexpected guest the following day. Around noon, Mr. Henwood visited Laurel Manor to thank the Phillips family for attending the wedding, but he came without his beloved bride. With her utmost sincerity (so as not to be mistaken for rudeness), Bess inquired over Mrs. Henwood's welfare, and with a heavy heart, Mr. Henwood replied that she had fallen ill. As if her words were exploding out of her, Bess insisted upon seeing her friend, but Mr. Henwood denied her request, beginning to speak of his brother instead.

"Benjamin was very pleased to have danced with you, Bess," Mr. Henwood started while hardly looking at her. "He is such a good man, and I don't want you—"

"I'm not in love with him," Bess interrupted, and then she changed the conversation. "Please let me go and visit Mrs. Henwood."

But Mr. Henwood acted as if he had not heard her, for he continued, "I do not wish you to speak with my brother anymore. He is an amiable creature, but I could *never* have you as a sister. He told me that he fancies one of the Phillips sisters, and you're the only one he's spoken to me about!"

Bess nearly laughed. "I do not wish to offend you, Mr. Henwood, but you must not worry." She paused. "However, you ought to keep me informed on how Mrs. Henwood is faring. Please have her or her sister write to me as soon as her health improves or worsens."

"At least we're clear about my brother," Mr. Henwood remarked, ignoring the reference to his sick wife. He then left Laurel Manor, and Bess turned to her sisters in astonishment.

"He hardly cared for his wife!" exclaimed Bess. "All he cared for was insulting me yet again!"

Abigail did not say a word, but Jane replied, "Mr. Benjamin Roberts *was* nice though. I had a dance or two with him, and I found him rather delightful."

"He *was* quite agreeable, but Mr. Henwood's intentions are terrible," Bess concluded before turning around and heading straight to the garden to finish reading *A Tale of Two Cities.* She did not wish to speak with anyone, and upon Jane's last-minute report that Alex was soon to arrive, Bess became even more motivated to exit the scene.

Not an hour later, a servant from Henwood Mansion arrived, delivering a letter addressed to Bess from Mrs. Henwood, reading—

Bess,

I understand that Charles visited you today, but I believe we all underestimated my sickness. I was ill last night, but now I am greatly ill, Bess, and I cannot determine if I will be well again. I could hardly even muster enough effort to write this letter to you, but I deemed it essential that you, my dear friend, must know. Doctor Coleman, Kent's best physician, just visited and said I have scarlet fever. I know it is horrible to say, but I cannot help but consider that my sickness is due to my spending time with Miss Elmsworth. I hope that I am the only one to catch this if my suspicions are correct. Bess, I heard that you are likely immune to scarlet fever, for you had it as an infant, so I would appreciate your visiting me. I would love someone with whom to speak. Thank you for your understanding.

Sincerely,

Your friend—Mrs. Emma Henwood

Without delay, Bess left Laurel Manor, neglecting a carriage or a horse with which to travel. She ran by Alex, who had just arrived. He gave her a puzzled look and shouted, "Where are you going, Bess?"

"Mrs. Henwood has scarlet fever! I must see her!" she cried. Alex glanced at the front door of Laurel Manor. He hesitated but soon raced toward Bess. Upon noticing her friend's floppy hair chase after her, Bess called, "Alex, go inside!"

"I'm coming with you!" he cried after taking a deep breath. "But you could have taken a carriage!"

Bess laughed but then a thought struck her. *I can no longer feel or show any affection toward Alex. My attention should be solely on Jack, and as difficult as this endeavor might be, I ought to be resilient. It's only right.* Another peculiar thought came to her mind, which she voiced. "You've never had scarlet fever, have you?" Alex shook his head and pleaded for Bess to slow down. Bess stopped running, for she, too, was growing exhausted. They decided to walk at a brisk pace instead as Bess reprimanded, "You shouldn't have come. You can catch it since you've never had it, and you should have at least told Jane where you were going."

"I wanted to come, and you would have been gone by the time I went inside to tell her." He paused. "Besides, Jane wouldn't have let me go."

Bess thought she saw him blush, so she quickened her pace in determination to forget about any feelings toward him. All the while, she could hardly help but smile at his folly.

Chapter 14

Upon their arrival at Henwood Mansion, Bess and Alex were startled to find an assembly of servants running around and insisting on complying *exactly* to all of "the doctor's requirements." Bess knocked on the front door but found it was unlocked. She pushed the door open and approached one of the less frantic-looking maids to inquire where she might find Mrs. Henwood. The maid directed Bess and Alex up a long staircase, and before she started ascending it, Bess heard Alex say, "I should wait down here."

Bess turned around to look at him. He was hunched over, attempting to catch his breath, and Bess could not help but smile and add, "I understand your concern for catching this illness, but part of me also thinks you are afraid that my stamina will prove greater than yours once I run up this staircase."

Alex smirked but was astonished to find that his friend was already halfway up the steps. Bess' face glimmered, for she was glad that she and Alex were on playful terms again.

Alex called, "Now you're just showing off!"

Bess let out a little squeal but dared not respond. She did not want to alert Mr. Henwood of her whereabouts. Thankfully, when she entered Mrs. Henwood's room, Bess discovered that her friend was alone, but like she had written, she was not in a good state. Her face was bright red, and her quasi pleasure from the previous day had entirely disappeared. She shook tremendously, and during every minor movement she made, red creases became visible across her skin.

When Mrs. Henwood's eyes caught Bess', a trace of a smile flickered across her face as she murmured a weak "Bess." Bess ran to her friend's side and heard her whimper, "Bess, I am pleased that you came, but you probably shouldn't stand so close. I know you are deemed immune, but I don't want to take any chances that the doctors are mistaken."

Bess stepped back and pulled a chair alongside her friend, but she did not know what to say. She had not known Mrs. Henwood for so long, so she was surprised that she was Mrs. Henwood's only guest. She would have thought that either her parents, her sister, Miss Henwood, or Mr. Henwood would have pledged never to leave her sight.

"I hope that I have not inconvenienced you," she began, and Bess anxiously replied that the occasion was no inconvenience. "Rachel has never had the illness, and I begged her not to come onto the property. Charles had scarlet fever when he was younger, but he's occupied with some important business." She took a deep breath. "Bess, I called on you because, well, there's something I've always wanted to tell you," she said before losing her breath. Bess quickly stood, preparing to find a maid to nurse her, but Mrs. Henwood told her to return to her seat. She continued, "Well, I never planned to tell you this, but based on my serious decline of health from yesterday, I do not know how long I will last—"

"Oh!" interrupted Bess. "No, Mrs. Henwood! Please don't say that!" she exclaimed, unintentionally wrapping her hands around her friend's.

"No, Bess. I must tell you." She paused. "And call me Emma—it sounds better. Mrs. Henwood makes me sound like an old maid." Bess chuckled before Emma continued, "You might remember meeting me the day of the Westfield ball. I never spoke because," she then lowered her voice before adding, "of Charles, of course." She took a deep breath and continued, "But that was certainly not the first time *I* saw you." She tried to sit upright but failed in her endeavors, growing paler at the attempt. "My father used to work at a haberdashery downtown, and when you were younger, you, your sisters, and your mother often went there. Do you remember?" Bess reflected and nodded. Emma added, "Well, you used to come in when you were perhaps seven or eight years old to find clothing for your father, and around that time, I was an adolescent. I would observe you and your sisters, and I always found your different dynamics interesting. Jane and Abigail seemed to emulate your mother, but you were much different—I could tell by your numerous, varied conversations. You were very disagreeable, but for an outsider like me, it was attractive. I always admired your individuality and your determination to follow your mind instead of others'." Bess smiled and replied gratefully, but Emma remarked she hadn't finished. "I wanted that determination for myself. And I often experimented with it. I became outspoken and generally disliked, but I preferred it much over conforming to everyone else." Emma paused and took a deep breath. "Then of course, to save my mother, I had to marry against my will, and I was forced into a long engagement that *made* me conform to Charles and his society. I became miserable, Bess, and you must have observed me that way at Westfield Manor." Emma pulled her hand away from Bess to brush her hand across her feverish forehead. She looked up again and said, "I never had the courage to tell you how much I've always admired you. If Charles ever overheard me, he would have suspected that I was fond of you. Then he might have ended the engagement and the medical payments for my mother." She hesitated. "I knew you didn't care to be a part of the wedding because you don't like Charles, and quite frankly," she lowered her voice again, "I don't blame you. But I was so pleased you came dress shopping with my bridesmaids and me." Emma's voice faltered, but without addressing her declining health, she continued. "You ought to have noticed that Jane was constantly talking to me then. She's a pleasant and kind girl, but she's nothing like you. We spoke of some trivial manner for which I hardly cared when I heard Miss Elmsworth and Mrs. Baldare talking to you. I knew what they said was wrong about your not being in the wedding, so I mustered the courage to make that curt response to them—I'm certain you remember, and you were probably taken aback by it—but I knew that it was something *you* would do for a friend. I was so pleased to become a friend of yours, and all I wanted was to cultivate a stronger bond with you, but now, this fever has ruined it all!" Emma paused for a few minutes, and a tear trickled down her face. Bess had not noticed that she was crying. Emma took a deep breath and continued, "And Bess, I cannot leave this world knowing that Rachel is left to Charles' hands. If I die, *please* promise me that you will look after her. I know she's older than you, but help guide her in the right direction. Be the example for her that you were for me."

Bess could hardly manage a reply. She was fighting back tears, and the best response she could make was a vigorous nod. Emma continued to cry, but this time, Bess noticed that it was out of pure happiness.

"Thank you," she said repeatedly. Bess held onto Emma's hand, and for the next hour, Bess watched her friend's laughter fade into sleep. Bess could hardly imagine that Emma had known her for so long. She tried to recall her former haberdashery days, but she could never remember the haberdasher's daughter. Bess' heart skipped a beat as she felt immense pride rise within her, and she resolved to care for Emma for as long as needed.

After Emma was sound asleep, Bess slipped out of the room and found Alex sitting on the steps where she had left him. Right away, he looked up and asked if Emma was doing well.

"She doesn't look well, but she was happy I came," Bess replied.

Alex remarked that he was pleased to hear that Bess' presence made her happy, and he carried on talking about how, while she was with Emma, he had some wine with Mr. Henwood. In a drunken state, Mr. Henwood said that if Emma passed away, he wouldn't care. He didn't like her anyway, and he would easily woo "the beautiful" Miss Rachel Barlette into marrying him. Mr. Henwood said that Miss Rachel Barlette seemed to love everything about her sister's higher marriage, so she would have no problem marrying her sister's husband.

Bess' face turned a bright shade of red, and she insisted that they begin their walk home. During the walk, Bess exclaimed how inappropriate Mr. Henwood had acted. First, Emma thought her husband was doing business work, not wallowing in alcohol! Second, Mr. Henwood's inconsiderate remarks about Emma and her sister were utterly dehumanizing. After Bess concluded her criticisms, she filled Alex in on all that Emma had told her, and throughout her description of Emma's praise, Bess could not help but notice Alex smile.

When the two of them returned to the outskirts of Laurel Manor, they came upon a furious Jane, who reprimanded them and yelled that Alex ought to leave the manor. When Alex had gone, Jane glared at Bess but said nothing. She marched back into the house and slammed the door behind her. Moments later, Bess opened the door and realized Jane was gone. Then when looking to discuss the day's events, Bess could not find Abigail.

Later that night, Bess caught Abigail sneaking into the house covered in dirt. She was not wearing one of her gowns; rather, she appeared to be wearing some old gentleman's clothing! Abigail's eyes widened when she spotted Bess, and she begged her elder sister not to say a word. When Abigail had cleaned up, Bess asked her where she had been all day, and she responded that she had gone to school to participate in some weekend lessons. Then she added that, after being run over by a horse-drawn carriage, she had fallen into the mud, but to her luck, a kind peasant woman offered her some of her husband's clothing to wear in exchange for a few coins.

Bess was dubious but too eager to tell Abigail about Emma that she ignored this fabricated tale.

Chapter 15

Early the next morning, Bess awoke and headed downstairs for breakfast. She found Jane eating alone in the dining hall. Jane glanced up, and when she saw Bess, she stood. She pushed in her chair and started to march away, but Bess cried out her name. Bess didn't know why, for she didn't want to speak with her. Perhaps she figured that making amends about going off with Alex would be the right thing.

Jane stopped, slowly turning to face her traitorous sister.

"Can I talk with you?" asked Bess rather timidly.

Jane didn't respond. She just stared at her little sister, trying to summon all the intimidating powers she possessed. However, in the end, she gave in and retook her seat. Bess sat down beside her. She opened her mouth to begin, but Jane interrupted, "If you're here to convince me that Alex isn't in love with you, then that's hopeless! I don't even know if Emma is sick. Perhaps the two of you just went to the town together or some other fiction like that!"

Bess pulled out Emma's letter, which she pocketed that morning in case she ran into Jane. She opened it up and held it out to her sister. Jane snatched the letter from Bess' hands and began to read it over. Bess watched her sister's face as she read through the message. She grew more distressed the further she read into it. By the end, Jane couldn't even look at Bess out of sheer humiliation for supposing that Emma was *not* ill. Bess took back the letter and said in the kindest way possible, "Jane, I was on my way to visit Emma, and I passed Alex as he was heading here. He asked where I was going, and he figured that it would be right for him to see if Emma was doing well."

"First," Jane pouted, "he could have at least *told* me where he was going—"

"It would have taken too long—"

"And also, *why* would Emma write that to you and not me? Emma and *I* are better friends! She hardly ever speaks to you, and you weren't even *in* her wedding!"

"That was Mr. Henwood's doing," Bess interrupted.

"Well, I'm sure her wishes could have overturned his." Jane frowned. Neither Bess nor Jane spoke for a few moments. Jane crossed her arms and stared at the table, evidently trying to figure out how to voice her next thoughts. Bess sat patiently, staring at her sister's arms, wondering when she would say more. Jane continued in a tremble, "But that doesn't address Alex's love for you. I've seen it in more ways than just this!"

Bess sighed. She readjusted her posture, rubbed her eyes, and cleared her throat. Jane watched nervously. "Jane," Bess started, "Alex and I are best friends." Bess felt a pang in her heart when she said this, for she knew that she and Alex *must* be in love with one another. However, Bess had, as of the other day, forgotten about her love for Alex and set her hopes on marrying Jack instead. Therefore, she continued. "We've always been such close companions, which is an observation I doubt you could have neglected. I suppose our relationship could be mistaken for one with romantic implications, but," Bess continued, hoping not to leave her elder sister in anticipation for much longer, "the two of you are indubitably soulmates," she hastily added. "You might remain unconvinced at what I'm telling you, but comprehend that best friends should *not* marry one another, which entirely negates the possibility of our matrimony. If my rhetoric is not fulfilling, take Alex's word over mine: he's told me that he loves you incredibly. He's never told *me* anything to that degree of consequence," Bess lied, finishing her confession with a sigh. "And if you *must* know, I wouldn't marry Alex—not for all the riches in England. For your mental comfort and romantic stimulation, you ought to know that I *would* consider marrying Jack if he proposed. *We* are in love," Bess added, more to convince herself than to convince Jane. "And I know," she continued rather hurriedly, "that I have never manifested any symptoms of affection— outwardly, at least—but this reasoning derives from a couple of points. First, I lack the ability to express my emotions in that regard. It might sound strange, but I believe that it is true. Second, I never wanted our family dynamic to break, so I resisted all possible romances. But now that I have seen that you and Alex are meant for each other, I have realized that, if we sisters cannot remain together forever, then I must move on. Lastly, I never recognized the type of man whom I could permanently fancy—until I met Jack, that is." Bess glanced down at the table after painfully revealing these false words, and when she looked up, Jane's face had brightened.

"Are you sure what you said is true?" Jane asked before acknowledging Bess' nod as an affirmative. "Well then—thank you, Bessie. Those words meant a lot to me," she said, standing up rather happily. "Now, I must go off and visit Emma. I suppose I'll have to stand far off since I've never contracted scarlet fever before, but I cannot believe that she hasn't yet written to me. Perhaps my letter got lost."

Then Jane departed from the table, leaving Bess alone to her thoughts. And as much as she wanted to revisit Emma, Bess knew that Jane would never allow her to come. This visit, to Jane, was meant to be personal. Bess knew that Jane would voice, in the kindest way possible, her concern that Emma's health had made her "forget" who her *real* friends were, which would account for her "mistake" in sending Bess a letter instead of Jane. But Bess didn't mind so much—Emma would understand.

After finishing her breakfast, Bess returned to her bedroom, anxious regarding the lies she had concocted. *At least they made Jane happy. But now, I've stated that Alex and I are not romantically involved. Further, I've completely attached myself to the notion that Jack and I are meant to be together. Jane would most likely voice these opinions to Alex, too, and oh, he would be devastated to hear them! But Alex had made his choice, and he could no longer hinder mine.*

At least she thought so.

Chapter 16

To her utter dismay, Bess watched the life slowly fade from Emma over the course of a couple weeks. She observed her symptoms exacerbating, a gruesome reminder of her mother's unhappy fate, but she never failed to consistently visit her friend every day.

Bess' fear ultimately came to pass in a letter she received from Miss Rachel Barlette about a month after the wedding.

Miss Elizabeth Phillips,

I am writing to report that my dearest sister, Mrs. Emma Henwood, has passed away this morning. There is no need for you to come and visit today. We aren't going to have a public funeral. Charles doesn't want to upset many people.

On another note, Charles and I are heading to his summer home in Brighton this afternoon. He proposed to me after the death of my sister, and we plan to elope. Please do not tell many people about this engagement; it is meant to be secret.

Anyway, thank you for all your love and care toward my sister Emma. I hope that we can meet again in the future.

Sincerely,

Miss Rachel Barlette

Bess' heart dropped, and she fumbled the letter between her hands. Once she had a solid grasp on the paper, she angrily tore it in two. She tossed both halves onto the floor and marched outside of her house. She slammed the door behind her and let out a loud, agonizing scream. She collapsed on the front porch step and dropped her head in her hands.

How could both Charles and Miss Rachel Barlette be so insensitive toward Emma's death? And now, I cannot look after Miss Rachel Barlette because she's leaving! I won't be able to fulfill Emma's final wish!

Bess took a deep breath. She slowly rose from her seated position before picking up her feet and racing to Henwood Mansion to stop Mr. Henwood and his new fiancée while seeing Emma, although dead, one last time. However, when she arrived, a servant reported that Emma's body was already gone, and Mr. Henwood and Miss Rachel Barlette had left hours ago. Bess immediately denied the servant's words and shouted, "Charles! Rachel!" She heard no response and was forcibly dragged out of the house. Bess escaped from the servant's grasp but chose to sulk back to Laurel Manor. When she arrived, she found Alex sitting on the front porch step. He looked up and noticed Bess' distressed countenance, and with a forlorn look, he stammered, "I came from there, too. I brought flowers for her, but then a servant told me—"

"Did you see Mr. Henwood or Miss Rachel Barlette?"

"No," Alex replied in an undertone. "But I know what happened." He paused. "I'm so sorry, Bessie."

Bess sat down beside Alex and laid her head on his shoulder. For the first time that day, she was no longer focused on Mr. Henwood and Miss Rachel Barlette's follies; rather, the weight of Emma's death was fully upon her. There had never been anyone who *truly* admired her. Emma, although she was a recent friend, was one of her greatest friends, and now she was gone.

"I can't believe Miss Rachel Barlette would do that to her sister," Alex said.

Bess removed her head from his shoulder and murmured, "I never knew her well, so I never judged her character. Perhaps this is *exactly* who she is," she sighed. "You know Emma's final wish to me, Alex. Perhaps Emma was working on helping her sister to change. Perhaps she figured this would happen, and I was her last hope."

Bess shed a tear, and when Alex saw this sign of sorrow, he put his arm around Bess' shoulder, whispering, "Bessie, this isn't your fault. There's nothing you could have done."

Bess laid her head back on Alex's shoulder and cried. She cried harder than she ever had before. She knew that she would be embarrassed to have cried so much in front of Alex when her misery subsided, but she could not help it. Every part of her body was screaming in pain and agony. Emma had been so kind to her, and her death was unjust. And not only had Emma unfairly died but so had Bess' mother. Bess pounded her fists on Alex's side and let out another cry. Then a climax of emotional pain overtook her: she cried over her mother, unintentionally changing Abigail, committing herself to Jack, and Jane's jealousy. Most prominently, she cried over Emma, her *only* real friend, for she knew in her heart that Alex was not *just* a friend.

Jane and Abigail must have heard her commotion because moments later, they emerged from the house and sat beside Bess and Alex.

"Alex?" Jane whispered, asking what the matter could be. "Is it Emma?"

Alex could only manage a nod, as he, too, was fighting back tears.

Upon Alex's confirmation of this news, Jane grew pale and released a tremendous howl. She reached for her fiancé, and Alex pulled her close, holding the two elder sisters in his arms. Abigail simply sat beside her family. She covered her face with her hands, but she did not cry. She rubbed her eyes but only stared blankly at her family, for they knew Emma's death was inevitable. It was no surprise.

"How did Mr. Henwood react?" Abigail asked Alex quietly. Alex responded by explaining the situation regarding Mr. Henwood and Miss Rachel Barlette's engagement. Abigail shook her head as a look of anger flashed across her face.

"At least," Alex began, hoping to lighten the conversation's mood, "Mr. Henwood will be gone for a while."

Bess lifted her head off his shoulder and managed a smile.

"He'll come home for his sister's wedding, I'm sure," Abigail said quietly.

"Yes," Bess began, wiping tears from her eyes, "when he does—"

"We don't even know when that will be," Alex added, but Bess never stopped talking.

"—none of you will wish to be at the scene," she finished. Abigail and Alex looked at Bess but did not say a word.

Suddenly, Jane yelped, which drew the attention of her family. She wiped away the waterfall of tears pouring from her eyes, and Bess watched with interest, for Jane hardly knew Emma. In fact, she had only visited her once while she was ill. Perhaps, like Bess, this outburst was a combination of many other factors, so Bess figured that it would be better not to judge.

When the weeping lessened, it was Abigail who spoke timidly.

"I wasn't sure when I ought to tell you all this," she began, and even Jane looked up. "But now that I see that none of you can become any *more* emotional, it's probably the perfect time." She took a deep breath with instant regret. "My extra school *lessons* are not lessons. Please don't tell Father or anyone else about this," she added before hastily concluding her speech, "but I have been playing this game called *football* with these boys at my school. It's loads of fun, but it's not a lady's game. All my teachers and the schoolgirls make fun of me, but I can't stop. It's why I cut my hair, you know," she said, emphasizing this final remark for Bess' sake. "I wanted to look more like my teammates."

"Callum," Bess replied, making the connection. Abigail nodded.

"I know football," Alex said. "I've seen some boys downtown playing it before."

"I just started playing it after the last break," Abigail added. "I couldn't keep lying to all of you about it. Just—Father cannot know. *Nobody* can know—or else, they'll make me stop. And I love it—I can't stop—I won't stop—I'd rather run away than stop!"

Bess wiped her eyes and examined her sister's countenance. Abigail had found something that was *truly* hers. This newfound love of football had come about after she had reprimanded Abigail for being too much like Jane, but this new passion was astounding. This hobby was not painting, reading, or anything else conventional. Abigail *was* becoming her own person, and Bess could not be prouder.

"You have my word," Bess said, mustering a smile. "I want to see you play, Abbie. Can I come and see a match?"

Abigail managed a weak laugh before adding, "Perhaps when I'm better."

"My word as well," Alex said, nodding to Bess.

Jane tucked a strand of hair behind her ear and looked away. Her eyes were beat red from crying, and she had tear stains all over her cheeks. Then she turned and examined her little sister with disapproval. Bess knew if Abigail had confided in Jane alone, then Jane would have outwardly disallowed the continuation of her playing. She would most

171

likely have taken the liberty to homeschool Abigail herself rather than sacrifice Abigail's ladyship. But Jane looked around, acknowledging Bess', and more importantly, Alex's acceptance of this, and she nodded.

"Good." Abigail smiled. She then stood up, gave her sisters hugs, and went inside. Bess looked at Alex, who was still comforting Jane and headed inside to allow her sister and friend some privacy.

Part II

Chapter 17

As the days wore on, Bess found it easier to forget about Emma's death. No longer did she awaken with tear-stained cheeks and red eyes, and no longer did she find herself wallowing in pain and regret. Through the consistent reassurances of Alex and Abigail, she would be all right, and Mr. Henwood and his new wife would soon face the consequences of their decision. Eventually, Bess managed to escape Laurel Manor for the first time since she had last visited Henwood Mansion. Abigail had requested Bess' companionship on a walk through the neighboring woods.

During their stroll, the sky maintained a grey, cloudy blanket, which encompassed the silent afternoon. Occasionally, a bird's whine traveled through the trees and interrupted Bess and Abigail's quiet chatter, but Bess remained pleased with the atmosphere. It was refreshing to breathe in natural air again.

When she returned home, Bess received a letter addressed from Jack, articulating vague details about *another* victim to scarlet fever. Frantically, Bess informed her sisters of this news while condemning Miss Elmsworth's negligence for causing yet *another* person to fall ill. Without delay, the three sisters made their way to Elmsworth Manor to learn who the latest victim was.

Upon approaching the manor, Bess' heart pumped heavily. As far as she knew, *her* immediate family, including Alex, was feeling well. Mr. Henwood and his new wife were long gone, so either one of them catching it was unlikely—or at least Jack's obtaining the knowledge of their potential illnesses was unlikely. Since *Jack* wrote the letter, then there was hardly a chance that *he* was sick. And of course, Miss

Elmsworth was already "sick," so she could *not* possibly be this mentioned sufferer. But because these people were only a fraction of her acquaintances, Bess could not help but worry.

With hesitation, Bess knocked on the front door of Elmsworth Manor. She took a step backward, not wanting to appear invasive, for she had not been invited. Moments later, the door swung open to the pale, weak figure of Miss Elmsworth! With a gasp, Bess cautioned her sisters from entering the house, but Miss Elmsworth, who Bess now noticed was red from crying, snapped, "I'm fine. I just have a little cough." After a momentary pause, Bess and her sisters entered the manor. Miss Elmsworth shut the door behind her guests and remarked that Jack would be arriving shortly. "And it's lovely to see you, Miss Phillips," Miss Elmsworth said to Jane before turning around to head upstairs.

Bess frowned. *Of course, she only cares to address Jane! I suppose Alex was correct in his negative assessment of Miss Elmsworth's character.* Bess tucked a strand of hair behind her ears and sighed. *Well, perhaps Miss Elmsworth is just so well-acquainted with the latest victim that she cannot think clearly and thus behave properly.*

Bess turned to relate her thoughts to Abigail, but she was interrupted by Jack, who dashed down the staircase and nearly jumped off the last two on account of his anxiety to report the news.

"It's Lydia!" he said, upon noticing the Phillips sisters' worried countenances.

Bess paused and exhaled with relief. She bit her lip and inquired, "Is she dead?"

"Bessie!" exclaimed Jane. "You needn't outwardly—"

"No," Jack said. "Not yet."

However, hardly a moment passed before he approached and embraced Bess. He moved his lips close to her ear and whispered that he was glad to see her again. Bess did not have the time to reply before Jack turned to hug Abigail then Jane. Jane's eyes increased to the size of golf balls, and her face turned a dark shade of red. She did not return the gesture but became speechless when Jack blatantly inquired about her upcoming wedding. Slowly, Jack's smile faded into a frown, and he turned to Bess, asking if she and her sisters would be willing to take a stroll around the garden. According to him, there were fascinating ducklings that he thought Abigail would love to see. Upon hearing this remark, Abigail twisted her face into a befuddled expression, but Bess neglected the oddness in Jack's words and opened her mouth to accept.

However, Jane cut in, "Oughtn't it be more proper to visit Baldare Mansion instead? I'm sure the grieving parents of Mrs. Lydia Baldare would not appreciate your interest in birds over their daughter."

Jack's smile rapidly disappeared, and he shrugged. Jane awaited a response, but upon hearing none, she prepared to leave. She took hold of her sisters' arms, but before she managed to escape the manor, she caught a glimpse of Miss Elmsworth descending the staircase. With tear-stained cheeks and beat red eyes, she said, "Miss Jane Phillips, we must have lunch soon."

And Bess, not caring to listen to Miss Elmsworth's final words, turned to Jack and asked if he had heard about Emma's death. Naturally, he must have heard, but she was eager to say *anything* that would distract her from Miss Elmsworth's immaturity.

Jack nodded and began to mutter a response, but he was interrupted by his sister, who abruptly ended her conversation with Jane to exclaim,

"Emma! How can one speak of Emma when my dear Lydia is almost dead?"

But the fire in Bess had already sparked, and she could no longer bear to accommodate Miss Elmsworth's horrid manners. She snapped, "She died less than a week ago from scarlet fever."

It appeared as if, for a half a second, a trace of penitence flickered across Miss Elmsworth's countenance. Her eyes appeared to glaze over, and a look of mourning was somewhat visible, but the momentary regret was soon extinguished. Miss Elmsworth whipped around and sprinted up the staircase to her bedroom. She could be heard whimpering about "poor Lydia," and Bess opened her mouth to exclaim, "I did not think sick girls could run!" but Abigail must have predicted this response, for she tugged Bess' shoulder, which proved to be a gesture strong enough to act as a distraction.

Soon, Miss Elmsworth's bedroom door slammed shut, and Jane and Abigail simultaneously sighed. Bess turned and glared at her younger sister but dared not say a word in front of Jack. A minute of silence ensued before Jane hesitated to ask, "How is your brother handling the situation, Jack?"

Jack exhaled and shook his head, staring down at his feet. "Curtis is unhappy—naturally." He took another breath, turned to Bess, and added, "Perhaps, though, if she dies, he'll find someone worth—"

"Jack, we ought to go now," Bess interrupted, predicting what the rest of his comment was likely to be and hoping to avoid Jane forming a negative image of him. *If Jane develops an aversion toward Jack, I suppose I could never marry him!*

Luckily, Jack comprehended Bess' implication and did not take her intervention to heart. Instead, he wished the sisters goodbye, and when asked by Jane if he wanted to come along, he said he was too tired, for he had already visited Mrs. Baldare earlier that day. In response, Jane asked and received directions to Baldare Mansion before stepping outside of Elmsworth Manor.

The door to Elmsworth Manor shut behind the three sisters as they made their way to Baldare Mansion. But as a period of silence prevailed, Bess could not help but get lost in her thoughts. *As awful as it may sound, I wonder how much better Jack's and even my life would be if Mrs. Baldare would pass away. Oh, but how terrible of me to think such a thing, yet—oh, no. I can't continue that thought. But what a shock it was to hear Miss Elmsworth prefer Mrs. Baldare, an awful creature, to Emma, an admirable one. I suppose Miss Elmsworth's judgment is still faulty, considering how ill she is, but I keep making these excuses for her. There's only so much I can do to ignore what I'm starting to realize is her dreadful character.*

Chapter 18

When the Phillips sisters arrived at Baldare Mansion, Bess stared at the abode in awe. If she and her family were well-off, then the Baldares must have been *royal*, for this mansion was massive. Constructed of stone, it possessed high arches, conical rooftops, and countless balconies. Large stained-glass windows, which Bess thought only existed in chapels, decorated the exterior. And surrounding the building were acres of trees and gardens, adding to its natural appeal. Bess ascended the staircase to the front porch and found herself delicately knocking on the door, which must have been made of some rich walnut wood.

What felt like an hour passed before the door slowly drifted open. Standing on the opposite side of the threshold was Curtis, who wore a mask of disappointment. Jane's eyes bulged out of her head, and she hastily inquired over the well-being of Mrs. Lydia Baldare to which Curtis sadly reported the recent death of his wife. Jane gasped, taken aback by the unfathomably quick succession of deaths. Curtis lowered his head, but Bess watched his countenance, which appeared neither pale nor tear-stained. She opened her mouth to ask how Curtis was *really,* but Abigail nudged her in the side. Instead, Bess took a step backward and admired this scene.

At best, I suppose my emotions are mixed. But what a terrible reaction to Mrs. Lydia Baldare's death! Oughtn't I be upset, not content, with the death of anyone... *no matter how much they harmed me?* Bess bit her lip, and a novel idea struck her. *I suppose I am sad, not for the sake of Curtis but rather Jack. He lost a sister-in-law, despite how awful she may have been.*

Jane perked up, "No," she began. Tears formed in the ducts of her eyes, and Bess watched in utter disbelief as her sister broke down in tears. Jane rubbed her eyes and said, "I'm so sorry, Curtis. We came over to wish her well, but…," she sniffled, "are *you* all right?"

Curtis looked down to his feet. He shrugged, and Bess pinched herself to stifle an amused smile. "My wife's death is tragic," Curtis began in a monotone "but what may be worse is that I am going to be sent away from Baldare Mansion. I will reluctantly return to my poor mother and father while living again with my intolerable brother and sister!"

No amount of Abigail's nudging could prevent Bess from rolling her eyes. She crossed her arms and glared at Curtis.

Jane answered, "I'm certain they will be glad to welcome you back." She hesitated but eventually reached out and rubbed Curtis' shoulder with the palm of her hand. Curtis accepted her sympathy with a hint of keenness, and Jane managed to grin.

"I don't want to return home," Curtis continued, and Jane listened to his whining with growing compassion. "I want to stay here, but Mr. and Mrs. Baldare won't let me." He paused. "I'm going to pack my things now. They won't even allow me to stay for the funeral next week."

"Oh! How—!" But Jane never managed to finish. Curtis returned her pity with a neutral expression, turned around, and walked away. He shut the door against Jane's flushed face, and she squealed with stupefaction. Slowly, she turned to face her sisters and said, "We better go now. I'm not acquainted enough with Mr. or Mrs. Baldare to greet them."

Then the Phillips sisters left the Baldare property, acting as if they had made no encounters with any of the mansion's inhabitants. Jane walked ahead in silence, for she was clearly exhibiting emotions of embarrassment and disappointment. The only remark she made was her request to *not* call a carriage. So, Bess and Abigail trailed behind with few thoughts rattling inside their heads. The evening had grown dark, and the younger sisters shivered as they skated along the dirt path. Jane, who was red and fuming, evinced no signs of being cold.

After having walked ahead for a while, Jane turned around and remarked, "Neither of you expressed any condolences to Curtis."

She swiftly turned back around and quickened her stride; meanwhile, Bess and Abigail faced one another and shrugged.

"He never cared for her," Bess muttered. "You saw him, Jane. All he cared for was living in the Baldare wealth."

Jane halted and whipped around to face her sisters. Her cheeks were red from either the temperature or her emotions—Bess could not tell. Nevertheless, she said, "I understand, Bessie, that you never really liked Mrs. Baldare. To be honest, I never really *loved* her either, but she's still a human. She still deserves your respect."

"We showed respect," Abigail interjected. "We visited. We expressed sorrow."

"It appeared to be indifference," Jane corrected.

"Well, would you like us to go back and beg Curtis to allow us inside just so that we can give an apology, which will mean *nothing* to him?" Bess cried out, startling both her sisters. She shook her head and took the liberty to march ahead.

"Bessie, stop!" Jane ordered, but Bess only increased her speed. "You don't understand."

Bess' heart fluttered with anger, but she kept her mouth shut. *I know Jane's right—I just cannot admit it.* Bess sighed. *Besides, perhaps there is someone other than Miss Elmsworth who truly valued Mrs. Baldare's life. To him or her, Mrs. Baldare's death would be just as tragic as Emma's was to me.* She bit her lip. *I know I ought to respect this notion, but I won't say a word to Jane.* Either she didn't want to admit fault or she didn't want to concede to the idea that Emma and Mrs. Baldare were esteemed equally—or both.

The three sisters traveled home without saying another word. When they arrived at Laurel Manor, they each parted their separate ways and spent the rest of the evening working on their respective studies.

Chapter 19

As the leaves turned golden and the days grew colder, Bess found herself trapped inside Laurel Manor. She had never experienced so much boredom in all her life, so every warm day that interrupted the cool weather was a blessing, and she indulged herself by reading outside, taking strolls, or visiting Elmsworth Manor. Two weeks after Mrs. Baldare's funeral, a series of warm afternoons occurred, and to her excitement, Bess received an invitation to dine and play croquet at Churlington House, the home of the Wheatleys.

With anticipation coursing through her body, Bess hastened to Elmsworth Manor to inquire if Jack had been invited. She had been so excited by an interruption to her monotonous lifestyle that she had forgotten about Jack's relationship to the Wheatleys of which she was soon reminded.

"Of course, I've been invited!" Jack laughed. "The Wheatleys are my family." Bess blushed, but this temporary embarrassment did not exceed her overall joy. Before she had the opportunity to reply, Jack added, "Most of our acquaintances are invited. However, my sister says she feels too ill to play croquet, and Mr. Henwood and his new wife are still away, so they will not be in attendance. And I must...," he began, stopping mid-sentence.

"You must *what*, Jack?"

He sighed, "My parents asked that I do not tell anyone."

"Of what?" Bess inquired, neglecting propriety due to her enthusiasm. "Does this matter regard your sister, who is often unwell?" Jack started to pace around the room, and Bess followed him. "Is her sickness now permanent? Jack, you must answer me, for I am growing impatient!" she laughed.

Jack managed a chuckle, but after hearing the sincerity in his voice, Bess' smile faded. She tucked a strand of hair behind her ear and bit her lip, praying that she did not cross the line by speaking of Miss Elmsworth's illness. Luckily, Jack turned around and reassured her, "The matter to which I'm referring has no direct correlation to my dear sister's curse, but since you're eager to know—"

"Oh, I'm only eager if it suits your confidence with your family," Bess added, attempting to mend her former overexcitement.

"It is of no problem, Bess," he continued with a sigh. "Perhaps it is better that you *should* know." He paused. "Very well. Curtis has run away—"

"Has he?"

"Three days ago. We found a note detailing his plans to seek a new life in America."

"America! But with the war—"

"I never said Curtis was intelligent." He shook his head. "Nevertheless, my aunt and uncle are hosting this tournament, I believe, to distract my parents from their loss." Then he added, "It would be best to refrain from mentioning the situation. If my mother knew I said—"

"Oh yes, of course," Bess replied, which concluded their discussion of Curtis. Following this mutual agreement, an uncomfortable period of silence ensued, so Bess thought it best to return home.

The morning of the croquet tournament arrived the following Saturday. Bess' excitement had kept her awake throughout the night, and when the sun rose, she dressed herself and skipped downstairs for breakfast. Jane was seated at the table, consuming a bowl of porridge, but it soon became clear that their father would not be joining them. Bess ascended the staircase once more and found her father half-asleep behind the desk in his study. She shook him awake and reminded him that they were to attend the Wheatley's gathering. Mr. Phillips sat up and groaned, mentioning that he was not planning on coming along, which sent Bess on a persuasive lecture lasting a quarter of an hour. But her rhetoric was to no avail, so Jane, Bess, and Abigail ventured to Churlington House. Upon their arrival, they explained their father's absence and apologized for their tardiness. Mr. Wheatley accepted their regret with kindness and began to detail the rules of croquet, which were relatively straightforward.

"And because this is a tournament," he added, "everyone will be part of a randomly-selected team of two. There will be a few elimination rounds of two versus two until two groups remain for the finals."

Juliette let out a massive squeal, and she started to toss around small pieces of paper, which she instructed were for the drawing. Everyone was to write down their name, fold their paper, and place it into a prepared hat. When everyone had complied, Juliette mixed the papers around and pulled out the first name, "Abigail!" she announced, digging through the hat again for another name. When she pulled out the next piece of paper, she announced with a smile, "And Leonarda—oh!" she exclaimed. "Come up with team names! Team 1, Team 2, Team 3—you understand—is dull."

With a grin and an uncharacteristic exclamation, Abigail said, "We'll be Notts County!"

Puzzled expressions filled the room, and Abigail blushed. An explanation seemed to be desired, but no words emerged from the youngest Phillips sister's mouth. Bess reclined in her chair and considered her sister's reaction with amusement. *Notts County—what a strange name to choose for a team. Everyone seems to be intrigued, but I bet it relates to her new hobby of football.* But as nobody was turning away from her sister, Bess cleared her throat and uttered, "Juliette, and the next team?"

"Oh, yes!" Juliette tossed her hair behind her shoulders. She made a dramatic motion with her arms before diving her hand into the hat to select the next piece of paper. Moments later, she shouted, "Father and Mr. Ashford! Huh—interesting. Think of a team name, Mr. Ashford. Father's not creative," she laughed, which triggered chuckling from the other guests, and during this time, she drew a few more teams. But Juliette soon commanded attention again, for she announced that only a couple of names remained in the hat. With a room full of anticipation, Juliette slowly drew one of the papers and said, "Alex and—" she shuffled her hand through the hat to select another, from which she then read, "Bess!"

Bess could almost feel the disappointment weighing on Jane's chest. She tilted her head slightly to gain a better view of her sister whom she soon noticed was pink with embarrassment. Bess watched Jane fiddle with a strand of her hair, sit up straighter, and pretend that she felt entirely content with the final selection. Bess looked away, hesitating to join Alex, who had already announced that his team would be called The Winners.

"Very original," Bess laughed, walking toward her partner. "But now we have expectations to live up to, and I've never played croquet before!"

Alex smiled. "Don't worry. *I* have."

Bess shook her head and chuckled. When she tilted her head, she caught a glimpse of Jack, who was partnered with his father. His eyes were gazing in her direction, and Bess pursed her lips. She tucked a strand of hair behind her ear and turned away before Juliette continued to speak. After a loud clearing of her throat, she announced the first match: Abigail and Leonarda were set to face Mr. Wheatley and Mr. Ashford. Without much interest in watching, the remaining guests found seats on the patio to drink some tea and chat.

Bess sat down beside Alex but soon found herself in the company of Jack, who sat on her other side. Bess refused to say a word unless spoken to, for she did not want to convey that she liked one friend more than another, but luckily, her discomfort was alleviated when Mrs. Wheatley said, "I heard of the deaths of poor Mrs. Henwood and Mrs. Baldare. With the utmost respect, I beg to ask, are each of you feeling well after having suffered the news?"

"Yes," started Bess quietly, but only Alex had heard her. She said again, "Yes. Yes, I'm fine." She nodded. "It's *very* disappointing, but I think…," but she refrained from continuing. She was close to hinting at Miss Elmsworth's responsibility in the matter, but upon noticing the Elmsworths sitting nearby, she held her tongue. Nevertheless, she noticed their faces grow pale, for they must have known their daughter had been the cause of these deaths.

To break the silence, Alex said, "It *is* disappointing."

Fortunately for the Elmsworths, the first croquet match had finished from which the cheers of Abigail and Leonarda distracted them from their guilt. Shortly thereafter, the second and third matches ensued then ended, and another loud exclamation emerged from field. Bess stood to prepare for her game but was alerted by Juliette that she and Alex had a "bye," which guaranteed their position in the next round without having to play a match now.

"Oh, all right," said Bess, who would rather play than sit around and talk.

"Bess, we made it past the first round!" Alex cheered, and Bess couldn't help but laugh.

She shook her head and teased, "Alex, you're an imbecile."

Alex opened his mouth to reply but was interrupted by the voice of Jane, which said, "Alex is *not* an imbecile." Bess rolled her eyes and turned to Jane, who was marching in their direction. "Also, I'm dreadful at this game. I don't have good coordination."

Bess sighed and made room for Jane to pull a chair between Alex and her. Jane smiled and tossed her hair behind her shoulder before planting herself beside Alex to whom she turned and began to speak. Bess tried to listen but soon noticed that Jane was excluding her from the conversation, so she stood up (neglecting the longing eyes of Alex) and walked toward Abigail and Leonarda, who were practicing a few yards away.

When she was within arm's length of her sister, Bess said, "I should applaud you for your victory."

Abigail laughed while finishing her strike. "No, you oughtn't. We were meant to win. Notts County doesn't accept defeat, and you should have expected that."

"Well," Bess laughed, "Alex and I are The Winners, so you ought to get used to losing."

Abigail shook her head, and after a moment's pause, she said, "I overheard you—Alex *is* an imbecile. And *you're* not as talented as I am.

189

There's no possible way you're pulling past Lea and me." Abigail swung her mallet to strike the ball again.

"Lea?"

Abigail smiled. "Leonarda. I never noticed that she's such a lovely companion. She's wonderful, and I'm glad we've become friends." She lowered her voice and said, "I used to think she was awkward. Perhaps, even, something was wrong with her, but she's just shy—quiet among large crowds. Once you speak to her, though, you'll find she's very agreeable and even quite witty—even at thirteen." But Bess was hardly listening. Her eyes were fixed on Jane and Alex, who spoke with such merriment. Jane laughed and kissed her fiancé on the cheek, which appeared to startle Alex, but he returned the gesture with a smile. Their companions laughed alongside them, but as Bess gazed onward at their cheerful facades, she was knocked in the side by Abigail. "Quit it, Bessie, won't you? Leave Alex to his fiancée—you're not missing much. And *how* did you end up with him? I suppose you must have rigged the drawing."

Bess shrugged, but it took another jab in the side before she returned to full consciousness. She opened her mouth to say, "It was meant to be," but she could not get the words out. Instead, she said, "You know very well I didn't." And then she added, "If I had, I would have paired myself with Jack." Abigail rolled her eyes and struck the ball again. This time, she hit it through the hole. Bess asked, "Can I try?"

"Hmm," Abigail started. "Should I give my opponent time to practice? I think not!"

"I'll be awful if you don't let me try."

"I was only kidding!" She smiled. "Go ahead." Abigail handed her sister the mallet, and Bess received it with a funny look. She lined

190

herself parallel to the cylindrical part of the mallet (like Abigail had done) and stuck the ball through a hoop. She brushed her hair aside. "Not bad," returned Abigail. "Perhaps if you—"

"It's not hard, Abbie," Bess laughed and hit another ball. Abigail took a step backward and Bess pounced, "Are you afraid that Alex and I will beat you now?"

"Alex can't do anything right." Abigail smiled. "Lea's good, too."

"Does Juliette call her Lea? Or is that just—"

"She thought my name was Gabrielle," Abigail snickered. "She called me Gabbie, so I called her Lea, and now it's stuck!"

Bess laughed and returned the mallet to her sister. "Juliette makes it seem like she and Leonarda don't get along well—or, at least, they don't prefer each other's company."

"That's nonsense," Abigail replied. "She might say that, but all elder sisters eventually tire of their younger siblings—at least temporarily. Juliette must be in that phase."

"Do younger siblings tire of their older siblings?" Bess smiled. Abigail returned Bess' question with a laugh, which caused Bess to laugh as well. "She's *very* good at the piano."

"She wants to become a composer. In fact, they have some school in, ironically, Nottingham—or was it London?"

Bess interjected, "Oh, I meant to ask: Obviously Alex chose our team name because we *will* win, but why did you choose Notts County?"

A smile flickered across Abigail's face. She looked down to the grass and answered, "You know. Football."

Bess nodded and prepared a response, but Juliette's voice projected across the grass, announcing the semi-final matchups: Notts County versus The Churlington Croquet Ladies (Juliette and Mrs. Elmsworth)

191

and The English Lions (Jack and Mr. Elmsworth) versus The Winners. rejoined her partner, and the three of them regrouped by the patio. Bess found Alex, and they trotted over to the field, where Jack and Mr. Elmsworth were waiting. When they arrived, Jack teased Bess that she would lose, for she hadn't yet played a match. Bess smirked and returned a smart reply but was interrupted by Alex, who whispered an apology for ignoring her to talk with Jane.

"Forget it, Alex. Let's play," she replied, but a line of thoughts entered her head. *I wouldn't want to marry anyone who would choose someone else over me. He could have incorporated me into the conversation. Jack would have done that—I'm sure of it.*

They began the match. It was a close game, and Jack complained that the (nonexistent) wind moved his ball off course a few times. Alex and Bess ended up with a resounding win, and upon seeing Bess' last hit go through the hoop to seal the victory, The Winners jumped up and down. They shook hands with their opponents, and a quarter of an hour later, Abigail and Leonarda were cheering for a victory.

So, Notts County was to face The Winners for the final. Bess looked to tease Abigail but found her on the other end of the pitch, rolling the balls with her foot back to the starting position! Bess watched with intrigue, for she had never seen the dynamics of any sort of football before. She opened her mouth to make known her thoughts, but she was interrupted by Juliette, who announced the commencement of the game. At the beginning, Abigail and Leonarda were dominating. Unfortunately, on one of her remaining strikes, Leonarda hit a ball too far off course, and this mistake gave Alex and Bess enough time to catch up and ultimately win the game. At the sound of Juliette's cheers, Alex leaned over and embraced Bess. Turning red, Bess broke away and did her best to avoid Jane's disappointed stares.

After the tournament, Mr. Wheatley invited his guests inside to feast on cake. Everyone was eager to try it—it was supposedly an excellent London recipe. Upon entering the dining hall, Bess sat down beside Jack, and then Abigail sat down beside her. A servant scurried around, serving slices of the cake, and before she took a bite, Bess took the time to admire the Wheatley's home. The inside of Churlington House was relatively small. The ceilings were low, the floors were uneven, and a small brick fireplace sat in the corner. Old, wooden furniture and a collection of scenic paintings decorated the interior, and most distinctly, a large, (perhaps) oak piano forte fashioned the drawing-room. Bess admired the piano forte and thought of Leonarda's ambitions to become a famous composer.

Bess' thoughts were interrupted when Jack nudged her arm and prompted her to take a bite of cake—it was lemon. She scooped a forkful into her mouth and agreed that it was *very* delicious. The same servant distributed the second round of cake before a table-wide card game began. Bess did not know how to play, so she, Abigail, Juliette, Leonarda, and Jack stepped outside, where they observed the darkening sky and subsequent sunset. Juliette and Leonarda seated themselves on the patio, and the others followed. Jack found a chair beside his cousins and spoke with them; meanwhile, Bess and Abigail grew rather bored and wondered when they would return home.

But their curiosities were peaked when Miss Henwood emerged from Churlington House. Upon noticing their gathering, she said, "I'm leaving now. Have a wonderful evening." She delivered a warm smile to her friends, but after receiving farewells in return, she dashed toward the street.

Abigail turned to her sister and whispered, "I wonder why she's so hasty."

"Perhaps she's meeting her *future fiancé*," Bess muttered, and they laughed. When their laughter died, they returned to silence and looked to see about what the others were talking.

Jack noticed their attention and interrupted Juliette's dramatic retelling of a former school story. "Now that Curtis is off to America—"

Juliette's eyes widened. "Curtis did *what*?"

Jack nodded. "Yes. I know it's absurd, but he and I were never very close, so it's not too much of a shame. I'm glad he's finally getting to start over. Perhaps he'll have a better life."

"But so soon after Lydia's—?"

"He never—"

"Oh, you're right! He never cared for her."

A period of silence ensued, and Bess turned to her sister. They both raised their eyebrows, seeming to communicate similar thoughts. *I know he doesn't care much for his brother, but I cannot fathom how he can be so indifferent toward this situation.* She paused. *Curtis is his brother! No matter how annoyed I could be with Jane or Abbie, I'd never want to part with them. I suppose*—but a loud exclamation from the dining hall rang through the garden. She heard Mr. Ashford yell, "Alex, fetch more wine from the kitchen!" and Mr. Wheatley cry, "Let Margaret get the wine!" Bess rolled her eyes and slumped back in her seat. "Thank you, Margie!"

Bess caught Jack's gaze and muttered, "I didn't know we were in the company of Mr. Henwood." Jack frowned, and Bess' heart sunk. *Alex would have—*

Then, to her utter surprise, Bess heard Jane exclaim her apparent loss to a round of cards. Bess had never seen Jane drink more than was necessary, so a mixed sensation of confusion and worry consumed her thoughts. She feared entering Churlington House, but Abigail urged her to check on their sister. When Bess stood, the others decided to join her. They had been outside for over an hour, and the sky was rapidly darkening, and the air was growing colder.

The inside of Churlington House was warmer than it had been before. A dark yellow aura from the fireplace made the dining hall feel tighter, and Bess grew more anxious to leave. She found Alex standing on the far side of the room and noticed his sagging eyes. When he caught a glimpse of Bess, his eyes grew larger, and he smiled. Bess tucked her hair behind her ears and began to smile but was taken aback by Jane, who cried, "No! That's not fair!" Bess whipped her head toward the table and found her sister climbing on top of it! "That's *unfair*! You must not give me a disadvantage, and clearly, you are!"

Alex swam through the drunken guests and tried to pull Jane down, but his endeavors worked to hardly an avail.

"Silly Jane!" cried Mr. Wheatley. "These are the rules, and they must be played as such!"

"*I* don't think—"

"Jane, please sit down," Alex's soft voice pleaded.

"*I* don't think," Jane repeated, and then she looked at Alex and frowned, "that anyone here knows how to play. *I* don't—"

Mrs. Wheatley exclaimed, "But we play all the time with family!"

"Family?" She paused. "Where's *my* family? Where are Bess and Abbie?" Mr. Ashford's intemperate remarks were added into this ridiculous conversation more than once as well, and the only person who seemed to be acting normal, or just plain tired, was Alex. Soon, Jane caught sight of her sisters, and she said, "Bessie, come play a game! Abbie, try this wine!"

Mr. Ashford interrupted, "More wine, Mr. Wheatley! The beautiful lady wants wine!"

Mr. Wheatley pushed his servant into the kitchen but stumbled over the uneven floor while doing so. Mrs. Wheatley and Mrs. Elmsworth howled with laughter. Bess crossed her arms and frowned. *At least the Elmsworths are distracted from their distress, but almost everyone is acting utterly absurd.* She turned to Abigail and whispered, "For how long were we outside?"

"I suppose a couple of hours." She shrugged. "Long enough for everyone to get drunk."

Bess added, "*Almost* everyone. Alex doesn't have a drink."

"Well," Abigail sighed, "I know why."

Bess bit her lip and looked away. She glanced toward Alex and watched his hopeless attempts at calming down Jane. She wrung her hands together. *No matter how much effort I put into trying to ignore Alex, I cannot. I try to replace the thought of him with the thought of Jack, but I don't know if that's realistic anymore. If only Alex would stop seeing me, but it seems like the world is pushing us together! It's incredibly hard to forget about him, knowing that he's always been* my *best friend.* She then made the promise for perhaps the second or third time to avoid Alex and focus on Jack.

She took a step toward Jack but was stunned when a glass shattered. Someone screamed. Jane cried out, for she had been splashed with a beverage. A minute of utter chaos ensued followed by an empty silence. It was almost as if, although still intoxicated, everyone had begun to realize how ridiculous they were acting. Jane looked down at her soaked dress and complained to Alex that she wanted to leave. Her wish was granted.

In the carriage, Bess stared outside of her window to avoid eye contact with Alex. She admired the glistening stars and the calmness of the night. She leaned her head on the wall and imagined living in another world where she and Alex could be together. *Oh, Bess, don't think such things! What you think is how you'll act and*—but she stopped. *For this one evening, I can dream. Tomorrow, I will rid myself of Alex altogether.* She took a deep breath. *Tomorrow, I will ask Jack what his marriage intentions are. If he gives me any indication that he wishes to be married soon, then I shall propose. I will be married to Jack, and I will never think of Alex again. Jane will be happy forever.*

The carriage jumped on the dirt road leading to Laurel Manor, and Bess sat up. With a layer of tears covering her eyes, she looked up and managed to spot a strange figure dashing down the road. Bess wiped her eyes and strained to see. She watched the figure dance down the street and thought the gait resembled that of Miss Henwood. Bess leaned over to Abigail and asked her sister if she could identify this person. Abigail shook her head.

"Doesn't it remind you of Miss Henwood?" Bess asked.

"I don't think so," Abigail answered. "She left hours ago. Why would she be here?"

Bess shrugged but could not rid herself of the notion that Miss Henwood was on their property. As the carriage parked in front of Laurel Manor, she found herself at a loss for answers. She considered asking Alex, but this thought reminded her of Jack, and then she was consumed with anxiety regarding tomorrow's potential engagement. She quickly forgot about the figure and went to bed without wishing anyone good night.

Chapter 20

Bess' heartbeat pounded as she ascended the staircase of Elmsworth Manor. The clock had not yet struck nine, but she had already eaten breakfast and journeyed across part of Kent. The cold autumn morning had stiffened her limbs, but her racing heart kept her warm, and she hastily knocked on the front door. For what seemed like a quarter of an hour, no one answered, and Bess turned around and wondered if she ought to leave. She noticed the colorful leaves outlining the manor property. And had it not been for the storm of thoughts running through her mind, she would have taken her time to admire the scenery.

But with imminent anticipation of everything that could soon transpire, Bess turned back to face the front door. When she entered, she planned to sit down with Jack and ask him what his marriage intentions were. If he were to reply that he was waiting to get married, Bess would happily comply with his wishes and let the entire idea drop. However, *if* he mentioned that he wanted to marry soon, then she would have to outright propose. Bess shivered and took a deep breath. She was starting to grow cold, and she reluctantly remembered Jane's final remark before she left Laurel Manor: *Bessie, bring a coat!* Naturally, Bess did *not* bring a coat, so once again, she considered returning to the warmth of her home. She rubbed her shoulders and glanced back to the path, but then Mr. Elmsworth answered the door with a broad smile.

"Bess!" he exclaimed, and Bess whipped around. "What a pleasant...," but he quieted at the sight of Bess' freezing figure and rushed her inside. Bess exhaled warm breath into her palms and thanked her host. After shutting the door behind her, Mr. Elmsworth asked, "Is Jack expecting you?"

Bess answered, "No. I came on short notice." Then she looked up and admired the portraits hanging on the walls of the entrance hall again. Due to being nervous and cold, she noticeably shook, and Mr. Elmsworth offered her a warm cup of tea. "That would be lovely. Thank you," Bess said, considering that the tea might also help her calm her nerves.

Bess followed her host into the dining hall and found Mrs. Elmsworth and her daughter eating breakfast. Miss Elmsworth looked up, acted as if she did not recognize Bess, and returned to eating her biscuit. On the contrary, Mrs. Elmsworth glanced up and smiled, welcoming Bess to the table.

"No, I don't care for a biscuit. Thank you," Bess replied upon Mrs. Elmsworth's offering to share the breakfast. Bess sat down beside Mrs. Elmsworth, and once she settled into her seat, a servant placed a cup of tea beside her. Bess took a sip, nearly burned her tongue, and returned the cup to the table. After a moment of silence, Mrs. Elmsworth inquired over Bess' welfare, happiness from winning the croquet championship last night, and reason for visiting Jack today. Bess answered each of these (except the last) with full honesty, reporting that she was a bit tired today but still happy to have won in croquet the previous night. Then she turned to Miss Elmsworth and asked, "How are you today, Miss Elmsworth?"

Perhaps if Miss Elmsworth responded cordially, Bess would have blissfully forgotten her apparent rudeness not five minutes ago. But Miss Elmsworth looked up, glared at Bess, and said, "Fine. I feel better than I did last night."

"It's strange," began Mrs. Elmsworth. "Liza is sick one day and feeling well the next. I've never seen anything like it."

Miss Elmsworth opened her mouth to respond, but she was interrupted by Jack, who hopped into the dining hall with a massive smile plastered on his face. "Bess! I'm pleased you've come! Are you here to see me?" Bess gulped down a mouthful of tea and nodded. Jack's face grew brighter, and he joined his family and friend at the table. He reached across the table to grab a biscuit (a gesture at which Mr. Elmsworth frowned), and Bess sighed. *There's no possible way I can propose here. If I am to propose, I must isolate Jack from his family.*

"Well," Mrs. Elmsworth said, clearing her throat. She sniffled, and Bess looked up, for she had not foreseen Mrs. Elmsworth's sudden change in spirit. "I apologize, Bess, for my emotions—I did not expect your presence, but don't fret! You're *like* family," she concluded, and Bess blushed. *Perhaps I shouldn't have come.* She prepared to excuse herself, but Mrs. Elmsworth cleared her throat. She unveiled and unfolded a sheet of paper with the words: *To Mrs. Hannah Elmsworth, My Dearest Mother* written on the front.

"Mother," Jack started, turning dark. "What is this?"

"I planned to read this to you yesterday, which was when it arrived, but we went to the Wheatley's, and I hadn't the opportunity," she said, rubbing her eyes. "Then we left Churlington House very late, and I was too tired to keep you up last night." Bess' heart sunk. She was no longer anxious about proposing. *Oh, I'm intruding upon a private family moment, and despite what Mrs. Elmsworth says, I don't belong here. I shouldn't have invited myself inside. I should have returned home even if it meant treading through the cold weather.* "I will now read it," Mrs. Elmsworth whimpered.

"No, Mother," Jack murmured. "*I'll* read it." Jack reached across the table (causing his father to groan again) and took the letter from his mother's shaking hands. He pulled the paper close to his eyes, gave a sigh of indifference to which Bess raised an eyebrow, and began without hesitation—

"*To Mrs. Hannah Elmsworth, My Dearest Mother,*

I hope that you, Father, Jackson, and Adeliza Lucille, in particular, are doing well. I feared that my brief letter reporting that I had run away to America was not enough, so I started drafting this letter to better explain myself. First, I wanted you to know that my love for each of you has not changed. You are not the reason I decided to leave.

I first married the late Mrs. Lydia Baldare mainly because of her beauty and situation. However, I grew to love her as I love you, Mother. There was nobody else whom I cared for more. I grew to love her family as much as I cherish my own. Mr. and Mrs. Baldare were my mother and father so much as you and Father are to me. Of course, you, Mother, hold the most special place in my heart, for you are the woman who produced me.

Nevertheless, I esteem both of my families equally, and the only reason that I stayed away from you while I lived at Baldare Mansion was because of the wishes of my dearest love, Lydia. When she passed away, I had to leave the Baldares. I could no longer live with them without my dear Lydia, but I couldn't return home. I couldn't leave one set of parents for another. I didn't think it would be right.

The only place left for me, I determined, was America. Now, they face a great civil war, but when that soon passes, I will live in the north where the industrial society is affluent with money and opportunity. I want to make something of myself. I don't want to be Mrs. Lydia Baldare's husband. Perhaps I will find another wife to love as much as I loved Lydia. I will continue to keep you informed on my safety, and I will undoubtedly inquire often about my first family.

The last point I have to make is a wish. Please do not visit the Baldares anytime soon. They are too distressed with the loss of their daughter to think clearly. Do not be fooled that they are as kind and welcoming as you and Father are, Mother. That is all I must say. Again, I apologize for any sorrow I have caused you. Right now, I have plenty of money to last me the trip, so unless you must, do not send me any.

Sincerely,

Mr. Curtis P. Elmsworth

When Jack had finished reading, Bess could not believe how strange Curtis' priorities were. *At least he recognized he only married Lydia for her wealthy background, but comparing his own family as being equal to the Baldares is incredulous! His reasoning for running away—that he couldn't leave one family for another—is utterly ridiculous. Yet, the strangest thing I gather from this letter is that Curtis left to better his own life. Instead of running to some wealthy county in England to marry a rich bachelorette, he wants to start over and make his own way in the world. For some reason, I cannot believe this explanation to be the full truth, so I ought to be prepared to hear of a letter in the future in which Curtis reports a change in his original plans.* Bess frowned but soon noticed that Mrs. Elmsworth was in tears. Mr. Elmsworth had the letter grasped between his fingers as he read and reread its content. Jack and Liza, however, appeared indifferent, a reaction which startled Bess.

"Bess and Liza, come with me," Jack eventually said. Bess rose from her chair and followed her friend to the hallway.

203

Once the door to the dining hall shut, Miss Elmsworth scoffed, "He's a pig. I don't care what his excuses are, but equating Mother, the woman who created him, to that woman is horrendous. I'd be glad to never see or hear from him again!" Miss Elmsworth tossed her hair over her shoulder and strutted to her bedroom, complaining that she felt ill again. Jack shrugged and turned to his guest, offering to take a stroll around the manor despite how cold it was. Bess anxiously accepted his request, realizing that this might be the ideal time to propose.

Jack found a spare coat and handed it to Bess, and after dressing warmly, they exited the house. Bess took a deep breath and prepared to speak, but Jack cut her off, "I hate him. I hate him with everything that I am. He was *never* a brother to me, and he's still proving that he hasn't changed." He kicked the ground, and Bess thought of an adequate reply.

"Well, he said he's starting over. Perhaps he *is* changing."

"No," Jack snapped. He raised his voice and said, "He probably stole money from Mr. and Mrs. Baldare on his way out. I guarantee in less than a month from now, we'll receive a letter detailing his newest proposal to a wealthy woman from New York City. A half a dozen months later, we'll hear of his divorce and another proposal—and then *another*. That's just who Curtis is. He's handsome and charming, and he'll *always* take advantage of that."

Bess shrugged and wished to disagree, but she knew that Jack was right. She had heard enough of Curtis and seen enough of his previous spouse to assess his character. Bess folded her arms across her chest and listened to the ensuing silence. Her heart began to pound, and she realized that *this* was her opportunity to propose. She took a deep breath and felt sweat running down her inner arm. She opened her mouth to speak, but no words came out. She tried again to no avail.

"I'm glad he left," Jack continued, and Bess pinched herself for not speaking sooner. "My parents are better off without him—although they don't know it. Did I ever tell you about Miss Martha Gilmore?" Bess shook her head. "Well," Jack started with a sigh, "during Curtis' final year of school, he met a girl from Surrey named Martha with whom he fell deeply in love. Martha didn't come from the most fortunate background, but Curtis didn't seem to mind for once. He was still an obsequious fool whom Liza and I passionately disliked, but he was more considerate." Jack paused in recollection. "He spent hours of every day with Martha in Surrey, and he even brought her back a few times. Martha was nice—perhaps too good for him. She wasn't as handsome as he, but that didn't matter. We were happy for Curtis because he found a good, caring person to return his apparent affection." Suddenly, Jack stomped his foot on the ground, and Bess jumped. His face grew red, and he continued. "A few weeks later, we received the news that Martha was pregnant. After disapproving of his sin, we forgave Curtis and made him promise to be a loving father to his future son or daughter. He promised that he would always be there for his child and Martha." Jack growled, and Bess recoiled with fear. "A month later, he came home talking about how he had met Martha's second cousin, Lydia. We never thought too much about Lydia, but one evening, we dined with the Gilmores and the Baldares, and we discovered the truth."

"Did Curtis—?"

Jack did not directly reply, but he took a deep breath and continued, "Curtis didn't pay *any* attention to Martha or her family. He spent the whole night flirting with Lydia. And to conclude this *marvelous* evening, he kissed her while we were dancing. The next week, we received the news that they were engaged, and we never heard of Martha or her child again!" Jack seethed. He wrung his hands together, and Bess stopped in her tracks. Jack walked ahead, and Bess feared to join him, for she had never seen him so enraged.

When Bess caught up to her friend, Jack took a deep breath and said, "Well, there *was* a rumor that she married a blacksmith from the western part of Oxford. I heard that they're taking care of Martha's *daughter*, who, I'm certain, is lovely and beautiful," he stifled. "But Bess," he said in a lowered voice, "please do not share this story with your family. My father is especially ashamed, and he does not want people to know *how* awful Curtis is." He paused. "Still, I cannot fathom that *any* human being could be *that* inhumane. And what irks me most about his letter today was that he never mentioned Martha or his daughter—a decent human being would find Martha and make amends with her." He shook his head. "Bess, you may have always thought that Liza and I are harsh in our judgments of him, but now you know the truth. He deserves our indifference. Father and Mother will continually forgive him because he's their son, but Liza and I could never."

Jack spoke no more. He led Bess to the entrance hall of Elmsworth Manor, and the two decided to part. Bess returned the coat despite Jack's insistence that she keep it and wished Jack and his family well. When the front door closed, Bess started her trek home, and never once did the thought of proposing come to her mind. *I never considered that Curtis could be* that *horrid. Jack was right in that I always thought of his and Liza's indifference with disapproval, but now I know their emotions are justified.* She frowned. *How awful I feel about making such incorrect judgments about Jack and his sister! I suppose, after all, that Jack isn't ignorant, and Miss Elmsworth isn't rude… despite what Alex said. Their issues with their brother have understandably taken priority over their demeanors.* Bess paused. *From now on, I should try to judge others less harshly.*

Chapter 21

It had been three and a half weeks without word from the Elmsworths. Bess must have written half a dozen letters, asking if Jack had available time, but she never received a response. Instead, she spent her days roaming Laurel Manor and reading books, for it was too cold to venture anywhere outside for long. One afternoon, her father organized a gathering, which the Elmsworths declined to attend. Alex, Miss Henwood, and the Wheatleys agreed to come, so Bess was pleased to have an activity in which to partake.

On the morning of the gathering, Bess received a letter from Mrs. Rachel *Henwood*. Anticipation and exasperation flooded into her system, and she exerted a massive sigh of frustration, which attracted the attention of her sisters.

"Upon my word, Bessie!" Jane exclaimed as she sprinted down the steps. "What is it?" When Jane arrived at Bess' side, she groaned, "Oh, it's *just* a letter."

Following Jane, Abigail chuckled, "It sounded like you died."

"It's not *just* a letter, Jane," Bess replied. "It's from *Mrs.* Rachel *Henwood*."

Jane gasped. "So, she *did* marry Mr. Henwood!"

"Why did she write to *you*?" Abigail inquired.

"I'm not certain," Bess said as she tore open the envelope. "I'll read it aloud, and perhaps we'll find out." She cleared her throat and read—

"Elizabeth Phillips,

My sister's dying wish was that I keep in touch with you. I didn't see the reason for it, but I respect my sister enough to fulfill her final

*request. Charles and I are in Brighton. We married a few weeks ago,
and we're happy together. We don't want any of you to be upset by our
decision. We were always in love. Emma (I loathe to say) was just in the
way.*

*Finally, I wanted to clear up the supposition that Mr. Augustus
Ashford and I were ever in love. Any conscious person ought to know
that rumor was false. In fact, Charles and I have been in love ever since
he was engaged to Emma.*

That's all I have to say. Leave us alone. We're happy here.
Mrs. Rachel Henwood"

Bess folded the letter in half, and Jane snapped, "That's it? That's all
she had the decency to report?" Bess nodded and turned the letter over to
confirm that there was nothing missing. "Huh," Jane thought aloud. "I
don't think I ever spoke to her. If I had, perhaps I would've been able to
discover her secret about Charles."

Abigail added, "I never spoke to her either. Frankly, neither will be
missed."

Bess read over the letter again, searching for anything that she may
have missed but found nothing. *I'm surprised that Mrs. Henwood, who
seems incredibly ill-mannered, is respecting Emma's final wish by
writing to me.* Bess smiled. *Actually, I'm more surprised (and flattered)
that Emma's final wish was for her to keep in touch with me!*

But Jane was bothered by this notion. She moaned, "And *why* would
Emma's last wish be to keep in touch with *you*? I didn't think you *ever*
spoke to her like I did, Bess."

Bess shook her head, knowing that Jane was too vain to accept that
she and Emma were good friends. Instead, she replied, "I'm uncertain."

Jane shrugged her shoulders and complained that she was tired. She wished her sisters a good morning and headed back to bed. Abigail, however, lingered around for a bit longer.

"Jane seems rather cheerful today," she started.

"I noticed," Bess confirmed.

Abigail hesitated before saying, "It's unusual."

Bess paused, watching the wheels in Abigail's head turn. "Abbie, what are you saying?"

Abigail sighed. She lowered her voice and said, "Bess, I think she and Alex set a wedding date. I assume she's both nervous and excited to tell us, which accounts for her rare behavior." Bess' heart nearly stopped. Abigail's intuitions were almost always correct, and if this supposition was true, then Jane and Alex's wedding was definite. Ever since the engagement, it had almost seemed as if the wedding was only hypothetical. They *wanted* to get married, but especially with Alex's mixed feelings, Bess didn't *really* consider their marriage a possibility. Abigail examined her sister's reaction and carefully said, "I thought you ought to know."

"That would be good for Jane then," Bess replied, and the subject dropped altogether.

Bess returned to her bedroom, and a few hours later, she heard a knock on the front door. As always, Alex was the first guest to appear at Laurel Manor, and Mr. Phillips heartily welcomed him inside. Soon after his arrival, Jane and Bess met him at the foot of the staircase, and Bess interpreted his odd smile as further confirmation of Abigail's supposition. Bess opened her mouth to greet her friend, but the Wheatleys followed, and Juliette and Leonarda's laughter distracted her.

Their giggling only briefly vanished at the arrival of Miss Henwood, who appeared less than a quarter of an hour later.

Once everyone had come, Bess led her guests to the drawing-room, where Abigail and her father were seated. The Wheatleys and Miss Henwood made themselves comfortable, and after clearing his throat, Mr. Phillips asked one of the servants to prepare a pot of tea. Then he blushed and after immense hesitation, began a conversation. "Well, first, I think it appropriate to apologize for not—not, I'm sorry—attending the croquet gathering," he sighed. "I hear that Alex and Bess were champions. How do you feel about the win, Alex?"

Alex's face reddened, and he avoided eye contact with Bess as he replied, "Oh, it isn't much of an accomplishment. Bess and I are simply good teammates."

"Extraordinary!" exclaimed Mr. Wheatley. "*No* team is *that* good on their first time!"

Alex and Bess both tensed.

Mr. Phillips muttered something to himself and blushed more heavily when the conversation suddenly died. He attempted to talk about Alex and Bess' general teamwork, but Bess, who realized that her father was putting Jane in an awkward position by talking about Alex and herself, changed the topic to that of politics. She inquired how the Americans were holding up in their "devastating civil war."

"Excellent question, Bess," Mr. Wheatley applauded. "I think—"

"You know," Mrs. Wheatley loudly interrupted. Bess had never really heard Mrs. Wheatley talk before, so she was startled by this outward intervention. "The other day I read that the Union is finally getting some hold on the Confederates. Some general named Grant—"

211

"General Grant!" Mr. Phillips exclaimed. "Yes! Ulysses Grant. I've read lots in the papers about him." But Mr. Phillip's joy soon subsided when the servant returned with a pot of tea and a tray of teacups. He was asked if his company required anything more to make their visit comfortable, and his guests replied that they were all right. Mr. Phillips blushed at the inconsistency of this conversation, but once the servant departed, the topic of the American Civil War returned. Mr. Wheatley and Mr. Phillips speculated over exactly *what* battle the Americans had last won. Mrs. Wheatley suggested many different battles, but Mr. Phillips adamantly replied that none of the ones she mentioned were correct. After becoming rather bored by this conversation, Juliette asked to speak with Bess privately. Bess agreed, for she did not want to sit around listening to politics.

"So," Juliette whispered once she and Bess were far from the other guests. She exchanged a childlike smile with her friend and said, "As you've probably noticed by now, I don't have many close friends except for Leonarda, which is rather unfortunate for me. But I've been lately taking the liberty to acquaint myself with you in the hopes of becoming your good friend." Bess bit her lip and nodded. "Well, you *might* be wondering why I asked to speak with you privately. And to answer your question, I must ask: don't you agree that there are just *some* things you can't tell your sister? Some things she couldn't possibly understand or bear to hear?" Bess raised an eyebrow but slowly nodded. Juliette giggled. She lowered her voice and added, "Well, I fear that—and by the way, this is wholly by my own supposition—that Leonarda is falling for Mr. Ashford!"

Bess, who was only half-listening to Juliette, did not comprehend the significance of her revelation. She looked away and replied, "And what is the matter with that?"

"Well," Juliette continued with a reddening face, "*you* know Mr. Ashford! He's always polite, but he's a bit odd."

Bess absent-mindedly nodded, but once she comprehended the weight of the matter, she turned skeptical. *I cannot believe that Gus would deign to show affection to someone like Leonarda Wheatley, whose family is not very wealthy. If that notion isn't enough, Leonarda is only thirteen years old. Gus could never truly consider marrying a girl that young! Juliette must be mistaken.* But Bess did not wish to upset her young friend's feelings, so she said, "What signs have led you to this conclusion?"

"Well," Juliette said with a brightening countenance, for this was a question she yearned to answer. "At croquet, I noticed him sitting beside her once, and they were laughing. Also, at the Henwood wedding, they danced together *twice*! Once, well, that would be just cordial. But *twice*! That's a sure sign of love, isn't it?"

Bess closed her eyes, took a deep breath, and responded in the kindest manner possible, "Juliette, I don't know too much about love and romance. Jane would be the person to ask. And do you really think that *Gus*, who is twenty-something years old, would fall for Leonarda, a thirteen-year-old girl?" Juliette blushed, and Bess realized that Leonarda was *not* the person whom Juliette supposed Mr. Ashford liked. So, she quickly added, "But of course, characters change. I would further evaluate the situation if I were you before making any substantial assumptions."

Juliette's face lit up again, and she thanked Bess, who led the two of them back to the drawing-room. *If I was closer to Juliette, I would have had to warn her to avoid Gus. He's only trouble, but Juliette may do as she likes, considering that we aren't so close. And who am I to declare that Gus hasn't changed after all?*

Once she stepped inside the drawing-room, Bess felt everyone's gaze land on her. With hesitation, she looked up and caught Jane's gleaming countenance and Alex's half-smile. She turned to Abigail and noticed her content grin.

"Oh, Bessie!" exclaimed Jane. "Alex and I are to be married in one month. Here! At Laurel Manor! Isn't that wonderful?" Bess wore an expression of utter bliss and enthusiastically nodded. "Oh, it shall be so exciting! Bessie, Abbie, Juliette, Leonarda, Miss Henwood—and oh, unfortunately not poor Emma—will be my bridesmaids! Alex has yet to pick his groomsmen, but oh, I'm so excited! I cannot wait to go to the village and pick out dresses, and—"

Jane went on *and on* for nearly a half an hour about her wedding preparations. The further she went into detail, the more painful listening seemed to be for Alex and everyone else. Occasionally, Bess and Abigail glanced toward each other with widened eyes, but nobody ever said a word. Eventually, Jane's excitement waned, which provided a perfect window for the Wheatleys to leave. Miss Henwood and Alex stayed, but the latter's remaining proved to be a mistake, for he was soon overtaken by Jane and her request to search the house for wedding accessories. Bess, who did not want to linger around much longer, wished everyone a farewell and headed upstairs to read.

Moments later, Abigail entered Bess' bedroom and remarked, "Tell Father I had lessons today."

Bess looked up from her book and noticed that Abigail was gearing up in her boy-like clothing again. Bess nodded and asked, "Is Miss Henwood still down there?" Abigail replied to the affirmative, and Bess added, "It's odd. She and Father seem to be good friends."

Abigail took a deep breath before responding with what seemed to be a prepared reply. "I think Father misses having Mother around the house and is glad to befriend Miss Henwood. Miss Henwood's family is mostly gone, and she's probably lonely, too."

Abigail's confirmation that her father's acquaintance with Miss Henwood was nothing requiring worry soothed her. When Abigail had gone, Bess returned to her book and was a page from finishing when she heard Jane exclaim something from the other room. Alex answered with fake laughter, and Bess sighed. *Perhaps Jane's too giddy with excitement to notice Alex's reluctance about this wedding.* She shook her head, looked down, and finished her book.

Chapter 22

The first of November was quickly approaching, and the weather grew colder each day. Alex became increasingly reluctant to visit Laurel Manor, for his family did not own a coach, and he did not want to travel in the cold. When a sunny morning finally blessed the county of Kent, Jane devised an idea to surprise Alex by visiting him. She recruited her father and sisters but was disappointed to discover that her father had plans. She inquired over what her father was up to, but he did not respond with specifics.

When the carriage was prepared, the three sisters climbed inside and enjoyed the short journey to Mulberry Cottage, Alex's dwelling. Bess peered outside of her window and thought how pleased she was that they did not have to suffer the chilly temperature by walking. Soon the cottage was within sight, and when Jane emerged from the carriage, she danced to the porch and ran her fist up and down until the door swung open. Mulberry Cottage was less than half the size of Laurel Manor. Like Churlington House, it was old-fashioned and cozy, but it was not meant for large gatherings. Bess had not visited Mulberry Cottage since she was a young girl, so just standing at the door gave her recollections of her childhood—the times when she was not anxious about her sisters, Alex, or anyone else. But when Bess shifted her gaze to the interior of the cottage, she found not Alex nor his parents but rather his sister Mrs. Henrietta Smith! Bess gasped and murmured, "Henni?" for she had not seen Mrs. Smith, who was a little over a decade older than Alex, since she married an older doctor from London *years ago.*

"Jane!" exclaimed a laughing Mrs. Smith. "Why, what a pleasure it is to see you!" She greeted Jane with a massive hug, but when her eyes landed on Bess and Abigail, she froze. "Is that Bessie Phillips?" Bess smiled, and Mrs. Smith lunged toward her to wrap her in an embrace. "Abbie, I didn't even recognize you, but you look *so* much like Jane!"

Abigail blushed. "Good morning, Mrs. Smith," she said while hugging her former friend. "But I thought I looked more like Bess."

"You don't look like either of us," Bess said, which ended the discussion.

"Oh, come in! Come in!" Mrs. Smith squealed. "And girls, there's no need to be formal. We'll soon be sisters, so *please* call me Henrietta, or Henni, like you used to." Henrietta did not leave time for a reply before she pulled her friends inside and sat them beside a burning fireplace. She plopped down into a large, wooden chair and continued, "My parents are in town purchasing groceries. Alex is upstairs, and I'm certain he'll come down quite soon." Henrietta held her palms up to the warmth of the fire and exchanged a familiar smile with Jane. "Evidently, I've come to visit for a few weeks. Doctor Smith is in Paris helping a man named Durham—is it Durham?—I believe so. I was incredibly bored and lonely, so I thought I'd come home early for Alex's wedding. In fact, I arrived yesterday—or perhaps it was two days ago," she pondered but continued without hesitation. Bess took a deep breath. She had forgotten how much Henrietta liked to hear her own voice. "Don't you remember the last time we saw each other, Bessie? You were *so* little, but you may remember seeing Doctor Smith before we married. I'm sure Jane remembers, but oh, Bessie, you've grown into such a beautiful girl—all of you have!" she chuckled. "Oh, Bessie. Truly, I cannot believe how much you've changed. Your physique, your countenance, your grace is—is astounding!" Jane widened her eyes but said nothing. "I'm sure you're wondering why I'm putting such an emphasis on my

217

reacquaintance with Bessie. Well, when we were younger, she and Alex played together *all* the time. Conversely, Jane—the mature one—spent time with the adults," she said with a grin. "Abbie was just a baby—I don't remember how old *exactly*. But oh! I'm *so* glad you've come to visit today. Perfect timing on my—"

"Yes," Jane interrupted with a smile. "We thought we'd surprise Alex. It's been hard for him to visit us due to the cold weather."

"Oh, I'm certain it *has* been! My journey to Kent would have been *much* less pleasant if I didn't come by one of Doctor Smith's carriages. He ordered it to be covered during the winter to prevent draught—or something like that. Still, every time we stopped for food or drink, I found it immensely chilling," she laughed, and Bess raised an eyebrow. "Of course, this topic brings me to another—Jane, *why* did you choose to have your wedding in November? Alex was telling me—"

"Oh," Jane said with a nervous chuckle. "We've been engaged for a while, and I wanted to marry sooner rather than later. I cannot wait to become Mrs. Alexander Cawdor."

Henrietta's face lit up. "Yes, I'm *very* happy for you—but you know, I'd always thought that Alex would marry Bess. I know that Mother and Mrs. Phillips planned your marriage, but I never thought it would come to fruition. Alex and Bess were just *so* close." Jane and Bess blushed, but Henrietta did not cease to talk. "Jane, do not fret! He's incredibly happy to be marrying you. Oh, I mean no harm to you, Bess— nevertheless, I'll always remember you and Alex playing together," she said to Bess. "You were silly—we couldn't let you roam around outside for too long or else you'd wander into the woods, you know, *frolicking* about." Henrietta laughed to herself and fell back in her chair.

Jane took this moment of silence to say, "Yes, I vaguely recall those days." She then straightened her posture and posed a smile, preparing for Henrietta's next recollection.

Suddenly, Bess felt a small object smack the side of her arm. She looked down to retrieve the object since Jane and Henrietta were again engaged in a conversation about Doctor Smith's handsome brother, but all she could find was a pebble. Bess glanced toward Abigail, who was looking leftward. Bess followed her sister's gaze across the room and saw half of Alex's face hidden behind the door. When Alex caught Bess' eyes, he waved his arms, indicating that he wanted to speak to her privately. Abigail groaned.

"Excuse me," Bess said, interrupting one of Henrietta's monologues. "I feel something stuck in my dress, and I need to get it out." She blushed and quickly stepped into the hall, where she met Alex, who silently redirected her to the kitchen.

Upon arrival, Alex placed his hands on the kitchen counter, looked down, and murmured, "Sorry about that."

"Oh, it's not a problem at all," Bess said quickly. "It's nice to see Henrietta again, but she and Jane can lead such boring conversations. Thank you for giving me an excuse to leave!"

Alex laughed, but his eyes did not deviate from the kitchen counter. He hesitated before saying, "I need to talk to you, Bess." He held his breath and said, "Why must Jane and I marry in November? It'll be frigid, and I don't need anything else to make me *more* miserable!"

"Miserable? Alex!" Bess exclaimed. "What in marrying Jane is *miserable*?" Alex shook his head and refused to make eye contact with his friend. Then Bess whispered, "Call it off." She approached Alex and thought of putting her hand on top of his. She hesitated, considering that

Alex may misinterpret this gesture as a sign of affection, which in this case, it was *not*. She simply wanted to comfort him, and eventually, she *did* decide to place her hand on his. She looked up at him and added, "She's already suspicious that you don't love her."

"But I *do* love her," answered Alex. He pulled his hand out from under Bess' and started to pace around the room. "I love the way she looks. I love her maturity. I love *lots* of things about her! But I—well, I mean, I'm looking forward to finally being a part of the Phillips family, but it won't be the same without you and Abbie around. I love Jane, but I just *cannot* see myself living alone with her."

"Talk to her," Bess said. She tucked a strand of hair behind her ear and blushed. "At least you can move the wedding to a warmer date. She's just so excited, but of course, that excitement will eventually subside."

Alex paused. He ran his hand through his ruffled hair and asked, "Could *you* say something about it to her, Bess?"

Bess took a step backward, and she looked up at Alex but was taken aback by what she saw. Rather than seeing the usual sloppy, nervous picture of her friend, she saw a red-eyed, trembling figure whose pungent smell indicated that he hadn't changed his clothing or bathed in days. Bess yearned to reach her arms forward and take Alex in her grasp, but she refrained from doing so. Instead, she cleared her throat and quietly agreed to his request. Alex smiled, and she said, "But at a minimum, you ought to *mention* it to her. If you don't, Jane will think I'm plotting some form of sabotage."

Alex laughed and agreed to *mention* it, but after a moment of silence, he said, "Bess?"

With a dying smile, Bess replied, "Yes?"

"Oh, it's—well," he hesitated to say. "Thank you."

He adjusted his messy hair, and Bess answered, "I know." She paused, and with increasing spirits, she added, "I ought to go now. I told Jane, Abbie, and Henni that I was removing something stuck in my dress. In theory, I should not be gone for long."

"That was your excuse?" Alex laughed.

"Yes," Bess replied. "I wasn't informed that I was going to be the ear for your darkest secrets." She smiled and led her friend back to the drawing-room. Upon seeing her fiancé, Jane jumped up and embraced Alex, who accepted this gesture without much emotion.

"Alex, I'm so pleased to see you! Did you see Bess in the hall fixing her dress?"

Alex nodded, and before he and Bess had the time to sit down, Henrietta said, "Alex, would you like to hear about an observation I've made?" Alex opened his mouth to answer, but Henrietta never stopped talking. "Why, *of course,* you do. Well, I've always known Jane as the reserved Phillips sister while, alternatively, I've known Bessie as the outgoing, even problematic one." She smiled. "But now, it seems that both of you have changed! A moment ago, Jane's immense zeal directed toward Alex, the man she sees almost every day, is completely out of character! And I've noticed that Bessie has seemed oddly restrained all afternoon, which I'm glad to see, for it is a testament to your growing maturity." Jane blushed, but Henrietta seemed utterly oblivious, and she started a new conversation. "I remember when Bessie and Alex pretended to be pirates. They would hide behind the large oak tree at Laurel Manor and plot their schemes, which were mainly to steal my mother's jewelry or kidnap little Abbie. It was quite bothersome, but they entertained themselves well."

"I *do* vaguely remember that," Jane said with a forced smile.

"I don't think you were there, Henrietta," Bess interrupted, changing the topic of conversation for Jane's sake, "when we attended one of the Rosemond's balls. Well, this was *years* ago, but while dancing with Jane, Alex ran into a large, old woman who subsequently knocked over a table of delicacies. It was perhaps the funniest moment of my life, but Jane responded so well! To make Alex feel less embarrassed (for his face was as red as an apple), Jane intentionally knocked over another table of foods," she laughed. "It was a mess—I would know, for I helped to clean it up—but it showed Jane's admirable qualities." Bess watched Jane's face light up, and she smiled. She turned to Alex, but he remained silent. *He's disappointed that I redirected the conversation from him and me, but he must have known that it was the proper thing to do.*

"It *was* a messy evening," Jane chuckled, interrupting Bess' thoughts.

"Upon my word, Alex," Henrietta exclaimed. "You've always been in such disarray! Once, you and Bess—"

"But Mr. Rosemond didn't mind," intervened Bess. "He laughed off the entire incident, and he was grateful when Jane offered to clean up the mess, which spared the servants the effort." Jane laughed, and Abigail smiled. Finally, Henrietta seemed to comprehend Bess' line of thought, so the remainder of the afternoon was fraught with conversations regarding London and Doctor Smith, *not* Bess and Alex.

When Bess grew tired of listening to Henrietta talk, she prompted her sisters to leave. Henrietta frowned at them "having to leave *so* soon," but she wished her friends farewell as they left Mulberry Cottage. The Phillips sisters soon arrived at Laurel Manor. They approached the front door but hesitated to enter, for they heard two voices conversing inside.

Gingerly, Abigail tapped open the door and stepped across the threshold. She listened closely to identify their father's acquaintance, and when she recognized the voice, she slammed the door. She whipped around to face her sisters with widened eyes.

"Well, who is it?" Jane hastened to ask, for she was cold.

"It's Miss Henwood," Abigail replied in a far-off voice.

"Miss Henwood?" Jane repeated, pushing her younger sister aside so she could enter.

Inside the drawing-room, Mr. Phillips was sitting beside Miss Henwood, discussing some seemingly important affair. When he caught Jane's eye, Mr. Phillips blushed and started, "Jane! What—are you home early?"

"Not particularly," Jane replied, slowly approaching her father. "It's good to see you, Miss Henwood," she added as she took a seat beside the fireplace. Miss Henwood made no reply, and Bess observed her father gulp. Suddenly, Bess' former suspicions collided. Miss Henwood's potential engagement, her dancing with Mr. Phillips, and her figure walking away from Laurel Manor all made sense now. Bess gasped.

"You're getting married," she stated.

"Excuse me?" Jane exclaimed as she sprang to her feet. She glared menacingly at her father and Miss Henwood, who wore a smirk. Abigail turned abruptly toward the pair, begging to know if this accusation was true. A dead silence ensued before Mr. Phillips mustered the courage to nod. Jane jumped on this gesture, squealing, "But what of Mother?"

"Don't you still love her?" Abigail added.

Mr. Phillips mumbled, "Of course, I do, but—"

"We're in love," Miss Henwood uttered.

Jane grew pale. She rubbed her eyes and managed to inquire, "For how long?"

But Abigail intervened, "Father, you should have told us! *Asked* us!"

Suddenly, Miss Henwood stood to her feet. She approached Abigail with confidence and said, "Your individual opinions should not dictate your father's choices."

Bess stood back and absorbed this scene with uncharacteristic self-restraint. Her mind was boiling with anger, for she couldn't comprehend many factors in this engagement. *First, how could Miss Henwood be attracted to a man twenty years her elder? Second, how could Father marry a woman right after the death of his wife? None of this seems sensible, but at the same time, so much has occurred over the past few weeks that I cannot deem this circumstance "unbelievable."* She paused. *And as much as I desire to exclaim my frustration as my sisters are, I cannot see how expressing my emotions could alter the situation.*

Miss Henwood noticed Bess' apparent indifference and asked, "Bess, are *you* content with this proposal?"

Jane eyed her sister with disdain, but Bess could not manage to say a word. She watched to see if Miss Henwood's stone-hard expression would change, and she frowned at her father's silent trembling. She yearned to remain quiet but knew that she would have to respond upon being directly addressed. She looked down to her feet and answered, "I'd rather keep my opinions to myself."

"*You*, out of all of us, would like to remain silent?" Jane exclaimed in disbelief.

"Then she must approve," Miss Henwood resolved with satisfaction.

"No," Bess said. "I wish not to speak, for my opinions would only exacerbate the situation." And to conclude her resolution, Bess turned around and headed upstairs. She was too overburdened with complications to completely comprehend this new matter, but she prided herself on escaping the drawing-room without blowing up. *If I hadn't left, then I wouldn't have been able to contain my frustration.* She paused. *Yet, how strange this engagement is! Miss Henwood is the sister of Mr. Henwood, so she must come from money. Therefore, her marrying Father from a pecuniary standpoint is out of the question. Father is certainly* not *handsome, so why in the world would she choose to marry him? Am I mistaken? Are they indeed in love?*

Chapter 23

Bess spent the following few days mulling over her father's engagement, but she remained clueless about why he would marry Miss Henwood. After Abigail had left for school on a foggy but peculiarly warm Tuesday morning, Bess met her father, who was reading, in the garden. She approached him, and when he heard her footsteps, he looked up and smiled.

"Bess," he said and closed his book. "I was wondering when you'd speak with me."

"Have Jane and Abbie—?"

"Yes. They've spoken to me plenty of times," he sighed and turned his attention to a rose bush. Returning his gaze to Bess, he hesitated. "Have you come to reprimand or encourage me?"

"Well," Bess started. She took a seat beside her father and said, "I suppose the former, but I would like to hear your stance. I'm trying not to be so judgmental."

Mr. Phillips chuckled, and Bess looked at him with a raised eyebrow. He wrapped his arm around her shoulder and said, "I'm so proud of you, Bess. I expected *you* to be the leader of this resentment against me, but I've been mistaken. You've demonstrated a type of maturity that I didn't know you had. It's a sign of immense growth, and I'm very pleased."

"Thank you, Father." Bess smiled, for she was glad her attempts to be civil were recognized. Mr. Phillips nodded and gazed at the rose bush again. He spent a minute in contemplation before mustering the courage to answer his daughter's question.

"After the death of your mother, I became lonely," he started. Bess turned to him but found that his eyes were locked on the roses. "I'm certain you noticed, for I became a shell of the man I once was." He paused, and Bess took hold of his hand and squeezed it. "I met Miss Catherine Henwood on the night of the Westfield ball. I was captivated by her tenderness and maturity, which are two traits your mother possessed. She reminded me so much of Emily, and I found myself bewitched by her. I struggled night and day with the thoughts of Emily's death, but I returned to myself around Catherine. She makes me *so* happy, Bess," he said as a tear trickled down his cheek. "For the longest time, I fought an internal battle regarding what I should do. I feared your reaction if I proposed, but Catherine's love for me only increased, and she persuaded me that our marriage would heal my open wounds. The evening you discovered our plan was the day I agreed to marry her." He held his breath and did not speak. Finally, he said, "I haven't been *this* happy for months, Bess. I loathe that Jane and Abbie have misinterpreted by actions as irreverence toward your mother, and I've spent the last few days wondering if it *is* too soon. I determined that when I heard your opinion, then I would make my final decision. If you supported the wedding, then I would marry Catherine. If not, I would call off the engagement."

"You plan to marry her then?" Bess stammered.

Mr. Phillips paused. "Is that what you want, Bess?" He shed a tear, and Bess took a deep breath. *I suppose that after Mother's death, I hadn't considered the welfare of my father. I've thought only of Jane, who seems content because of her upcoming marriage, and Abbie, who now has football to entertain her. I've befriended Jack, but Father did not have anyone on whom to rely.* She sighed. *I suppose I've always held a relatively high opinion of Miss Henwood. It isn't as if Father is marrying someone as insensitive as Mrs. Baldare.* She paused. *Yet, part of me feels that this engagement isn't right. My feeling goes beyond Miss Henwood's situation, but I cannot devise a* true *reason to call off the wedding. If it makes Father happy...*

"Yes," she answered and felt a sudden pang of regret. Mr. Phillips' red eyes shot up. He started to tremble, and then he nodded, and a weak grin spread across his face. He covered his face with his hands and began to cry. Bess kissed him on the forehead and whispered, "Father, you deserve all the happiness in the world."

Through his wall of fingers, Mr. Phillips choked, "Thank—thank you, Bess."

Chapter 24

Eventually, Bess convinced her sisters that their father's engagement to Miss Henwood was not as horrible as they had first presumed. They arrived at the consensus that their father was in dire need of healing, and his marriage to Miss Henwood was the best remedy. So, to repair her previous behavior toward Miss Henwood, Jane drafted an invitation, which invited her future stepmother to tea.

The following morning, Bess dressed in humble attire. She did not want to display any of the opinions that were rattling around in her mind. She thought of dressing elegantly—in such a way that would intimidate Miss Henwood, but she decided that by doing this, her father's happiness would be at stake. Still, Bess felt that this marriage was not right, but she did not know why, and because she had no reasoning, she could *not* be a barrier in the way of the wedding.

Having finalized her appearance, Bess met her sisters in Jane's bedroom. Like Bess, Abigail wore a modest dress that suited the occasion, but when Bess turned to Jane, she was taken aback. It was clear that Jane's mindset matched Bess' original thoughts, for she wore a refined gown, which was draped in flashy accessories. Bess frowned. She cleared her throat and suggested, "You may want to wear something less, well, *grand*."

"I told her that, too," Abigail said. "But she keeps refusing."

Jane admired her picture in the mirror. She sighed, "I cannot change."

"Jane, you'll look ridiculous," Bess said.

"But if Miss Henwood enters dressed *better* than I—well, I *cannot* let that happen."

Bess and Abigail shook their heads. Jane pretended not to notice and led her sisters downstairs to await the arrival of their guest. A quarter of an hour passed without any notice of Miss Henwood. Jane opened her mouth to complain when, suddenly, she heard a knock. Abigail stepped forward and opened the door, revealing Miss Henwood, who wore attire that matched that of the younger Phillips sisters. Jane blushed but graciously greeted their father's fiancée before leading her to the dining hall, where fresh appetizers were prepared.

Jane took hold of a slice of bread and said, "You look lovely, Miss Henwood."

Miss Henwood smiled. "Thank you, Jane." She paused. "The three of you look beautiful as well. Truthfully, I've never seen such beautiful sisters."

"Oh, you needn't *flatter* us," laughed Jane, taking another slice of bread.

"I don't mean to exaggerate," Miss Henwood replied. She glanced toward Bess and Abigail, who had remained silent thus far. "My brother's late wife and sister-in-law—well, who's *now* his wife—were gorgeous creatures, but I cannot say that they were any lovelier than the Phillips sisters."

Jane laughed again. "Since you mentioned it, how *are* Mr. and Mrs. Henwood?"

Miss Henwood shifted her position and sighed. "Oh, they report their whereabouts and wellnesses every few weeks. I believe that you know they first headed to Brighton?" Jane nodded. "When they first arrived, Rachel contracted a fever, but she spent a few days at the sea, which healed her."

"I'm glad to hear that."

Miss Henwood nodded but said nothing more. Silence filled the dining hall for a couple minutes while its four occupants finished their appetizers. Bess admired Miss Henwood's graceful way of eating, which was another trait of her mother. In some respects, she even resembled Jane, but Bess shuttered at the thought that her father was marrying someone young like her sister. Eventually, Miss Henwood lowered her fork and said, "Girls, I must address the reason for which you invited me. It is no surprise that you are disappointed with my engagement—"

"On the contrary," Bess interrupted, "we're quite content." Miss Henwood raised an eyebrow and Bess continued, "However, out of sheer curiosity, I wished to inquire *why* you chose our father. Certainly, more suitable gentleman *must* have caught your fancy."

Miss Henwood smiled. "I *can* address that concern. In short, I've found myself in love." Abigail sighed, and Bess' heart sank, for she yearned for a permanent change in her sisters' demeanors. Yet, Miss Henwood continued, "Please allow me to recollect my childhood days before judgment." Abigail folded her arms across her chest as she listened to Miss Henwood begin, "I was born and raised in Derbyshire by a single mother with an elder brother. When I turned three years old, my brother, who was much older, abandoned us for a woman in France, and my mother married my stepfather, Mr. Charles Henwood VII. You may not believe it when I tell you that I was always well-off. My mother's father owned a wealthy estate, which he passed on to my mother in his will. Nevertheless, the next portion of my story is rather complicated, so I will relate it slowly. A year before my mother married, my stepfather's wife, Charles' mother, had a child out of wedlock. They named him Benjamin Roberts—I believe you met him at Charles' wedding. Ben's mother divorced my stepfather to marry her lover;

however, they both died a couple years later, and Ben returned to us. In short, I am the *stepsister* and Ben is the *half-brother* of Charles. Perhaps these difficulties played a part in Charles' development, but I wanted to ensure that you knew of my proper background." She took a deep breath before continuing. "After my mother's marriage, I started to attend a wealthy co-educational institution. I was a quiet, reserved child, so I found it difficult to make friends. My stepfather was well-acquainted with the Elmsworths, so he arranged for Curtis and Jack to be my friends. Curtis was arrogant, so I did not spend much time with him. Jack was a rather exuberant child, but we connected well, and although I was a couple years older than him, we grew to be close friends." She paused and took another deep breath. "Eventually, Jack and I had a disagreement, and we drifted apart."

"What happened?" Jane asked.

"Oh," Miss Henwood sighed. "I would prefer to avoid discussing that matter." Jane nodded her head, and Miss Henwood continued, "Then I met a man named Mr. Elliot with whom I thought I fell madly in love. You see, youth makes one irrational and blind to reality, and I later learned that Mr. Elliot only wanted to marry me for my money. I broke off our engagement once I discovered the truth, but I became awfully lonely again." She sighed and readjusted her position. "Eventually, my mother and stepfather passed away. Then Ben bought a house to the west, so I was forced to live at home with Charles. When he met Emma, I often accompanied them to balls, but nothing more came of my life until I met your father." She paused to take a deep breath. "Your father pitied my plights. He listened to me, which is something nobody has ever done for me before. As you know, he's very kind and admirable, and I don't think I'll ever find a man whom I could love more." She turned to Bess. "Bess, *you* uncovered our secret, so forgive me if I am repeating information you know. Oftentimes, when your father was home alone, I would come over. For instance, I left early from Churlington House to see him, which was an idea we planned in advance." She paused. "Our relationship was mainly a secret, but your father is such a good gentleman, and I was tremendously pleased when we agreed upon the engagement."

"Did the agreement occur just before we arrived?" Jane asked.

Miss Henwood nodded. "I sincerely hope that I've enlightened each of you with my troubles. I believe that I love your father, and I beg you overcome the difficulties regarding our engagement. It's no secret that we have a great age disparity, but please know that it doesn't matter to me."

Realizing that Miss Henwood had finished her monologue, Bess answered, "I'm happy that you and my father found each other." She sat back in her chair and managed to half-listen to the next replies. Ever since Miss Henwood mentioned Jack, Bess could not keep questions from racing through her mind. *What disagreement broke them apart? What sort of relationship did they have before then? Why do they still seem friendly if they hadn't seen each other for years?*

Bess' thoughts were interrupted when Miss Henwood asked, "Then are each of you satisfied?" The Phillips sisters nodded, which caused a large grin to spread across Miss Henwood's face. As if on cue, a servant arrived with tea, and for the remainder of the gathering, Jane and her future stepmother spoke of the latter's childhood. Jane listened with a perpetually red face, for (Bess supposed) the embarrassment of misinterpreting Miss Henwood's intentions was almost too great to overcome. Soon, the evening arrived, and Miss Henwood decided to

233

leave. After wishing their guest final farewells, the Phillips sisters closed the front door and turned to each other.

"I suppose she'll make a decent stepmother," Abigail observed. "She's not as dreadful as I thought she'd be, and I regret making such a prejudice."

Jane blushed. "Well, *I* don't. She might appear all right, but she *cannot* replace Mother."

"Jane, she might be the *best* replacement for Mother!" Bess intervened.

"Others could replace her better," she huffed. "By the way, her age is unfathomable! It's almost like *I'm* marrying Father."

Bess shook her head. "Jane, don't you care for Father's happiness?"

"Of course, I do," she answered. "But I suppose it doesn't matter. Soon, I'll live in Mulberry Cottage, and I won't be bothered by her presence."

"She doesn't *seem* bothersome," Abigail interjected.

"Outward appearance *hardly ever* indicates inward character, Abbie!" Jane cried. "I've seen girls like her before! Despite *what* she says, she's only marrying Father for money or something to that equivalent. Father's been swindled, and—"

"Jane, I thought you'd be content," Bess interrupted. "Did you *listen* to what she said? You were red afterward, and I thought it was because you were embarrassed for misinterpreting her—"

"*Embarrassed?*" Jane laughed. "She just made me awfully uncomfortable."

"And what if they're truly in love?" Bess asked.

Jane shook her head. She turned to the front door and muttered, "You *think* that a *gorgeous* woman like her could *ever* really like our *old, utterly plain* father?"

"Jane!" Bess exclaimed.

But Jane continued as if there had been no interruption, "Perhaps you and Abbie don't get it, Bess. *I*'ve known Father the longest, and—"

"Jane, that doesn't mean you know him better than Abbie and I do."

"Well!" Jane exclaimed. She was on the verge of tears, so she took a deep breath. Once the blood started to drain from her head, she moaned, "I apologize. I didn't mean it. It's just—"

"It's hard. I know," Bess sighed. Then she and Abigail embraced Jane. "But *your* wedding is upcoming, and there's always the chance Father *won't* marry Miss Henwood. It's only a supposition."

Jane dug her head into her sister's shoulder and nodded. Eventually, she pulled out of the embrace and wiped her eyes. The cosmetics she wore were smeared across her face, and her elegant gown seemed dull, but she still looked beautiful. She sniffled, "And suppose that Alex and I don't get married. What if that's *only a supposition*?"

"Oh," Bess started. She reached out to hug Jane again and said, "You and Alex are meant to be together, Jane. Father *just* met Miss Henwood a few months ago." Bess sighed. *Perhaps I shouldn't mention Alex's request to change the wedding date. This matter does not involve me, and besides, Alex ought to stop confiding his secrets in me. Sooner or later, he'll have to open up to Jane, and for once, I need to put my sister's needs before my friend's.*

"But lately, I feel detached from him," Jane moaned.

"It'll be all right, Jane," Bess reassured. "Everything will be all right."

Chapter 25

As the end of November drew closer, Jane's anticipation heightened. She visited Mulberry Cottage twice a week, allowing neither Bess nor Abigail to accompany her. Bess did not mind being excluded from these visits. She had never spoken to Jane about delaying the wedding, and she did not want to face Alex's wrath about her unfulfilled promise.

Soon, the week of the wedding had arrived, and Jane was more anxious than ever. She had instructed the servants to clean Laurel Manor thrice, and she had arranged for several teams of workers to prepare the garden, which was groomed to perfection. Jane's uneasiness, however, had its advantages. She never heard (or listened) to the many complaints about the November temperature, for she was too anxious to consider anything other than the wedding preparations. When the wedding was within forty-eight hours, Bess recruited Abigail to help arrange the seating by the altar. Bess had heard rumors of Alex's imminent arrival, so yearned to be as far from him as possible. She prepared to bear the chilling weather for however long Alex stayed, but when she walked outside, she was surprised to find that the temperature mimicked that of a spring day.

Bess turned to her sister and asked, "Do you think this weather will last until Sunday?" She took hold of a chair and set it upon the carpet of beautifully groomed grass.

Abigail picked up another chair and answered, "I do. We—well, Jane and Alex—need a good omen, and I think the weather will comply."

Bess pursed her lips and looked away. She set down another chair and changed the subject, "Are you still playing football in town?"

"Yes," Abigail replied without hesitation.

"Even in *this* weather?" Bess straightened a crooked chair, and Abigail laughed.

"What do you mean? *This* weather is magnificent," she said, pointing to the sun. Bess chuckled and playfully nudged her sister in the side. "But yes, when I'm running around, I hardly feel the cold."

"How's—what's his name—the boy to whom you introduced me at Lady Madeleine's? Does *he* enjoy the cold weather, too?"

Abigail laughed, "*Introducing* Callum to you was the last thing I wanted, but he's doing well. He doesn't mind the temperature either. Perhaps you should come watch us play together." She blushed and turned away. Bess recognized this sign of affection and replied that she would be happy to watch her sister play.

When Sunday arrived, Abigail's prediction had proven accurate. The weather was indubitably superior to that of the typical November day, and this positive development improved everyone's mood. Jane appeared happier than ever, and from what Bess heard, Alex was optimistic as well. Bess and Abigail, though, hardly had time to admire the weather because they were overwhelmed with last-minute wedding preparations. At ten o'clock in the morning, they were dancing around in Jane's bedroom, ensuring that everything regarding her appearance was well in order.

"What if I trip and fall?" Jane trembled. "What if I forget what I'm supposed to say?"

Bess adjusted a lock of her sister's hair and assured, "Nobody'll be at the wedding whom you don't love, Jane. *If* any of these situations was to occur, you wouldn't disappoint anyone." Jane only frowned, and Bess took a step back to admire her sister's beautiful figure. She was draped in silky white cloth that appeared neither modest nor gaudy. She wore jeweled accessories that used to be their mother's, and her face was adorned with cosmetics. Bess tilted her head to view her sister at another angle, but she appeared only *more* dashing.

Abigail continued, "I promise that you *won't* mess up. I've never heard of anyone who has." Yet, these words only further flustered Jane.

She covered her face with her hands and moaned, "But I'm as likely to as anyone else! What if I do something crass, and Alex decides not to marry me?" She threw her hands to her side and said, "And what if I grow *so* nervous that I sweat?" She glared at her dress. "Perhaps I ought to cut off these sleeves. It would do me—" But Bess and Abigail shook their heads and persuaded their sister to drop the idea altogether. "And what am I supposed to do after we marry?" Jane exclaimed, which startled both sisters.

Bess raised an eyebrow and replied, "You'll move to Mulberry Cottage, Jane."

"Oh, but I couldn't leave you two and Father!"

"We won't be far," Abigail reassured, placing her hand on Jane's shoulder.

Bess shook her head. She glared at her sister and said, "Jane, you love Alex. The weather is perfect, and everyone is in high spirits. Everything will be fine." Jane gulped and turned to Abigail, who confirmed Bess' words with a nod. Bess opened her mouth to continue, but Abigail scowled, and Bess said nothing more.

Jane sighed. "I've always wanted to marry. Are you sure today isn't a dream? Am I *actually* marrying Mr. Alexander Cawdor?" She laughed. "I cannot wait until your weddings!"

Abigail shook her head. "Huh—we'll see about that."

Bess did not reply, and Jane asked, "Bessie, are you *still* set on never marrying?"

Bess rolled her eyes. She murmured, "Yes, but perhaps I'll marry Jack."

"Oh, Jack would make a lovely husband!" Jane squealed. "I'm excited to help plan them. They'll be big white weddings—even bigger than mine!" Bess and Abigail turned to one another and exchanged doubtful expressions. Within moments, they burst into laughter, and once Jane realized how foolish she sounded, she chuckled as well. Bess wiped her eyes of tears and thought of how wonderful it was that she could spend this quality time with her sisters before Jane left. Eventually, their humor dissolved, but Jane was no longer tense. She admired herself in the mirror and watched as Abigail pinned back her hair into a braid. Suddenly, a frown spread across her face and she moaned, "Bessie, could you please go downstairs to see if all of my bridesmaids are here? This morning, Miss Henwood told me that Miss Elmsworth fell ill again."

"How would *she* know?" Bess interrupted.

"She visited Elmsworth Manor earlier."

"Why?"

Jane shrugged, "I'm unsure." Bess hesitated to leave, but eventually, she resolved to fulfill Jane's request. She descended the staircase, and as she heard the volume of chattering voices increase, she spotted the Wheatley sisters whispering in the drawing-room. She approached them, and opened her mouth to seek their services upstairs, but Juliette interrupted.

"Good morning, Bess! How are you?" she asked in the midst of dying laughter.

"I'm doing rather—"

"It must be *tremendously* exciting having a sister marry! It'll be a while before Leonarda's wedding day, but I'm certain I'll be elated. And—"

"Uh-huh," Bess interjected. She turned around and glanced toward the dining hall.

"Oh, I'm sorry! Do you have something you wish to say?" Juliette faltered. "Am I keeping you from doing something or being somewhere?"

Bess nervously chuckled. "Jane asked me to send the bridesmaids upstairs. I should be returning there shortly with Henrietta and Miss Henwood."

"Oh, of course!" Juliette replied, standing up. "Do you need help finding Henrietta and Miss Henwood?"

"Oh, no," Bess said. She glanced toward the dining hall again to look for either of her two targets. As she started to turn back to the Wheatley sisters, she noticed Alex standing among a crowd of his family. When he caught her eye, he signaled for her to meet him.

With a dying smile, Juliette replied, "All right. We'll be upstairs then." But Bess hadn't heard her reply. The thought of Alex sidetracked her, and she left the drawing-room without another word. She met Alex midway in the dining hall, and when they were within an arm's length of each other, he wrapped her in an embrace. Bess tensed and waited until her friend unwrapped his arms.

He whispered into her ear, "I'm so glad I found you."

Bess took a step backward. She looked into her friend's blue eyes, which showed no trace of anger at her refusal to relay his former request. She hesitated, but when she chose to respond, she did so with a chuckle.

"Are you *that* bored of being the center of attention already, Alex? The wedding hasn't even yet begun!" Alex laughed, which confirmed Bess' suspicion that he was in good spirits. Then he led her outside, and when he had found a neighboring, isolated wooded area, he sat on the ground and buried his head in his hands. Alarmed at Alex's sudden change in demeanor, Bess knelt beside her friend and said, "Alex, is everything all right?"

Alex shook his head, but no words emerged from his mouth. Bess hesitated to comfort him, so she watched his figure slowly melt into the earth. Finally, his voice shook as he said, "I can't do this, Bess. I *really* can't do this."

Bess stood to her feet. She folded her arms across her chest, and her throat tensed as she replied, "I can no longer put your emotions ahead of my sister's, Alex." She lowered her eyes and added, "Do what you wish, but I beg that you do *not* get me involved." She turned to go inside, but Alex stood up and took a firm grasp of her hand. She swiveled back around and stared into her friend's glossy eyes. She pulled her hand away to rub her eyes, which had begun to form tears. She tried to take a deep breath and swallow but could manage neither.

"Bess, you're my best friend," Alex choked. "I can't do this."

Bess turned away, fearing that he would see her cry. She managed to collect herself, and she opened her mouth to make a sharp reply, but nothing emerged. She heard a thud and whipped around to see that Alex had fallen to the ground again. He wrapped his arms around his body, buried his head in his legs, and began to shake. Instinctively, Bess fell to his side. She managed to outstretch her arms and pull him into an embrace.

"I'm sorry, but you must marry Jane. I would rather you marry my sister than hurt her," Bess whispered. Alex lifted his head, revealing a red face coated in tears. Bess took another deep breath and said, "If you won't do it for Jane, do it for me."

Alex replied with a moan, but eventually, he resolved to stand to his feet. He brushed off his attire and wiped his eyes, but he still shook as if he were cold. He looked up and said, "At least the weather's nice." Bess grinned as she saw a trace of a smile flicker across his face. She started to depart, but Alex interrupted, "Do you have to go now?"

Bess nodded. "Jane told me to gather the bridesmaids."

"I shouldn't keep you then," Alex murmured. He rubbed his eyes again and looked down to straighten his attire. Bess turned away and left without saying another word. Once she shut the front door to Laurel Manor behind her, she leaned back and covered her face with her hands. She wiped her cheeks to rid herself of any evidence of tears. Then she took a deep breath, straightened her posture, and walked into the dining hall, searching for Henrietta and Miss Henwood. From the corner of her eye, Bess caught a glimpse of Miss Henwood, who was deep in conversation with Mr. Phillips. Bess pushed her way through a crowd of guests, for she could not bear to delay Jane's request any longer. By the time she reached her father and future stepmother, she was out of breath.

She huffed, "Miss Henwood, Jane wants you upstairs."

"Is she assembling the bridesmaids?" Miss Henwood asked. Bess took another deep breath and nodded. She watched as Miss Henwood squeezed her fiancé's hand before wishing him farewell and heading toward the staircase. Bess started to follow, but then an idea struck her. She turned around and watched a hopeful, happy expression fade from her father's face. She smiled to herself and continued to follow Miss Henwood through the crowd of guests until she found a clear pathway to Henrietta and Doctor Smith.

When Henrietta noticed Bess approaching, her face lit up. She outstretched her arms and exclaimed, "Bessie, do you remember my husband Doctor Smith?" Bess sighed and exchanged a faint smile with the thin, aging gentleman accompanying Henrietta. Although Bess knew that she had once met Doctor Smith, she did not recognize him. Henrietta detected this lack of familiarity and continued, "Well, in any case, Doctor Smith managed to escape his business trip to attend the wedding, and—"

"I hope you had safe travels," Bess intervened.

"I did. Thank you," replied Doctor Smith in a feeble voice.

"Oh," Henrietta continued, "before you arrived, we were discussing a fascinating piece of news that Doctor Smith heard while he was away. Well, to be precise, he heard it *mentioned*. Apparently, this is *old* news, but I had no prior knowledge of it." Henrietta took a breath. "Well, I'm no pundit of politics, but a group of American feminists back in 1848, I believe, assembled at what they call the—the—oh, Doctor Smith, what was it called?"

"The Seneca Falls Convention," he answered. "The leaders created the Declaration of Sentiments to promote women's rights."

Henrietta interrupted, "Isn't that such a remarkable achievement for the women's movement?"

Bess bit her lip. "Yes, I believe it is, but—"

"In a country with freedom and independence as its motto, it's astonishing to think that women *still* don't have equal rights! You know," she added, lowering her voice, "*I* don't mind. If *I* was left to make my own political decisions—well, if *everyone* were like me, then I think our nation would fall apart! I can hardly decide what shoes to wear, so how is someone like me supposed to make major political decisions by voting?" She paused to take a breath. "Perhaps the women's movement, then, isn't such a good—"

"I'm sure anything promoting equality among individuals is a step in the right direction," Bess intervened. She had completely forgotten about Jane's request, for she had been focused on Henrietta's narrow political views.

"Do you propose then that the slaves be freed?" Henrietta asked. "Truthfully, I don't have much of an opinion." She tossed a lock of her hair over her shoulder and gave a placid smile.

"Did you ever read *Uncle Tom's Cabin* by Harriet Beecher Stowe?" Bess asked as she folded her arms across her chest. The blank look on Henrietta's face signified that she was clueless, but Bess caught a glimpse of Doctor Smith nodding from the corner of her eye. "It shows the immense cruelty of the institution of slavery. *I*, for one, could *never* support something as horrid as—"

"Oh, but it doesn't apply to us, does it?" Henrietta interrupted with a naïve grin. "If there were slaveholders in London, then perhaps I *would* have an opinion. But because we don't have that *American issue* here, I don't see why I would need to read somebody's uncle's book."

Bess sighed and rubbed her eyes. She looked over to Doctor Smith, who wore an amused expression on his face, and Bess pursed her lips. She shook her head, and he frowned, but this pause in conversation redirected Bess' attention to Jane's request. With a sudden jolt of energy, Bess opened her mouth to speak but was interrupted. "Oh, that sounded cruel," Henrietta added. "I hope I don't sound crass. I haven't been in school for so long." Then she turned to her husband. "How many years, Doctor Smith, would you say have passed since I was last in school?" Doctor Smith opened his mouth to reply, but Bess took this opportunity to intervene and request Henrietta's presence upstairs. Doctor Smith shut his mouth, but Henrietta did not seem phased, and her cheerful countenance prevailed. She briefly apologized for being a cause for delay, wished her husband farewell, and followed Bess upstairs.

"It's been, huh, perhaps a decade since I last attended an institution. I can hardly remember," Henrietta continued. "I used to *love* going to school. I loved to learn, and I loved to spend time with my friends. Once, I had a friend named Miss Leighanna Walcott, and we were inseparable, but—oh wait, wasn't it Miss *Lucilia* Walcott?" But Bess and Henrietta had reached the assembly of bridesmaids at the second-floor landing, and the latter stopped talking. When they arrived, Bess looked up and caught a glimpse of Jane, who was pacing about the hallway with a bright red face.

"Bess, what took you so long?" Jane reprimanded. "*Only* one hour remains before the ceremony!"

Henrietta blushed. "Oh, I sincerely apologize, Jane. I was talking about politics and—"

"I stopped to chat," Bess said, relieving Henrietta of her embarrassment.

"Well, I hope you enjoyed it," Jane groaned. She narrowed her eyes before turning to her bridesmaids, beginning to give directions as to where their dresses were located. "Prepare as soon as possible," she emphasized. "I'll need help straightening up my appearance when you're finished." Bess raised an eyebrow, wondering why Jane wasn't yet ready. She was on the verge of voicing her opinion but kept her mouth closed for the sake of her sister's sanity.

When Bess entered her bedroom, she spotted her dress hanging beside her wardrobe. She eyed the light pink color with distaste, for she had never worn anything similar. She groaned as she removed it from its hanger and imagined herself dressed in its material. *It's winter; why does this look like a spring ball gown?* She reluctantly pulled the clothing over herself, and once she was dressed, she gazed at herself in the mirror. *I suppose I look a bit bloated, but so long as Jane likes it, I am satisfied.* Bess straightened the skirt and took a deep breath. She returned to the hallway where she awaited the arrival of the other bridesmaids. About a half an hour elapsed before everyone, including Jane, reconvened. Jane applauded the appearances of her friends and then requested Abigail's help in finalizing her appearance. A quarter of an hour passed before Jane opened her bedroom door and revealed her dashing figure, fully prepared to grace the aisle.

Henrietta gasped and said, "You look *so* beautiful, Jane."

This remark started a train of compliments from the remaining bridesmaids, and Jane smiled with relief. After the final remark was made, Bess turned to her sister.

"Jane," she said. "I've never seen you look more beautiful." Half a second passed before tears formed in Jane's eyes. She outstretched her arm and pulled Bess into an embrace.

"I'll miss you, Bessie," she whispered into her sister's ear.

Bess felt a lump forming in her throat, but she managed to say, "I'll miss you, too, Jane." The two eldest Phillips sisters remained clutched in each other's arms for the longest time. Eventually, Abigail broke them apart, reminding them that the ceremony was about to begin. Jane pulled away and wiped her eyes with the back of her hands.

She trembled, "Oh, have my cosmetics smeared?"

Bess admired her sister's beautiful countenance and shook her head. Jane wiped her cheeks and turned to the steps, preparing to descend and approach the altar. She looked back to her bedroom and hesitated. Bess grabbed onto her sister's right arm, and Abigail reached out and took hold of her left. Then the two youngest Phillips sisters led their elder sister down the staircase.

Chapter 26

When Bess rounded the corner from the manor, she was taken aback by the scene. Her father had hired a local carpenter to make the venue appear like a proper church, but this was not the only feature that amazed her. Not only had a garden of wintry flowers bloomed in time for the wedding, but wooden trellises draped in flowering dogwood formed a spectacular centerpiece for the altar. Behind this spectacle stood a pentagonal construction, dangling a holy cross from its point. And standing amid this decor was Alex, anxiously beaming as he awaited his bride.

Anticipating her turn to descend the aisle, Bess clasped hands with Abigail, who faced the groom and minister. She watched as Henrietta and her father pranced toward the altar, and she stumbled forward as Abigail started to follow them. Bess grabbed hold of her sister's side so as not to fall, which caused Abigail to snicker. Then she collected herself and started making elegant strides toward the altar. When she arrived, she turned away from Alex and admired the guests. Unlike at the Henwood wedding, she recognized almost everyone, and when she spotted Jack seated in the middle, she smiled. Soon, the music quieted, and Bess caught a glimpse of her father and sister strolling down the aisle. As always, Jane looked beautiful. The flowers behind her perfectly complemented her gown and veil, and when Bess peered over to Alex, she saw a look of awe pass over his face.

To everyone's relief, the wedding proceeded as planned. Neither Jane nor Alex forgot their lines, and at the end of the ceremony, they locked lips to signify their union of marriage. When they broke apart, they had joyous tears settled in their moon-shaped eyes. Bess saw Jane's mouth form the words "I love you," and as if on cue, they embraced once more in a final kiss. The crowd applauded.

When the ceremony had finished, Mr. Phillips led his guests to reconvene in the dining hall, which he and Jane had flawlessly cleaned and prepared. The servants wasted no time in serving food and beverages, and the professional musician from earlier made no delay in playing music on the piano forte. After the first course was served, Bess turned to admire the musician and found Leonarda seated to his left, watching as his fingers danced across the keys. A quarter of an hour elapsed before Alex and Jane performed a waltz, which prompted the other guests to join when the next song arose. Bess watched as the number of dancers exponentially increased, and as she took a bite of her food, she heard a distant voice ask her to dance. She set down her fork and knife and turned to find Jack's beaming countenance. She smiled and replied to the affirmative.

Jack took Bess' hand and led her to the center floor, where they joined a dance of French origin. Bess started with a twirl and performed the choreography with perfection, for Jane had insisted she learn it as a child. And for perhaps the first time in months, Bess reveled in the music. She led the others, especially those unfamiliar with the dance, throughout the routine. In one instance, she caught a glimpse of Alex and Jane's dancing figures. They moved elegantly together, and Bess turned away. She managed to sneak another glance and found that Alex's attention was solely focused on Jane. His wandering eyes seemed forever lost, and Bess forced a smile.

The first song finished with a crescendo, and Bess held her final stature before bursting into laughter. She reached forward to embrace Jack while catching her breath. When she pulled away, she said, "I haven't danced like that in years!" Jack doubled over in laughter, and when he stood upright, he took a deep breath. Bess took hold of his hand and asked, "What did you think of the ceremony?"

"It was beautiful," he answered.

A massive grin overtook Bess' face, and she sputtered, "Jane said she's excited for Abbie and me to get married. As if *that* would ever—"

"Why do you make fun?" Jack interrupted with a frown.

"Oh." Bess paused. "It was only, well, I suppose that if I find the *right*—"

"I see," Jack intervened. He looked down to his feet and refused to say a word throughout the second song. Bess bit her lip but continued as if nothing had occurred. When the dance concluded, Bess took a step back and felt a tap on her shoulder. She turned around, fully expecting to see an either exuberant or anxious Jane but found a smiling Miss Henwood instead.

With an empty champagne glass dangling from her fingers, she giggled, "Would you like to dance with me? Jonathan—I apologize, your *father*—and I did the last one, but now he's tired, and I *yearn* for a partner." Miss Henwood set down the glass, and Bess raised an eyebrow but felt a sudden sense of relief, for dancing with Miss Henwood would alleviate her tension with Jack. She nodded and told Jack of Miss Henwood's request. He frowned and stepped away.

Soon, a unique melody rang through Laurel Manor. Miss Henwood whispered that *this* song was Italian, and before Bess had time to reply, she was taken up by Miss Henwood, who grabbed hold of her arm and began to dance. Bess followed her partner's steps since she was unfamiliar with the choreography. *How silly I must look dancing with my father's fiancée!* But Bess did not have much time to consider how she looked, for she stumbled over her feet and fell to the floor. Miss Henwood's lips turned upward into a smile, and she started to laugh. Bess found her feet and brushed off her gown but could not help but to join her friend in chuckling. When the musician altered tunes to that of an Austrian waltz, Bess and her partner were radiating liveliness. They no longer followed the traditional choreography; rather, they made up their moves as the song progressed. As she heard the crescendo approaching, Bess mocked the opposite sex by bowing, clearing her throat, and prancing around with an imaginary top hat. Miss Henwood joined her fun, and Bess laughed aloud—perhaps harder than she had for months. Bess closed her eyes to absorb the moment, and when she opened them, she expected to find Jane, Abigail, or even a friend like Emma, not the face of Miss Henwood!

Eventually, the song drew to a close, and Bess paused to catch her breath. She exhaled with a final jolt of laughter and asked, "Do you want your wedding to be like this?"

Miss Henwood took a deep breath and looked away. She said, "Let's not talk about my wedding. This is Jane's special day. Mine will arrive soon enough." Bess smiled at her partner's good-natured reply, but she did not have much time to commend Miss Henwood. The musician started to play an upbeat song in which Bess was soon engrossed. She took Miss Henwood's hand, and the pair danced like they had before. Guests surrounding them paused to glare at their nonsense, but neither partner minded. Even when Jane and Alex stopped to watch them, Bess never faltered. As the music grew softer, Bess cast her gaze toward the bride and groom, who had moved into the chairs adjacent to the dancers.

"Bess, is everything all right?" inquired Miss Henwood, who noticed Bess' hesitation.

"Oh," Bess started, whipping her head back to her partner. "Yes. Why?"

Miss Henwood looked to her feet and chuckled. "Well, I thought—I had in mind—oh, pay no attention to me." Bess raised an eyebrow, but her suspicion was confirmed when Miss Henwood glanced toward Jane and Alex.

For the next quarter of an hour, Miss Henwood and Bess danced until they could no longer feel their legs. Bess forgot the names of Alex, Jack, Jane, and any other problematic character. She felt free—perhaps even happier than ever before. The sky soon turned dark and transmitted light from the moon and stars. Miss Henwood whispered a farewell to Bess, but as she started away from the ballroom floor, Bess called out her name. She hesitated, but the slight grin encompassing her partner's face prompted her to ask, "Could you stay to talk?" Miss Henwood nodded, took Bess by the arm, and led her to a nearby table. "Thank you," Bess began. "I apologize if you had former—"

"Plans?" Miss Henwood asked. "No. None." She smiled and leaned forward in her chair. "Bess, if your dilemma is what I suppose it to be, I've seen heartbreak before and—"

"I'm *not* heartbroken," Bess interrupted. "In fact, I'm beyond happy for Alex and Jane."

Miss Henwood opened her mouth to continue, but she hesitated. She nodded her head, but after a minute of silence, she cleared her throat and took a deep breath. "A former friend of mine was a decent fellow. His admirable qualities negated his flaws, but I need not go further." She sighed, "Once, he fell in love with a beautiful woman whom he impregnated. To spare this woman's identity, I'll omit her name from this story. They were not married, so the matter was a complication.

252

Luckily, both sets of parents forgave them, and any problem seemed to be resolved." Miss Henwood paused to take a deep breath. "My friend—well, truthfully, he wasn't much of a friend, rather the brother of my suitor—fell in love with another woman. He left Mar—oh, I apologize—the *woman* by herself with the child." Miss Henwood folded her arms across her chest and frowned. "Eventually, the woman married a blacksmith. She became better off without my friend's brother, but I daresay the situation *ruined*, in a way, her life. I do not mean to say that having a child is ruinous," Miss Henwood corrected. "But being left to raise a child alone at such a young age certainly complicates life." Miss Henwood paused and turned to her young acquaintance. She said, "Bess, I've seen how you admire Alex. Everything will turn out all right. I promise."

Bess bit her lip but was unable to conceive a response, for Miss Henwood had already given her a reassuring touch and bid her farewell. Bess watched her future stepmother return to her father, but once she was out of sight, Bess felt charged with perplexity. *Miss Henwood's story sounds familiar, but where have I heard that tale before?* She sighed and tried not to overthink, for she was here for celebration, not contemplation.

Bess returned her gaze to the crowd, choosing to observe the guests rather than dissect Miss Henwood's anecdote. First, her eyes landed upon Juliette and Leonarda, who appeared to be mimicking Bess and Miss Henwood's ridiculous choreography. Bess sighed; despite what Juliette reported, she and her sister seemed to get along perfectly well. Bess turned her head and spotted Mr. Ashford, who was chatting with one of Alex's female cousins. She shook her head and rolled her eyes while turning her head back to her father and his fiancée, who were drinking champagne. She found Jack dancing alongside his mother, Alex waltzing with Abigail, and—

"Bessie, what are you doing?" Jane's voice inquired. Bess turned around and smiled when her elder sister came into view. Without awaiting a reply, Jane settled into the chair beside Bess and complained, "I'm *exhausted*." She waited a moment before chuckling, "You seemed to be having fun with Miss Henwood."

Bess laughed. "Yes, she's a good dancer."

"I hesitate to say *good*," she replied. She glanced down to the floor, and after a long pause, she added, "I asked Alex to dance with Abbie. I needed to sit down, but he seems to have an unlimited amount of energy. I simply can't keep up!"

"You looked magnificent today," Bess said, changing the subject.

Jane chuckled at her sister's directness and replied, "You have no idea *how* many people have told me that."

"Oh, but it's true, Jane," Bess emphasized. "And with all of the flowers—"

"Yes, *the flowers matched me perfectly*," she quoted. "I know." She smirked and continued to repeat the numerous compliments she had thus far received. Bess leaned back in her chair and half-heartedly listened, but Jane did not seem to notice. She sat upright and spoke with such animation that she often laughed to herself. "And this one man—I don't even know who he is—told me—" She paused and covered her mouth for fear of laughing too hard.

"Jane," Bess said, taking this momentary opportunity to interrupt. Jane looked upward with curiosity. Bess took a deep breath and said, "I'm so happy for you." She exchanged a warm smile with her sister, who shut her eyes to hold back tears. Yet, her efforts were to no avail, and she began to cry. She outstretched her arms to grab hold of Bess, and once she managed a solid grasp, she pulled her into an embrace.

"You have no idea how much your words mean to me. I love you, Bessie," Jane whispered. Bess squeezed her sister tighter and did her best to hold back tears. She wanted to tell Jane that she loved her, but she couldn't formulate the words. Instead, she simply returned Jane's hug, and for now, that was enough.

Part III

Chapter 27

The Christmas season had dawned upon the county of Kent, but the inhabitants of Laurel Manor were slow to partake in the holiday preparations. Jane had settled at Mulberry Cottage, Abigail spent most of her leisure time in town, and Mr. Phillips constantly locked himself away with Miss Henwood. These developments led Bess alone to decorate, which was typically her mother and Jane's responsibility. On numerous occasions, Bess determined to hang up a wreath or two, but she could never find her mother's former stash, and she found herself longing for Jane's knowledgeable albeit fastidious presence.

To Bess' relief, her monotonous lifestyle had frequent interruptions due to the busyness of the holiday season. A fortnight after the wedding, she received both written and verbal invitations to attend a gathering at Mulberry Cottage. Doctor Smith and Henrietta were no longer temporary residents in Kent, so only Miss Henwood and the Phillipses were invited. Bess did not mind the size of this party; she was simply excited to have *something* to do. And her enthusiasm was further peaked when the shock of Mr. Benjamin Roberts' imminent arrival was made known to her. It did not take much effort for the Cawdors to make accommodations for their additional guest, but Bess spent her time leading up to the gathering wondering why he had decided to come.

It was with immense disappointment that Bess learned that the Cawdors had rescheduled their party to the date of Mr. Roberts' delayed arrival. Again, Bess grew weary of the boring winter season, but as the twenty-third of December approached, her excitement reinvigorated. Then she learned that Mr. Roberts would be residing at Laurel Manor, not Mulberry Cottage, and her already twisted Christmas exacerbated, for she despised changes in tradition. There was nothing that could fully please her this year, but she felt a sliver of hope when Mr. Roberts' carriage did *not* arrive on the morning of the twenty-third. Her selfish emotions later pained her when she caught sight of Miss Henwood's anxious demeanor, but this Christmas season was nevertheless strange.

As she stood perched at the top of the staircase, awaiting Mr. Roberts' arrival, Bess overheard her future stepmother remark, "I hope he will make it by tomorrow. A Christmas without Ben is tantamount to an awful Christmas." Bess pursed her lips and returned to her bedroom, but not an hour elapsed before she heard commotion resounding from the entrance hall. Bess dropped the book she was reading and dashed downstairs to greet her guest, but she soon found herself in awe. Standing before the threshold of Laurel Manor was a figure Bess had *never* seen before. Nevertheless, Miss Henwood threw herself onto this tall, thin gentleman draped in neat, modern attire. She turned to Bess and asked, "Bess, do you remember my brother Ben?"

Bess returned her gaze to her guest, and when the realization struck her, she took a step back. Mr. Roberts, who was once overweight at the Henwood wedding, was *almost* unrecognizable aside from his now visible, handsome face, and charming smile. Bess beamed and replied, "Of course."

Mr. Roberts sighed with relief and thanked Mr. Phillips for hosting him. He set his luggage down on a table, and Miss Henwood said, "Ben, would you like me to show you around the manor?" Mr. Roberts nodded, and as he started toward the dining hall, Bess caught a glimpse of his deep-set, blue eyes and blushed.

Mr. Roberts nodded in her direction and said, "It's lovely seeing you again, Miss Phillips." Bess opened her mouth to respond, but it was too late, and she remained in the entrance hall utterly dumbfounded.

On the morning of Christmas Eve, Bess headed downstairs to eat breakfast but was surprised to see Mr. Roberts occupying the dining hall with a book. She tiptoed around the kitchen to avoid disturbing him but eventually resigned to sit across from him. She kept her eyes to herself, but once she took a bite of her meal, Mr. Roberts spoke. He lifted his head, set his book aside, and asked, "Do you like to read, Bess?"

"Yes," Bess answered while chewing, for fear of not responding promptly. "I'm about to begin *Oliver Twist.*"

"Ah, Dickens," Mr. Roberts said, turning *Our Mutual Friend* toward Bess.

"How is it?" she asked, setting down her breakfast.

"Long," he said, flipping through the book. Bess wanted to chuckle, but she was afraid that his comment wasn't intended to engender laughter. After a moment of hesitation, Mr. Roberts added, "It's all right—you can laugh." And Bess, albeit feeling awkward, expelled a chuckle. Mr. Roberts scratched his head and continued, "Other than its length, I cannot complain." He paused again, allowing Bess time to admire his gleaming eyes and sharp jawline. "Is there a library in town? On my ride here, I didn't pass one."

"Yes," Bess answered, shaking off her infatuation. "I can take you there if you'd like." Mr. Roberts returned Bess' smile but didn't respond. Bess waited for another minute, but upon hearing nothing more, she excused herself from the dining hall. As she made her way to her bedroom, she grew embarrassed about leaving and moments later, she returned with a pen and paper, preparing to draft a holiday letter to the Elmsworths.

Mr. Roberts glanced up and inquired, "For whom is that?"

"The Elmsworths. I'm wishing them a happy Christmas," Bess replied, refusing to meet her guest's eyes. Mr. Roberts nodded.

Suddenly, he set down his book and said, "I heard your sister married Mr. Alexander Cawdor." Bess did not meet his eyes, but she murmured in the affirmative. "How is she coping with the change of scenery?"

Bess finally turned her attention to Mr. Roberts. She took a deep breath and answered, "Truthfully, she hasn't yet told me. But you'll see her this evening for dinner, and I suppose you may ask her then."

Without hesitation, he added, "How interesting it is that so many people are getting married. Not only has my brother been married *twice* this year, but soon, my sister and your father will wed." He paused, caught in contemplation. "Yesterday, when I arrived, Catherine seemed uncharacteristically energetic, and I was clueless as to why. Now, I comprehend—your father will make a suitable husband for her." He paused. "Catherine has a history with failed engagements, but I believe that finally—"

"Oh, she told me," Bess intervened. Suddenly, she grew red again as silence coursed through the dining hall. She stuttered, "I apologize—I didn't mean—"

"Do not fret, Bess," Mr. Roberts reassured. Bess bit her lip and asked if he knew where his sister was, and he answered, "Elmsworth Manor. Upon what business, I'm unsure. But she said she'd return by noon."

Bess glanced down at her blank latter and sighed, "Well, I'm certain she's wishing them a lovely holiday. Perhaps I ought to head over there, too." Without awaiting a response from Mr. Roberts, Bess stood up from her chair, wished him farewell, and headed to her father's study. After explaining where she was going, Bess made her way toward the front door when she ran into Abigail, clad in her boyish clothing. Bess opened the front door and asked, "Football?" Abigail nodded. "In *this* weather?"

"Well, *you*'re going for a walk," Abigail shot back. "I don't see how you can judge."

"You're heading into town?" Bess asked, and when she received Abigail's confirmation, she added, "Elmsworth Manor is on the way. I'll walk with you."

Once they escaped Laurel Manor property, the younger Phillips sisters felt the severity of the cold upon them. Bess shivered and folded her arms across her chest. Each sister had only brought a thin coat, so every step they took shot a surge of sharp pain through their bodies. When drops of rain began to fall from the sky, they quickened their pace. Bess' teeth chattered, and despite not being keen to chat, she inquired, "For how long do you plan to play football?"

Abigail rubbed her palms together and answered, "Not sure." Then the sisters added another hop to their step.

Elmsworth Manor was approximately a quarter of a mile closer to Laurel Manor than the town. Upon reaching her destination, Bess recommended that Abigail stop inside for a hot cup of tea, but Abigail declined the offer. The sisters parted, and Bess, still shivering, pranced toward the front door to keep warm. Once she reached the entrance to Elmsworth Manor, Bess knocked loudly, and hardly a minute passed before Mrs. Elmsworth answered.

"Oh, Bess!" she exclaimed. "Did you walk in this weather? Come in, come in!" Bess shuffled into the house and followed Mrs. Elmsworth to the drawing-room, where she took a seat beside the burning fireplace. She rubbed her hands close to the flames while thanking her hostess, who smiled and called for her youngest son. As she awaited Jack's presence, Bess glanced around for any sign of Miss Henwood but found none. She listened intently, and as she heard footsteps approaching, she tried to distinguish if there were two sets rather than one. When Jack entered the drawing-room alone, Bess started and stood up.

"Jack, I was going to send a letter."

Jack sat down and chuckled, "Why didn't you? It's awfully cold outside."

"Mr. Roberts told me that Miss Henwood was here, and truthfully, I didn't want to seem inferior to her," she answered, biting her lip.

From the dining hall, Mrs. Elmsworth shouted, "She was foolish to put her health at stake like that—and so were you!" Mrs. Elmsworth laughed aloud, and Bess sighed with relief.

Jack shook his head. "Cath—Miss Henwood came by to wish us well."

"I thought that I'd do the same," Bess said. "I don't intend on staying long."

"Oh, you'll stay until I can ensure a warm carriage," interrupted Mrs. Elmsworth.

"I *really* appreciate it," Bess intervened, considering that she might watch Abigail play football today, "but I'm heading to town after this, and I don't want to bother your coachmen." Mrs. Elmsworth sighed but did not respond. Bess smiled and returned to Jack, asking, "How is Miss Elmsworth? I'd like to—"

"She's ill again."

"Again?" Bess blurted. "Well, how is your father?"

"He's in town," Jack hastened to reply.

Bess frowned and folded her arms across her chest. "Please wish him a happy Christmas for me." Jack nodded but did not reply. *What could have brought about Jack's sudden discourtesy? He's never seemed so indifferent toward me before. Well, I suppose Curtis' absence* has *started to affect him—perhaps, then, I ought to go.* Bess shifted her position and glanced toward her friend, who was tapping his foot and holding his breath. *He looks like he has something to say.* Bess paused. *Therefore, I shall remain here until he says what he ought to.*

Soon after Bess made this resolution, Jack lowered his voice and asked, "Did you hear about Curtis?" Bess shook her head, and her enthusiasm heightened. *Perhaps his behavior has* nothing *to do with me.* "We received a letter communicating his late marriage," Jack said and took a deep breath. "Her name is Miss Francesca Telley. She's American, and so is her father—I'm unsure how far back their lineage goes. Nevertheless, they're all unionists living in Boston—I assume he docked around there. I'm not surprised, though," he added, glancing toward the fireplace. "He says that she's rich, and her deep roots make her family fairly reputable. Miss Telley—now Mrs. Elmsworth—knows about Lydia, but I doubt Curtis mentioned Martha and their child to her," he concluded, shaking his head. Bess pursed her lips, lost for words on how to respond. She opened her mouth to sympathize, but Jack said, "However, I'm somewhat happy for him. He's settled down, and he seems to be doing well. Perhaps his wife is a good person, who will respect him. Perhaps when she realizes how terrible he is, she'll feel obligated to stay married, and perhaps her positive influence will affect him." Bess nodded, unsure of what else to say. She sat in silence for about a quarter of an hour before finally deciding to leave. She wished

Jack and his mother, who insisted on lending her a coat, a farewell before making her way to the town in now rainless conditions.

Chapter 28

When she had reached the outskirts of the town, Bess was pleased to hear resounding cheers reverberating to her left. After crossing the creek, passing Lady Madeleine's, and turning a corner, Bess reached a square packed with about half a hundred gatherers. Amid the crowd was a dirt court with uneven chalk marks outlining the perimeter to indicate boundaries. At the corner of the street, Bess stood beside a young boy, who was cheering for one of the teams. With a smile, Bess looked up but was shocked to find half of the boys shirtless! To her greater astonishment, they were neither pale nor restive from the temperature. Bess scanned the shirtless boys and was relieved to see that Abigail was *not* among them.

In fact, Abigail was standing by the opposite boundary line, jumping on the balls of her feet. Bess looked away from her sister and returned her gaze to the game. Although she couldn't understand what was so exciting every time a player did a neat trick to maneuver around a defender, she applauded. Bess glanced over to see if Abigail, too, was clapping, but instead, Bess found her younger sister engaged in a playful conversation with the familiar figure of Callum.

A few minutes elapsed before Abigail and Callum, both with dying laughter, entered the game. And for the third time in the last five minutes, Bess' mouth dropped. Abigail had stripped herself to short sleeves! *In fairness, I suppose she'll be warm from running around, but her being casual in front of so many people is unfathomable!* Bess tried to ignore Abigail's absurdity, and instead, she returned her focus to the game. Truthfully, she had no idea what was going on, so she decided to watch her sister's body language. Abigail seemed very natural every time the ball arrived at her feet. She would do some neat trick, pass the ball, and the crowd would cheer. Out of curiosity, Bess scanned the other players and noticed that Abigail was the *only* girl playing. She smiled.

Halfway through the match, the teams paused. Bess watched as some players removed their shirts while others reclothed themselves. And to Bess' relief, Abigail remained on the shirted team. Soon, the second half began, and as Abigail ran down the line next to Bess, she turned her head and caught her sister's eye. Out of sheer surprise, Abigail tripped and fell to the ground. Bess covered her mouth with her hands and instinctually took a step forward to help her sister. But Abigail stood up and brushed herself off. Some of her teammates and opponents began to laugh, and Bess' face reddened, for she didn't think that it was right for these *kids* to make fun of her sister. However, to Bess' surprise, Abigail smiled and laughed at herself, too.

"Bess!" she exclaimed. "I didn't know you'd come!" Bess hardly had time to reply before Abigail received the ball and dribbled down the pitch. She made an excellent shot, scored, turned, and ran into the arms of her teammates. Bess couldn't help but smile.

Shortly thereafter, the match ended. Bess had been too intrigued by the unfamiliar dynamics of football to focus on the length of the game or how cold it was outside. In fact, by the end of the match, she was cheering alongside the crowd. Before long, Abigail, who was somehow sweating, approached Bess with her hands casually placed on her hips.

"Well done," Bess applauded, pulling her sister in an embrace.

"Bessie, I'm hot!" Abigail laughed, pushing Bess away.

Moments later, Bess noticed Callum running up behind her sister. When he was within a short distance, he tapped Abigail on the shoulder and said, "Abbie, we're meeting tomorrow to play. Can you come?"

"Ah," Abigail stammered, "I don't think so. I'll see, but it's Christmas."

Callum interrupted, "The day after then?" And before Abigail replied, Callum turned to Bess and said, "Hi, you're Abbie's sister, right?"

"Uh-huh," Bess said with a smile, for she was captivated by Callum's appearance, despite having seen him before. His dirty blonde hair, blue eyes, and crooked smile gave him a boyish charm, which stupefied her. Bess turned to Abigail, whose face was red with embarrassment. But before anyone could utter another word, a crowd of players approached Callum, insisting on competing in another match.

A handsome, dark-haired boy, who was leading the group, stepped forward and asked, "Abbie, do you want to play?"

Abigail pursed her lips. "I've got to head home with my sister, but—"

"Go ahead. Play another," Bess interrupted. With crinkled eyes, red cheeks, and a priceless smile, Abigail thanked her sister. Bess watched as she and her friends returned to the street. Fewer boys remained, and thus, fewer people were in the crowd, but Bess didn't mind. Once Callum organized the newest teams, they began to play.

While observing the second game, Bess crossed her arms to keep warm. Approximately a quarter of an hour later, she watched the ball roll out of bounds, and within that instant, she spotted an old couple standing beside a run-down house. Yearning for social interaction, Bess approached them, and when she was within a few yards, they looked up and recoiled. *I suppose they can tell that I'm from a wealthier part of town.* She paused. *I am wearing two coats compared to their thin ones, but never before have I seen anyone recoil at my presence.* In a quiet voice, Bess asked the couple, "Do you have a family member who is playing?"

With a look of surprise, the old woman, who was shivering, replied, "Our son Daniel." And after a momentary pause, she sneered, "Do *you*?"

"Yes," Bess replied. She took a deep breath, smiled, and added, "My sister Abigail."

Suddenly, the old man exclaimed, "*You're* Abbie's sister?"

"Oh," Bess laughed, turning to the man, "Yes. Why are you surprised?"

"She's such an unusual girl," the woman continued. "But I must admit she *does* have a passion for the game. Daniel talks about her all the time."

"Yes?" Bess asked, watching as Abigail maneuvered around an opponent.

"Lucy," the man interjected, "she's much better than—"

"Now, Eugene—"

"She is?" Bess jumped.

"Oh yes," he continued, despite his wife's glare, "everyone *loves* to watch her play. She's very talented, and it's admirable that she spends so much time here considering that—"

"She's rich," his wife retorted, crossing her arms.

"Oh," Bess laughed nervously. "Truthfully, our father doesn't know about it, but she loves playing with them." Bess turned to the woman but noticed that her nose was stuck in the air. Bess tried, "Which one is your son?"

"The one closest to this goal," she answered, pointing to the dark-haired boy whom Bess had previously seen. Bess nodded but chose to cease talking, for the woman did not seem fond of associating with her.

A half an hour passed in silence before Bess turned to check on the man and his wife. Noticing their shivering, Bess stepped toward them and took off her coats.

"Here," she emphasized, offering them each a coat. "Take these. I'm rather warm."

"Thank you," the man trembled. He extended his arm, but his wife interjected.

"No, Eugene. We don't need charity."

Bess blushed and thrust the coats farther forward. "I insist. We have plenty."

"No," the woman resolved, and Bess frowned. *Perhaps I shouldn't have emphasized that we have "plenty."* Bess held the coats in the crook of her arm to prove that she wasn't cold, but after a few minutes had passed and dark clouds hovered over the sun, she shivered. She made a second offer to the man and his wife, and the former, despite his wife's reluctance, accepted. A strong, cold wind drifted through the town, and soon enough, the wife agreed to take a coat, too.

"What is your name, Miss?" asked the man.

"Bess," she replied, exchanging a smile with her newest acquaintance. She extended her hand for the man and his wife to shake, but only the former returned the gesture. As if on cue, large drops of sleet began to fall from the sky, and the game was abandoned. Abigail ran off the court, pulled her coat over the upper half of her body, and turned around to greet her sister but was stopped by Callum. Despite being unable to hear what words passed between them, Bess stood and curiously watched her sister squeal with excitement.

When Abigail parted from her friend, she skipped toward Bess. Before addressing her sister, she said to the man and woman, "Good afternoon, Mr. and Mrs. Cobbler." Mr. Cobbler bowed his head, but his wife didn't budge. As the sisters started walking away, Abigail asked, "You gave your coats to Daniel's parents?" Bess nodded, and Abigail removed her coat, placing it around her sister's shivering, red arms. At first, Bess declined this gesture, but her younger sister insisted. And before Bess was able to express her gratitude, Abigail started, "I had *no* idea that you were planning to come, Bessie! I was going to suggest it, but I thought that it was too cold, and you wouldn't want to stand around for so long. In any case, I hope you enjoyed watching me play. I think that I did better than usual, and that's because you were there. At the end, even Callum told me I was exceptional today!" she laughed. "And letting me stay longer made me *so* happy—you have no idea!"

"I'm glad that I came," Bess replied with a smile. "Mr. Cobbler told me that you're well known in that area of town."

"Oh, you got along well with them?" Abigail inquired as her face brightened. "Mrs. Cobbler was especially difficult for me to get to know."

"She certainly was!" Bess agreed, but neither sister continued on that subject. After a momentary pause, Bess asked, "What did Callum say that made you so happy?"

"Oh," Abigail said with a pause. "I told you—he said that I played well." Bess nodded, but she was too numb to respond.

Standing before the threshold of Laurel Manor, Bess returned Abigail's coat. After Abigail had safely placed it in the crook of her arm, Bess opened the front door to discover her father, Miss Henwood, and Mr. Roberts on the other side of the entryway, dressed in their best attire. Abigail tried to hide, for she did not want to be seen in boy's clothing, but she was too slow. Mr. Phillips said, "Abigail, what are you wearing?

We have to leave soon, and Bess," he choked, turning to his older daughter, "where is your coat?"

"Father," Abigail murmured, "sometimes I like to play with friends in—"

"We visited Elmsworth Manor to wish Jack and his family a happy Christmas," Bess interrupted. She caught a glimpse of Mr. Roberts, who was quiet in contemplation, and turned away. Mr. Phillips took a deep breath and glanced sideways at Miss Henwood before allowing his daughters to return upstairs and change into proper dinner attire.

Chapter 29

Once the front door to Mulberry Cottage opened, Bess and Abigail pushed past their father to embrace their elder sister, who was wearing uncharacteristically modest attire. She chuckled and greeted her sisters, but upon glancing up at her other guests, she blushed. When she was able to break away, Jane welcomed her father and Miss Henwood before turning to Mr. Roberts, "It's a pleasure to see you again," she said, bowing her head but unable to hide her surprise at her guest's loss of weight.

Mr. Roberts' tone deepened as he replied, "I'm glad to see you, too, Jane." Bess stood back, admiring this strange encounter but thought nothing of it when her eyes landed on Alex. Since the wedding, Bess had not seen her closest friend. He had never accompanied Jane to Laurel Manor, so Bess was cautious about approaching him. She was unsure how he would react.

With a massive smile, Alex stepped forward and pulled the younger Phillips sisters into his arms. "Happy Christmas, girls!" Once she was able to break away, Bess took a step back. *Does he mean to be so degrading by calling me* girl *instead of Bess?* She frowned. *At least he seems happy, but is this how we'll forevermore behave toward one another?*

Once the introductions had concluded, Alex's father Mr. Cawdor invited his guests to the dining hall, where the first of three courses was almost assembled. Bess took her seat beside Abigail while noticing Alex opt for a chair at the opposite end of the table. Bess frowned before redirecting her attention to the end of the table where Mr. Cawdor sat. *If I was married, I wouldn't want to live with my husband's parents. And*

Jane, who's fantasized over marriage longer than anyone I know, probably doesn't either. Bess looked around with dismay. *Jane has always looked forward to the grander parts of marriage, so living in a cottage must not be ideal for her. I wonder if she's happy.*

Once everyone had settled, Miss Henwood spoke, complimenting the Christmas decorations, which consisted of an ornamented tree and ribbons dangling from the ceiling.

"That's Jane's work," Mr. Cawdor replied, turning to his daughter-in-law with a smile.

"They're charming. And oh—the tree is absolutely...." Miss Henwood continued, and for the next quarter of an hour, Jane was flattered with compliments. Bess turned to Alex, whom she hoped would exchange an irritated look with her, for this topic of conversation was useless, but she found him gazing at Jane. Bess sighed. After some confusion, the Cawdor's servant hastily served the first course: carrot and ginger stew.

"Excellent stew," Mr. Roberts applauded, looking upward. "Jane, did you prepare this?"

With a blush, Jane replied, "No. Mrs. Cawdor made it, for it was her mother's recipe."

"It's delectable," responded Mr. Roberts, nodding toward his hostess. A few minutes elapsed before he added, "It's been so long since I've seen many of you. Jane, I'd like to formally congratulate you and Alex—" he started, turning to the couple, "on the—"

"Thank you," Alex interrupted, and despite being cut off, Mr. Roberts smiled.

Jane glared sideways at Alex but continued, "Mr. Roberts, do you plan to marry soon?"

Mr. Roberts chuckled, which caused Bess to glance up and raise an eyebrow. Then he paused and considered his answer before saying, "I had one person in mind, but I don't believe it'll work out." Before she could help it, Bess looked to Mr. Roberts, whom she hoped was looking in her direction. *He seemed to fancy me at the Henwood wedding. And we had a pleasant conversation this morning. Besides, at this rate, my relationship with Jack is stagnant. Perhaps I ought to—oh, but I couldn't!* Bess frowned. *He's Mr. Charles Henwood's brother!*

Then, in a quiet voice, Alex mentioned, "Bess is supposed to marry Mr. Jackson Elmsworth soon." All eyes turned toward Bess, and in return, she looked at Alex, whose glossy eyes were glued to the table. From the corner of her eye, Bess noticed Abigail shake her head.

"Oh," Bess stammered. "No. We're not getting married."

"What a shame," Mr. Roberts said. "He's a handsome man, who seems to like you."

Bess frowned. "Of course, it *could* happen," she said, glaring at Alex, who remained stiff.

With sudden amusement, Miss Henwood put down her spoon and said, "Yes?"

"I suppose," Bess fumbled. "We're good friends, so we're as likely to marry as any good friends are."

"Oh," Miss Henwood sighed, returning to her stew.

"Well," Mr. Roberts said, "I wish you the best."

"Thank you," Bess mumbled. Over the next hour, the second and third dishes came out. Roasted goose, Yorkshire pudding, mince pies, and other assortments decorated the table, and the same compliments Jane had received at the start of the evening were given to Mrs. Cawdor and her servant. After dinner, Mr. Cawdor invited his guests to reconvene in the drawing-room, where Mr. Roberts announced that he had gifts to share. Despite feeling guilty for not having a gift in return, Bess watched as Mr. Roberts removed about a half a dozen little packages and cards from his overcoat.

When Bess received hers, she examined the package with intrigue. *Why would Mr. Roberts hand out gifts to people he hardly knows?* Moments later, the sound of paper ripping filled the room, and Bess soon discovered that Mr. Roberts had made her a charm out of strings and gemstones. The note attached read: *I hope this charm gives you the best of luck as you learn to adjust to an environment without your sister Jane. Happy Christmas.* Bess smiled, noticing that Abigail had received a matching gift. Indeed, when she looked up, Bess saw that *everyone* received a charm with a letter attached. While each recipient thanked Mr. Roberts, Bess couldn't help but notice that Jane was *still* reading her letter, which was, to Bess' surprise, an entire page long! Bess watched her sister with skepticism, but Jane made no reaction. *I wonder if Jane's letter relates to Mr. Roberts' interesting personality. Until now, I've never seen him do anything seriously suspicious, but Miss Rachel Henwood once held an awful opinion of him. Perhaps she* wasn't *mistaken.*

The remainder of the evening was fraught with badinage and other needless discussions. At one point, Curtis' marriage, which surprised many of the guests, was announced. Bess voiced her knowledge, but otherwise, she hardly spoke. When Mr. Phillips was preparing to leave, Bess hugged her elder sister and wished her the happiest of Christmases. But when she turned to address Alex, she found that he wasn't anywhere to be seen. With a sense of longing, she said, "And tell Alex I wish him the same."

"Of course," Jane replied.

During the carriage ride back to Laurel Manor, Bess occasionally glanced at Mr. Roberts, who was sitting across from her in the carriage. *Despite how suspicious he might be, he's an admirable gentleman. How thoughtful it was of him to make a gift for everyone!* Bess yearned to ask him what he wrote to Jane, but she refrained from doing so, for he was staring through the carriage window, deep in thought. Instead, she thought of how handsome he was. *I'm glad he lost weight, for he's much more attractive now.*

When the carriage halted, Mr. Roberts allowed everyone to exit ahead of him. Bess and Abigail hastened toward Laurel Manor, for they were bubbling to chat.

"What do you think Mr. Roberts' letter to Jane said? Did you see it?" Abigail asked.

"Oh, I saw it," Bess confirmed. "But I have no idea. And I couldn't guess, for Jane made no overt reaction to it."

"That's *exactly* what I thought! And Jane never keeps anything from us," Abigail said in a flustered manner. Then she corrected, "Well, she never keeps anything from *me*."

Bess rolled her eyes and said, "She didn't even *hint* at something?" Abigail shook her head. But by the time they reached the entrance to Laurel Manor, they were too close to Mr. Roberts to finish their conversation. Even when Mr. Roberts and Miss Henwood returned to their bedrooms, the younger Phillips sisters held their tongues, for they didn't want their father to overhear their suppositions.

Chapter 30

The new year offered a chance for Bess to reestablish her friendships with Jack and Alex, among others. Although this resolution was optimistic, her plans did not come to fruition. She frequently penned letters to Jack but never received any in return. And she could never bring herself to send anything she had written to Alex, for none of her words sounded right. She and her father grew slightly closer, however, since he was the only one who was ever available to accompany her in her daily pursuits, such as outdoor walks and book discussions.

At the height of Bess' frustration and boredom, she decided to walk over to Elmsworth Manor to demand a response from Jack. She started to make her way toward her front door but was surprised to hear a knock resounding from outside. Curiously, she peaked through an adjacent window and found Juliette standing alone. Bess swung the door open and started to inquire over Juliette's presence, but Juliette did not allow her the time to get halfway through her question. She stepped forward and embraced Bess, exclaiming, "Bess! How happy I am that you are here! I don't return to my schooling until next week, and—is Abigail here?"

Bess shook her head. "She's at school."

"In town?" Juliette inquired, and when Bess nodded her head, she continued, "I would have guessed that you'd have governesses, not—"

"Jane and I were taught by an old governess who passed away before she could complete Abigail's curriculum."

"Oh, yes. Of course," Juliette interrupted. Then she lowered her voice and added, "Lately, I've been thinking a lot."

Bess sighed, "About what?"

"The subject I told you about last," she said, raising her eyebrows.

And with sudden irritation, for Bess had been bored and thus too impatient to tolerate Juliette's silliness, she snapped, "Would you *just* tell me? I can't remember *everything* you say."

"Oh." Juliette drew back. Bess blushed and opened her mouth to apologize, but her young friend continued, "I meant to address Leonarda's liking of Mr. Ashford."

"I apologize," Bess interjected. "I didn't intend—" She sighed, "How *is* that situation?"

"Oh!" Juliette giggled, seeming to neglect Bess' rude remark. "It's marvelous! Mr. Ashford visited for Christmas Eve dinner, and he and Leonarda got along very well. They spent half the evening in intimate conversation," she said, smiling in recollection. During Juliette's narration, Bess led her guest to the drawing-room, where she lit the fireplace and ordered the servants to make two cups of tea. With increasing enthusiasm, Juliette bounced around before settling onto the sofa beside the fireplace. "I think that their relationship is progressing! Perhaps they'll be married soon and—"

"But Leonarda is *so* young," Bess intervened, sinking into the chair across from Juliette.

"Yes, but they seem perfect for one another!" She nodded before taking a deep breath. "Do you recall when I said that Mr. Ashford seemed odd? Now, I rescind my remark, for he's certainly the nicest gentleman in the world! For Christmas, he bought me—I mean, Leonarda—one of these lovely diamond necklaces, and the only explanation I can devise is that it's a sign of affection. Bess," she said, and Bess, who was losing her concentration, snapped awake, "once you meet someone, how long is it until you're married?"

280

Bess covered her mouth with her hands to conceal her laughter. *Oh, how naïve Juliette can be!* Then she paused and bit her lip. *I've known Alex for forever, and Jack and I have been acquainted for months. Perhaps Juliette's question isn't as ridiculous as I first thought.* Bess sighed. "I suppose it depends, Juliette. But as I said before, *I'm* not the person to be asking. Consider talking to Jane, for she's married."

"Oh, but Jane's so—" Juliette stammered. "I could *never* talk to her!"

"What do you mean?" Bess asked, leaning forward and furrowing her brow.

"Oh, I mean that Jane is—I feel like she is—well, she's *untouchable*. She's beautiful, older, married—I c*ouldn't* ask her. But you, Bess, are perhaps the greatest friend I've ever had," she gushed. "You listen to me, which is much more than I can say about anyone else, and you give such good advice. I don't feel… *intimidated*, I suppose, when I talk to you."

Bess sat back, examining Juliette's countenance. *She can't possibly admire me. Earlier, I insulted her!* Bess pursed her lips as she watched Juliette's genuine smile fade into a sigh. *Yet, somehow she* does *look up to me. And how strange! Before Emma and Juliette, I've never received such wonderful compliments before!* Then Bess sat forward. "And you truly mean to compliment me?" she asked, unable to conceal a smile.

Juliette giggled. "You're like a sister to me, Bess."

Bess beamed. "Well," she chirped, "I suppose, concerning Gus, anything could happen. Although Leonarda *is* young, if this situation involves true love, I would expect an engagement soon. I think," she said, recalling the first time she met Mr. Ashford at the Westfield ball, "Gus is straightforward when communicating his affection. I'm certain he'd like to settle down and marry once he finds the right woman."

"Oh, but *how* soon will that be? Leonarda isn't even out of school yet."

Comprehending Juliette's true intentions, Bes chuckled, "I'm unsure. How long has this quasi relationship lasted?"

"A few weeks," Juliette answered, sitting at the edge of her seat. "Well, perhaps it's been a couple of months."

"You could always ask him what his intentions are," Bess suggested.

"No!" Juliette exclaimed. "If I asked him and all of my suppositions are incorrect—oh, I *couldn't*, Bess!" But realizing her error in revealing that *she*, not Leonarda, fancied Mr. Ashford, Juliette blushed. "It's me!" she cried, covering her face with her hands. "*I* like Mr. Ashford." She took a deep breath before starting to shake. And Bess, who had never been a good sympathizer, sat still and watched this scene unfold. Finally, Bess sighed, stood up, crossed the drawing-room, and sat down beside her friend. She reached across Juliette and started to rub her back. But Juliette's whimpers only heightened. She uncovered her red eyes and moaned, "Oh, but I could never admit to liking him." Bess opened her mouth to question Juliette's assertion but was too slow. "Because if I admitted my feelings to him or anyone else, I'd be humiliated! Even if I lost interest, I'd be *known* for having liked him," she sniffled. "Also, I've never seen the value in courtships or marriage, so by fancying Mr. Ashford, I'm going against my nature!" Suddenly, Juliette grew silent. Bess wiped a tear from her friend's eye, but it didn't take long for Juliette to continue. "I've always said I don't like dances." Juliette paused. "*That's* true—I don't enjoy dancing *with gentlemen*, but I love to dance. I love to dance with Leonarda, and if I had other female friends, then I would like to dance with them." She frowned. "But by dancing with a gentleman, I'd feel out-of-place. If I danced with Mr.

Ashford, I'd be falling into the societal convention that females *must* depend on gentlemen, and I'm an individual. I can't—" But Juliette fell silent. She stared at the fireplace, looking hollow. "If I could pretend Leonarda liked him, then I could experiment. I'd watch how society would react. I'd observe how *Mr. Ashford* would react. But now," she sighed, turning to Bess, "*you* know. I trust that you won't say anything, but now, my secret is out. Oh," she cried, "this situation is so difficult to explain! Essentially, I *like* Mr. Ashford, but I couldn't be with him! If he liked me, too, then I'd have to reconsider. But oh, then I could never be myself again, and—"

"I understand." Bess nodded. "And it's all right." But Juliette's flustered expression communicated that this message was *not* what she wanted to hear. Bess paused. "What if we forget about Gus and society, and instead, we dance together?" she suggested with a smile. "Afterward, we can indulge in what you *truly* want and see if Gus likes you."

With dried tears dotting her cheeks, Juliette looked up and smiled. Moments later, Bess started humming to a song, and the two girls joined together, dancing an improvised jig. When she had run out of notes to hum, Bess took Juliette's arms and twirled her around. Juliette laughed and returned the gesture. And until the clock struck to indicate that an hour had passed, the girls danced as if their lives depended upon it. Then Juliette hopped out the door after accepting Bess' invitation to visit the next day.

"Tomorrow, we can plan out what you'll say to Gus!" laughed Bess when Juliette was halfway down the walkway. Juliette blushed and wished her hostess a farewell. Bess closed the front door and smiled, for tomorrow, Juliette would be a lovely companion.

Chapter 31

When the following morning arrived, Bess received a letter from Jane. She tore the envelope open and skimmed the contents, discovering that Jane was in *urgent* need of company. Bess felt a surge of anxiety course through her as she reluctantly wrote to Juliette, detailing her reason for having to postpone their plans. She instructed a servant to deliver the message, and then she spent the remainder of the afternoon wondering what Jane's cause of distress could be. *Perhaps Alex isn't displaying the proper affection for which Jane yearns.* Bess bit her lip in contemplation. *However, this explanation would be unwarranted, for I had made it very clear to Alex that we could not continue our usual level of intimacy. And other than myself, there's no one whom he fancies more.* Bess frowned. *Well, I suppose that Jane could be upset about the Cawdor's situation in life. Yet, I'm sure Jane's too polite to make this the chief cause of her seeming anguish—right?* But luckily, Bess' considerations were addressed a few minutes after Jane welcomed her into Mulberry Cottage.

Once Bess crossed over the threshold, Jane leapt forward and held her sister in a tight embrace. Bess laughed and returned the gesture, despite being anxious to hear of Jane's concern. When she took a step back, Bess observed her sister, whose clothing was covered in paint droplets. She cocked her head. "Have you been painting?" Jane nodded, and Bess smiled.

As Jane led her sister to the drawing-room, she made the usual inquiries about Bess and her family's well-being. Of course, Bess returned this show of manners when she asked about Alex and his parents. After ensuring that nobody was nearby, Jane took hold of her sister's hands and whispered, "Bessie, I'm—I'm—" She paused and took a deep breath. She glanced down at her paint-covered attire and mumbled, "I'm unhappy."

Bess' thumping heart stopped. She looked around as if expecting someone to enter the drawing-room. Then she whispered, "What?"

Jane took a deep breath. She rubbed her eyes with the back of her hand and whispered in a wavering voice, "The first few days of our marriage went well. Alex and I enjoyed ourselves, but (and I'm sure you noticed at Christmas) we're *so* distant. I've always thought that we had this special connection, but for a while, it's felt like we don't even live together! He spends time with me when we have guests over, but other than that, he's never around." She sighed. "I've had to occupy myself with activities, such as painting, but I miss home!" she cried. "Is this what marriage is like, Bessie? Because I would much rather be at Laurel Manor with my—my *real* family."

"Oh, Jane!" Bess frowned and rubbed her sister's trembling back. "If it helps, at Christmas I thought the two of you were perfect for one another, and I'm sure—"

"It's almost as if he's in another world," Jane continued as a tear ran down her cheek. "And when I *try* to rekindle our connection, it becomes hard for me to remember what we had in the first place!"

"Did he say anything to you after the first couple of days? Did *you* say anything that would have made him... worry?" she hesitated to say.

"No, no," Jane sobbed, burying her head in Bess' shoulder. Bess took a deep breath. She lifted her head and stared at the opposite wall in contemplation. Then she heard a strange noise from outside of the drawing-room. Bess hesitated to inspect its origin but was soon

285

enlightened when she caught a glimpse of what seemed to be Alex running by.

Bess rolled her eyes and started to move Jane aside. "Excuse me, Jane," she whispered, placing Jane's head on a cotton pillow beside the sofa. "I'll be right back," she said as she exited the room. Once she was far enough from her sister, Bess whispered, "Alex?" Suddenly, she took a step back as the pale face of Alex rounded the corner. He opened his mouth to greet his friend, but Bess was the first to speak. "Alex, *why* am *I* the one comforting your wife?"

Alex sighed before trying to create some humor. "You're her sister." But Bess only frowned. Alex placed his hand to his forehead. He murmured, "Bess." Then in a weaker voice, he repeated, "Bess—Bess, she wants to have children." And once these words emerged from Alex's lips, Bess froze. She had never considered being an aunt before, but because Alex didn't seem pleased with this notion, she grew both curious and confused. "She told me two days after the wedding," he added.

Bess folded her arms across her chest. She replied, "*I* wouldn't mind being an aunt."

"I'm not ready to be a father," Alex uttered.

"Did you tell Jane that?" Bess shot back, and Alex didn't reply. After a few seconds, he shook his head, and although Bess was interested in hearing his explanation, she turned around and returned to comfort Jane, who was still in tears.

When Bess entered the drawing-room, Jane looked up and murmured, "You spoke to him?" Bess nodded, and she whimpered, "And he told you about—"

"Mhm."

"I apologize that I didn't tell you before, but I was embarrassed," Jane moaned. She sat up and wiped the tears from her cheeks. "But I don't understand. I thought that he would be *just* as eager as I am to grow our family."

"Jane," Bess interrupted, "you and Alex *just* got married."

"So, I shouldn't have said anything?" she asked. "I *knew* I shouldn't have—"

"No, it's *good* that you said something. It's *good* to establish a line of communication."

"Oh, it's *all* my fault!" Bess was taken aback by this remark, and she asked for an explanation. Jane continued, "If our marriage falls apart, it will *all* be my fault!"

"Jane!" Bess cried, turning impatient. "Your marriage will *not* end after two months! All you must do is learn to communicate better. *I* shouldn't have to keep being the mediator."

"*Keep* being the mediator?" Jane started, and Bess froze.

She blushed and hastily added, "Is that what I said? I don't believe I said that, and if I did, I didn't *mean* it." She rubbed her eyes, feeling immensely guilty but knowing that *this* response was the only plausible solution. To ensure that she wouldn't have to lie anymore, Bess stood to her feet. "I ought to go home now." Jane glanced up at her sister with worry plastered across her face. "Jane, I *know* that you can figure this out." Jane opened her mouth to respond, but Bess had already left.

Chapter 32

Bess climbed the staircase to the entrance of Laurel Manor with raging thoughts bouncing around in her mind. She swung the front door open and slammed it shut but paused when she heard movement in the drawing-room. She tiptoed across the entrance hall, poked her head around the corner, and to her utter surprise, discovered Juliette sitting at the tea table. Bess started making her way toward her friend, but Juliette turned around with a pen clutched between her fingers and squealed, "Bess—!"

"Didn't you receive my letter? I tried to reschedule."

Juliette shook her head. She held up a yellow slip of paper on which she had been writing and said, "And if you were curious, one of your servants let me inside." She laughed, "I didn't just let *myself* in." Bess took a deep breath and managed to chuckle. She sat down beside her friend and picked up the letter. Then she cleared her throat and read—

"My dear Mr. Ashford,

I beg you don't assume that I'm a hopeless romantic. I've never manifested any signs of affection before, so I sincerely pray my feelings are returned. Well, I love you, Mr. Ashford—or Gus, shan't I call you that now? I'm only joking, not about my emotions, but regarding the nickname. For months, I've kept this secret, and what a burden it's been! My dearest friend, Miss Elizabeth Phillips, encouraged me to write to you. She's given me hope that you like me, too, and—"

Bess sighed, putting down the letter.

Juliette blushed and asked, "You don't like it?" She grabbed hold of the paper and read it over. "Should I rephrase *I beg*? Oh, yes—it makes me sound like a pauper." Analyzing Bess' neutral expression, she added, "Oh, no. *That's* all right, but do you mean that I ought to omit *pray*? Does it make me sound too pious? Is Mr. Ashford an atheist?"

"Juliette—"

"Oh, Bess," she interjected, "*don't* tell me. You *hate* being called Miss Elizabeth Phillips," she concluded, scratching the paper with the tip of her pen. "I'll just write Bess."

"Juliette!" Bess interrupted with a frown. She sighed, "I'm no expert, but I thought, perhaps, since we're trying to figure out *if* he likes you, we should be subtle."

"Oh, of course, Bess." Juliette nodded and flipped the letter to its back side. She shook her head, reprimanding herself for giving way to such ridiculous ideas. "*To my Mr. Ashford....*"

"*To Mr. Augustus Ashford* will do. You don't want to sound so eager."

"Of course," Juliette said, scribbling down these words. She paused and looked up.

Bess shrugged, "Tell him why you're writing."

"Oh, all right. *I am writing to you because*—" Juliette looked up to Bess again.

"I don't know!" Bess threw her arms up in the air. Then she cringed, realizing that she was starting to sound like Jane. "Perhaps: *Some of our friends have noticed that you appear to fancy me and*—I don't know, Juliette. I'm not great at this."

"Do you think this is a bad idea? Because the more I think about it, the less I want to do it. I'm *perfectly* happy living at home with Leonarda and my parents. I don't know if I—"

But a knock on the front door interrupted Juliette. Both girls looked at each other with widened eyes, for they were doing something uncharacteristic of themselves. *If Alex is at the door, I'd hate for him to see me writing a love letter.* Bess shuttered. She hesitated but soon excused herself. Walking through the hallway, she turned red at the sight of Jack's silhouette. Her heart pounded, for she had not seen Jack in weeks, and she gingerly opened the door.

"Jack?" Bess questioned. She smiled and let him inside, but her mind started to race. *Jack has never visited me at Laurel Manor before—aside from at Jane's wedding. And now that it's on my mind: how inconvenient it's always been to walk to Elmsworth Manor! How impolite of Jack to always make me—*but Bess shook her head, doing her best to neglect these accusatory thoughts. For all she knew, she and Jack could marry one day. *Yet, there* must *be something wrong, for why else would he come?*

Jack scratched his head, looked down at his shoes, and answered, "Thank you for letting me inside." He glanced around, not to admire the building but to see if anyone was in the vicinity. Upon confirming that he and Bess were alone, he removed his hands from his pockets. He took Bess' chin in his palms and kissed her on the lips. It was a short kiss, full of affection, but Bess pulled away in shock. She blushed and hastily turned around to see if Juliette was watching. Jack bit his lip and asked, "Is someone here?"

"Juliette," Bess exhaled as her eyes bulged out of her head.

"Juliette? My cousin?" Jack repeated with a frown. Bess opened her mouth to mention the kiss, but Jack pushed her aside and found his way to the drawing-room. When Jack and Bess entered, Juliette looked up from her letter. She gasped, folded the paper, and slipped it under her chair, but Jack had already caught a glimpse of the header. He turned to Bess and exhibited a coy grin. Then he snatched the note from Juliette and read, *"To Mr. Augustus Ashford—I am writing to let you know that in addition to some of our friends' remarks that we would be a great couple, I, too, believe this to be the case. I've always admired you as a handsome man, and if you—*If you what?"

"Well, I was *going* to tell him," Juliette stuttered, "that—that if he's available to marry, he would be my ideal—"

"Marriage?" Bess exclaimed, turning red. She turned to examine Jack's reaction and found that he was exploding with laughter.

"Well, yes. I thought that—" Juliette stammered.

"We were going to inquire," Bess clarified, "if Gus fancied Juliette because she—"

"Well, just ask him." Jack shrugged. He returned his hands to his pockets and added, "His house is only a mile away." Juliette blushed but refused to say a word. She turned to Bess for advice, but Bess didn't flinch.

"I suppose you *could* simply ask him, Juliette," Bess started.

She lowered her eyes and groaned, "Could you come along then?"

Bess raised an eyebrow, "To Gus'?" Juliette nodded, and Bess sighed. She tucked a strand of hair behind her ear and turned to Jack. She inquired if he cared to join them, but he shook his head and complained that he was too tired. Apparently, the journey from

Elmsworth Manor to Laurel Manor was exhausting enough, and another trip would "nearly kill him."

"You two can go together, or Juliette can go alone," he insisted. "I want to stay here and—"

But Juliette, who was quivering with anxiety, moaned, "I don't know my way—"

"We'll go," Bess concluded. She exchanged a smile with Juliette, and from the corner of her eye, she examined Jack's reaction. He frowned but said nothing more, and Bess found herself lost in thought again. *Jack's behavior this afternoon has been very unusual. I cannot even begin to pinpoint his reason for traveling here, and he has offered no explanation to his outward signs of affection.* She took a deep breath. *Quite frankly, I'm bubbling over with too many emotions today, and I cannot focus on him.* She clenched her teeth and tried to block Jack's complexity out of her mind. She marched into the entrance hall, approached the door, and perched her hand over the doorknob but was startled to find the door swing back into her. Crossing the threshold was the frail figure of her father chuckling alongside Miss Henwood.

Amid laughter, Mr. Phillips nodded toward his daughter and inquired after her plans. Bess replied that she and the others were heading to Mr. Ashford's house, and Mr. Phillips smiled and waved them away. Bess rolled her eyes. *I suppose I could have said that I was planning on running away to join the American Civil War, and he wouldn't have minded.*

As she made her way down the walkway to the carriage in which her father had recently ridden, Bess overheard Jack ask Miss Henwood how she was. Miss Henwood ceased to laugh. She cleared her throat and replied that she was doing well, but Bess could hear the peculiar smile in her tone.

During the carriage ride, nobody said a word. Juliette stared at her trembling hands while Jack glared out the window. More than once, Bess tried to capture his attention, for he had seemed so adamant about his affection, but her efforts were of no avail. *Did I say something wrong? Is he upset that I made him go to Gus'?* Bess reached toward him and stroked his arm. He acknowledged Bess' gesture with a smile but soon returned his gaze to the window. Bess frowned, but it was not long until the carriage halted before a small, run-down, one-story cottage. Countless dead trees lingered around the house's outer walls, and as Bess emerged from the coach, she noticed that the pathway leading to the entrance was covered in overgrown shrubbery.

She started forward but overheard Juliette murmuring something to Jack. She tried to listen but couldn't decipher a word and resolved that it was of no importance. Then she led the hike through the thickets and debris, and when she reached the front door to the Ashford's home, she knocked. A few minutes elapsed before Mr. Ashford, dressed in torn, faded clothing, answered the door. Bess' eyes widened and she took a step back. Disregarding the exterior of the cottage, she assumed that Mr. Ashford would uphold his affluent impression. She turned to assess Juliette's reaction, but Juliette was still on edge and seemed indifferent toward Mr. Ashford's appearance.

"Miss Phillips?" Mr. Ashford started. "Mr. Elmsworth? Miss Wheatley?" Upon mentioning his final guest, Mr. Ashford glanced at his attire and blushed. He shook his head and continued, "Were we expecting you? I apologize, for I was unaware."

Bess answered, "Oh, no. We arrived on short notice."

"Very well," Mr. Ashford said with a sigh. He straightened his clothing and readjusted a lock of his hair before inviting his guests inside. Once everyone had crossed the threshold, Mr. Ashford cleared his throat and shut the door. He rubbed his large nose and offered his guests some tea. Bess' first reaction was to decline, for she was skeptical about Mr. Ashford's method of preparing tea, but she overcame her judgment and accepted the warm beverage.

Mr. Ashford led his guests to the drawing-room while remarking that his parents were out of town. Bess occasionally nodded while examining her host's tight, dark abode but eventually found a seat on a three-legged stool. She watched as Mr. Ashford lit a fireplace before turning to check on Juliette. But to her surprise, Juliette's lips were poised an inch away from Jack's ear as she was whispering something discreet. With increasing curiosity, Bess analyzed her friends' body language and noticed that Jack was fidgeting with a box-shaped item in his coat pocket.

And Bess' jaw dropped. Her heart ceased to pump, and she turned pale. *He wants to marry me! No wonder he's been so distant lately—he's been planning the proposal. And oh!* She nearly fell off the stool with animation. *He kissed me because he must love me!* She settled herself on the seat but could not conceal her reddening cheeks. A smile encompassed the bottom half of her face, and she could not help but steal glances toward Jack, who had just broken apart from Juliette. He maintained a neutral expression, but Bess admired how well he could hide his emotions behind an indifferent facade. Mr. Ashford excused himself to prepare a pot of tea, but Bess was too busy fantasizing to notice.

When Mr. Ashford returned, and Juliette started talking, Bess remained oblivious. *I'll have to say yes. Jack and Alex are the only gentlemen for whom I've ever cared, and considering that I'm growing older, it's about time to get married! Mrs. Elizabeth Elmsworth....* Bess couldn't help but snatch another glance at Jack. Once again, he was staring off into the distance, but Bess smiled. *For the first time in a while, I know what he's thinking!* She blushed and readjusted her seated position, ensuring that there could be *no* cause in her appearance that could prevent Jack from fulfilling his plan.

And after what felt like seconds since they'd arrived, Juliette whimpered Bess' name.

"Hm?" Bess murmured as she cast her eyes toward her friend. But when she caught a glimpse of Juliette's tear-stained face, she came to her senses. She stood to her feet as her heart dropped, and she insisted that they return to Laurel Manor. She wished Mr. Ashford a hasty farewell and led her friends back to the carriage.

"And what he said—!" Juliette agonized as they entered the coach. "He said—did you hear it, Bess?" But to Bess' relief, Juliette continued without delay. "He said that he couldn't marry someone with such low—such little wealth!"

Jack's eyes shot up. He wore an irritated look as he scorned, "Does he *see* his house?"

"He wants to marry rich, and when I told him that being rich of mind is the equivalent, if not greater, to being rich regarding wealth, he laughed! Now, what gentleman does that?" she cried. "Well, he apologized for leading me on," she whimpered. "Oh, I'm so humiliated, and I never want to see him again!"

Bess bit her lip and reached over to comfort her friend, who was sitting on the bench beside her. "If he truly thinks that, then he's not good for you. Right, Jack?" Bess added, trying to gauge Jack's attention.

Jack's attention snapped back into the conversation, and he sputtered, "Uh-huh."

"But I was *so* certain!" she sobbed. "I'm glad I didn't send a letter. Then he would have had a record of it." Bess nodded and allowed Juliette's head to drop onto her shoulder. Her cheeks were hot and wet, but Bess didn't mind. She whispered consoling words to her young friend while noticing but not judging Jack's lack of concern.

Chapter 33

Upon entering Laurel Manor, Jack caught a glimpse of Miss Henwood, who was sitting in the drawing-room, and offered to escort her back to Henwood Mansion. Mr. Phillips protested, but his fiancée's consent quieted him. Then, with longing eyes and a furrowed brow, he watched the pair escape the manor. Bess watched this scene unfold with little intrigue. Jack's suspicious behavior would typically have been a mystery for her to contemplate, but now she *knew* why he had acted as such. *He must be asking Miss Henwood for her opinion on his marrying me! Because Father is disappointed, it seems that Jack hasn't communicated his intentions to anyone other than Juliette.* Bess felt a surge of excitement run through her, and as she headed to her bedroom, she almost forgot about Juliette, who was trailing behind her.

After closing the door behind her friend, Bess observed as Juliette sat on the bed and stared out the adjacent window. She grew startled by Juliette's mellow demeanor, but her considerations were shortly addressed. Juliette cleared her throat and started, "Crying is inappropriate. I should have never let myself get carried away." She paused. "Yet, I'm unsure why he gave the impression that he liked me. Perhaps I was too afflicted with excitement to distinguish between his friendship and seeming love."

Bess frowned, regretting her partial responsibility in this matter. She said, "You never seemed *so* convinced that you liked him. You said you might prefer to remain home with your family."

"Oh, yes," Juliette moaned. "I suppose I said that." Bess opened her mouth to inquire further, but Juliette continued, "Bess, I didn't want to articulate the whole truth, but now I see there's no other route to take."

She paused. "Honestly, I'm awfully lonely. I've spent my life alongside Leonarda and my parents with no other outlets. You might argue that the Elmsworths were a different sort for me, but only lately have I grown close with them." She sighed, "Bess, I'm coming upon the age wherein marriage is a necessity. I have no prospects, and truthfully, no *ideas*, but a few months ago, my parents told me that I ought to find a husband soon." Bess' languid eyes shot upward. *Never have I considered Mr. and Mrs. Wheatley to be absorbed in the conventional ideals of marriage. I had no idea that Juliette was feeling this pressure, but how lucky I was! Growing up, Mother and Father never spoke of marriage. Mother preached that she wanted us to do what makes us happy, married or unmarried.*

Bess sputtered, "Oh, Juliette—"

"Bess, I know that I needn't listen. I try to avoid conversations that revolve around institutions like marriage. It makes me feel commonplace, but I couldn't overcome this message. It hung over me like a dark cloud, and ironically, Mr. Ashford visited the following day. Perhaps my fantasies began then." She sighed, "Perhaps there was encouragement from my parents. I cannot recall—"

"Oh," Bess repeated. She lifted her arm and wrapped it around her friend, but Juliette did not notice. Bess' arm hung stiffly like a loose coat, and it soon fell back to her side.

"I'm the elder child, so it is my responsibility to be Leonarda's proper role model." She paused and glanced down at her hands. "Well, and if anything ever happened to my parents, I'd have to care for her, and if I wasn't married, then I—I *couldn't*."

Bess mumbled, "I wish that I could say something to help."

"Oh, Bess!" Juliette exclaimed. "Your listening is plenty! You needn't say a thing." Bess nodded. A moment of silence ensued before Juliette murmured, "Thank you, Bess, for all you've done." She rubbed her glossy eyes and continued, "Now that we've grown closer, there's something I ought to tell you." Bess bit her lip and felt her heartbeat rapidly increase. She considered that the subject of Jack's proposal was in the air, but when she caught a glimpse of her friend's solemn face, she frowned. Juliette tensed her shoulders and cleared her throat. Bess tilted her head with curiosity. "It's not *so* awful, but up until now, I've had to keep this from you for Jack's sake," she continued. Bess' heart fluttered, for perhaps she was mistaken. Could the subject of marriage be on the— "Jack and Miss Henwood are in love—*were,* I apologize. They *were* in love. Something came between them, and they broke it off." She paused in recollection. "I thought that you ought to know." Bess took a deep breath but didn't reply. *I had once suspected this fact to be true, but I have long since ridden myself of the idea. I suppose Juliette's confirmation is unsettling, but their former love shouldn't matter. Jack and I are to be married, and now that I know his secret, I'm not unsatisfied.* Juliette waited for Bess to reply but soon asked, "You haven't anything to say?"

Bess managed to laugh. "No, your situation with Gus is worse—*much* worse. This news hardly matters to me," she exhaled. "What, though, makes you say this?"

"Oh," Juliette said, returning a chuckle. "Well, I assumed that you and Jack were going to marry sometime, and I thought that you ought to know." She took a deep breath and smiled. Bess returned her grin and embraced her friend but not without the thought of marriage on her mind.

Chapter 34

Eventually, the wintry season of February arrived, but Bess' boredom had not waned. Her father and Miss Henwood had been busy planning their wedding for April. Meanwhile, Abigail and Juliette returned to school, and Jack was supposedly out of town. According to a letter he sent, he was visiting family and friends near Derbyshire, so Bess assumed that he was confirming his proposal plans before alerting her. With increasing anticipation, Bess mentally readied herself for her future marriage to Jack, and she spent her days roaming Laurel Manor with the expectation that she would soon reside at Elmsworth Manor.

Constant reading was not a sufficient pastime, and Bess often groaned to her father about her perpetual boredom. Mr. Phillips answered his daughter's complaints with an offer to organize a theater trip among their acquaintances. A new theater had recently opened downtown, and according to the critics, the shows were magnificent. Bess quickly accepted his proposition, for she hadn't seen any shows since her mother's death, and at this rate, *anything* was better than reading.

Accordingly, Mr. Phillips sent invitations to their usual acquaintances, including Mr. Roberts. Mr. Ashford and Miss Elmsworth, who felt ill, replied that they could not come, but Bess' intrigue enhanced when she learned that Jack would be arriving home in time to attend. She then resolved that he *must* be planning on proposing at the theater—it was a perfect location!

When the mentioned evening arrived, Bess dressed as well as she could. She imagined Jack wearing handsome attire, lowering himself to one knee, and confessing his undying love for her. Excitement ran through Bess' body as she exited her bedroom and encountered her father and Abigail. Mr. Phillips wore a waistcoat and trousers—his usual theater garments. Abigail, however, wore a plain yellow dress that matched her nest of half-heartedly braided hair. She seemed to have already lost Jane's aesthetic influence.

The carriage ride to the theater lasted longer than anticipated. A light snowstorm had overcome the region earlier that week, so the roads remained covered in a thin layer of snow and ice. Bess watched the winter scenery bypass the carriage as she stared out the window and thought of her expected proposal with animation. Her musing eventually ceased when she spotted the novel brick arena at large. She exited the carriage with an extra hop in her step as she greeted the rest of her friends and family, for the Phillipses were the last to arrive.

Mr. Elmsworth cleared his throat, and Bess redirected her attention toward him. She had not yet seen Jack, so she observed her friend's father with suspense. *Did he make the journey safely? Did he catch a cold?* Bess bit her lip with fear, and she soon discovered that Jack *and* Miss Henwood had been unable to come. Their reasoning for being absent was unknown. Bess cast her eyes to the floor, but she was not the only one who exhibited frustration. Mr. Phillips sighed and started ahead toward the entrance to the theater, disappointed that his fiancée could not accompany him.

Despite feeling downcast that her anticipated proposal would not come to fruition, Bess searched and eventually spotted Jane and Alex to the left of the entrance. She found Abigail's arm and led her to their family but was interrupted by Juliette and Leonarda, who wore broad smiles across their faces. Juliette laughed, "Bess, I've never been to the theater before. I'm awfully excited!" She danced from foot to foot before whispering, "I feared that Mr. Ashford would come, but my comfort has immensely increased now that he hasn't."

Bess replied, "My father invited him, but he provided no explanation for his absence."

"It certainly must regard our quarrel," she said. "He's never missed a social gathering before then." She paused. "Bess, I told Leonarda about the incident, so we may talk freely."

"Do you care if Abigail overhears?"

"Abigail?" Juliette questioned. Bess turned to her right, where Abigail was standing, but found an empty space. She turned around but saw no notice of her sister.

"She was here a moment ago," Bess replied. "Perhaps she went inside with Father."

Juliette nodded and continued to chat, but Bess glanced over top of her friend's head toward Jane and Alex, who were whispering among themselves. Neither countenance conveyed happiness nor excitement about the theater, but Bess rationalized that *at least* they were communicating. With half an ear listening to Juliette's rambling about how she had only *thought* she liked Mr. Ashford because of her parent's remark, Bess analyzed her elder sister's body language. Despite having dressed like a queen, Jane had a frown planted on her face. She opened her mouth to make some seemingly rude comment to her husband, who received this remark with what appeared to be disgust, and Bess bit her lip. Within minutes, Mr. Roberts approached them, and their changes in attitude were astounding. Their postures straightened, their smiles brightened, and they even appeared disappointed when Mr. Elmsworth announced that everyone ought to end their discussions to go inside.

As Bess headed into the theater, she searched for her younger sister but was unsuccessful due to the dense crowd of guests. She eventually settled at the end of a long row of seats beside Juliette, who had not ceased to talk. This seating arrangement made it difficult for Bess to continue her prolonged stares at Jane, Alex, and Mr. Roberts while occupying Juliette's attention, so she reluctantly surrendered her focus to her young friend.

"Bess, I don't think that I'll ever marry. Marriage is a complicated institution of which I hardly care to have a part." She paused. "I spoke to Leonarda about the matter, and she begged me to never give up my happiness because of her. *If* a situation arose in which we became alone, we would figure it out together." Juliette laughed to herself. "Leonarda and I are *such* good sisters. I know that I complain about her a lot, but she has so many wonderful qualities. For instance, consider her musical abilities...." Bess nodded, but her focus soon shifted to admiration of the theater. The design and architecture were sharp and lustrous, evincing its novelty. There must have been about a thousand seats with all angles to view the show, and there were large, red curtains decorating the frame of the stage that reminded Bess of her former theater days. She recalled attending shows with her mother, who had made it a monthly trip to take one of her daughters to lunch before seeing a performance. Bess felt her eyes begin to gloss over, and she pinched herself to avoid choking up. Again, she looked around unsuccessfully for Abigail.

But Bess' thoughts ceased when a tall, thin man wearing a top hat announced the start of the show. Finally, Juliette quieted as the lights dimmed, and the first act began. As the first scene unfolded, Bess enjoyed listening to the actors recite their lines with ardor. She recalled that her mother used to love the actors' passion, and she even imagined that her mother was relating her opinions on the show's ghostly plotline. But Bess' happiness was cut short when Juliette leaned over and asked Bess to translate what was occurring. Shakespeare's verbiage was difficult to comprehend for those unfamiliar with his works, so Bess understood her friend's troubles. With a sigh, she provided an explanation, but these constant interruptions disrupted her discernment of the story. Eventually, Juliette must have recognized that she had become bothersome, and she stopped talking altogether.

During the curtain call, Bess stood and cheered, which signaled for Juliette to do the same. But Bess ignored her friend's imitation, for she was overwhelmed with the *true* magnificence of the show. She wiped a tear from her eye and smiled at the notion that her fascination with theater stemmed from her mother's innate love of performances.

Before departing for Laurel Manor, Mr. Phillips reconvened with his acquaintances to discuss the show. The consensus seemed that Bess, Alex, and Mr. Roberts enjoyed the performance while the remainder of the guests could not follow Shakespeare's language. Curious about her sister's opinion, Bess looked for Abigail but could not find her. She wandered the perimeter of the theater's property in search of her sister but came to the frustrating conclusion that she was *nowhere.* She returned to the others with a furrowed brow and listened as her father gave his final farewell. She opened her mouth to inquire if anyone knew where Abigail was but was startled to find her smiling, blushing, deeply breathing sister standing beside her. Bess took one look at her sister's animated countenance and understood where she had been—or, more accurately, with *whom* she had been.

After settling into the carriage, Mr. Phillips stared out the window and asked, "Well, Abbie, how did you enjoy the performance?"

Abigail's eyes widened. She looked to Bess for help, but Bess only chuckled and shrugged.

"I liked it," she said.

"What was your favorite part?" he murmured.

"Well," Abigail stammered, imploring her sister for assistance.

Bess smiled at her sister's failing deception but reluctantly answered, "Abbie told me that the witches intrigued her. In fact, she liked the announcer's remark that back when Shakespeare wrote the text, he included witches to impress the king, who was fond of the supernatural."

Mr. Phillips turned his gaze toward his daughters and said, "I didn't think you liked reading Shakespeare, Abbie."

"Oh!" Abigail exclaimed, doing her best to avoid laughing. "I hate *reading* it, but *watching* the show was something else!"

"So, would you like to go again?" he asked as he returned to the window.

Abigail looked at Bess with her eyes bulging out of her head. She slowly replied, "Well, not anytime soon—"

"The theater reminded me of Mother," Bess interjected, altering the focus to what was *really* on everyone's minds.

Mr. Phillips sighed but did not flinch. A short period of silence ensued wherein his stagnant figure started to tremble. Finally, he mumbled, "That's all that occupied my mind." And although Abigail hadn't seen the show, she understood why the theater had been sentimental. The younger Phillips sisters then reached out to hold their father's hands as he fought back tears. *It must have been a challenging year for Father.* Bess pursed her lips as she rubbed the back of her father's hand with her thumb. *He didn't have Mother with whom to share these latest experiences like Jane's marriage. He's cared for us by himself. And oh!* She exhaled. *I haven't made it easy.* Despite how difficult this evening had been for him, Mr. Phillips managed to contain his tears during the ride home. Bess and Abigail expected him to burst upon their arrival at Laurel Manor, but his brief "good night" was enough to communicate that he would handle his emotions by himself. So, each member of the Phillips family parted ways, thinking only of Mrs. Emily Phillips.

Chapter 35

The pounding sound of heavy rainfall awoke the residents of Laurel Manor. Bess rubbed her eyes and hid her head under a pillow in an unsuccessful attempt to recover from a sleepless night. Eventually, she trudged downstairs for breakfast and encountered the groggy faces of her sister and father. She hardly acknowledged her family as she slumped into a chair and rested her head on the table, and she startled when a servant placed a slice of toast with marmalade before her. Abigail's red eyes fell onto Bess, and she whispered, "Would she have liked the show?" Bess closed her eyes and rocked side-to-side but was reawakened by a nudge from her sister.

Bess pursed her lips and contemplated a response, but Mr. Phillips speedily replied, "She loved the theater. She would have loved *Macbeth*." He cast his eyes downward and spread marmalade over his toast with a sigh. Bess nodded to confirm her father's remark, but the momentary silence did not last. Mr. Phillips took a deep breath and mumbled, "Do you think that it was wrong of me to ask for Catherine's—Miss Henwood's—hand in marriage?"

Suddenly, Bess' gloomy countenance brightened. Her eyes shot up, and she bit her lip with hesitation. *Had Father asked this question months ago, Abbie and I would have truthfully replied that yes, his marriage to Miss Henwood would be like a sacrilege to Mother's memory.* She sighed and set down her toast. *But Miss Henwood has made Father unbelievably happy. I haven't seen him laugh like he's had for months. She's like an angel, blessing Father when he needs it.*

Bess opened her mouth to answer, but Abigail first said, "No, Father. Miss Henwood's lovely."

"She's made you *so* happy," Bess added.

Mr. Phillips slightly nodded as he fought to hold back tears. He managed a deep, trembling breath and thanked his daughters for their honesty. "You don't think Emily—your mother—would be upset?" he quivered.

"Not at all."

"Mother would want what makes you happiest."

Mr. Phillips sighed. His anxious demeanor transformed into one of pure relief, and he took a large, appetizing bite of his toast. He laughed and lifted his crust into the air, pretending to toast his daughters. Bess and Abigail chuckled at their father's clever wordplay and returned his gesture, but the room soon fell to silence. Abigail set down her glass of water and changed the subject of the conversation. "Father, are you looking forward to your wedding? At least it's in April, not November. It'll be much warmer than Jane's wedding was."

Mr. Phillips smiled to himself. "Yes. In fact, I sent an invitation to my half-sister Josephine, who lives in Ireland. I haven't seen her for years."

"Aunt Josephine?" Abigail inquired. "Father, you never told—"

"Abbie, he mentioned her when we were young," Bess intervened. "After having Father, Grandmother divorced her husband, moved to Ireland, and had Aunt Josephine."

"Yes," Mr. Phillips continued. "I was raised by my father, and we kept the divorce a secret. Otherwise, we would have been deemed outcasts." He paused. "Despite the circumstances, I never failed to write to my mother, and she never failed to respond. Once a year, I journeyed to Dublin to see her and Josephine. They survived well on their own, but I believe that my mother faced shame for producing Josephine out of wedlock." He sighed, "I never learned the cause of my parents' divorce, but it must have been serious to drive her to leave."

Abigail said, "I've never heard of a divorce *actually* occurring."

"It's unconventional," Mr. Phillips added. "Nevertheless, your grandmother passed away years ago, and Josephine now resides in Dublin by herself. I am looking forward to seeing her again in addition to introducing her to my daughters." He smiled, but amid his reminiscence, a firm knock sounded at the door. The Phillipses jumped in surprise, and a servant rushed to the entrance hall to greet the handsome figure of Mr. Roberts, who pounced inside and sped toward the dining hall. Bess' eyes caught her guest's grave look of concern, and she stood, expecting the worst news.

But Mr. Phillips exhibited a blithe disregard for the fearful anticipation that now encompassed the room. He smiled and asked, "Ah, Mr. Roberts, has Catherine come along?"

"No," Mr. Roberts answered with a crackling voice.

"What is it?" Bess hastily inquired.

Mr. Roberts took a deep breath and stepped toward Bess, who instinctively cowered. With a reddening face, she listened as her father continued his cheerful monologue before Mr. Roberts interrupted, "Mr. Phillips, there is something that you must know."

"Well," Mr. Phillips whined, "if it doesn't have to do with Catherine—"

"It does."

Bess watched as her guest took a seat, and as she sat beside him, she inquired, "Do you mean to relay the message that Miss Henwood and Jack were in love? Juliette told me, so if this is your reason for coming, you mustn't act so concerned. I know about it, and I'm satisfied."

Mr. Roberts hesitated. "She said that they *were* in love?" Bess slowly nodded. Then she watched as Mr. Roberts took *another* deep breath. He reached into his coat pocket and removed a piece of paper covered in messy cursive. He turned it over and slid it across the table to Abigail. Fighting back tears, he mumbled, "Abigail, go on. Read it aloud. I cannot." Abigail eyed Mr. Roberts before languidly unfolding the letter.

She cleared her throat and began—

"Ben,

First, let me apologize for my recent secrecy. Over the last few months, I was keeping something immense from everyone, including yourself. Although I deeply regret hiding the truth, I believe that this matter is beyond your comprehension. And Ben, I mean not to insult you; your mind is too pure and beautiful to understand my sins. I could not risk your finding out and denying me this opportunity." Abigail looked up with a muddled expression, but Mr. Roberts waved her onward. *"My love for him never ended. I told you that it did, but I lied—to you and to everyone. A few months ago, I confessed my feeling to him, and he felt the same. It was a miracle, but I suffered in his long-spent time of contemplation. Eventually, he proposed. And believe me, Ben, our decision was not light-hearted. We spent day and night in deep consideration, but we resolved to fulfill our true desires. My deepest condolences to all parties involved, particularly Jonathan and the other Phillipses. Fear not for my safety and well-being, and I beg that you do not search for us. Ben, I love you wholeheartedly, but I must go.*

With dearest affection—always,
Catherine"

Mr. Phillips gasped when Abigail read aloud the name of his fiancée. Bess turned to her father and noticed his paling face and tear-filled eyes. He froze in shock, and Bess felt her face redden as she clenched her teeth. She bit her bottom lip, and with the smallest voice she could muster, she whispered, "With whom did she leave? Was it—?"

Mr. Roberts nodded. "I'm *so* sorry, Bess."

Bess jumped up from the table, and Abigail reached over to take hold of her sister's hands. Mr. Phillips started to rock forward and backward with widened eyes, and when Mr. Roberts opened his mouth to apologize again, Mr. Phillips bolted upright and threw his chair to the ground. In a deeper voice than either of his daughters had ever heard him conjure, he cried, "Catherine's gone! She left with Mr. Jackson Elmsworth!"

Mr. Roberts gulped and cowered in his chair before attempting to formulate an explanation. "Mr. Phillips, I had *no* idea. I didn't see her this morning, but once I saw the note, I searched the town for her, and she wasn't anywhere. I believe that they left last night while we were at the theater. I went to Elmsworth Manor, but Miss Elmsworth, who was the only other person at home last evening, wouldn't say a word. Mr. Phillips, I wish I'd known."

Bess broke free from her sister's grasp and began to pace the length of the dining hall. She trembled, "He—he kissed me the other day. Was my reaction unsuitable? Did I turn him away?" But nobody seemed to notice her remarks. Even Mr. Phillips, who would have been most offended by this unorthodox romantic gesture, kept mulling over his own thoughts.

"We were planning our wedding just *yesterday* morning!"

And suddenly, Bess sprinted from the dining hall. The front door slammed shut, and Abigail knocked the chair out from under herself to start chasing her sister. Yet, she had been too slow, so she first searched the garden. She found no trace of Bess and made her way toward her sister's only other possible destination: Mulberry Cottage.

Running to the Cawdor's home on the rocky, dirt roads was a challenging endeavor. Halfway through the journey, Abigail rolled her ankle, but she ran on, determined to support her sister. When she reached Mulberry Cottage, her ankle was throbbing, and her calves were burning. Nevertheless, she climbed the steps to reach Bess, who was standing before the front door, hopping from foot to foot to keep warm. With a furrowed brow and a shaking voice, Bess managed to scold, "You shouldn't have followed me." She wiped a tear from her eye. "I didn't want you to come."

"Bessie," Abigail started. She placed her hand on Bess' arm and took a deep breath. "Just—are you looking for Jane or Alex?" Bess didn't say a word, but her contemptuous glare conveyed that she was searching for the latter. The door crept open, and to the shock of both Bess and Abigail, a tear-stained, red-faced Jane emerged and embraced her sisters in a massive hug. Bess momentarily stopped crying, and she observed her elder sister, who looked tired and anxious. It appeared that she had been crying for much longer than Bess had.

"You couldn't have come at a better time," Jane wept. Bess clutched onto her elder sister and reached to caress the back of her head. Abigail took a step back and examined her troubled sisters. She tilted her head to the side, trying to figure out *why* Jane seemed upset about a matter that only partially concerned her.

312

"Jane," she started, "are you *this* upset about Jack and Miss Henwood?"

Jane hesitated but eventually turned to her youngest sister. She wiped her cheeks and murmured, "Jack and Miss Henwood?"

"Why are you upset then?" Abigail asked, crossing her arms.

"Oh," Jane sniffled, wiping her nose. "It's nothing—nothing at all. What happened between Jack and Miss Henwood?"

But before Abigail had time to respond, Bess broke away from her sister's grasp. She covered her face with her hands and exclaimed, "Misery upon misery! Jane, they left!" Jane's eyes bulged out of her head. She immediately forgot her previous dread and begged Abigail for a better explanation, which was reluctantly given and awfully received.

"No," Jane replied, covering her mouth in disbelief. "No," she said more firmly. "Miss Henwood was supposed to marry Father, and Jack was supposed to—"

"I know," Abigail interrupted, and both sisters turned to Bess, who still possessed a hollow look. Then Abigail asked, "Why were *you* upset, Jane?"

Yet, Jane seemed immune to whatever had aggravated her before because she simply replied, "No—no, it's nothing." She outstretched her arms to take hold of Bess' shoulders. "Bess, you mustn't despair. Tell Father that as well. If they dared to treat both of you like that, then they are entirely undeserving of—"

"He kissed me," Bess muttered. She still hadn't blinked. "I thought that he was going to propose. I saw this box-shaped item in his pocket, and—oh!" she cried. "That was for Miss—"

"He kissed you?" both sisters cried.

But Bess could only manage to nod. She lowered her head into Jane's arms while fighting back tears, but eventually, she pulled away. She wiped her eyes and took a deep breath as her hollow look started to dissolve. Finally, she sputtered, "Quite frankly, I didn't think that he was meant for me. I know I look ridiculous getting emotional over a *man*, of all things." Abigail smiled, but Bess never faltered. "Honestly, Jane—Abbie, I'm just—I'm just *so* lonely. Jack was a fine friend to me, so I thought—I thought that—that would be enough. And when he kissed me—I thought that it was certain that we would marry. Why did I do it, Jane?" Bess cried, burying her head again into her sister's shoulder.

"Bessie, why did you do *what*?" Jane murmured with quivering lips.

"*Why* did I let myself fall for Jack? *Why* did I let others believe that we would be good together? I was setting myself up for—for this!"

"No, no," Jane breathed into her little sister's ear. "No, Bessie. *You* didn't do this. I'm certain that there are plenty of others who are *much* more deserving of you than Jack ever—"

"It's *humiliating*, Jane!"

"Father's case might be worse, Bessie," Abigail interjected, adjusting her arms from across her chest to her hips. "I wonder if Miss Henwood ever cared for him—"

"I wonder if *Jack* ever loved *me*!"

"Oh, yes—yes, I'm sure he did," Jane said, caressing Bess' hair. "Bessie, you're beautiful, smart, confident, and *so* many other things. He would be inane to have never loved you."

"*I* was inane for thinking that I loved him—"

314

Abigail sighed, "Bessie, I know that this must be difficult, but Father's going through the same situation, so if we could *just* go home to see if he's—"

Suddenly, Bess overheard footsteps approaching from the road leading to Mulberry Cottage, and she shoved Jane away. She wiped her eyes with the back of her hand and watched as Alex, with a look of concern, raced toward her. She felt the urge to cry again, but she wiped her eyes for a second time and forced herself to say, "Everything's fine, Alex." Jane glanced toward her younger sister and shook her head. When Alex reached the top of the steps, he received Abigail's whisper that Jack and Miss Henwood had run away. His eyes widened in disbelief, and he turned back to Bess with bewilderment plastered across his face.

He pressed his palms together and took a deep breath. Then he offered to make Bess some tea, adding that *this* tea was his mother's, and it was used to cure his and his sister's childhood misfortunes. Bess refused and insisted that she and Abigail return to Laurel Manor. Truthfully, Bess had come to speak with Alex. She had come to convey the horrid message and perhaps her disappointment, but she had *certainly* not planned on manifesting any sincere emotions. Both Alex and Jane frowned, and they begged Bess to stay, but nothing they said could convince her to change her mind. Moments later, Bess was dragging Abigail down the pathway toward the road. Once she had escaped Alex and Jane's view, she sighed. She covered her face with her hands and wailed. Abigail watched but said nothing.

Bess peaked through her fingers and observed Abigail's awkward stance. She was balancing on her left leg since she had injured her right, but Bess shrugged and neglected this potential injury's connotation. *How aggravating her behavior is! Jane has the sympathy to care for me, but all she offered was logical advice that only further angered me.* Then she stomped ahead without noticing Abigail's sizable limp.

.

Chapter 36

The remainder of February passed without cheer for Bess and her father. Their local acquaintances neglected their distress, so they remained trapped inside Laurel Manor. Mr. Phillips looked as miserable as he had when his wife died, and Bess suffered with immense humiliation. Abigail, however, did not dwell over her family's misfortunates; rather, she continued attending school and playing football once her ankle felt better.

The first of March proved to have considerably warm weather, so Abigail invited her sister to watch her play football. Bess agreed, feeling glad that she could venture someplace where nobody knew of her embarrassment, so the younger Phillips sisters subsequently made their way into town. Upon arrival, Abigail met her teammates on the far side of the street, and Bess nestled herself in the corner. She admired the players, who were warming up, and from a distance, she caught sight of the Cobblers. She hesitated to approach them but eventually recalled Mrs. Cobbler's former behavior and decided to leave them alone.

The game began around a quarter past noon, and the weather was perfect for comfort. Bess noticed that one of the teams still ran about shirtless, but instead of gawking at this spectacle, she found it humorous. And to her pleasure, on the first time Abigail touched the ball, she drove down the sidelines and crossed it to the center of the pitch for Callum to finish. Callum raced toward Abigail, who was celebrating by the post, and the two embraced. The rest of Abigail's teammates surrounded them with cheers while the crowd of spectators, which was considerably smaller than before, burst out in encouragement. Bess smiled and applauded. Callum turned around to run back to his side of the pitch, but

Abigail paused to admire him. Bess smiled at Abigail's affection, but she could not help but feel a bit jealous.

At the end of the match, Abigail's team had defeated their friends by a close score of five goals to four. As Abigail gathered her belongings, she turned to her elder sister with a massive smile. Bess waved, but just as Abigail took a step in her direction, she was stopped by Callum. The two exchanged a few words before Abigail broke free, leaping with excitement.

"How did you like it?" she asked.

"It was wonderful," Bess replied. "Abbie, you've got an incredible talent."

Abigail laughed at Bess' compliment before inquiring how she felt about being among others again. Bess chuckled, remarking that *this* crowd of people was certainly not as daunting as their friends in front of whom she was humiliated, but Abigail reassured her that it was all the same. As the sisters started to depart, Abigail suggested, "Should we go see Jane? You seem fairly comfortable now, and it might be a suitable time." Bess shook her head, but Abigail was one step ahead of her sister, for she nodded toward a window in a building they were passing. Bess followed her sister's gaze, and to her surprise, she saw Alex speaking to a gentleman inside. Bess turned to Abigail, who shrugged, and the two girls agreed to make a stop at Mulberry Cottage.

Like their last visit to the Cawdor home, Jane was the first to crack open the door and invite her sisters inside. Her cheeks were red and stained with tears, but she refused to explain why she seemed miserable. To ease the silence, Abigail explained that she had just returned from playing football, which accounted for her being dirty. Jane raised an eyebrow and asked how the game had gone, but Abigail urged Bess to

318

answer. Bess then recounted their sister's excellent skills that led the team to a victory. And after a moment of hesitation, Jane said, "Oh, Abbie, I'm awfully proud of you—*truly*. And I'm pleased that you chose to come here. I haven't seen either of you in a while, and I've *really* missed you." Bess turned to Abigail. They exchanged their concern for Jane within a glance, but they deemed it best not to pry at her emotions. *I suppose that she's upset about some long-standing but trivial dispute between her and Alex.* Abigail seemed to agree.

Jane invited her sisters inside, and without any questions, she prepared a pot of tea. When she returned from the kitchen with a full pot and three cups, she sat down and smiled. She continued to sit and smile without saying a word, so Bess turned to Abigail, who was equally confused. Then a few minutes passed before Jane started to shake and tap her foot.

"Jane, is everything all right?" Abigail conceded.

"Oh, yes," Jane hastened to reply. She stood and peered into her sisters' teacups, wondering if they needed more tea. Upon realizing that they had hardly taken a sip, she sat down and rubbed her palms together. She took a deep breath and asked again, "How was the game?"

"Well," Bess started. She glanced toward Abigail, who pursed her lips. "Her side won five goals to four."

"Oh, of course—I apologize," Jane replied. She playfully hit herself in the head and laughed, but neither of her sisters found any bit of her jest amusing. Jane recognized her sisters' increasing concern, and she took a deep breath. "Have either of you heard anything from Jack or Miss Henwood?" By now, Bess had loomed over Jack's absence for far too long, so Jane's mention of his disappearance did not bother her too much. She took a deep breath and tried to convey absolute normality, but

Abigail, who seemed to notice Bess' slight change in emotion, seethed a short "Jane!" to quiet their eldest sister.

"Oh," Jane murmured. "I apologize; that subject must still be sensitive."

Abigail lifted her eyebrows, and Jane jumped to her feet. She danced across the room, picked up a jewelry box, and set it down before returning to her seat. Abigail reached over to lay her hand on Jane's twitching leg, but Jane flinched and turned away. "Abbie, I'm fine!" She paused. "Have either of you heard anything about Mr. Henwood and Mrs. Henwood—Charles and Rachel, not Charles' parents? I'd imagine they're doing fairly well. They're by the sea, they're together without the trouble of dealing with friends and family—oh, I could go on."

"We haven't heard a thing," Abigail remarked.

"And Mr. Curtis Elmsworth—someone *must* have received some form of notice—"

"He married," Bess started. "But I'm sure you already heard of that."

Although having known this fact, Jane yearned for something to talk of other than her private affairs, so she seized this opportunity by gasping, "No! Really? To whom?"

Bess sighed, comprehending Jane's ploy, but she answered, "Her name's Miss Francesca Telley, but *honestly,* Jane, Curtis is the *last* person of whom we should be talking! Considering that he left England without making amends to Miss Martha Gil—"

"Amends to whom?" Abigail looked up with confusion.

Suddenly, Bess realized that nobody else knew of Curtis' history. She sighed but decided that Jack no longer deserved her promise of secrecy. "He ought to have made amends to a woman named Miss Martha Gilmore." She looked up and noticed her sisters' intrigued countenances, so she continued. "When Jack and I were friends, he enlightened me on his brother's past. I suppose his story could be false, considering that everything I ever knew about him is now up in the air, but—"

"Go on," Jane urged.

Bess sighed again and began to relay the tale of Curtis' past. She started by explaining how she had always been skeptical of Jack and his sister's intense dislike of their elder brother. Then she mentioned how Jack had entrusted her with this personal information, but both Jane and Abigail were craving to hear the story, so Bess cut out the insignificant details and continued. She explained how Curtis used to fancy a certain pauper named Miss Martha Gilmore. The pair grew close, and even the Elmsworths began to accept that their eldest son, although possessing an awful character, could have his love reciprocated. Shortly thereafter, Miss Gilmore announced that she was pregnant—a grave sin for unmarried couples. Nevertheless, the Elmsworths forgave their son, who promised to dedicate the remainder of his life to Miss Gilmore and his child. However, Curtis eventually met Miss Gilmore's cousin, Mrs. Baldare, and he abandoned the mother of his child for the wealthy Baldare family. The rest of the story, she concluded, they knew.

A few minutes elapsed in utter silence before Abigail murmured, "As horrid as this incident is, I'm not surprised."

"What happened to Miss Gilmore and her baby?" Jane inquired to which Bess replied that Miss Gilmore married a blacksmith, who now helps look after the child.

"What a horrible family," Abigail muttered. "Curtis, Jack—oh, and their sister is *much* worse than them!"

"Miss Elmsworth?" Bess asked, and Abigail nodded. "Upon what grounds do you make this discernment?"

"Frankly, Curtis and Jack's ignorance has never led to anyone's death," Abigail answered, and Bess paused. *Well, I suppose that Abigail could be correct. Ever since I've known Miss Elmsworth, I've justified every rude remark that she's made or every ignorant deed she's done. Considering that she's ill, she should be more mindful about spending time with those who aren't immune. Unfortunately, those like Emma and Mrs. Baldare have suffered—and oh, Mrs. Baldare and Miss Elmsworth were good friends! Shouldn't that enough have made me despise her?*

"Yet, I don't think that Mr. and Mrs. Elmsworth are awful," Bess said.

"Yes. I suppose not," Abigail agreed. "But I've never spoken directly to them, so I wouldn't know for certain." Bess and Abigail turned to their elder sister to see if she had anything to add about Mr. and Mrs. Elmsworth. To their surprise, they found that Jane had returned to a hollow state, for she was staring off into the distance. Abigail reached over and prodded her sister's shoulder, and Jane shook awake, asking what the matter was.

But before either sister could answer her question, Jane asked, "So, if I understand correctly, both brothers' running away didn't necessarily make them bad people. They were always awful beings, who probably did everyone else a favor by leaving. I mean," she continued upon noticing Bess and Abigail's surprised expressions, "Mr. Curtis Elmsworth was horrible, and by him leaving, we don't have to deal with him anymore. Miss Elmsworth never ran away, but she, too, is—"

"But not Jack," Bess quickly responded, despite being unsure why. "I can't allow you to think that he's always been a disagreeable person. We spent countless hours together—"

"But he lied to you," Jane interrupted, and Bess pursed her lips, understanding that her sister was likely correct. Then Jane took a deep breath and settled deeper into her chair. "Well, then I suppose that Mr. and Mrs. Elmsworth ought to be terrible parents. Clearly, they disregarded teaching their children how to sympathize." Jane's logic made sense, so Bess and Abigail were forced to nod. *Yet, there's still a nagging part of me that loathes talking ill of Jack and his family, particularly his parents. His follies aren't nearly as great as his siblings' are. He's a nice gentleman, and if the only person he ever hurt was me (and perhaps my father), then I can cope with that. I had only fantasized about marrying him. If he and Miss Henwood were truly in love, and to make their relationship work, they had to be secretive, then I suppose I can accept that.* But Bess didn't voice these opinions to her sisters for fear of reigniting the fire of Jack's leaving. So, she simply nodded and pretended to fully agree.

A moment of silence ensued, but the sound of Alex's footsteps brought Bess to her feet. Jane stood, brushed off her dress, and helped Abigail up. She frowned and said, "I suppose that it's time for you to go." She turned and embraced Abigail, whispering, "I love you, Abbie." Her hug seemed to last a second longer than usual, and when she turned to Bess, she embraced her sister in the same firm manner.

"Jane, are you certain that—?"

"Yes, yes," Jane sniffled, breaking away. "Everything's fine. I love you both *so* much," she said, waving her sisters off with a smile.

Bess pursed her lips and pushed open the front door. Alex was on the other side of the threshold. He opened his mouth to greet Bess, but she pushed past him, neglecting to say a word. Abigail, though, whispered a hello. When both sisters were far from Mulberry Cottage, they pondered the real reason for Jane's distress. But unable to come up with anything plausible, they left that topic alone, assuming that everything was all right. Abigail then continued talking about her football game, detailing each of her noteworthy plays and how Callum was "magnificently" involved.

Chapter 37

Juliette remained a frequent guest at Laurel Manor. She and Leonarda arranged visits for every Saturday where they would spend the afternoon chatting with Bess about generally unimportant matters. Occasionally, Juliette relayed news that she received during her family visits to Elmsworth Manor, which revolved mostly around Jack and Miss Henwood. Bess learned that ever since leaving, Jack sent weekly letters to his mother and father to assure them of his happiness and safety. He had married Miss Henwood and moved to a town, which he neglected to name, in Scotland. In his new settlement, he found a job as a tradesman. Frankly, these details failed to increase Bess' spirits, but she viewed the Wheatley's company as a positive influence on her overall dreary lifestyle.

Aside from the letters, Juliette dedicated a large number of their conversations to describing how the Elmsworths were coping with the loss of their second son. As one would suppose, they were not doing well. They hardly left their house, and the only social interaction they received came from their family, the Wheatleys. Furthermore, Miss Elmsworth's illness was getting worse. Jack had been her chief caretaker apart from the servants, but now that he was gone, her morale (in addition to her physical health) had rapidly declined. In fact, the Elmsworths had hired a nurse from London to care for her, but Juliette mentioned that she had overheard the nurse say that her cousin's death was forthcoming.

A few weeks after this unfortunate news was wrought, a visitor arrived at Laurel Manor with another dreadful message. Alex's footsteps sounded on the pathway, and after three brief knocks on the front door, he entered. He met Mr. Phillips, who was reading an update on the American Civil War, in the dining hall. Alex's anxious countenance frightened Mr. Phillips, who directed his son-in-law to gather Bess and Abigail's from their likely locations: the garden and drawing-room, respectively. When she reached the dining hall, Bess took a seat beside her father, and for the first time that afternoon, she recognized Alex's corpse-like demeanor. Printed on his pale face and beneath his drooping, red eyes were dark, heavy bags. The hair spiking from the lower half of his face and neck was immensely overgrown, and he expelled an odor, which suggested that he hadn't bathed in weeks. His cheeks were coated with dried tears, and when Mr. Phillips opened his mouth to inquire over Alex's welfare, he became speechless.

"Alex?" Bess wondered as her eyes caught a glimpse of his repulsive appearance.

Alex stammered, "I—I have three unfortunate—unfortunate—pieces of news."

"Alex, what is it?" Bess asked. She stood to her feet and tensed.

Alex covered his face with his hands and choked, "First, I received information—regretful information that Miss Elmsworth passed away yesterday—yesterday evening." No one from the Phillips family flinched. *This report is no shock. I feel awful for Mr. and Mrs. Elmsworth, who have now lost* all *their children, but by looking at Alex's face, I know that this cannot be the worst of his news.* Alex took a deep breath. "Second, I must tell you that—no, I cannot," he cried.

"Alex!" Bess chastised, stepping toward him and noticing that he carried a letter. She outstretched her arm to grasp onto it, but he managed to pull it away in time.

Suddenly, he exclaimed, "Jane and I have—have divorced."

Bess sighed. *In truth, Alex's proclamation of divorce is rather underwhelming. I suppose that this is a concrete explanation for Jane's strange behavior, but after considering all the reasons she could have been upset (she was terminally ill, she was on the verge of killing herself, etc.), this reality seems the least dire. Of course, the entire divorce process must have been difficult for both Jane and Alex, considering that divorces are only supposed to occur on account of a dreadful happening. Therefore, I suppose that Alex's tears are justified—at least to some extent.*

However, Mr. Phillips's reaction was not as subtle as Bess'. His face turned red, and his demeanor grew cold as he started to formulate an explanation. Immediately, Alex pleaded, "Mr. Phillips, *I* didn't want the divorce—Jane did. Over the past few weeks, I—I had been going to town fulfilling her request. Believe me," he cried, shedding another tear. "I love Jane with all of my heart. I would never—"

"What is the last piece of news?" Mr. Phillips roared. His face was darker than either of his daughters had ever seen it. And before reporting this final piece of misery, Alex took a long, deep breath. He opened his mouth to sputter this final update, but his voice fell short. He fumbled and eventually dropped the letter in front of Abigail. Then he covered his face with his hands and wailed. Carefully, Abigail unfolded the note and read—

"My dear Alexander,

I think there comes a time in a young woman's life when she realizes her purpose for living. I've spent the last few years believing my reason for being on this earth was solely to marry, create a family, and foster a loving environment among all those whom I undoubtedly cherish. Ever since we were young, Alex, you were the man whom I dreamt of marrying. Alex, please know that I never lost any love for you over these past few months. Our marriage was miraculous, but even before then, I had uncertainties. You must know that especially over these past few months, I've come to fully comprehend that family doesn't have to mean building a new circle of relatives. Lately, I've learned that family means caring for those whom you already love. It means putting the desires of those whom you love above your own wishes. I think I had forgotten that. When we married, I spent a considerably smaller amount of time with the three people who made me happiest, and I learned to value their opinions, follies, and idiosyncrasies that used to drive me mad. I would do anything right now to have one more quarrel with Bessie about appropriate ballroom clothing! And Alex, I'm certain you think that I could always just squabble with Bessie again or spend more time with my family, but by doing that, I wouldn't be honoring my newest family, the Cawdors. Alex, there was nothing in your character that urged me to ask for a divorce: it was the concept of marriage that broke my relationships with my sisters and my father. And even now, as a divorced woman, I could never rekindle those broken bonds. It'd be different. I understand that my decisions will label you and the others as undesirables among society, but I cannot hold back. My choices will, overall, benefit rather than hurt you. Believe me, Alex. I would never do anything to engender harm without proper reasoning and eventual success.

"Also, Alex, I'm tired of ignoring the obvious barrier in our relationship." Abigail paused. She skimmed over the next few lines of the letter and shook her head. Bess looked over to inquire why she had stopped reading but noticed that her younger sister had tears streaming

down her cheeks. Bess closed her mouth and resolved to listen without intervention.

"Abigail, carry on!" Mr. Phillips barked.

"Yes, I apologize, Father," Abigail sniffled. "*Alex, it is these two points*—oh." She paused and caught Bess' gaze before returning to the letter, "*and a third upon which I've made my current decision. Alex, I know that both of us have been unhappy. Married persons are supposed to love one another with all their hearts, and I'm not entirely certain about you, but I apologize, Alex. I never loved you like I wished I would. I loved you like a best friend, not a romantic partner. There is another gentleman who has taken my fancy for quite some time now. I tried to ignore him the best I could to achieve a successful marriage with you, but in the end, hiding my true emotions was too much for me to handle. I do not feel that it is right to pursue him, but he was a factor in my decision, which I thought you ought to know. Recently, Juliette visited while you were finalizing divorce papers and asked if I was as happy as I could be. Everyone knows, Alex. I'm not certain about my father, but surely Bessie and Abbie must! And I cannot continue to live in Mulberry Cottage. I have no home here. I cannot live with my ex-husband just as I cannot return to Laurel Manor. So, I've been corresponding by letter with a relation I have that lives far from here. I am going to live with them now. Please relay the important aspects of this letter to my father, Bessie, and Abbie. And please know, Alex, that these decisions had absolutely nothing to do with your admirable character. I love you, Alex, and I always will.*

Also, do not, by any means, search for me. I intend to restart a life without the stains from my past. I will write to my family so that we do not lose touch. Hug my father for me, tell Bessie that she may have all of

my old schoolbooks, and let Abbie know that she can have my wardrobe.
Just know, Alex, that I am doing this for the benefit of everyone.

  Always,
  Jane"

Abigail held the letter in her trembling hand and scanned the document again to ensure that she hadn't missed any critical details. When she was certain that she had conveyed all that needed to be said, she looked up and returned the letter to Alex. At this point, Alex had stopped crying, as the reality of Jane's disappearance was finally setting in. Bess sat down and held her head in her hands, but Mr. Phillips bolted upright. His face was an impossibly dark red, and without a word, he marched upstairs to his study. The door slammed behind him.

Alex turned to Bess and Abigail, who were still processing this information, and he mumbled, "We've got to find her."

"Yes, but we've no idea where she is!" Bess exclaimed. "Alex, how could you let her go?" Alex cowered as he murmured something about her leaving in the dead of night. He apologized continually, blaming the entire ordeal on his "being a bad husband," despite Abigail's insistence that *none* of Jane's reasoning had anything to do with him. Then Alex tore himself away from the younger Phillips sisters and departed for Mulberry Cottage. Once he had left, Bess turned to Abigail. With anticipation of being blamed for Jane's leaving, she bit her lip and asked, "You skipped a portion of the letter. What did it say?"

Abigail looked up sharply from the table. She clenched her fists and gritted her teeth, nearing Bess with an animal-like aggression. And without even a word of explanation, she raised her hand and smacked Bess square in the face.

Football must have toughened Abigail, for her smack had contained enough power to knock her sister to the ground had it not been for Bess' instinctive grasp of a table leg. A stinging sensation spread from her head to her chin, and her anger boiled, as she wanted to retaliate. But Abigail's brief comment silenced Bess' thought of returning the punch: "There was nothing else in that letter, Bess. Enjoy those books. One sister gone is tantamount to having none at all."

Chapter 38

Bess suffered a sleepless night, but when the sun rose, she trudged downstairs and started toward Elmsworth Manor. She trekked until daylight had consumed the earth, and she reached her destination with enough fatigue to collapse at any given moment. With swollen, red eyes, she knocked twice on the front door and swayed in her stance until Mr. Elmsworth answered.

Gazing down at his guest, Mr. Elmsworth trembled and refused to speak. He stepped aside and allowed Bess to walk across the threshold and for the last time, she admired the Elmsworth's entrance hall. The grandeur of its marble floors and lavish, red carpets still fascinated her along with the collection of family portraits lining the staircase. She stood with a vague recollection of the first time she had seen them, and she managed to smile.

"Mr. Elmsworth," she began. The recipient of her remark startled, and when he turned to her, Bess noticed a teardrop twinkling in his eye. She leaned forward to touch his arm and murmured, "I apologize about your daughter."

Mr. Elmsworth whipped around, and with his back to Bess, he took a deep breath. He choked, "Thank you, Bess." He paused. "And I am very saddened to hear about your sister."

But Bess ignored her host's final remark and said, "You and your wife have always been good to me, and I wanted you to know that I am very grateful for your many kindnesses." Mr. Elmsworth tried to respond, but Bess reached for the doorknob and concluded, "Take care, Mr. Elmsworth. And if you hear from Jack, please tell him that I forgive him."

Part IV

Chapter 39

A year had passed since Jane's departure, and the Phillipses remained clueless as to where she was. In his everlasting misery, Mr. Phillips had concluded that she must have run to America, where she was firsthand witnessing the American Civil War. He dejectedly announced that she would *never* be seen again, despite his other daughters' wholehearted belief that she would one day be found. The only consolation he received was Jane's frequent letter, which documented how she fared without leaving a trace of her current location. Bess had analyzed everything she sent but remained oblivious as to where she was, for Jane had gone to extreme lengths to keep that component hidden. Whether she had hired an independent mailing service that did not require a postmark or delivered the letter herself, nobody knew. The best that the Phillips family could do was wait and hope that Jane would accidentally give a hint, providing a stepping stone for them to find her.

The first letter that Jane wrote was the longest. As the months wore on, her notes grew briefer until the latest message only contained a sentence. Nevertheless, each letter was a pleasant surprise, and it slowly returned Mr. Phillips to sanity.

LETTER ONE:

To my loving family,

This is the first time that I'm directly corresponding with you regarding my running away. Now that I have had time to come to terms with my actions, it is easier for me to write about them. I am confident that Alex read you at least a portion of my letter, which detailed my reasons for leaving, but you must know that I did what I did for the benefit of everyone. I know it's strange to say that, but it's true. Anyway, I've been settled in my new home for quite some time, and I'm happy. I've met some new friends (some better than others, of course,), and I've even retained a job! Please do not worry about me. I am feeling happier and freer than ever before.

Love,

Jane—April 1864

The following letters were also vague, but at least she confirmed that she was safe and happy.

LETTER TWO:

My dearest family,

I think that I'm even happier than I was before. I hope that each of you are reaping the benefits of my absence—as odd as that is to say. I've met a great friend whose name, for privacy reasons, I do not wish to mention, but he and I have become very close. Bessie, I think you'd find him humorous. I've got to go, but I will keep in touch.

Love,

Jane—August 1864

The next letter brought some distress to Mr. Phillips, but after his other daughters assured him that Jane was *still* safe, he calmed down.

LETTER THREE:

Loving family,

I hope that all of you are doing well. Tell Alex I say hello.

I wish that I could write to you more often, but recently, I have been plagued with great anxiety. You must know that I will accept and even cherish this cause of my concern one day. Otherwise, I've been safe and happy. I love you all.

Jane—November 1864

It was cruel that Jane mentioned that she wasn't doing well without providing a deeper explanation, but Abigail supposed that her grief may be related to the American Civil War. She considered that perhaps Jane had lost a friend in battle. Bess disagreed, for it was impossible for their sister to "cherish" the death of anyone. Nevertheless, Jane's latest letter brought massive relief to her sisters and father.

LETTER FOUR:

My dearest,

I am doing well, happy, hope you are all good, too.

Jane—March 1865

Before the arrival of this last letter, Mr. Phillips had locked himself in his study. He ventured downstairs for breakfast and dinner, and the extent of his socialization included greeting his daughters each morning. He no longer invited acquaintances to visit. The humiliation he felt from Miss Henwood and Jane had transformed him into a pariah, and nothing Bess and Abigail did could lighten their father's mood. He was often heard crying or praying, asking for penance for his part in Jane's absence. No number of reassurances from his daughters could satisfy him, and Bess was left wondering: if Jane knew how much havoc she caused, would she return?

Despite the absence of her sister, Abigail had continued pursuing her daily activities. Bess frequently watched her play football in town, and from what she could gather, her sister's skills were greatly improving. She scored many goals and often performed tricks that left her opponents in awe. Aside from football, Abigail hardly spoke. She had spent a year talking to Bess about nothing more significant than weather patterns. Bess supposed that these emotions related to the missing link in Jane's message, but Abigail still refused to detail what she had deliberately omitted.

Therefore, Bess determined that her life had never been duller. Alex became a scarce visitor, for he feared being blamed for Jane's actions. The Wheatleys prohibited their daughters from coming over. According to a letter Juliette had sent, her parents didn't want her and Leonarda to "contract some of the prevailing misery at Laurel Manor." So, Bess spent her days reading, walking, and occasionally watching football. Yet, her countless months of boredom were filled with desire to find Jane. She was plagued with guilt, for she knew the missing portion of the letter dealt with her relationship with Alex, but she had no idea what to do about it.

The warmth of summer soon arrived, which provided Bess a better atmosphere for her daily walks. She remained solemn, but one mid-July afternoon brought her some excitement. She had been reading in the garden when Abigail, who had just returned home from playing football, approached her. Bess looked up and noticed Abigail's unusual smile. She set down her book and watched as her sister took a seat beside her. Abigail started, "Bess, we've been so miserable lately, but there has been this—this, well, *thing* that I've avoided sharing with you. However, I think that knowing it will bring you joy." She paused. "You'll understand after I say this to you, but I couldn't tell Father—not yet, at least."

Bess leaned toward the edge of her seat and exclaimed, "Abbie, what is it? I'm in desperate need of some good news!"

Abigail took a deep breath. "Last winter—I think it was the first day you saw me play football—did you notice that Callum said something to me that made me very happy?" Bess nodded. She opened her mouth to make a supposition, but Abigail continued, "He told me, well," she giggled, "that he—that he wanted to marry me!" Bess' jaw dropped. "You must know that it wasn't a formal engagement. His family hasn't much money, but he said that he would save up to buy me a ring, so long as that would be all right with me. And of course, his financial situation isn't much of a concern of mine (despite what society says), so I agreed. But Bessie," she said, shifting her position, "I wanted to tell you because our lives have lately been so dreary. Father cannot know because it's not official, but I will certainly tell him when it is." She paused. *Naturally, I'm beyond happy for Abbie. Her relationship with Callum seems perfect, and although I don't know him very well, he seems like a wonderful person. Yet, I cannot rid myself of this sense of jealousy. It was so easy for Jane and Abbie to find someone, but—oh, I shouldn't think of such things. It's better to congratulate Abbie without holding hidden feelings.* She embraced her sister and voiced her happiness.

Henceforth, Bess watched Abigail play football more often. She made it a habit to take particular notice of Callum, whom she eventually came to adore. *He must be the best footballer here. He scores the most goals, and he seems to be involved in every play.* And off the pitch, Callum was equally as amazing. One day, he invited Bess and Abigail to have a drink after a game. They agreed, so he led them to a tavern called

The Swallow, where he ordered a round of drinks. Despite Callum's protests, Bess declined to have a taste of anything, but Abigail conceded and took a sip from her glass.

"Ah, it's strong!" she exclaimed, and Callum laughed.

She took another sip, and Callum turned to Bess. He cleared his throat and said, "Abbie told me that you know about our unofficial—"

"Oh, yes," Bess interjected. "And I'm pleased, Callum. Abbie lights up every time she's with you."

Callum laughed, and Abigail playfully hit him. He added, "The townsfolk who know don't like the notion." He set down his drink. "They don't want a member of a wealthy family around. They know and like Abbie but might feel intimidated by her constant presence." Bess pursed her lips, unable to gather the proper words to reply. Callum took another sip of his whiskey. "So, I want to ensure that she will feel welcomed." Abigail raised her eyebrows and smiled, but Callum ignored her. He peered over her head and waved. Bess turned around and watched a man, who seemed about fifty years old, approach them. Had it not been for his wrinkles and grey hair, this man could be described as handsome. He possessed attractive facial features and thick, lean muscles that ran down his arms. When he reached the table, his smile radiated, and when he spoke, his voice sounded sweet and soothing.

"Good day," he said to Bess, who was too startled to reply. The man then turned to Abigail, extended his arm to shake her hand, and said, "Welcome, Abbie." Bess furrowed her brow and turned to her sister, who wore a massive smile.

But Callum soon clarified, "Bess, this is my father—Mr. Samuel Lewis. He's the owner of this pub." And for the first time since she had arrived, Bess admired The Swallow. The tavern had low, wooden ceilings but many windows and dim candles, which emitted a warm, comforting sensation. There were old pictures, hats, scarves, chalices, and other antique-looking items displayed on the walls, which Bess looked at with intrigue. The building was packed with friendly faces, who sang jingles and splashed around their drinks, but Bess was captivated by its overall character and British culture. For the first time in a while, she felt tears glistening in her eyes and wished to share this moment with Jane.

From that day onward, Bess and Abigail visited The Swallow after every match. Abigail had a beer, and Bess, who still never drank alcohol, ordered a sweet lemonade, which Mr. Lewis created in her honor. And to Bess' delight, by the autumn of 1865, the menus had a selection called "Bess' Specialty Lemonade (non-alcoholic)."

One September afternoon, Bess and Abigail returned to Laurel Manor from The Swallow, and a servant informed them that their father had received exciting news. With immense anticipation, the sisters dashed to their father's study and were shocked when he unveiled a letter sent from his half-sister in Ireland. He closed his eyes and cried, "Oh, go on—read it!" Abigail's eyes widened, and she took the letter from her father's shaking fingers before reading—

"*Jonathan,*

This is, by my count, the twenty-seventh note I have drafted. I've tried to write to you before, but your daughter is insistent that she read over every letter to ensure that none are addressed to Laurel Manor. She is currently on a last-minute excursion, so I took my opportunity.

341

As you have indeed gathered, Jane is with me in Dublin. Please come and retrieve her. I won't have the money to support her much longer. I must be brief, so I wish you farewell.

Your Sister Josephine"

Mr. Phillips clapped his hands and exclaimed, "She's safe! She's with Josephine!"

"Father, how are we supposed to retrieve her? Dublin must be a day's travel by train, and you would be much too weary to go on the journey by yourself," Bess hastily remarked. This news was too overwhelming for her to immediately process, but she always knew that if the opportunity arose, *she* would have to be the person to fetch her eldest sister. The thought that Jane's absence was due to her relationship with Alex had been lingering in her mind for far too long, so it was her duty to mend what she had broken.

Mr. Phillips took a deep breath and said, "I won't go. I wrote to Alex."

"Alex cannot go alone," Bess resolved. "I'd like to go." She paused and glanced toward her younger sister. "And I'm certain that Abbie would like to go as well."

"If Alex is going, then I would like to bring a good friend of mine for company," Abigail chirped. "Father, his name's Callum Lewis, and he's a school friend."

"Callum Lewis?" Mr. Phillips repeated.

"Let him come," Bess said. "We'll all go."

Mr. Phillips leaned back in his chair, and it must have been his happiness in knowing that Jane would soon come home that made him agree with his two daughters. Both girls smiled, and without delay, Abigail left to inquire if Callum was available. When she had gone, Mr.

Phillips described that the plan was for everyone to leave this evening. They would travel to Dublin during the night, head to Josephine's house for which he possessed the address, and bring Jane home. He would purchase multiple sets of returning tickets for different dates. It did not matter *when* Jane came home; it only mattered that she did.

Chapter 40

Bess occupied the next hour in scavenging her house for belongings to pack. She did not want to carry too many items, but she also did not want to forget anything. She did not want to wear attire that could possibly impact Jane's decision to return home, so she found herself at a loss. In the end, Bess decided upon two changes of clothing. She rationalized that she could not predict Jane's attitude, so she ought not to spend so long considering the matter. In fact, Abigail had an equal amount of difficulty in preparing her luggage because half of what she owned used to be Jane's. Every dress, shoe, and scarf was a reminder of her elder sister. So, neither sister walked out of their bedrooms without having shed some tears in the process of assembling their baggage.

At sunset, Alex and Callum arrived at Laurel Manor. Had it not been for his excitement in rescuing Jane, Mr. Phillips would have conducted a thorough inquisition of his youngest daughter's guest, but luckily, Callum was let off without even a greeting. About a quarter of an hour later, a carriage came to take the four travelers to the train station. Upon hearing that a carriage was the vehicle being used to transport everyone, Callum exclaimed, "Oh, Abbie, I've never ridden first class before!"

The coach for which Mr. Phillips had called was relatively small, so attempting to fit four guests along with four sets of luggage was a challenge. To worsen their dilemma, Alex must have brought the *largest* bag imaginable. *I suppose that he is like Jane in some respects.* Bess shook her head. *He certainly has a large wardrobe!* The travelers eventually nestled themselves comfortably in the cabin, and Mr. Phillips sent them off with a blissful wave. He was so confident that Jane would want to return home that the thought she may refuse never occurred to him.

In any other setting, this group of people would have spent their journey in a light-hearted, jovial manner. Yet, the ominous supposition that Jane may not want to return home, the awkwardness between Bess and Alex, and the tightly packed compartment were all factors in their silence. The subsequent train ride started no differently. Once again, Callum was in awe of the first-class cabin Mr. Phillips had reserved. Every detail from the complimentary meals to the gold buttons lining the servants' vests intrigued him, and for the first hour of the ride, he wouldn't stop talking about how thankful he was for being invited. As the sun began to set, Callum's dialogue lessened until he had fallen asleep on Abigail's shoulder. Soon, Abigail, too, placed her head against the wall and fell asleep. Alex and Bess remained awake.

But Bess didn't want to fall asleep. She was too overwhelmed with the notion that she would see Jane tomorrow. As she stared out the window into the darkness, she considered what she would say to her sister. *Should I apologize? Or would that simply remind Jane of the reason she left?* She bit her lip, but the sound of Alex moving thrust her back into reality. She frowned, realizing that it was only a matter of time before Alex said something to her. And she certainly did *not* want to talk to—

"Bess," Alex murmured. Bess pretended that she did not hear Alex's whispers, but when he repeated her name louder, she had no choice but to answer.

"Mhm?"

"Do you think that I shouldn't have come?" he asked. Bess took a deep breath but refused to turn away from the window. She opened her mouth to reply, but Alex cut her off. He hesitated before saying, "Jane left me. Would she *really* want me seeing her again?"

This conversation seemed deeper than superficial chatter, so with reluctance, Bess turned to Alex before making her honest reply, "Alex, you and Jane are friends. You've always been friends, despite your recent troubles. She won't see you as a former husband; she'll see you as a childhood confidante."

Alex relaxed his tense muscles, and although Bess yearned for this conversation to end, he said, "Do you think that Jane knew from the start that she would want a divorce?" he mumbled, unsure whether Bess would view his question as serious or silly.

Bess rolled her eyes, but when her gaze landed on Alex's anxious countenance, she faltered. She took a deep breath and chose to listen, not pity nor judge, her closest friend. "No," she concluded with a shake of her head. "Like you, Jane always wants to do what's best for everyone. She left because she thought it was the *right* decision to benefit *everyone.* Therefore, she wanted to make your marriage work; I'm certain of it."

Alex stammered, "Did we both know that, truly, it wouldn't work? Even if we tried our best, would we—?"

"I cannot speak for Jane." Bess hesitated. "She often kept her feelings to herself. When Abbie and I visited during your marriage, we could see something was wrong. If we could have figured out—"

"Oh, she wouldn't tell me either," Alex said, looking down to his palms. "I knew that something was wrong. I think—I think she knew right after the wedding that if she didn't do something to make everything better, our relationship would fall apart. So, I suppose that's why she wanted children. If we had a child, then neither of us could leave." Bess paused, contemplating Alex's comment. "But I would never have left her," Alex continued. "She might have thought otherwise, but I know it would have been wrong. Also, I couldn't have left you and Abbie behind. You two are as close to me as Jane ever was. Perhaps she overlooked that."

"Perhaps," Bess repeated. But the more she thought of it, the more she realized that there were *so* many good reasons for Jane to have left. *The decision for her must have been relatively easy, for the complicated dynamics of romance and friendship have always been so intertwined—it must have been difficult to distinguish what was right and what wasn't. And then I suppose that society is at fault. For if it hadn't been for those foolish dances, shallow friendships, and relationships that everyone thought should have worked but never did, then everything would have been all right. Nobody would fear telling the person they love that it's he or she that they are fond of. Nobody would believe that running away is the only solution to restarting life. If people just learned to accept others' flaws and opinions without judgment, then the world would be a lot better of a place.*

"Alex," Bess suddenly started, "you must know that I, too, have always loved you. Even when we were apart, I thought of you. Even when I was with Jack, I only really considered you. I've done lots of silly things to try to push you out of my mind, but somehow you never left." Bess couldn't believe it. These lines had played repeatedly in her mind over the last few years, but she had never mustered up the courage to voice them. She was afraid that she would be judged. She was worried that she would change her mind and be unable to forgive herself. But now she knew not to care. She didn't mind what Abigail thought of this confession (and although she was unaware, Abigail *was* listening). She had come to realize that the truth was all that mattered.

Alex didn't speak. He had spent the last *years* of his life prodding at Bess' feelings, trying to attain her affection. He took a deep breath and chuckled, "You've no idea how long I've waited to hear you say that. Did it have to take a marriage, a divorce, and a rescue-mission train ride for you to come to this?" Bess couldn't help but smile. She shook her head, but before she was able to respond, Alex hurriedly remarked, "When we return home, will you marry me, Bess?"

And as if her moment of relief and happiness had never occurred, Bess' heart dropped. Her head began to boil with anger. *We're on a search to find the woman whom he divorced, and he dares to ask me to marry him!* Bess' muscles tightened. She took a long, deep breath and uttered, "Alex, with all due respect, do not mistake me; I love you. I've always loved you, Alex, but I couldn't do that to Jane."

Alex froze. His face turned white. He wouldn't respond, and Bess returned his reaction by turning toward the window. But pretending she wasn't sitting beside him wasn't enough, so she excused herself. She left the cabin in the middle of the night to sit in the hallway. She collapsed to the floor, buried her head in her hands, and sobbed. But without her knowing, Abigail smiled at her sister's courage.

This was just another reminder that family preceded everything.

Chapter 41

Rays of light from the sunrise streamed through the train's windows and fell across Bess' sleeping countenance. She awoke but kept her eyes closed as she listened to a steward report that they were due to reach Dublin later that evening. Bess rubbed her eyes and grudgingly stood to her feet. She swung the compartment door open and climbed over Alex and Callum, who were both asleep. Abigail's eyes were wide open and glued to the passing trees outside her window, and when Bess sat down, she turned to her elder sister with dark bags set under her glimmering eyes. Bess started, "Abbie, did you get any sleep last night?"

But Abigail didn't hear her sister. Bess listened for a response, but after thirty seconds of nothing, she asked again. She reached across the aisle in which they set their feet and tapped her sister on the shoulder. Abigail shot her swollen eyes toward Bess and said, "No. I was up all night thinking."

"About what?"

Abigail pushed her back against her seat and moaned. She rubbed her eyes, yawned, and murmured, "Lots of things. Of course, Jane was on my mind." She paused. "What if she doesn't want to come home, Bessie? What if she sees us and resents us for coming?"

"No," Bess said and shook her head. "Jane wants us to find her. She needs to know that she's still loved despite having run away. If we seem adamant enough, she'll come home."

"But how do you know that?" Abigail whimpered. "What if we arrive, and she's mad at me and doesn't want to—?"

"Mad at *you*, Abbie?" Bess exclaimed. Callum twitched, and Bess lowered her voice, adding, "Why would Jane be mad at *you*?"

349

Abbie sniffled and rubbed her eyes, "All of my life, she's supported me with practically everything. Lately, I haven't been capable of sympathizing well (I don't know why), but if I had tried harder to get Jane to open up, then I know—"

"Abbie!" Bess whispered, placing her hand on her sister's shaking knee. "Jane *wouldn't* have told anyone. You ought to understand that."

"But a couple of years ago, when you said that I was like her pet, she told me *everything*, Bess. And then I became this football-playing, inconsiderate, unsympathetic—"

"Abbie! Don't think that you had *anything* to do with Jane's decision to leave. Both of you have grown in different ways, and the Jane we know now is not the same as the unmarried Jane we used to know."

Abigail took a deep breath. She closed her eyes, processing everything that Bess had said. In a quiet voice, she uttered, "The missing portion of Jane's letter dealt with you." She paused and reached into her back pocket. "I brought it with me." Bess pursed her lips, watching as Abigail unfolded the paper and whispered—

"Also, Alex, I'm tired of ignoring the obvious barrier in our relationship. I know, and I'm certain others do as well, that you and Bess would be wonderful together. Every day since it became clear to me, I've abhorred myself for being your obstacle. Alex, when I leave—marry her. Don't worry about me; I'm going to make a better life for myself. But promise that you will make her happy."

Abigail folded the letter in half and returned it to her luggage bag. Bess opened her mouth to reply but noticed that her sister had fallen asleep. She sighed, leaned her head against the window, and closed her eyes. She thought of what Abigail had read, and she felt satisfied for making the right choice in refusing Alex's offer of marriage. And then, for a few hours, she slept.

Suddenly, the train shrieked and grinded to a stop. Bess' eyes flung open, and she noticed that Alex, Abigail, and Callum were already awake, bracing themselves for the arrival. Bess put one hand on her luggage and another on the window as the train pounded to a halt. As soon as their compartment had steadied, a steward opened the door and instructed them to exit the cabin and take two lefts until they reached the platform. Alex looked pale, and he hastened to exit the train. Bess followed him, but she overheard Callum mention how amazing first-class traveling had been, and she smiled.

When she reached the platform, Bess gathered her friends and led them through the crowd of passengers. She reached into her bag to ensure that her Aunt Josephine's address, which her father had given her, was still there, and she removed and unfolded it. She examined the paper and said, "I'm not entirely sure *where* her house is, but Father said it isn't far from the station."

"Can we make a brief detour? I'd like to head to the city center and purchase something for the pub," Callum said.

Abigail touched her friend's arm and sighed, "Callum, we're here to find Jane. Can you wait until, at least, we locate the address?"

Bess glanced toward Callum, whose furrowed brow and set jaw communicated that he was lost for words. He flashed an imploring look toward Bess, who eventually conceded, "Go ahead, Callum. I'll write down the address for you," she said, pulling out a scrap of paper on which she scribbled Aunt Josephine's address. She handed it to Callum, who thanked her, pocketed the paper, and started toward the center of

Dublin. Once Callum had vanished, Abigail jumped toward Bess and retorted that she hadn't wanted her friend to venture off alone. Bess sighed and did not even attempt to justify her decision. She turned away and examined the address before heading toward the first neighborhood that she could find.

As Bess surveyed the city, she determined that Dublin was a place in which she would never wish to live. Gentlemen, ladies, and even working children (to Bess' horror) packed every street. Some bustled about the city with a clear objective, but most others, who wore pieces of cloth, sauntered about without any purpose. Most buildings appeared old-fashioned and run down, but there remained some novel, high-rising structures, which emitted thick, black smoke. Bess shuttered at the city's vast differences to Laurel Manor. *I'm certain that Jane will be glad to return home. There's no way she could prefer Dublin over our peaceful, country-style living.*

As Bess journeyed deeper into the neighborhood district, she encountered numerous rows of disintegrating houses, which appeared stacked on top of one another. Each abode was poorly built with broken windows and tilting roofs as its defining features, and Bess feared that the city would collapse. The stench arising from the streets was horrendous, and she couldn't help but recoil in disgust. Mr. Phillips had told Bess about an industrial revolution materializing across the continent, leaving many people destitute. Since then, child labor and pollution persisted throughout all major cities. Dublin hadn't seemed to fully embrace the revolution yet, but Bess still watched in awe as children covered in soot walked among gentlemen in top hats. She shuttered, for in no country was it right for children to be laborers while wealthy men walked about as if the world was perfect. But she shook her head. *I'm not on a humanitarian mission. I have one task: to bring Jane home.*

To Bess' relief, the walk from the train station to her aunt's house was relatively short. She soon reached the general neighborhood written on the address, but she found herself lost when identifying the exact house. She spotted an old man walking alongside his wife, and she approached them with the question. The man replied in a broken English tongue (with a hint of distaste on account of their entering *that* area of Dublin) that they needed to travel straight for another three blocks then make a right.

Like the man had indicated, Aunt Josephine's street made Bess recoil in disgust. As she, Abigail, and Alex ventured down the road, they examined the impecunious environment with intrigue and a bit of fear, for they wondered how Jane had managed to exist here. The air reeked of unbathed citizens, who infested every building, and Bess pinched her nose. But when she came upon Aunt Josephine's house, she sighed with relief, for it was the largest abode on the block. Located at the end of a long string of buildings, Aunt Josephine's house had a large, front porch, which hosted a set of rocking chairs. Bess gingerly walked up the steps, and with a racing heart, she knocked twice on the front door.

At first, nobody answered, so Bess took a step back to examine the house with more attention. The front door was freshly painted a shade of white, and unlike the surrounding buildings, no paint chips or cracks existed on the exterior. Bess walked to the edge of the porch and surveyed the neighborhood. The adjacent house had a broken porch upon which it was almost impossible to stand, so Bess turned and sighed with relief when she recognized that her aunt's porch was completely steady.

Suddenly, Bess heard the door crack open. There was a large gasp, but before the person inside could grab hold of the doorknob to shut the visitors out, Abigail stuck her arm across the threshold and threw it open. Standing on the opposite side of the doorway was Jane, dressed in modest robes with her long hair draped around her. She held a child in her arms.

And before a look of concern flashed across Jane's face, Bess thought she saw a smile.

Chapter 42

Jane stepped back and turned around to hide the child from her family's view, but she had been too slow. Abigail thrust open the door and exclaimed, "Jane, whose is that?"

Jane shifted her body toward her guests and cast her swollen eyes, which sat above thick, dark bags, toward the ground. She took a deep breath and replied, "Why did you come? How did you know that I'm here?"

Bess followed her younger sister through the doorway and said, "Aunt Josephine sent us a note." She hesitated before continuing, "She said that she cannot accommodate you here anymore."

Jane blushed and stroked the baby's head. The child let out a whimper, and after a moment of silence, Jane whispered, "She's mine." Her guests froze, and Jane shut her eyes in embarrassment. She opened the front door wider so that the doorknob hit the adjacent wall, and she murmured, "Come inside."

Like the exterior of the house, the interior of Aunt Josephine's abode was rather well-done. Plenty of chairs and sofas decorated the drawing room, allowing for accommodation of numerous guests. A large fireplace crackled in the corner and emitted a warm, comforting sense, which reminded Bess of Laurel Manor. The walls were decorated with bright red flowers and vine-like designs from which wooden picture frames hung. Bess approached the closest frame she could find and admired a fuzzy drawing of her father and aunt. She found it difficult to distinguish in what location they were, but she recognized her father's glimmering eyes and smiled.

Once her guests had settled in the drawing-room, Jane headed into the kitchen to prepare a pot of tea. Bess stood to examine a second frame, which presented a clearer picture of her aunt. Aunt Josephine was a rather beautiful creature, who (in her younger years) possessed dark hair and light eyes. Bess related her aunt's appearance to Jane's, but before she could voice these opinions to Abigail, Jane returned. Bess returned to her seat to receive a cup of tea, but she soon developed a puzzled expression. She cocked her head and started, "Jane, where *is* Aunt Josephine?"

Jane cleared her throat and replied, "She's in town, but she should be back soon." She handed the final cup of tea to Alex before settling herself in a large, wooden rocking chair. She moved her child from her hip to her lap but refused to say a word to her visitors. Bess examined the child and observed that it must have only been a couple of months old. She considered approaching the baby, but her thoughts ceased when Jane suddenly broke down in tears. Immediately, Bess and Abigail stood and ran to their sister's side, but Alex did not move.

Jane wrapped the child close to her chest and covered her face with her hands. She sniffled but as her crying diminished, she managed to say, "Once I decided that I wanted to leave, I knew that my destination was Aunt Josephine's, whom Father had occasionally mentioned." She removed her hands from her face and returned them to her child. "During the last time I visited Laurel Manor, I found her address in Father's study. I wrote down the information, and when the opportunity arose, I wrote to Alex and escaped." She paused. "When I arrived, I was taken aback by the scenery. I yearned to return home, but I met Aunt Josephine, who immediately accepted me. She was shocked to discover that I had left my family, but I described my situation, and she understood. I made her promise to *never* write to Father." Jane took a long, deep breath. She closed her eyes from which tears kept trickling and prepared herself to detail the second half of her story. In a shaky voice, she said, "Then, as I wrote, I earned a job and met some wonderful people in Dublin." She paused. "There's a boy with whom I worked who is also English. We became very close, but after our relationship ended, I discovered that I was going to have...," Jane started, looking down at her child. She turned to her sisters, who were waiting to hear the name of their niece. She took a deep breath, bit her lip, and said, "Emily."

Jane cast her eyes to the floor, but she listened as her sisters gasped at the realization that their niece was named after their mother. Jane sighed with relief and smiled. She shed a few more tears, but this time, they were tears of joy. She had known that her sisters would eventually discover the news of her daughter, but she never imagined that they would be forgiving. Having a divorce certainly made one a pariah, but having a child out of wedlock was equally disreputable. She took a deep breath as Abigail extended her arms and offered to hold Emily. Jane smiled as she transferred her little girl to her little sister.

The child smiled, and Abigail turned to Bess. Both sisters laughed, filling with pride and satisfaction. Jane rubbed her glistening eyes, but forced herself to turn toward Alex, who remained frozen in disbelief. He sat hunched forward with his hand glued to his chain as he attempted to comprehend everything he had heard. Jane took a deep breath and murmured, "Alex, I apologize." And for the first time that afternoon, Alex leveled his eyes to Jane's. No words were exchanged, but he nodded.

As she felt a massive smile looming, Jane covered her mouth with her hands. She broke away from Alex and watched as her sisters played with her daughter. Bess caught Jane's invaluable expression and knew that her elder sister could relish in this moment forever. *Jane has always lived by societal rules and obligations, but Emily's birth has changed her. By the way she looks at her daughter, I know that Jane wouldn't trade Emily's life for any social acceptance. She doesn't care that she's an outcast. She's finally happy but in a different way than anyone could have expected.* Bess leaned back in her chair and admired her niece. Emily had brown puffs of hair and sharp blue eyes, which matched Jane's. Her smile had the ability to light up a room, and Bess could not help but imagine the person whom she would become. Suddenly, Bess sat forward and asked, "Jane, does she have a middle name?"

Jane startled. She blinked twice before turning her attention away from Emily. Then she whispered, "Mhm. Josephine." Bess smiled, but when Jane returned to her daughter, she delved back into contemplation. *Aunt Josephine is my only aunt, but she was never around to watch me grow up. How am I supposed to behave toward Emily if I never had someone to show me? I can support her in all her endeavors, but I—oh, I shouldn't fret. I already love Emily Josephine Phillips with all my heart.*

Suddenly, Bess caught sight of Abigail's nervous countenance. She was preparing to ask the crucial question, which encompassed the reason for their journey, so she no longer admired Emily. She bit her lip and trembled but eventually stammered, "Won't you come home with us, Jane? Laurel Manor is a much more suitable place for Emily to grow up. Besides, *we'll* be there," she added, nodding toward Bess. Jane took a deep breath. She pressed her back against the rocking chair, and her eyes fell on Alex. Abigail glanced toward Bess and uttered, "Jane, we're not leaving until you and Emily are with us."

Jane bit her lip and brushed off her robes. She took another deep breath, but Bess already knew her answer. She tucked a strand of hair behind her ear and nodded. Upon seeing this gesture, Abigail's entire face lit up. She kissed Emily on the forehead before yelping with excitement. Jane laughed at Abigail's enthusiasm, and Bess calmly brought her sisters into a tight embrace, which even Alex joined.

"Then we shall leave now," Abigail resolved, but Bess was skeptical.

"Shouldn't we greet Aunt Josephine?"

"Oh," Jane murmured. "She'll be gone for a while, but I can leave her a note." Although dubious, Bess nodded and proceeded to help her sister collect her belongings. Once Jane had stored her items into a single bag, Alex hauled it over his shoulder and trudged toward the front door. Bess held open the door, and Alex crossed the threshold but stumbled into Callum, who was bent over to catch his breath. He wore a small sack slung around his torso, and when Abigail caught sight of him, she laughed, remarking that he had almost been too late.

"I ran *all this way*," Callum complained. "Are you heading back now?"

Abigail nodded and laughed again, but Jane silenced her. She wore a mask of confusion as she inquired who Callum was. After some explanation, Abigail concluded that he was *just a school friend* of hers. She hadn't wanted to overwhelm Jane with the mention of the unofficial marriage proposal. Nevertheless, the return to the train station was filled with happiness and relief. Abigail and Callum walked beside Jane and her daughter, asking countless questions about the city and the events of her last year. Bess remained beside Alex as she discussed how incredible their day had been. Once, she mentioned that she was curious about where her aunt Josephine was, but Alex didn't seem to think too much of her suspicions.

When they reached the train station, the afternoon had turned into the evening. Everyone boarded the train, and once she was settled, Bess took one final look at the city of Dublin: the unknown place about which she had spent the last year obsessing. Soon, she placed her head on the window and drifted off to sleep, dreaming of reaching Laurel Manor and mending the family she felt she had broken.

Chapter 43

The train compartment felt considerably smaller than the previous day. Six people unlike the recommended four were packed inside the cabin, but this notion did not distract Callum from his fascination with first class travel. He fell in love with the velvet seats and top-notch service, and he and Abigail spent the first quarter of their journey reveling in their happiness. Emily had difficulty falling asleep, so she cried on Jane's lap, which added an even greater volume of noise to their trip. But as darkness settled across the horizon, almost everyone drifted off to sleep. Even Emily shut her eyes and cuddled in Abigail's arms, yet Jane remained awake. Bess' eyes had not yet deviated from the night sky, so Jane whispered, "I cannot remember the last time that Emily was quiet. She must love her Aunt Abbie." Bess rubbed her eyes and smiled. She outstretched her arms, managing to avoid touching Abigail or Emily, and yawned. Jane giggled, "You're tired then?"

Bess smiled again and replied, "I've just had lots on my mind."

"Oh! Is any of it gossip?" Jane whispered. "I haven't heard anything fun in years."

"Well," Bess laughed, thinking of Alex's proposal. She paused and admired her beaming sister. Then she hesitated before saying, "While we were traveling to Dublin, Alex proposed to me."

"Oh," Jane startled. She glanced sideways toward Alex whose eyes remained shut. She twisted her mouth into an odd shape, which caused Bess to hold her breath. Then she whispered, "Well, what did you say?"

"No, of course!" Bess answered.

Jane frowned. "I think you should have said yes." Bess furrowed her brow, but Jane continued with a smile. "Bessie, I've always been your obstacle, but I've realized that your happiness means more to me than anything." She paused. "Now that I'm certain of Alex's affection, my former marriage to him *cannot* stand in the way of your happiness." Then she chuckled, "If Emily were not here, then I would shout to every compartment in this train, exclaiming that you and Alex are to marry."

"Oh, Jane," Bess murmured, "You *say* that, but Alex and I could never—"

But Bess was unable to finish. Jane shook her head and placed her hand on her sister's knee. Her face had transformed into one of worry, and she started, "And Bessie—"

"You've changed your mind already? That's fine."

"No," Jane laughed. She bit her lip and continued, "It's—well, this has been bothering me for a while. I apologize for interrupting our previous conversation, but I cannot hide this any longer." She paused, and Bess leaned to the edge of her seat. "Aunt Josephine passed away a couple of months ago." Bess raised her eyebrows. "I apologize—I had to say it. I couldn't lie anymore." She sighed, "When I arrived in Dublin, she was ill. A reason why she gave me residence was so that I could care for her. But once I announced my pregnancy, *she* took care of *me*. She looked after me like I was her daughter." She paused. "I don't care to continue—I just needed you to know the truth. I cannot be completely happy for you and Alex unless I've been fully honest." Then she ceased to talk. Bess expressed her condolences, but she no longer felt eager to chat. *Oh, how devastated Father will be! He will have Jane back just to discover that his sister is gone!* She sighed before a strange idea came upon her. *Aunt Josephine had sent the letter, which informed us of Jane's whereabouts. But Aunt Josephine died months before this letter was sent.* Bess smiled at her deduction but didn't wish to worry Jane.

After taking a deep breath, Jane closed her eyes. Bess leaned her head against the window but was unable to fall asleep. *How am I supposed to tell Alex that I will marry him? And despite what Jane says,* should *I marry him? Growing up, I never imagined falling prey to society's expectations by concluding my adolescence in marriage. Of course, Alex understands my mentality, for I've told him countless times, which further substantiates the notion that we are brother and sister—nothing more.* She paused. *Upon greater consideration, I loathe to confess that Alex has been on the forefront of my mind for far too long! I will, however,* not *admit that I've obsessed over him—I've only ardently thought of him. When Jane attempted to pair me with Gus (whom I never wish to see again), perhaps I was too prejudiced. Then I discovered Jack, who was an excellent distraction from my apparent affection toward Alex. I was convinced that we were in love, but only lately have I comprehended my mistake. Lastly, and ashamedly, I think I fancied Mr. Roberts. Yet, only my love—as one may call it—for Alex remains.* She paused. *How has it really come to this?* Bess sighed, and another novel idea struck her. *Every momentous event that has recently occurred must have played a role in my change of character. Otherwise, I wouldn't have changed* for the worse *on my own!* She hesitated. *Every death, every running away, and every heartbreak must have led me to be the person I am today. Before she died, Emma taught me to trust in who I am. The absences of Mr. Henwood, Curtis, Mrs. Baldare, and Miss Elmsworth have allowed me to focus my raging emotions, as Jane considers them, elsewhere. And Jane's disappearance has made me fully comprehend the value of family.* She hesitated. *I cannot claim that Mother's death resulted in anything worthwhile, but if I'm reaching for something, then there might be a positive. I've learned so much about independence, friendship, family, and love—if she had been here, would I have learned these invaluable lessons?*

A sudden whispering snapped Bess back into reality. She kept her eyes close but listened intently as Callum removed an item from his sack. She heard Abigail gasp and was unable to prevent herself from peeking—and what she saw, took her breath away. Glistening before her sister, who cried silent tears, was a diamond ring. Callum murmured, "I bought it in the city." He hesitated. "Abbie, will you marry me?" Abigail opened her mouth to answer, but Callum continued, "Before we departed for the train station, I pulled your father aside and asked him for his blessing because I figured that he was too pleased about Jane to decline my offer."

Bess shifted her body to attain a more comfortable position, but Abigail noticed. She elbowed her sister in the side and squealed, "Bessie, don't say a thing!" Bess smiled and closed her eyes, but when she overheard Abigail accept the proposal, she opened her eyes in time to see them kiss.

Chapter 44

The front door to Laurel Manor stood within a dozen yards of the Phillips sisters. Jane froze and admired the unchanging atmosphere of her home. She pressed Emily against her chest and watched as Abigail and Callum started forward. Bess lingered behind and offered to hold Emily, so that their father's first glimpse of his daughter had no connection to a baby.

While Jane handed over her daughter, Abigail banged her fist on the front door. Hardly a minute elapsed before Mr. Phillips' eager countenance greeted the newly engaged couple. He laughed and reached forward to hug Callum and then Abigail, but it didn't take long for him to brush his youngest daughter aside. He pushed past Alex and caught a glimpse of his eldest daughter, who ran to embrace him. Mr. Phillips clutched onto his first-born child with tears glistening in his eyes. He whispered praises to the heavens, but Jane soon silenced his delight.

She pulled away, sniffled, and murmured, "Father, you oughtn't be *too* happy."

Mr. Phillips raised an eyebrow and asked, "Whatever do you mean, my dear? You're home!" He stretched his arm to graze Jane's face, but she turned away.

"Father," Jane insisted. "Aunt Josephine is dead."

Mr. Phillips took a long, deep breath. He lowered his eyes to the floor and said, "Jane, I receive this news with immense sorrow, but I anticipated her death long ago. She had a habit of writing to me once a year, and in her last letter, she explained that her chronic illnesses would soon overcome her. Do not mistake me: I am unhappy to hear of her passing, but it is no shock to me."

"If it's any consolation, Father, I was *there*," Jane interjected. "I took care of her, and I assure you that she passed in peace and happiness." Mr. Phillips tenderly touched his daughter's arm, but Jane continued with a blush, "Father, there is something else you must know. I fear to say what I must, for it could bring you intense criticism and isolation, but—"

Yet, it was too late, for Emily had begun to cry. Bess tried to shield the child from her father's view, but he had already caught a glimpse. Jane's reddened face turned pale, and she watched her father's expression grow confused. Mr. Phillips furrowed his brow and whispered, "Jane, is it yours?" Jane replied with a small nod, and Mr. Phillips pushed past his daughter to greet the child. He took a deep breath, lifted Emily from Bess' arms, and asked, "Is it a girl?"

"Yes," Bess answered.

A tear ran down Mr. Phillips' cheek and splashed onto his granddaughter's nose. Emily smiled, and Mr. Phillips murmured, "She's beautiful, Jane. What did you name her?"

Jane descended the porch steps to approach her father. She rubbed her eyes and pet her daughter's head, whispering that Bess ought to find her niece a place to sleep. Mr. Phillips asked again what the name of his grandchild was, and with a quivering lip, Jane answered, "Emily Josephine Phillips."

Mr. Phillips trembled and could not contain the smile which overcame his face. He tickled his granddaughter's cheek and whispered, "Emily, you're so beautiful—just like your grandmother." He refused to look away from the child as he started toward Laurel Manor. He brushed past Abigail, who held open the door for him, and laughed as he dangled his finger over Emily's head. He began strolling around the house, giving his newest guest a tour of the property.

When Jane and Bess had stepped over the threshold, Jane looked around with nostalgia. She smiled and said, "Well, not much has changed."

Bess chuckled, "Without you, Jane, this manor has been—" But Jane ignored her sister. She started toward the dining hall and ran to catch up to her father and daughter. Bess shook her head and smiled.

It was wonderful to have Jane home.

Chapter 45

In his everlasting joy, Mr. Phillips invited his usual acquaintances to dine on the following evening. He intended to celebrate Jane's return, Emily's birth, and Abigail's engagement, but he was disappointed to discover that most of his invitations were rescinded on account of his being an outcast. Mr. Phillips' dismay, however, did not last long. His general elation caused him to forget about his friends' discourtesy, but Bess felt slighted by these rejections. She was especially upset to hear that Juliette and Leonarda would not be coming.

When the subsequent evening arrived, Mr. Phillips remained optimistic that at least *one* of his guests would come. His enthusiasm was further fueled when Alex, Callum, *and* Mr. Roberts appeared at the proper hour. He shuffled his visitors inside and arranged for their beverages to be made as his daughters prepared for the dinner. Jane was the first to enter the dining hall, and upon noticing Alex and Callum, she greeted her friends with warmth. But when she turned to take a seat, she caught a glimpse of Mr. Roberts and blushed. Mr. Roberts' face lit up, and he said, "Jane, I haven't seen you—"

"Mr. Roberts, I'm very pleased to see you, too," Jane replied. She approached him, took hold of his arm, and led him to the drawing-room, where Emily was situated. She took a deep breath and recounted her year in Dublin, and Mr. Roberts listened in earnest.

When the dinner was ready to be served, Mr. Phillips regrouped his family and guests in the dining hall. He pulled out his chair to take a seat but was surprised to hear a knock on the door. Because she sat the closest to the hallway, Bess stood but hesitated to see who had arrived.

She walked to the front door, but after noticing two familiar silhouettes, she eagerly invited Juliette and Leonarda inside.

"Oh, Bess!" Juliette exclaimed. "I'm terribly sorry about what my parents wrote in response to your father's invitation! I knew that they had insulted you and your family, so I convinced Leonarda to sneak away with me." Bess opened her mouth to reply, but she was interrupted by Jane, who emerged from the dining hall with Emily cradled in her arms. Juliette's voice heightened as she cried, "Jane, is it—?"

"Yes," Bess intervened. "Her name's Emily."

"Well, I would have never supposed such a wonderful surprise!" Juliette exclaimed as she pushed past Bess to see the child.

When the Wheatley sisters reached the dining hall, Mr. Phillips squealed with excitement. He delivered a hearty welcome to each of his guests, but once his monologue concluded, the room fell silent. The first course was served, and minimal chatter began, but halfway through the meal, Mr. Roberts set down his fork and knife and inquired if he could speak to Mr. Phillips in private. Mr. Phillips, who had no reason to decline, happily agreed, and once the two gentlemen left the table, the remaining guests erupted into supposition.

"Could he be moving someplace?" Juliette asked Bess. "Could he be reuniting with either of his siblings—do you think?"

Bess chuckled and cast her eyes to her partially finished dish. "I do not believe that Mr. Roberts would rejoin either Mr. Henwood or Mrs. *Elmsworth*."

"Oh," Juliette replied with a blush. Bess felt everyone's concerned gaze land on her, but it wasn't long until they were distracted by Juliette's next reply. "Could he dislike the food? I don't see how, for *I* think this steak and kidney pudding is delectable!" Bess laughed and shook her head, but in doing so, she caught Abigail's eye. Drawing as little attention to herself as possible, Abigail mouthed the word "marriage." Bess' eyes widened in disbelief. She turned to Jane, who was quietly feeding Emily at the end of the table. *Abigail's intuition is excellent, but it seems that Jane has no idea.* She paused. *Could she be correct? I've never thought of Mr. Roberts as her husband!* And then the notion dawned on her: *The person to whom Jane referred in her letter was Mr. Roberts! Their relationship was undoubtedly kept discreet, but his dedication to improving his appearance, his long letter to her at Christmas, and his continued friendship were all clear indications of his affection. How could I not have realized?*

When Mr. Roberts and Mr. Phillips returned, Juliette ceased to talk. Every eye turned toward Mr. Roberts' amused countenance and Mr. Phillips' enormous smile, but nobody said a word. The second and third courses were soon served during which Mr. Roberts requested to speak with Jane in private. Bess leaned her head close to the hallway to eavesdrop on their discussion, but all she could gather was muffled voices. A few minutes passed before Jane returned to the dining hall. She cleared her throat and with a laugh, she announced her engagement to Mr. Roberts. A chorus of cheering and clapping erupted, and even Alex congratulated his former wife, remarking he was glad that she had found true happiness.

Mr. Roberts thanked the guests for their enthusiasm and assured the Phillipses that he would be more than happy to accept Emily as his own daughter. Then he concluded with the exciting news that he had retained ownership of a beautiful abode within a half a mile of Laurel Manor property. Mr. Phillips leapt up with tears of joy, for this was not news of which he had been aware, and the remainder of the evening was fraught with cheerful conversation. Bess' sisters occupied their time with their fiancés, and Bess half-listened to Juliette's chatter while thinking about Alex's marriage proposal. *If I was to marry Alex, then Father would be alone. I suppose that I could visit him every day, but that would be such an inconvenience. I couldn't allow him to suffer in that manner.*

Suddenly, Bess overheard Abigail tell her father about Alex's offer of marriage. Bess whipped her head around and caught a glimpse of her father's impossibly large smile. He instinctually replied, "Well, of course, I approve!" But Bess crinkled her eyes and covered her face with her hands. *The entire institution of marriage proposals is distorted! Why must gentlemen offer their hands to women? Why can't it be the other way around? Alex should have known better than to ask me!* Then she started to pant. *And what is the purpose of marriage? Isn't it just a way for society to normalize people? Alex should have known that I don't like involving myself in these conventions!* But Bess' thoughts were interrupted by Abigail's squeal. Every other guest, excluding Alex, chimed in and voiced their opinion that Bess ought to marry her best friend.

Juliette climbed onto her chair and laughed, "I knew this would happen! I just *knew* it!"

Bess uncovered her face and bit her lip. *Don't they understand that pressuring me to accept Alex's offer makes me* more *resistant? I certainly don't want to lose Alex's friendship, and I don't want him to marry anyone else, but the concept of marriage repels me. Can't we simply be life-long friends?* Bess turned to Alex and caught a glimpse of his dejected countenance. She pursed her lips. *Yet, as I look into his glimmering blue eyes, I see no other end to my story. It's always been Alex.* She paused. *What right do I have to send him down a tunnel of despair by rejecting him? I know well enough that his happiness means more to me than anything. If I decline, my sorrow in rejecting him will certainly exceed my satisfaction in retaining the integrity of my values. For my own happiness, I have only one solution.*

"Alex," Bess started, and Alex finally turned to her. "I shall accept your proposal. My only request is for us to reside at Laurel Manor, for I wish to keep my father company." But the first line of Bess' response was enough. Alex's dispirited look transformed into an enormous grin, and moments later, Bess found herself locked in a kiss with her best friend. Bess pushed Alex away and laughed before pulling him into an embrace. "And our chief priority is to care for Emily," Bess whispered into her fiancé's ear. "The act of marriage is something I've always mocked, but being an aunt is—"

"Oh, quit it, Bessie," Jane moaned. "Shouldn't you be pleased that you're engaged at the same time as your sisters? I mean... who would have thought it possible?"

But Bess could no longer quarrel with her elder sister, for she was right. There *was* no better way for the Phillips sisters to unite than being engaged at the same time to the men they loved. A tear trickled down Mr. Phillips' cheek, and he gushed, "Oh, your mother would have been so proud."

Chapter 46

Within the year, the Phillips sisters were married. Because she insisted on having her wedding first, Jane married in October. Shortly thereafter, Abigail celebrated her wedding at The Swallow, where both wealthy and impoverished guests joined hands to commemorate the union of two fellow footballers. Several months later and clad in a blue gown (for she had wanted to be as unconventional as possible), Bess walked down the aisle to greet her best friend.

Jane and her husband moved into Woodbury Manor, which neighbored Laurel Manor, and raised two beautiful daughters, who were gratefully named Marietta Elizabeth Roberts and Lucretia Abigail Roberts. Of course, Bess called them Maria and Lucy.

Abigail and her husband occupied a small house that bordered the football court. They assisted Callum's father at The Swallow, and eventually, they had a daughter and a son.

Like her sisters, Bess lived a fulfilling life. She spent her days alongside her father, visiting Jane and Abigail, or watching her nieces and nephews play football. As time passed, Alex mentioned the prospect of having children, but Bess rejected this idea, for it was another convention society expected of her. But as the years wore on, Bess felt like a part of her life was missing, and she agreed to have a child. By the end of her life, she and Alex had *four* children, which was certainly a surprise to everyone.

And life carried on just as well. The insanity of the Phillips sisters' young adulthood had faded, and there was almost nothing left to prevail but happiness.

About the Author

Erin Sullenberger has been an aspiring author since the age of five. She lives in Collingswood, New Jersey with her parents, sister, and dog Kai. Erin has read four of Jane Austen's six novels, which provided the foundation for this novel, and she plans to read the final two this upcoming summer. Erin will study public relations and play soccer next year at Boston University, where she hopes to become a distinguished student-athlete and writer.

Instagram: erinsullenberger5

Twitter: esullenberger5

Website: erinsullenberger.wordpress.com